(347) 35

MOM

Windward Heights

Also by the author

Segu
Children of Segu
Tree of Life
I, Tituba, Black Witch of Salem
Crossing the Mangrove
The Last of the African Kings

Windward Heights

Maryse Condé

Translated from the French by
Richard Philcox

First published in this translation in 1998
by Faber & Faber Limited

Copyright © 1995 by Maryse Condé
Originally published as *La migration des coeurs*,
Editions Robert Laffont, Paris, 1995
This translation copyright © 1998 by Richard Philcox

Published by
Soho Press, Inc.
853 Broadway
New York, NY 10003

Library of Congress Cataloging-in-Publication Data
Condé, Maryse.
[Migration des coeurs. English]
Windward heights / Maryse Condé : translated from the French by
Richard Philcox.
p.   cm.
ISBN 1-56947-161-4
I. Philcox, Richard. II. Title.
PQ3949.2.C65M4913   1999
843—dc21   98-52071
                                                            CIP

10 9 8 7 6 5 4 3 2 1

To Emily Brontë
Who I hope will approve of this interpretation of her masterpiece.
Honour and respect!

Death has separated us
My death will not reunite us

—Simone de Beauvoir,
La Cérémonie des adieux

Contents

Part Three: Marie-Galante

Part Four: Roseau

Part Five: Guadeloupe

Windward Heights

PART ONE

Cuba – Guadeloupe

1 The Procession at Epiphany and the Events that Followed

Melchior headed the procession carrying the banner of his god, Chango.

He was dressed in the god's favourite colours, with a red and white striped jacket and red cotton cambric breeches cut just above his spindly calves, which looked like guava twigs in their bobbled silk hose. A necklace threaded with glass beads, shells, dogs' teeth, alligator molars, shards of bone and pieces of flint, swung low over his belly that was as hollow as a famished wild animal's. From under his white sombrero spiked with red feathers his eyes flashed haughtily at the crowds thronged along the streets as far as the governor's palace – an edifice recently completed after hundreds of slaves had worked on it for over half a century under the orders of architects who had come all the way from Castile. Idle onlookers crammed windows and balconies of the houses that were fortunate enough to be on the route of the procession – the procession at Epiphany that marked the start of the new year. All the *cabildos*, the secret societies, were in attendance. Behind Melchior came the Congos and the Lucumis in blue and black, the Araras in dishevelled raffia skirts, their cheeks striped with scars slashed with a knife or a red-hot iron, and lastly the Mandingos, so elegant in their baggy breeches and the yards and yards of indigo cloth wrapped around their heads. The entire procession danced and swayed in rhythm to the

3

worldly beat of the drums. After the Mandingos, however, the procession broke up. A motley crowd of women and children of all the colours of the rainbow, from Congo black to pass-for-white, cavorted in any old fashion. The children, boys and girls alike, showed off everything Nature had given them at birth. The women displayed the most oddly assorted rags. Some were waving lighted torches whose flame the wind flattened and sometimes even blew out; others were brandishing rara rattles or striking cymbals. Some of the dancers had pieces of mirror pinned to their breasts and wore masks of animals whose noises they imitated. Occasionally, Melchior could not help turning around and casting angry looks at the tail of the procession. Nobody paid him any attention and the bacchanal continued.

The nine arches and ten Ionic columns on the western façade of the governor's palace filled one side of the Plaza de Armas. It was the architect Antonio Fernandez de Trevejo y Zaldinas, a man of great renown, who had begun building the residence. Sick with haemorrhagic dengue fever he had returned home to Castile to look death straight in the eyes. His young successor, Pedro Medina, had faithfully kept to the original plans, and pink marble had been imported from Italy, precious wood from Mexico and translucent blocks of madreporian stone from the Isle of Pines. In order to enhance the patio, he had recently commissioned a statue of Cristobal Colon from the sculptor Giovanni Cucciari, thinking it was time that one Italian paid homage to another.

With the sun setting in his eyes, Excellentissimo José de Cépéro, Grand Cross of the Orders of San Fernando and San Hermenegildo, lieutenant general of the armed forces, political head and military governor of the province of Havana and captain general of the island of Cuba, watched the

4

procession as it bounded towards him in a cloud of dust. With one hand he clutched the wrought-iron balustrade of the palace balcony; with the other, he leaned on the velvet coat of his adviser, the effeminate Silvestre de Reina, whispered to be his lover. His mask of benevolence contradicted his inner feelings. His heart was not at peace. The deaths of that troublemaker, José Martí, and the mulatto, Antonio Maceo, had done nothing to help the political situation, and the battle for independence raged on in the Sierra del Cristal. A column of Spanish soldiers had just been hacked to pieces by the so-called Liberation Army, and dozens of coffins were lined up in the cathedral under heaps of lilies and frangipani blossom. How much longer would he remain in Havana? His wife, Maria – for he was married and father of three sons – had already set sail. Above all, José de Cépéro hated these crowds of negroes and turned up his nose in disgust at the smell of sweat and filth lurking under the velvets and silks. Under pressure from the other European nations, Spain had finally abolished slavery. Now the illiterate barbarians fleeing the plantations were crowding into the hovels and gambling dens in the towns.

He motioned to Silvestre to throw coins to the revellers, who were now dancing shamelessly under the balcony and bawling their miscreant songs that resounded noisily off the paving stones. Motionless, standing aloof from the mêlée of stooped backs, was Melchior. Leaning over, José dropped a bulging purse at his feet. For Melchior was no ordinary mortal. He was a *babalawo*, a high priest of *santería*, son of the *omo-koloba*, who, with the pomp due to his rank, had departed this life several years before to join Chango. José had consulted him on several occasions concerning matters of great urgency, and was about to call on his services again. In this age of chaos and calamity, a look into the future was

5

no mean gift. Melchior thanked him with a blink, and with figure erect, disappeared under the silk-cotton and palm-trees lining the square.

Soon the Plaza de Armas emptied.

Congos, Lucumis, Araras and Mandingos began to swarm into the surrounding streets and *paseos*, and only a few tireless masked dancers remained gesticulating under the balconies, together with the women and children who took advantage of the situation to indulge in their obscenities with impunity.

Turning his back on the palace, Melchior walked briskly to the cathedral built on the site of the former church of San Ignacio. Passers-by hurriedly made the sign of the cross when they saw him, while Melchior walked straight ahead like an automaton, heeding nobody.

The cathedral was deserted, save for a few worshippers in the chapels, staring at the saints with tears in their eyes, kneeling on their silk handkerchiefs spread out on the marble floor, their faces drained of colour under their black mantillas forming a terrifying, baroque frieze. Melchior passed in front of a row of empty confessionals, then stopped at the chapel to Santa Barbara. By a strange twist of collusion, this frail virgin in her white dress and red cape, holding a heavy sword with both hands, was one of his god's manifestations of power. In fact her image could be seen in every temple dedicated to *santería*, depicted as a young Yoruba girl, her forehead haloed in frizzy hair, her cheekbones scored with scars, seated on a horse, clutching against her breast a bunch of plantains, Chango's favourite food. Melchior fell to his knees. A dream he had the previous night was plaguing him. He had seen himself suffocating in a river of his own blood. But Santa Barbara responded with a smile. At the same time a streak of lightning followed by the thunder of Chango flashed through

6

the vividly coloured stained-glass *vitrales*. The interior of the nave gleamed white.

Comforted, Melchior got up off his knees.

When he emerged from the cathedral, red streaks dripped across the sky, the colour of sacrificial blood. This too was a good sign, and he felt fortified.

In the calle de Mercaderes the silence was as heavy as a bundle of wet washing. The only lighted window displayed rows of motionless fans, like butterflies poised for flight. Two streets over, however, the gambling houses and dens were swarming with life. In front of the bodega La Estrella, the nightwatchman hurried to open the door. Inside, the smoke was so thick that at first nothing was visible through the dark blue coils. Then the faces of the customers emerged, blacks and mulattos, all with a cigar or a pipe stuck between their teeth, dabbing their foreheads with squares of blue batiste. Melchior needed no help from the proprietor, who was watching every movement of a young barmaid's breasts as she washed the glasses in a trickle of water. He spotted the man immediately.

As usual, Razyé was drinking alone.

He was dressed all in black in the French fashion, from his tightly-laced leather boots to his felt hat sewn with a large hem stitch. His skin too was black, that shiny black they call Ashanti, and his hair hung in curls like those of an Indian half-caste, the Bata-Zindien. Nobody could hold the gaze of his languishing eyes, where churned who knows what pain and solitude. His expression was that of a man attending the wake of his own mother. On meeting him, you knew that you had come face to face with a soul that could find no rest, neither day nor night. Melchior could not help comparing him to a spirit of the dead, an *egun*, but an *egun* prevented by an abominable crime from joining the other invisible spirits in the afterlife and who wandered restlessly among the living. Razyé waited for him to sit down and order a *mojito*, before asking him in a low, rough voice: 'Well?'

Melchior avoided his gaze and drew a handful of leaves out of his shoulder pouch.

'Wash yourself with these. For two days you must have no dealings, do you hear me, no dealings with women, and then come and see me. It will be time for the ceremony.'

Nobody could say exactly when Razyé had arrived in Havana nor where he had come from. They only knew him by this odd name, as if his parents had not bothered to give him a saint's name on the day of his christening. Consequently, imaginations ran riot. Some said he was already on the island when Governor Pezuela had recruited free men of colour into the Spanish army to fight the rebels, and had thereby miraculously escaped the gallows despite having committed an horrendous crime. Others said that he had engaged in tobacco smuggling together with a Creole of mixed blood, and that after his associate had mysteriously died, he had spent some time in jail. For the time being he was operating a laundry business with an unscrupulous Chinaman and his carts could be seen all over town. It was said he was as rich as El Dorado. But you would never have thought so from appearances. He lived just off the Campo Santo in a dilapidated house guarded by a mangy dog, a house so dark that even in the middle of the day his quarteroon scullery-maid had to light candles. Every morning, at the same hour, Razyé walked to his business on the calle Obispo, dragging himself along under the burning sun, looking as nightmarish and bilious as the dregs of night.

Melchior had met him the same way he met everyone else

in Havana, from senior functionaries to humble citizens, one day when Razyé had sought him out to fathom his future. Melchior had immediately yielded to Razyé's strong willpower, which had taken him places he had had no intention of going. That was how he had revealed to him involuntarily the secrets reserved for *babalawos*, the priests of *santería*. He had recently undertaken to initiate him and hang around his neck Chango's five necklaces of red and white beads. When he was in his right senses, he realized just how dangerous his undertaking was. Razyé would be able to get in touch with those *egun* of which he was the very image, and use their powers for his own ends. And yet he was unable to resist him.

Without removing the cigar from his mouth, Razyé began to speak in a fog of smoke.

'I'd like you to advise me on the voyage I'm planning.'

Melchior was taken aback.

'A voyage? You're planning a voyage?'

'Yes, it's time I went back home.'

For the first time Melchior ventured a question that he had been turning over and over in his head.

'Home is where?'

Razyé gave one of his mournful smiles.

'I say "home" to speak like the rest of you. But I have no home. I was found in Guadeloupe as naked as the day I was born, on the barren heath and cliffs – the *razyés* – hence my name.'

Razyé said not another word and his attention wandered elsewhere, so Melchior got up and took his leave. Razyé did not even notice. While darkness tightened its grip around his shoulders, Razyé remained in solitude, locked in smoke and silence, downing glass after glass, getting more drunk by the minute, but also heavier and stiller, like a rock or a desert isle lost in the midst of the ocean's waves.

Meanwhile, pondering on the ceremony he could not make up his mind to proceed with, Melchior walked up the avenida de Las Misiones that encircles Havana in a tight clasp. Not a star shone above his head. In the huge, Indian ink-coloured sky, the clouds jostled each other. The houses too had donned their night façades, and the *babalawo* strode on, draped in the blackness that he pierced with his lofty gaze. On reaching the church of Santo Cristo del Buen Viaje, he saw a shape steal furtively out of the shadows. He fingered the bulging purse that José de Cépéro had thrown him, for he recognized Jaruco, a dangerous individual commonly known as the Footpad, quick with a knife, who respected nobody, not even the dead.

2   The Burial of the Babalawo

The murder of Melchior fired the popular imagination.

Everyone was asking the same question. How could a mere mortal, a man born of a woman's womb and destined to end up in the earth's, be so bold as to lay a finger on the powerful *babalawo*, rob him of all his money, even the ring he wore on his little left finger to symbolize his association with Chango, and leave him sprawled on the flagstones, drained of his blood like a common slaughter-house animal? Some people really fear nothing and nobody. And Melchior, who could read Tom, Dick and Harry's future, why couldn't he predict his own end and avoid the calle where death was lying in wait for him?

As for the police, they did not go to much trouble to track down the murderer; for day after day in Havana one crime followed another. Blood was flowing in every neighbourhood, from the smartest to the shadiest. There was no telling political assassination from a sordid stab in the back. Every morning Captain General José de Cépéro received death threats in his mail, which meant that he never went out without his bodyguards and never let any food touch his lips without its having been tasted three times. Already several of his tasters had passed on from this world to the next. A certain General Blanco was due to arrive who would bring the rebels to heel and perhaps restore law and order.

For the time being, Melchior's house, a stone's throw from the Zuerzuela, was too small to hold all those who had come to pay a last homage to his remains. In the room barred to visitors, even to his wife, Madrina, nine *santeros* were seated around the funeral bed to ensure that the soul of the deceased would not linger on earth and cause trouble for the living. They were preparing to bury the *babalawo* with his cowries, his palm-kernels and divining dish. That morning they had marched to the mouth of the Chorrera and thrown into its muddy waters his fetish stones, his razor, his necklaces and every one of his ceremonial adornments. Melchior himself was laid out on his bed, his face serene and smiling, oblivious of such an unworthy death. A gourd had been placed against his left side containing the rice, okra and unsalted meat he would need for his journey that would take nine days; his arrival on the ninth day would be marked by a wake of prayers similar to the one preceding the funeral.

Outside, the drums beat in mourning.

The biggest one, the height of a man, rumbled, while the little ones wailed like tiny infants abandoned by their mama.

Razyé was standing as rigid as a candle in a corner of the yard. Unlike the men and women around him, his face showed no grief, because deep inside he was furious and exasperated, as if Melchior's death had played a trick on him. Now he would never realize his childhood dream; he would never communicate with the dead. He would never have access to the secrets of the invisible world, and he would never refashion the world to his liking. In his irritation a muscle throbbed along his cheek, adding to the macabre nature of his features. Nevertheless, he had made up his mind. Protected by the spirits or not, he was going to leave. He was going to return to Guadeloupe. The time for revenge had come. And what's more, he sensed that Cuba was going to live through even more dangerous times. That morning, when he had gone to the port to book a passage, he had seen the *Maine*, a huge battleship flying the American flag anchored alongside the Castillo del Morro and blocking the roadstead. Blond, pink-cheeked sailors climbed up and down the accommodation ladders while officers dressed in white gazed at the town through binoculars. What was America up to now?

Meanwhile the doors of the funeral chamber were opening, and carrying the heavy, unvarnished wooden coffin on their shoulders, the nine *santeros* crossed the yard. The procession formed behind them and the wailing intensified, for the moment of separation was near. Seeing the birds dressed in black perched on the terraced roofs and hearing their croaks, people knew that they were the spirits in disguise come to accompany the deceased. Razyé joined the procession and stared at the coffin with his narrow eyes, whose lids lowered like the slats of shutters. He envied the dead man. How many times had he wished it was all over for him too and his mouth and eyes were closed under six feet of earth in an abandoned graveyard, where Guinea grass grew haphazardly along the paths and here and there pushed up the flagstones. Flowers thirsting for water withered among the crosses and the dusty pearl embellishments. The photos of the dead yellowed and crumbled to dust in their frames.

Why did he continue to walk along the road of the living? The girl who meant more to him than life itself had turned her back on him. Her cries of protest had never stopped echoing throughout his life: 'I could never, never marry Razyé. It would be too degrading. It would be like starting to live all over again like our ancestors, the savages in Africa!'

On hearing these terrible words he stood stunned. Then he had fled the house. For days and nights he had run like a madman, oblivious to where he was going. The sun rose and set in his company. The rain soaked him. The clearing skies dried him. Then one morning he found himself in La Pointe, facing an ocean of indifference. Tall, burly men were loading a ship. He had mingled with them and at nightfall crept aboard. When they discovered him it was too late. The green hue of the shore propped against the horizon was like a mirage. The churches and palaces of Havana were silhouetted in a halo of light. They kicked him off the boat, but he had escaped jail by signing up with the army to fight the rebels.

Soon the procession left the courtyard and, cutting across the fields, headed for the church of San Eusebio; for however much a *babalawo* he might be, Melchior was nevertheless a staunch Catholic. The procession resembled a sinister snake as it coiled gloomily under the dying sun.

Leaving the Campo Santo, Razyé paid a visit to his mistress, Doña Stéfania Fonséca, widowed at the age of twenty-four by a rich planter. In polite society she passed for inconsolable because she had refused all types of men on account of Razyé. They kept their liaison secret for fear of slander, and twice she had had an abortion to douse any scandal.

In the little peony drawing-room, so called because of the design on the wallpaper, she was in tears. This was unusual, for knowing him as well as she did, she generally hid her feelings under her mask of painted porcelain, except for their moments of pleasure together.

'I hear you're leaving for Guadeloupe. What are you going to do on that tiny speck of an island where they don't even speak Spanish? You told me yourself that the hearts of people over there are harder than flint and never watered by compassion.'

Razyé stood erect against the velvet curtains of the windows carefully closed against prying neighbours.

'You wouldn't understand!' he retorted contemptuously. 'People of your colour have no passion in their veins. They don't know what it's like to burn with fire at the thought of a person breathing, eating and sleeping with another on the opposite side of the ocean.'

'Do you really believe that?' Doña Stéfania murmured. 'You think I can't understand. When it comes to feelings, whites and blacks are one and the same. There's no difference between their trials and tribulations. All humans dream of being reunited in Heaven with those they have lost.'

Razyé was no longer listening. All he could hear was his own voice and the chaos of his inner self.

'I must take my revenge. On the man who took the woman I loved and the man who made me unworthy of her love. My plan is all worked out. I've toiled three years in Cuba to have enough money to put it into effect. I'll bring the second man to his knees and if I have to kill the first with both hands, I will.'

'If you leave,' Doña Stéfania said in an even quieter tone, 'I shall not stay in Havana. I'll go home to Spain. Besides, José Martí has died for nothing. Soon Cuba will be a colony of America. Her soldiers are already in the port, awaiting the moment to hurl themselves upon us!'

3   Nelly Raboteur's Tale

The *Veracruz* had been at sea for two whole days. No sight of land. Not even a speck of an isle with its ring of coral and coconut-palms. Everywhere you looked there was nothing but a great expanse of water that changed colour with the moods of the sun; sometimes a sparkling turquoise green, sometimes grey, sometimes as black as soot. At times shoals of flying-fish flashed through the air, dressed in their gleaming jerkins, and whales spouted furious jets of water. Apart from that, nothing. Nothing but water. Water.

In order to pass the time the men played at quoits on the deck or drew deeply on their Havana cigars in the smoking-room. As for the women, with their faces half-hidden by their fans of woven raffia, their sole subject of conversation was the presence, albeit discreet, of a dark-skinned negro in first class. He had come aboard when they had called in at Havana and avoided any contact with the other passengers, his eyes never wandering, eating all alone at his table and returning to his cabin once his travelling companions were fast asleep. But his very reserve was offensive. They would have liked him to dare a smile, to attempt to shake hands, for the pleasure of putting him in the place his colour deserved. Yet, deep down, the ladies on board fell victim to that inexplicable, mysterious attraction white women feel for the black male. They were forced to admit that such an indifference combined with an acquired arrogance in an elegantly tailored coat, that strong torso under a frilled shirt and those firm curves under the fine serge of his trousers, quickened their pulse. How charming this inscrutable face would be if lit up by a smile! But Razyé – for it was indeed our hero – passed haughtily by. In the morning he would draw up a deck-chair next to the life-boats and gaze at the infinity of the sea. In the evening, under one of the lamps in the smoking-room, he frowned over a book in French, Victor Hugo's *Bug–Jargal*.

It was so depressing!

Everything changed when they docked in Martinique.

At Fort de France the passengers who were continuing on to Guadeloupe had to disembark and take a passage on board the *Kalenda*, a steamship of smaller tonnage, anchored at the other end of the wharf. All this took place amidst the din of the coalwomen's shovels, the clamour of porters, the shouts of the market women who never missed a chance to sell their coconuts or cane-juice, the cries of infants and the rush of latecomers. Razyé collided with a stout, handsome, middle-aged woman, dressed like a *da*, a nursemaid from a respectable family, in a flowery, loose-fitting dress over a lace petticoat that stopped short above a pair of mauve velvet slippers embroidered with silver flowers.

'Monsieur Razyé!' she cried. 'Is it really you? I almost didn't recognize you.'

Razyé did not say a word, and she hurriedly added: 'Don't you remember? Nelly Raboteur!'

Razyé raised his hat, grumbled an answer and quickly disappeared. This short interlude had not gone unnoticed, and Mademoiselle de La Cossardière, who more than the others perhaps had spied on our mysterious traveller, walked over to the *da*. Nelly needed no further invitation, and while the sun continued its games with the sea, she began her story.

*

17

Our life is traced out for us long before we are born. Depending on the cradle that rocks us, we are given the gift of wealth or poverty, life's happiness or life's wickedness. I was born into a poor family in Morne-Caillou, a few miles from Anse-Bertrand, in the most desolate part of Guadeloupe. We were seventeen children around the table, and we seldom ate meat. So when I was sixteen I was only too happy when the priest, Monsieur le curé Poissaudeau, found a place for me working for Hubert Gagneur.

Hubert Gagneur was a tallow-coloured mulatto who had inherited from his white Creole father his pretentiousness and l'Engoulvent, an overseer's house almost in ruins at Grand-Fonds-les-Mangles, situated on the Windward Heights. It was called l'Engoulvent because the winds seemed to rush in from the horizon, sweeping over the limestone bluffs, the columnar cactus and the heath. You could tell the force of the wind by the way the bent trees grew, stunted and shrivelled like old folk. When there was a hurricane or simply a storm or tropical depression, it was as if hundreds of wild horses had been let loose in a howling stampede. The sea came over from La Désirade, swelled up and flooded the Heights. The closest plantation, the great house of Belles-Feuilles, the estate of a rich white Creole family, the Linsseuils, was situated about twenty miles distant on the edge of the sugar-cane fields. Except for the postman who grumblingly had to drive his horse that way, nobody ever visited l'Engoulvent. Hubert Gagneur had a bad reputation. He did not believe in the Good Lord and lived like a miscreant. He had recently lost his wife, whom he had treated badly, and lived alone with his two children, a boy and a girl, Justin and Catherine, Cathy as everyone called her. The boy was somewhat sad and taciturn, with a fair skin, fair enough for him to earn a place for himself in white folks' company through sheer hard work. As for

18

Cathy, she was the colour of hot syrup left to cool in the open air, with black hair like threads of night and green eyes. You couldn't help but love her. Yet the day after I arrived at l'Engoulvent I realized she was the true daughter of her papa. At the age of six she respected nothing and nobody. She was bossy, headstrong, always ready to answer back, and artful. And what's more, she was convinced she was the most beautiful creature on earth. Always admiring herself in the mirror, imitating the ladies in polite society by pinning up her hair. I told her: 'Mademoiselle Cathy, beauty won't get you nowhere! If you want to find a husband who will get you out of here, that's not the way to go about it.'

By way of reply she made the most terrible faces, and I myself was ashamed at what a little person like her, no bigger than a guava twig, made me feel.

One morning Hubert Gagneur saddled his horse to ride to La Pointe. He went there about once every two months to attend the meetings of an association that did its best to defend the interests of the small sugar-cane planters. The abolition of slavery hadn't changed anything at all, you know. It was still the rich white planters who laid down the law and the blacks who lived from hand to mouth. People said that Hubert Gagneur took advantage of his visits to La Pointe to have his fling with Amélie, a vivacious *capresse* who lived on the Morne-à-Cayes and who had been his mistress as long as people could remember.

Since the children clung to his legs and prevented him from leaving, he said to them: 'Behave yourselves. What shall I bring you back? You may choose what you like.'

They hesitated. Then Justin chose a fiddle. Once his papa had taken him to La Pointe and he had seen a violin in the shop window of the Luthier de Crémone and had become infatuated with the instrument. He managed all on his own to play tunes he composed himself. Cathy chose a whip. Not surprisingly. At her age, she would gallop under the sun like a real girl of the islands. Hubert Gagneur could not have got further than Petit Canal when a hurricane blew up. Throughout the week there had been no ominous signs except for an unusually calm sea and the shameless blooms on the cactus, swollen with blood-tinged lips. Shortly before midnight it seemed the house was about to lie down and die, while groans issued from every crack. The wind burst open the doors we had done our best to nail down. The rain lashed the wooden boards and gushed in everywhere.

I set about looking after the children.

When I went up to her room, Cathy was standing in front of a wide open window. Her nightgown ballooned around her like the sail of a boat out at sea, and it looked as though she was about to take flight. Where to? I wondered.

'Cathy!' I cried. 'Are you mad? Close that window at once!'

Do you think she obeyed me? She calmly went back and lay down in her soaked bed, and I was the one who had to struggle with the shutters, the wind and the rain. The hurricane fought with us all night long. In the morning the wind dropped all of a sudden and the fine weather returned with its peace and quiet. Blue everywhere. The sky had cast off its old grey, leaden clothes. Not a fleece of a cloud over the sea. All that remained to remind us of what had happened was the mud and the piles of leaves and broken branches that had been swept over the paved yard by some unknown force. With shovels, buckets and brushes, Carmélien, the handyman, and a few freed slaves – the so-called new citizens, but still as pitiful and working in the fields for two slices of breadfruit – started to clean up all that muck. I had my hands full in the house.

The day after, around noon, Hubert Gagneur turned up.

He surprised us for we were not expecting him home so soon. When he left like that for La Pointe we would go weeks without seeing him. He had been frightened for his family on account of the hurricane, he said, and had turned back as soon as he could. The whole of Grande-Terre had been devastated, he told us. Three-quarters of the houses in Petit-Canal and Anse-Bertrand had collapsed like cow-pats. He had heard that in Le Moule all that remained were heaps of corrugated iron and wooden planks. To tell the truth, I was hardly listening. I was looking at what he was clutching between his knees: a dirty, repulsive, seven- or eight-year-old boy, completely naked, with a well-developed sex, believe me; a little black boy or Indian half-caste. His skin was black, and his tangled curly hair reached down his back.

Hubert Gagneur noticed my curiosity.

'I found him among the *razyé* – on the heath – and he bit my hand like a mongoose. It must have been the evil spirits hidden in the wind of the hurricane that brought him our way.'

He handed me the horrible creature.

'Take him. Wash him, dress him. Try to make him look like a Christian.'

'Where will he sleep?' I asked. 'There's already not enough room in the house.'

He shrugged his shoulders.

'Let him sleep with Cathy. I'm sure she'll adore him.'

'What shall we call him?' I persisted.

Hubert Gagneur climbed down from his horse and burst out laughing.

'How about Razyé!'

At that moment Justin and Cathy ran out of the house and threw themselves on their papa.

'Look what I've brought you,' he said jokingly. 'Isn't this better than all the fiddles and whips in the world?'

21

And that's how Razyé entered l'Engoulvent, on a day of wind, terror and rain.

You shouldn't play with the hearts of children.

Justin had always thought himself to be the little master of the house. He worshipped his papa like the holy sacrament. It was as if he had transferred to him all the feelings he had had for his maman, who died so young. He copied his every move. Since Hubert Gagneur only spoke Creole and swore like a field nigger, he imitated him. I told him: 'That's not how you'll get into polite society. They'll take you for an uncouth, uneducated savage.'

From one day to the next Justin had to share his place with a ragamuffin, come from goodness knows where, for Razyé had found a special place in the heart of Hubert Gagneur. The master treated him like a plaything. He taught him the words to the most obscene biguines. He split his sides with laughter at the sight of him shaking his behind and thrusting forward his sex as he danced. He encouraged him to masquerade as a carnival *mas' à congo* or a *mas' à goudron*. He had him imitate animal sounds: squeal like a pig, bray like a donkey, cackle like a hen that's just laid an egg, and moo like a cow. Unlike her brother, Cathy began to worship Razyé. All day long the two of them would romp and gallop on horseback across the limestone heights that surrounded l'Engoulvent. They caught bush-rats they roasted on an open fire. They dived into the sea and fished with their hands for the crayfish that hid among the holes in the cliffs. I never understood why their favourite place to play was the little graveyard where rested Irminette Boisgris, Hubert's wife, a fatherless mulatto like himself; Joséphine, his black mother, so mouth-watering that a white Creole could not wait for her to reach sixteen to taste her delights; Félicité and Emmanuel, his sister and brother, twins laid to rest by typhoid fever at the age of four; and

Julien and Eloise, his grandparents, a deserving couple who never got over the calamity that befell their only daughter. They cavorted and climbed over the graves, sat down among the wreaths of pearls and leaned their heads against the cool tombstones as if they were trying to listen to the secrets of those disappeared under the earth. In the evening, sitting in the paved yard, Razyé beat the *gwo-ka* like a true drummer and Cathy danced like a field girl. Then, aching all over, they would climb up to their room and sleep in each other's arms. When I went to wake them I looked at their bodies tangled up in the sheets and said to myself nothing good could come out of such a friendship. I would have liked to tell Hubert Gagneur what I thought, but I was afraid to.

I must admit that after living with us for three months, Razyé was transformed. You couldn't say he was handsome because of the colour of his skin, his facial features and his big purplish mouth. But his height and build had developed. With his black hair braided into a plait down his back, he looked like Otaheite, the Indian hero you see in picture-books.

Neglected by father and sister alike, because of this newcomer, Justin inevitably came to hate Razyé.

Nelly Raboteur was stopped at this point in her story by a commotion of voices. They had just learned through the Morse system on board that the battleship *Maine* had mysteriously exploded in the port of Havana.

Accident? Attack? Perpetrated by whom? And why?

Whatever the case, two hundred and sixty sailors were dead and the United States of America was calling for revenge. There was already talk of declaring war on Spain. What lay in store for Cuba?

4 *Nelly Raboteur's Tale (continued)*

In fact, Nelly Raboteur was only able to continue her story the following morning. They were a few hours away from landing at Pointe-à-Pitre and she would have much preferred to pack her trunks and the wicker baskets with the clothes of the family from Le Moule she was working for. But she was assailed by her eager young lady listeners.

Life would have gone on that way for years and years if Hubert Gagneur hadn't been struck down in the prime of life, in his forty-first year. We think a mason-wasp must have crept into the ear of his horse which took fright, galloped madly across the savanna and tossed him over the cliffs. Two fishermen mending their nets beside their boat saw him take a nosedive. They ran as fast as they could but to no avail. His brain had squirted out and his arms and legs lay broken on the rocks. They picked up what they could, put the remains into a basket and brought them back to l'Engoulvent on the stroke of noon. Justin and Cathy were having their lunch.

Nobody bothered to give Hubert Gagneur a wake, even less a *vénéré*, nine days after. He was merely the illegitimate son of a mulatto without a bank account or a cent to his name. The priest came in his rumpled surplice together with two half-asleep choirboys, poured some holy water on the rough pinewood coffin, mumbled a bit of Latin and took to his heels as if he were afraid of meeting a blood-sucking *soukougnan* in the savanna. Then without taking the trouble to remove their *bakoua* hats pulled low over their foreheads, a group of labourers dug him a hole next to the grave of his late wife.

So ended the life of Hubert Gagneur.

While Cathy cried her heart out, Razyé remained quite unmoved and perfectly dry-eyed. It was as if the death of the man who had so spoiled him meant absolutely nothing to him. Hubert's death slid off him like water off malanga leaves. Out of respect for Cathy, he did not say a word, and stood next to her, as stiff as a scarecrow, a *bwa-bwa*, waiting to be burnt on Ash Wednesday. It was at that moment I think I realized his true nature. Only one person counted on this earth and that was Cathy. At the same time I had the feeling that he was especially flattered by the exaggerated way she clung to him and that he had nothing in his heart but pride. Now I'm wondering if I wasn't mistaken about him, and if, out of the two, he wasn't rather the victim.

As for Justin, he became a different person overnight. He drew himself up and blossomed like a sunflower that had finally found the sun. Hubert Gagneur had hardly been laid under the earth than Justin did everything he had never been allowed to do. He sold a strip of land along the cliffs to the colonial authorities who had been requesting it for years to make a panoramic route. With the money he set about repairing l'Engoulvent, which sorely needed it, and hired four Indians from Calcutta. They arrived in an ox-cart from Le Moule, the women wrapped in their golden veils and the men bearded and broad-shouldered. On orders from Justin, they abandoned the sugar-cane that had never really thrived over our way, and by cartloading buckets of water and wheelbarrows of cow-pats they grew lettuce, endives, peas, tomatoes, cabbages and carrots. Every week baskets of vegetables were sent off to the markets of Grande-Terre. Then Justin went to find the school-teacher at Grands-Fonds-les-Mangles. Hubert Gagneur had never set foot inside a school or even thought of sending his children, because he thought education a waste of time. Every evening, by the light of the hurricane-lamp in the dining-room, Justin toiled over his reading, arithmetic and natural science books. So much so that he passed some examination or other, and proud as a peacock, started at the school in Anse-Bertrand in a uniform I washed and starched for him. From then on he only returned to l'Engoulvent at the end of the week, giving orders left and right like a real Monsieur.

One Saturday when the devil was beating his wife behind the church, as we say, and it was raining our way but the sun was out over La Désirade in the distance – I have kept the memory of that day in my head as if it were yesterday – he came home from Anse-Bertrand and found Razyé and Cathy sitting in the kitchen. Their cheeks were stuck together as they ate Jamaica plums. With one arm slipped around Razyé's neck, Cathy was popping them one by one into his mouth in fits of laughter. Razyé was swallowing and groaning with pleasure. At first Justin remained rooted to the spot, as if his eyes could not believe what they saw. Then he rushed over to his sister and with one cuff sent her sprawling to the ground. At the same time he revived his Creole that he had been neglecting somewhat and shouted: 'Kimafoutiyesa! Ti-ma-fi, sé on vant a krédi, ou vlé poté ban mwen? E épi yon nèg anko?'

She tried to get up, but a second slap sent her flying again with a bloodied mouth. Justin turned to Razyé and shouted at him like a dog.

'Dèro! Dèro, mwen di-w! Maché!'

From that day on Justin forbade Razyé to set foot inside

the house and confined him to the fields with the Indians. He hired an elderly nun from Petit-Canal, as withered as an over-ripe passion-fruit under her grubby winged coif, to teach Cathy French, a little reading, a little writing, but above all embroidery, sewing and good manners. At first Cathy locked herself in her room on the day of the lessons, but the nun did not give up and drummed on the door for hours so that in the end Cathy gave in. I felt sorry for her when I saw her sitting on a bench in the dining-room pricking her fingers as she awkwardly tried to thread her needle. But gradually she seemed to like being with the nun, who told her stories of when she was in France during the Revolution and how the fanatics wanted to snip the nipples off all the Sisters. I could hear them giggling together.

As for Razyé!

You would have expected him to buck like a horse against the whip. For at that time he was fifteen or sixteen years old and the size of a locust-tree. But nothing of the sort! L'Engoulvent had a stable that had never housed more than one horse and leaked all over. That was where he now spent his nights, after having toiled with the Indians and eaten his root vegetables out of the same gourd. It was as if he took pleasure in his abjection. I watched him with his chin down to his chest as he watered, weeded, hoed and lit bonfires. He no longer washed. A comb never touched his hair. Whenever I passed him by, my nostrils revolted at his smell – a mixture of dirt, sweat and cow-pats. All the liveliness and boldness had gone out of him. He had become sullen and uncouth, a repulsive animal.

The only person who did not seem to notice this transformation was Cathy. Once the nun had left she managed to escape Carmélien's attention and join Razyé in the stables. She stayed there until I hung a hurricane-lamp out in the yard to frighten the rats away. Sometimes even much later. The moon had time to light up the whole expanse of sky. What went on when they were together? I couldn't help turning this question over and over in my head. Yet when I came up with an answer, the only answer possible, I convinced myself I must be mad.

How could such a lovely girl bear to be embraced by such an individual? And how could he possibly appreciate such delicacy? For a monster to be happy, doesn't he need to meet his match?

At the end of June, when an embroidered indigo hand-kerchief was stretched to the four corners of the sky above our heads, Justin assembled us all in the dining-room, all of us, even the Indians, even Razyé. It was then I could see how changed he had become on reaching manhood. He was as different from his father as first light is from dusk. Slim, tall, as straight as a whistling pine. With his light brown hair and his grey eyes he could be mistaken for a white Creole. He looked us straight in the eye and declared: 'I am going to be married. Not to just anybody. To Marie-France La Rinardière, heiress to one of the best white Creole families, related to the Linsseuils. So I want everyone of you to be on your best behaviour in her company. I shall not tolerate any bad manners.'

The following Sunday a procession of tilburies rolled up to l'Engoulvent. Nothing but white Creoles. Ladies in straw hats and veils, gentlemen in gloves and gaiters, children with hair in ringlets. Never had we seen such a gathering at l'Engoulvent.

Marie-France La Rinardière had the figure and waist of a

ten-year-old, the complexion of a tallow candle and white-blonde hair that fell right down her back. She perspired and was ready to faint at the slightest effort. For generations the sons and daughters of La Rinardière had been carried off by tuberculosis, and there was no counting the number of tombs scattered down one side of the plantation of La Grivelle in the shade of the casuarina-trees. Since she only had one or two years to live, the family had let Marie-France marry Justin so as to procure her a little pleasure before she left this earth. But you could sense the contempt veiled by the smiles and the sugary words. All this high society made merry with Cathy as if they had not noticed her colour, and Cathy smiled, whirled round and showed off her beauty as if she did not know that they would never forgive her for what she was. At one point, Huberte de Linsseuil, who was her own age, with her maman's permission invited Cathy to stay with her at the Belles-Feuilles plantation, and she accepted with delight.

Just when they were about to take their seats around the banquet table – and you should have seen what expense Justin had gone to, ordering from the caterers in La Pointe crab and conch pâtés, curried colombo vol-au-vent, grilled crayfish, red snapper in its jelly, stuffed goat, christophene croquettes, purée of green pawpaw, guava tarts, soursop, coconut and passion-fruit sorbets, and goodness knows what else – I realized that we hadn't seen Razyé since morning. I went to look for him and found him in the stables, his head between his hands, filthy and disgusting as usual. I caught myself taking pity on him. I took his hand that was as rough as a yam peel and said: 'Wash yourself, clean yourself up and come and join the fun. Justin has given you permission to join us.'

'What's she doing?' he merely replied.

'Cathy?' I answered. 'She's enjoying herself!'

He looked up, and I noticed his eyes were brimming with tears.

'Oh, how I wish I were white!' he shouted. 'White with blue eyes in my face! White with blond hair on my head!'

I shrugged my shoulders.

'When you go to church don't you hear the priest preach from the pulpit that the colour of your skin doesn't matter; all that counts is the colour of your soul?'

'Liar! If I was white everyone would respect me! Justin like all the rest!'

'And I'm telling you that everyone would like you if you behaved more pleasantly. . . . and if you washed a bit more often.'

To console him, for he was really in a sorry state, I added, half-jokingly: 'You know you're handsome in your own way, with that Ashanti black skin, that fine curly hair and all those marks on your cheeks. Perhaps your ancestors were princes and princesses? Who knows what our parents were before we were brought here as slaves!'

But nobody could have changed his mood, except perhaps Cathy – and her thoughts were far away at that moment – and he began to scream like a savage.

'Go away, leave me alone!'

I did what he told me to.

Getting ready to accompany her new friend, Huberte, to the plantation of Belles-Feuilles, Cathy was packing her things, singing at the top of her voice. As my feelings for Razyé had somewhat changed since our conversation in the stables, I was shocked at her lightheartedness and could not help venturing the question: 'Why are you so happy? If I were you I'd be wary of the friendship of those white folk.'

She spun round.

'I'm going to listen to Mozart. I bet you've never heard that name before! I'm going to dance the quadrille; I'm going to speak French with people who are not common and boring. Like all of you here!'

'Like Razyé?' I scoffed.

Her face fell instantly. I thought she was going to start crying like a baby.

'Razyé? Promise me, Nelly, that you'll take good care of him while I'm not here, for I cherish him more . . . more . . . than myself.'

I burst out laughing.

'Well, this is a fine way to show it!'

Thereupon I left the room, without bothering to listen to any more, and slammed the door.

Cathy spent a whole month with Huberte de Linsseuil and I reproached her brother for letting her stay for so long with strangers. Who knows if these white Creoles had not invited her to their house for the pleasure of making fun of her, her family and her manners? But Justin was too preoccupied with savouring his honeymoon to listen to me. All day long, it was 'my little darling', 'my doudou', 'my sweetie'. In the evening the twittering and bellowing that came out from under their bedroom door told anyone who was listening what they were up to. Even so, I could not help noticing that the bride was becoming frailer and frailer, a real wisp of a girl, that the handkerchief she brought to her pallid lips was stained with blood when she mounted the stairs, and that her forehead was damp with drops of sweat every time she walked more than a few yards or made the slightest effort. I tried to mention this to Justin, but every time he sent me packing.

'Thunder and lightning! What are you on about now? There's nothing wrong with Marie-France! People are jealous here, always ready to gossip and spread their nonsense!'

The day after Cathy left, Razyé disappeared. As he still hadn't returned after a week had gone by, I managed with some difficulty to convince Carmélien that we should go and look for him. We walked all over the Heights; we scoured the countryside as far as Petit-Canal, Anse-Bertrand and even Le Moule. I was imagining the worst, when some scamps told us about a beast that was hiding in one of the caves in the cliff. They had tried throwing rocks to make it come out, but to no avail. I guessed immediately what beast this must be. When I saw Razyé with my own eyes I almost ran a mile, for he really was frightening. His eyes were as red as hot peppers and I understood why when I saw all the bottles of Belles-Feuilles rum piled up on the sand in the cave.

Suddenly Nelly Raboteur looked up and cried: 'Good Lord, we've arrived!'

Indeed a multitude of islands had floated up to the surface of the water, like trails of confetti, decorated with rickety shacks balanced on four stones, leaning coconut-palms and sea-grape trees. The town of La Pointe sprawled around the bay. Its patchwork of red and grey roofs huddled round the cathedral against a background of blue-tinged hills. On the right the chimneys of a factory spewed columns of dirty smoke. On the wharf you could already see the commotion of ox-carts drawn by horned zebus, grey donkeys, and porters wheeling their barrows between the legs of the crowd come to meet the boat. On deck there was a rush of feet, and those who had stayed behind to listen made a dash for their cabins.

5   The Return of Razyé

At four o'clock in the afternoon, the folks in Petit-Canal, those who were out on their doorsteps, saw a black man gallop by, astride a black horse. Although his mount was strong and handsome, its hoofs echoed through the silence of the town in a limping, unequal fashion like the three-legged horse of the Bête à Man Ibè that usually only ventures out under cover of night. People took fright. Tearful children ran to hide in their mothers' rags. The men immediately recognized who this could be and shouted at the top of their lungs: 'Mi Razyé, mi!'

At the Bois-sans-soif rum-shop tongues started to wag. The most inebriated of the rum guzzlers recovered their wits. They guessed that Razyé had returned to this desolate land for some serious business. He had a mission to accomplish. They settled down comfortably in the bar and watched for events to unfold.

Razyé reined in his horse at the crossroads and contemplated the landscape where he had grown up. Nothing had changed during the three years he had been away and one got the feeling that in twenty years' time everything would be the same. The same pitiless sun. The same coolie-plums, the same guava-trees, the same *tét à nèg*, the same *razyés* growing lopsided in an arid soil. The same cabins, ashamed of being so ugly. With their bony oxen and goats. Ever since vegetable-growing had been the death of sugar-cane, the sugar-mill had gone to ruin. Its stones were stained with a greenish growth, and a rough crown of acacias grew out of the top. The sea encircled all this desolation with a deep blue line. This is where he had suffered martyrdom, with never a kind word, never an embrace to soften his heart. The girl he loved had trampled him into the dust with little thought for his feelings. Nothing could have separated them, neither the Good Lord nor his saints, neither the devil and his demons nor any other creature on earth. Nobody, except her. And she had done it deliberately.

Who can read the heart of a woman? What had she gained by sacrificing him? She had entered the world of whiteness, of course, she bore a noble name, she owned acres of sugar-cane land and sat in a centre pew at church! But what did she put in her bed every night? A spineless individual!

His return would really shake her up. She must have forgotten about him by now. The first few weeks she must have worried about him. Every morning, on waking, she would have examined her dreams for a sign from him, for this was how they used to communicate. As youngsters, when Justin's spitefulness had separated them, and forced them to sleep far from each other's arms, he had joined her in his sleep and they had done everything they always did together.

And then gradually she had forgotten him.

Suddenly the horse set off at a trot and soon began to gallop as if it were eager to arrive at its destination. The sound of its hoofs striking the limestone road brought back all the echoes of the past, with its inextinguishable suffering.

When Cathy had returned from her stay with Huberte de

Linsseuil, nobody recognized her. The wild girl who laughed at the top of her voice, spoke too loudly, massacred the French language, wiggled her *bonda* and danced the *gwo-ka* every evening in the yard, was dead and buried. A respectable young girl had taken her place. She pouted in just the right way. She didn't walk, she glided, her feet now firmly encased in shoes. She had pinned up and rolled into a chignon her thick black hair that used to tumble down her back. She worried about her complexion, shaded herself under a parasol and hid from the sun. Instead of leaping onto the back of a horse and galloping under the sun, she sat on the veranda leafing through the pages of a book. One lunchtime Nelly Raboteur stood in front of her, watching her savour a fish stew. She skinned the head of the fish with her fork, sucked the bones, the gristle and the eyes one after the other, then placed the remaining bits on the edge of her plate. When she had finished, she sent for some household soap and a bowl of lukewarm water floating with lemon slices and washed her mouth and hands. Justin was certainly proud of her! Every afternoon he would sit his sister in the tilbury next to Marie-France and go visiting all the white Creoles in the vicinity. They would receive him out of pity for his wife, but took offence behind his back at his bad manners. Marie-France was pregnant and thrust her calabash of a belly in front of her. All those who had eyes to see realized that she would not have long to watch her child grow up. But Justin saw nothing of the kind.

Despite her new appearance, Cathy had not forgotten her Razyé. The day she got back, she rushed out to him in the stables. But once there she looked at him in disgust and addressed him sharply.

'You could wash yourself a little. Cut your hair. It looks like a cow's tail.'

He did not answer, wiped his wild-looking face, and

Cathy continued nervously, as if his silence were an accusation.

'What's Nelly been telling me? You ran out of the house after I left? I bet you went drinking rum and running after the girls!'

He found his tongue again.

'In all my life I've never looked at another girl but you.'

She spun round the way she liked to do.

'I'd be surprised a girl would want anything to do with you, the way you look. Listen! Tomorrow I want you to clean yourself up and get dressed so that I can introduce you to Aymeric de Linsseuil.'

Without waiting for a reply, she dashed out into the yard where Justin was shouting for her. They were invited for coconut sorbet at the d'Hérouville's, a white Creole family who were living in style at Anse-Bertrand. This afternoon tea extended late into the evening and it was around eleven o'clock and pitch dark when they returned to l'Engoulvent, cackling, laughing and singing the latest mazurka. That night Razyé waited for Cathy in vain. Around three in the morning, tired of tossing and turning on his straw mattress, he left the stables. It was the month of September, midwife to hurricanes and ill winds. Yet the sky was crystal clear and the air was dry. Outside was as bright as day. An obese moon sprawled high in the sky and lit up every corner of the landscape. The wild and desolate savanna. The waves surging in from the sea. The jagged edges of the rocks. The cross high on the cliffs erected for the three fishing-boats lost in the deep with their cargo of men without a grave or a *Dies irae*. On the horizon, the island of La Désirade, isle of lepers and outcasts like Razyé himself. Who was this Aymeric de Linsseuil Cathy wanted to introduce him to? Huberte's older brother? Why did she seem so infatuated with him?

The next day he tried to make himself look presentable. All his clothes were too short, too tight, stained with mildew and years old, but he did his best and went so far as to look for Nelly Raboteur to cut his hair.

Unfortunately, just as he was about to enter the kitchen, Justin bore down on him and erupted in a fit of anger.

'What are you doing around here? I thought I told you never to set foot inside the house. Get back where you came from and double quick!'

He was forced to beat a retreat and he had to watch from the stables as the Linsseuils' elegant tilbury trundled up to the house. Aymeric was accompanied by his sister Huberte whom he curiously resembled, but in a more effeminate way. It was because he was so blond, his complexion so pink and his eyes so blue that his family had nicknamed him 'heavenly Cherub'. As for the malicious gossips they called him quite simply 'Dolly'. He had studied tropical agronomy at university and spent several years in Bordeaux with his father's older brother, which meant that he spoke elaborate French but not a word of Creole. Because of that, and the colour of his hair and eyes, all the eligible white Creole girls dreamed of walking out of the cathedral on his arm to the tune of Mendelssohn's Wedding March. But his mother was keeping watch, for Aymeric was her only son and the apple of her eye. As far as she was concerned, he had only one flaw, the result of his natural goodness. During his stay in France, he had read too much Montesquieu and other philosophers and believed in the equality of the human races. He believed in eradicating the very memory of slavery and transforming the Belles-Feuilles estate into a model plantation where there would be no white Creoles, no mulattos, no blacks, but free men, equal in the eyes of the law. In his student days he had perpetrated a short essay on 'The White Creole Class in Guadeloupe', which he was rather proud of.

The visit by Huberte and Aymeric lasted for hours.

After having eaten the guava tart, Nelly Raboteur's speciality, and drunk the vanilla-flavoured chocolate, Aymeric took Cathy's arm and they walked to the very edge of the savanna, where the void takes over from the land and the mind is seized by vertigo. They seemed to be deep in conversation. Looking at their silhouettes in the twilight, Razyé dreamed of stealing up on them and with one slit of the throat, getting rid of Aymeric. Oh, to see his blood run thick and red. To send him to his grave and make sure he never returned among the living!

Once again that night he waited for Cathy in vain. Around midnight he walked down to the beach in despair and stretched out on the seaweed. The seagulls contemplated him in astonishment and perched on his body for a better look. Why didn't he have a maman like all the other human beings? Even the slaves in the depths of their hell knew the womb that had carried them. He wondered what face he should give to his dreams and who was this mother he was never to know. Sometimes he told himself she was an Indian who had arrived in this land of exile and misfortune on board the *Aurélie*. Other times she was an African, treading the island paths in search of lost gods. Or else a mulatto girl, torn like Cathy between her two races. Had she been raped and then set about despising the child of the man who had assaulted her? What father's crime was he paying for? How could he explain his abandonment? Razyé was suffering agony. There was a time when Cathy had been a papa, a maman and a sister to him. Her body had protected him. When he curled up against her he found the softness of the breast and the womb he had never known. Now she had deserted him.

He cried for hours and took refuge in a cave.

When he emerged the sun was at its station, as implacable

and tyrannical as usual. Half-naked in their rags, the Indians were cracking open the dry belly of the earth and planting their seeds.

From that day on Aymeric was a regular visitor. He no longer took the trouble to have himself chaperoned by his sister. As the Belles-Feuilles estate was not too far from l'Engoulvent, you could hear the bell on his tilbury tinkling from a distance and he would turn up all alone at any time of day, as if he owned the place. He would sit on the veranda with Cathy and show her picture-books or else read her the magazines from Paris. He taught her to play croquet and other society games. He gave her a little poodle with curls as tight as his that he called Pompom. Once he brought his fiddle and played some Italian capriccios for her. Razyé wondered how Cathy could put up with all these antics. If only they could split their sides laughing once Aymeric had left. But, alas, he could not even get near her. During the day she deliberately made sure that she was always with company. In the evening he would wait for her in vain. Hidden in the shadows, however loud he croaked like an ungainly toad under her window, she would not open her shutters.

One day he took advantage of a moment when Justin had gone to Petit-Canal and a doleful Marie-France, a few weeks away from giving birth, was asleep once again, to slip into the house. He went through the kitchen, where some quails with an occasional flap of the wings were being drained of their blood in the sink, and tiptoed to the threshold of the dining-room. Nelly Raboteur was teasing Cathy while she served her cassava cakes and her morning hot chocolate.

'You're very quiet this morning! You haven't yet flown into a fit of anger, insulted anyone or come to blows! I'd almost say it wasn't you sitting in front of me. What's the matter?'

Sullen and pale, as if she had spent a sleepless night, Cathy seemed to hestitate then made up her mind.

'Yesterday Aymeric de Linsseuil asked me if I would like to marry him.'

Nelly had trouble hiding her disbelief.

'Did he say marry?' she exclaimed.

Cathy nodded. Nelly had been watching Aymeric prowl around Cathy like so many other sons of good families before him. But she expected nothing good to come out of those affected manners and never once dreamed it was for the right reason. A belly, that's all Cathy would get out of it! For there is a golden rule that knows no exception and it is this: the white male will never marry a mulatto girl, though she may be his mistress. Guadeloupe was full of mulatto women who had been given a house, a carriage and a few acres of land in exchange for their reputation.

'Monsieur Justin will be pleased, that he will!'

Cathy put her cup down on her saucer with a clatter.

'Not so fast! I haven't made up my mind yet.'

'What are you waiting for?' Nelly jibed. 'It's not as if you had a stream of suitors to choose from.'

Cathy burst into tears, and it was so unusual for her that Nelly put her arm around her and quietly asked: 'Do you love Monsieur de Linsseuil or don't you?'

Cathy looked up. She seemed to be in agony.

'I do love him. . . . How could I not love him? . . . But can someone like me marry a heavenly Cherub? You know me and you know I'm no angel. Anything but. It's as if there were two Cathys inside me and there always have been, ever since I was little. One Cathy who's come straight from Africa, vices and all. The other Cathy who is the very image of her white ancestor, pure, dutiful, fond of order and moderation. But this second Cathy is seldom heard, and the first always gets the upper hand.'

40

Nelly Raboteur shrugged her shoulders.

'Don't start talking nonsense. Just think, if you marry Monsieur de Linsseuil you'll have everything you never had and more! You'll be the envy of Guadeloupe!'

Cathy sighed.

'I know, I know! And that's why I'm going to marry him. I'll get out of l'Engoulvent that's nothing but a hole full of rats and bats. I'll have silk dresses, wide-brimmed Italian straw hats and servants at my beck and call. My children will be white and rich.'

Yet the longer she listed her future happiness, the darker her face became and she seemed about to burst into tears.

'If Justin hadn't done what he did to Razyé, I wouldn't even be thinking of this marriage. But the way Razyé is now, I could never marry him. It would be too degrading! It would be as if only Cathy the reprobate existed, stepping straight off the slave-ship. Living with him would be like starting over as savages from Africa. Just the same!'

The memory of these words opened up the same old wound inside Razyé. It was on hearing these words that the calabash of his heart had been smashed, and he'd never managed to piece it together.

With its lights glowing behind its louvred shutters, l'Engoulvent loomed up from the savanna like a ship in peril on the sea. The hurricane-lamp that used to light up the outside was long gone, and for an instant Razyé was swallowed up by a mouth full of shadows. The air was filled with the squeaking of bats, whirling around their nests, and the endless din of the night insects. Razyé dismounted, and the famished horse searched in vain for some grass between the cracks in the paved yard. Then he walked up to the entrance, whose door was wide open despite the late hour, as if the inhabitants possessed nothing of value that needed protecting or guarding, and crossed the kitchen where the smell of saltfish lingered sullenly. The dining-room was even dirtier and shabbier than he remembered. An odd assortment of furniture fidgeted on the dusty floorboards in all four corners. A piano sat bored under its dust-cover. A man sitting in front of a glass and a half-empty bottle of rum looked up, and Razyé almost didn't recognize him, he was so altered. Justin was haggard and aged. From light brown his hair had turned to a yellowish white. A beard the same colour was eating up his face, in which his eyes flared red like distress signals.

'Well! The devil has crawled out of hell!' he sneered.

Razyé put down his heavy sack, sat down opposite him and drank from the bottle.

'Well that makes two devils meeting again in hell.'

Justin looked him over with eyes that no longer conveyed hostility, merely weariness and a bottomless despair.

'Where have you been all this time?' he asked. 'You look like you've been a soldier. You're as stiff as a broom.'

Razyé drank from the bottle again.

'I've made my fortune. I can pay you what you like for board and lodging if you let me stay here.'

Justin expressed surprise.

'You want to stay here? You've got no scruples, like a dog with fleas. You want to stay here after the hellish treatment you got from us? Me, and specially Cathy.'

He began to laugh wickedly.

'You sat on the egg for years but another has come to eat the chicken fricassée.'

Razyé leapt on him and threw him to the ground, his neck in a strangle-hold, shouting: 'Don't talk like that, do you hear, or I'll shove you back in your mother's c—'

Holding him brutally like a hog about to be slit open, he asked: 'Where is she?'

'First, let me go,' Justin said calmly.

Razyé reluctantly obeyed and Justin got up.

'Where do you think she is? At the Belles-Feuilles estate. With her husband. Didn't you know she got married?'

He helped himself to another glass of rum and started to speak in a cracked voice without nuance or inflection.

6 Justin Gagneur's Tale

'For once I've got you in front of me, and I'm going to tell you what I think. And even if you don't listen to me, I'm going to tell you and you'll have to hear it.

'You see, I got off to a bad start in life. All those I loved abandoned me, one after the other. First maman. Maman was beautiful, like a rainbow over the sea after the rain. I remember her wake and her funeral as if it were yesterday. On the news of her death nobody took the trouble to come over from Petit-Canal or Anse-Bertrand, because people don't like mulattos like papa, who have nothing to their name but lord it over all those who are blacker than they are. So there were not many people around her bed. Maman was dressed in her wedding-gown, a little tight around the breasts and belly. Her face had been made up. There were white lilies in her hair and arums strewn all around. Old Juminie who never misses a wake and its thick soup led the prayers and mumbled on, caring little about the words:

"For everything its season, and for every activity under heaven its time: a time to be born and a time to die."

'The few mourners were half asleep and the few friends of papa were gossiping on the veranda where Théobalde was telling a story, though nobody was listening.

'In the morning the corpse started to smell as though all sorts of poisons had come up through the skin. Papa jumped on his horse and went to fetch the priest and the undertaker. But all to no avail. He couldn't find them since they had gone to bury someone else in Grands-Fonds-les-Mangles. So we had to stay here and wait for them right up to the afternoon. By that time the corpse stank so much we couldn't go near it. When they arrived, the undertaker's men hurriedly laid it in the coffin and everybody had their handkerchief pressed to their noses. That's what I've never been able to forget: the smell of maman's decaying corpse.'

However hard Razyé cleared his throat to indicate he was somewhat bored by the speech, Justin took no notice and went on talking.

'Secondly, from the very moment you set foot inside l'Engoulvent, both papa and my sister ignored me. I became a nonentity. I couldn't dance or sing or beat the drum like you could. Only play the fiddle, and the violin is white folks' music that doesn't get your blood tingling. I was convinced that if I fell down and died, nobody would notice. Life would go on as usual. All through my adolescence I had this feeling of being unwanted. I thought the Good Lord had finally taken pity on me when He gave me Marie-France. In fact, He was making fun of me, as He always makes fun of us humans, and He took her away from me before I could realize what was happening. Life with her flew by like a dream. You open your eyes one morning and ask yourself: "Did I really live that or was I dreaming?"

'One evening – she had just given birth to our son, Justin-Marie – I was sitting at the head of her bed. I was holding her hand and telling her a silly story she was fond of, the one about a princess who ate a slice of poisoned apple and was laid to sleep in a glass coffin. Suddenly her hand became all soft and limp in mine. I thought she had fallen asleep, but no, she had just passed away like a candle being snuffed out. I wanted to die; I couldn't. What was I going to do with all the rest of my days, what was I going to do?

'People prattled on about my son and his future. They told me a grammar school had just been opened in La Pointe where I could send him to study and become a doctor. Insufferable chatterboxes. Now that Marie-France was gone I had no attachment to this whimpering child. Fortunately, there is rum, our friend, our confidant for every day of the week, staunch and faithful . . . '

After having rambled on, Justin pulled himself together and resumed the thread of his story.

'When you disappeared and we realized that it was not a question of days before you came back, but that you were never going to come back, Cathy almost went out of her mind. At first, I took no notice, I was so absorbed in my own grief. But I finally realized it was a serious business. She had to be watched every minute of the day so that she didn't go out and jump over the cliffs or drown herself in the sea, and she had to be tied to her wooden bed that she clawed with her nails. At night she would scream without catching her breath, like a dog that sees death go past. And then she fell into a sort of stupor. She stayed in bed. She refused any food, solids or liquids. In the mornings Nelly brought her a tray of coconut milk, fresh eggs, cassava and coconut cakes and fine wheaten cookies with guava jelly, but she wouldn't touch a thing. When they took her out onto the veranda to get some air, she would shrink from the daylight and keep her eyes tightly shut as if the sun hurt them. At the same time she kept her head obstinately turned towards the stables, as if she was expecting to see you. Aymeric de Linsseuil did not become disheartened. He came to see her every day the Good Lord made. Doctor Louisor, the family physician, was beyond understanding her sickness and consequently called for a certain Doctor Lacascade, who was well-known in La Pointe. But even he with his leather case, his paunch, his glasses and his self-importance was of no use. As much use as a poultice on a wooden leg. Aymeric was trying to find a way to take her to France to see a specialist when he came up with the answer: Mama Victoire. She was the one who put Cathy on her feet again. Of Nago stock, she was as black as the bottom of a cooking-pot and as tall as a bunch of Guinea grass, and lived in Le Moule in the Bois-Sergent district. Apparently her mother was a healer before she was, and her mother's mother, too, with practices straight out of Africa.

'Yes it was Mama Victoire who brought Cathy back to life. Cathy had become a zombie and she gave her salt.'

Thereupon Justin took another swig of rum, then continued his story.

'Cathy was married to Aymeric de Linsseuil on 13 April 18—. Obviously the Linsseuils were against it. The white Creoles never want us. They have no intention of mixing their blood with ours. They want to keep their plantations for themselves and all the money they got from sugar-cane when they were still whipping their slaves. But Aymeric looked his maman straight in the eye and told her: 'That's how it is. You either accept her or else I go back to France and you'll never see me again.' His maman cried her heart out, and finally she had to give in.

'During the two weeks prior to the wedding it poured with rain, something you never see in our region, especially during the month of July when everything is so dry it goes up in flames like a piece of candlewood. The sky pissed down like a drunk who never quite finishes pissing. For the first time in years the desolate savanna was coated in a fine cover of green and bloomed with the mauve corollas of the creeper used for rabbit food. The water butts and barrels beside the cabins overflowed. This strange phenomenon started off malicious gossip. People said that rain like this meant tears would mar the wedding to be celebrated in silk and gold. The rain would drown it in grief from the very start. It's a fact, love is blind. It's a fact, it gouges out its eyes rather than look truth in the face. But even so, who was Aymeric de Linsseuil going to fool that he did not know what everyone knew – that he was eating Razyé's leftovers?

'And that's why he dismissed Nelly Raboteur. Nelly Raboteur had been in Cathy's service for years. She had kept her clean and tidy and done her hair. She had taken care of her like a maman when she was sick. Nobody knew her whims and fancies better than she did. Nobody but Nelly could get Cathy to laugh at her own bouts of anger and sulking fits. But she also knew too much. So Aymeric got rid of her, on the pretext that there were already enough servants twiddling their thumbs at Belles-Feuilles and that he had hired a certain Lucinda Lucius to take care of his new wife. Without saying a word, Nelly packed her bags and went back to her family. I heard she found work with some mulattos in Le Moule.

But, miracle of miracles, on 13 April the sun rose in all its splendour, so bright over the sea that as early as eight in the morning it was impossible to support its glare. It blinded two fishermen who had the nerve to look up at it and burnt the eyelids of some kids who had done the same.

'Hate the white Creoles as much as you like, you have to admit that they stick together. Not like the mulattos and specially the blacks, always ready to tear each other apart, run each other down and do the dirt on each other. The Linsseuils had ended up accepting Cathy, even though she was a penniless mulatto girl, and consequently, the white Creoles rallied when they were called. Even those from Matouba and Saint-Claude, who hang their great houses on the steep slopes of the volcano, and every morning screw up their eyes to inspect the colour of its smoke. Even those lost in the depths of the forest seldom pierced by the sun's rays. All those who have grown rich from the prosperous sugar-cane regions. The people round about, who were not used to seeing such a multitude of white folk, thronged the side of the roads and their doorsteps, grumbling: "It's been almost fifty years since slavery's supposed to be over and yet the blacks only find misery at the bottom of life's bowl. Meantime the white Creoles are still parading around with the same wealth and haven't suffered one bit."

'Seeing this silent crowd massed around them, the white Creoles took fright, but hid their feelings under their smiles and embraces, under the kisses and hand-kisses they gave each other. They hadn't yet got over the freedom the slaves had won by torching the plantations, poisoning the masters and the cattle. They hadn't got over the speeches by the first mulatto politicians, who were popping up everywhere and claiming to deny what whiteness had always meant. Was this a sign of the end of the world? Were families, one after the other, going to marry into mulatto families like the Linsseuils were doing today? Or worse still into black families? And who knows, one day into Indian families? Was Guadeloupe going to become one vast pig-swill where you couldn't tell one colour or origin from the next? Rather be dead, the patriarch de Saint-Riveaux said to himself, as he descended on arthritic legs from his tilbury. Rather be dead, the dowager Dormay swore to herself, as her jowls touched the velvet of her dress.

'How beautiful Cathy looked in her yards and yards of crêpe de Chine and Alençon lace, with a diadem in her hair and a diamond necklace around her neck, a present from Aymeric, for the Gagneurs owned nothing, not even a vulgar *grenn-do* neckband. How pale she was too, as if she knew on that day she was turning her back on everything that had made her life enjoyable. Under the crystal chandeliers she waltzed with Aymeric over a floor that

49

generations of slaves, her ancestors, had polished, and the music sounded in her ears like the tears of a requiem. For the house of Belles-Feuilles was filled with the sighs and sorrows of black, mulatto and white women united in the same subjection. Slaves raped by sadistic planters. Mistresses poisoned by a rival and dying in unspeakable suffering at the banquet table. Virgins sold to old men for money and parcels of land. Sisters lusted after by their brothers. Mothers by their sons. A week after her marriage, one bride had thrown herself headfirst from the second-floor circular gallery, and the flagstones in the hallway were still stained with her blood. The servants covered it up with pots of flamingo flowers and red ginger. After slavery was restored by the infamous Richepance, some Mandingo women strangled themselves rather than go back into irons. And discerning these wails and sighs amidst the echoes of the wedding feast, Cathy realized she was taking her place of her own accord in a long procession of victims.'

Razyé measured the amount of rum remaining in his glass and asked in a tone that cut short any further rambling: 'Where can I sleep tonight?'

Lost in his thoughts, Justin remained silent for a while and then answered: 'In your old room, the one where you used to sleep with Cathy when you were children. That way you'll be bound to have sweet dreams.'

7   The Belles-Feuilles Plantation

A drive over a mile long bordered with royal palms led to the steps of the great house at Belles-Feuilles. This, together with its park of trees mostly unknown on Grande-Terre, such as *mapous*, candlewood and mahogany, was its only claim to beauty, for the house was fairly commonplace. Each generation of Linsseuils had added to the original building dating from the seventeenth century – a music-room, a child's bedroom, a greenhouse, an ornamental pond, sometimes an entire wing, depending on its fancy. On several occasions the house had been put to the torch by rebellious slaves. Each time it had been rebuilt, massive and identical. A wrought-iron balcony ran along the first floor, but only reached half-way round, stopping up against a strange statue of a young woman with both arms raised, apparently in anger. They nicknamed her Joséphine in memory of a temperamental ancestor who had whipped her slaves herself whenever she felt like it. A Linsseuil infatuated with stars had pierced the ceiling with the dome of an observatory and night after night looked for his heavenly bodies through a telescope. Another had perched an astrolabe on the roof.

The abolition of slavery had not diminished the wealth of the Linsseuils, who still employed a hundred or so free negroes in their sugar-mill at Sainte-Marthe and as many farm workers in their latifundias that covered almost the entire area of the sugar-cane basin on Grande-Terre. They took pride in saying that a man on horseback could travel three days and three nights among the sooty waves of sugar-cane without coming to the end of it. Since the premature death of his papa Alix, victim of an attack of apoplexy, Aymeric, despite his youth, had been in charge of everything. He was a good master, even a very good master, one of the best on the island. He had been one of the first to install steam-driven mills. His black shack alleys painted in bottle-green under galvanized roofs were a model of their kind. They were aligned in parallel rows under the shade of mango-trees and were all fitted with zinc gutters channelling the rain-water into earthenware jars. Behind them stood the latrines, one for every six cabins, regularly disinfected with quicklime. Not far from the great chapel that had witnessed the services and prayers during slavery, Aymeric had recently erected a school that could match Petit-Canal's. A monk paid monthly with money from the estate conscientiously taught the little negroes to recite: 'Our ancestors the Gauls ... ' Beside the dilapidated and run-down infirmary he was planning to build a dispensary, where the workers would be inspected for parasites such as ascarides, pinworms, amoeba and hookworm, and treated for the dysentery that was causing too many to be laid in coffins. Despite all this, nobody liked him on the plantation. Faces scowled when he appeared on horseback. They said he was always on their backs and never let them alone. Secretly, they uttered the insult *makoumè*. Those who had known him much preferred his papa, who gave up counting his illegitimate children and as drunk as a lord would roll in the sawdust of the rum-shops with his slaves. In short, he had been a man who had what it takes between his legs.

Aymeric had always despised the company of women

and feared that of men. The adulation of his maman, his seven sisters and the gaggle of white Creole girls who had only one idea in mind – to catch him and keep him tied to their apron-strings – had cured him of their artificial poses, their dreamy looks and their false modesty. Moreover, when he was twelve his cousin Déodat, almost forty and already bald, had savagely sodomised him in the attic, while on the lawn below they were drinking the traditional *chodo* after the confirmation of his eldest daughter. During his years as a student in Bordeaux he couldn't walk the streets without being bothered by indecent proposals from strangers. During classes on tropical agronomy, male students with a crush on him would slip him passionate love letters. Despite the grief it would cause his mother, he was vaguely thinking of taking refuge in a presbytery when, entering his sister's boudoir, he had caught sight of Cathy. Sitting next to Huberte, she was awkwardly jabbing her needle into a tapestry. This young girl, who was visibly bored in such insipid company and casting looks around her like a trapped mongoose, had sown in his heart for the first time the desire to conquer. The ardour of his gaze had troubled her and in her clumsiness she had pricked herself. In the blood he had caused to flow, he had seen the prelude and the symbol of the blood that would redden the fine linen of their wedding sheets. When he discovered she was not the girl he thought she was, he had not been disheartened. On the contrary! The more he learned about her, the more he desired her. No, she was incomparable, and this passion for Razyé, which cast a shadow over her reputation, likened her to the scandalous Erzulie-Fréda and not to that gaggle of geese dreaming of children, silks and wicker baskets filled with 18-carat-gold jewels.

After three years of marriage, his feelings for her had not lessened. She had remained frail after her illness and had to be treated with great care, but she gave him no serious cause for reproach. She did everything possible to satisfy him, even if she didn't always succeed. She had given him two boys, Déodat and Isidore, as blond as the Linsseuils could be. She sewed and embroidered diligently. She sang in tune (a little too loudly, and Madame de Linsseuil, the mother, rightly reminded her that shouting was not singing). After high mass at the church in Petit Canal she accompanied him to the chapel on the plantation and nodded her head in agreement when, after the sermon by the priest for the negroes, he reproached his workers for their fornication and adultery, in a word, the enduring wickedness of their lives. But he had understood it was useless keeping a woman imprisoned by his side, morning, noon and night, and then in his bed after dark, if her spirit roams wherever it pleases. He realized that Cathy did not belong to him and all he would ever have was a hollow mannequin painted in her image.

That afternoon, when he entered the pineapple-living room, so called because the walls were covered in a white brocade with startling bright blue pineapples, he was covered in sweat and beside himself with anger. A terrible accident had just occurred at the sugar mill. A worker had had half his arm crushed by a machine and had almost died of pain and bleeding. It reminded him of the darkest days of slavery when the lives of the slaves were sacrificed for profit. Aymeric had already spent a fortune modernizing the machines. Apparently it was not enough. However, after a short while, Cathy's smiles, the gracious face of Irmine, his young sister, the sparkle of the silverware and the delicious prospect of the coconut tart on the tea-table soothed his nerves. He regained his usual verve, for he read a lot of French journals and was thought to be extremely witty and knowledgable. He was being offered a cup of

54

vanilla chocolate by a young maid when Lucinda Lucius, the beanpole of a girl he had chosen to replace Nelly Raboteur, rushed into the living-room. She dashed up to Cathy and panted: 'There's someone asking to see you.'

'Who is it?' Cathy asked, slightly irritated.

Lucinda bent down and whispered in her ear. Cathy turned deathly pale, got up so quickly she knocked the table, making the silverware clatter, and ran out of the room. While the young maid busied herself trying to mop up the chocolate that was dripping everywhere, Aymeric turned to Lucinda and asked: 'Who is it?'

She seemed to hesitate then murmured: 'Razyé.'

At the same moment, Cathy entered, beside herself with laughter, arm in arm with an athletic, well-formed man of towering height and upright carriage. His tight curly hair fell over his forehead; his eyes were full of black fire, his cheeks shaven and his skin so black that the cloth of his coat seemed light by comparison. Aymeric had never seen Razyé with his own eyes and from what he had heard, he'd taken him for a common scoundrel. He was stunned by his dignified manner and at a loss for words when Cathy crushed his hand into his. Then his upbringing prevailed and he managed to stammer: 'I am delighted to make your acquaintance at last.'

Razyé openly mocked him.

'Now there's a lie you'll have to admit to in the confessional.'

But Cathy covered this answer with a stream of words, cries and hysterical laughter.

'I shall think it a dream tomorrow. And yet I know it's not a dream because in all these years I haven't dreamed of you even once. Not once! Even in my dreams you abandoned me. Where have you been? Your heart is really like a rock, a boulder, a cliff in the middle of your chest to have left me so long without news. Jesus, Mary and Joseph, I think I shall go mad with happiness. When did you get back? Where are you living?'

'At l'Engoulvent,' he managed to get in.

'At l'Engoulvent!' she exclaimed. 'You have made your peace with Justin?'

Razyé laughed. Gradually the happiness he felt at seeing Cathy, and especially the effect his return had on her, illuminated his entire countenance and he was transformed.

'I wouldn't say that. I'd say he thinks he's found a drinking companion.'

Then he asked, almost in a whisper: 'So you're married?'

At the tone of this question, a mixture of reproach and extreme tenderness, Aymeric broke in.

'Cathy, are you going to serve the tea or are we going to stand here and take root?'

Cathy pulled herself together.

'Let's sit down. Let's sit down. Razyé, sit down here beside me. Let me hold your hand because I don't want you to disappear again. Let me introduce you to Irmine, Aymeric's little sister.'

Irmine, the last of the seven Linsseuil daughters waiting to be married, had just completed her studies with very poor marks at the Catholic boarding-school of Saint-Joseph de Cluny at Versailles. She had a reputation for being impertinent and capricious. What exasperated Aymeric was the way she looked at Razyé. Her eyes sparkled with curiosity and excitement, like a child peeping at something she had been told not to.

He choked on the second cup of chocolate that had just been served him, almost suffocated, and got up furious.

'I apologize, I don't feel very well.'

Then he turned to Razyé, who was watching him in amusement.

56

'Stay, make yourself at home.'

Ever since he was quite small, the vexations of his mind had translated into sicknesses of his body. A bad mark at school and his temperature soared. A scolding from his papa and he lost his voice. He closed the door on Cathy's exclamations of joy that felt like daggers, and mounted the huge stairway lined with potted ornamental palms that led to his mother's quarters. He found her sitting in a rocking-chair, wearing twisted leeches for earrings, for with old age her blood was thickening in her veins and Doctor Louisor constantly prescribed for her castor-oil and blood-letting.

'Misfortune has just entered this house,' he said darkly, as he sat down.

Madame de Linsseuil did not answer. For her, misfortune had entered the house of Belles-Feuilles a long time ago, in the shape of Cathy; she had only to count the number of calamities that had befallen them ever since she had come to live with them. Two years ago, just before Christmas, during a family outing to the waterfalls at Moreau, the son of Amédée, her husband's brother, had broken his neck on a boulder. The following Palm Sunday, Eléonore, her first cousin, had fainted in church shortly after the *Agnus Dei* and had died in the tilbury that was hurrying her home. On 15 August, her eldest daughter's twins had drowned in a pond under the eyes of their nursemaid. Three days later, a fire had started in the cane-fields and left a hundred acres scorched, bristling with burnt stumps. At the church in Petit-Canal there was a nigger priest who sat down in the confessional and gave communion like a white man. What worse could happen?

'This Razyé has come back,' he explained gloomily. 'Well dressed, from head to toe. If it weren't for his colour, his face would let him into any respectable salon.'

One of the bloated leeches detached itself from the ear of

57

Madame de Linsseuil and dropped onto her satin peignoir. She slipped it into a glass jar, commenting: 'Well, he must have changed then. I caught sight of him once at church with the late Hubert Gagneur and he looked like Satan in person.'

She hesitated.

'With the reputation he's got around here, aren't you going to stop him from setting foot inside this house?'

Aymeric shook his head.

'It's impossible. You know that Cathy loves him as if he really were her brother.'

Her brother? Come now! But Madame de Linsseuil cherished her son too much to let herself say what she thought in the secret of her heart.

Cathy lay with her eyes wide open in the dark, overwhelmed by the violence of her emotions.

All around her the shadows of the room, curtained off in heavy repp, locked her in like a tomb. She could hear the spasmodic breathing of Aymeric as he lay with his back to her in bed. He had declared himself sick with fever and a servant had had to bring him a tea of soursop leaves. She was no fool. All this had been caused by Razyé, the return of Razyé. How tiresome men were. Good Lord! What was he blaming her for? For having shown her happiness at finding the man she thought she had lost for ever? Had she ever kept her feelings for him a secret? If he loved her as he said he did over and over again, if he wanted her to be happy, he should not have received him so coldly, with a worried, forced expression, but with a burst of friendship.

She slipped out of bed.

Under her feet the century-old floorboards creaked. At night the old house groaned and shook and resonated with all the sounds of its secrets locked in its dressers and cupboards. Rapes, murders and theft of all sorts. Sometimes it would wail like a widow or a maman separated from her infants. Sometimes it jabbered like a mad woman.

Suffocating, Cathy quickly crossed the bedroom and went out onto the landing. An oil-lamp that was always kept burning downstairs cast grotesque shadows on the framed portraits of Linsseuils in rows along the walls.

Cathy entered her sons' bedroom and immediately caught that smell of children coddled, lotioned and perfumed that had never been hers. However hard poor Nelly Raboteur had worked on her, she had still smelled rancid and sour. As a wild young girl her skin cracked like pottery that had stayed too long in the oven. She would scratch herself, and the scratches would become infected under the scab and swell with pus and dead skin. She had *lotas*, fungus spots, all up her legs and sunburn all over her face. Her hair tied in two braids was singed, spiked with stickseed and tiny prickles. Sometimes when she scratched her head she would crush lice under her half-mourning nails. From mounting Toussine without a saddle her buttocks were hard and calloused. She urinated standing up, legs wide apart, the way she had seen Razyé do it, and sprayed the jet of urine onto the mad ants that went crazy. On Sunday mornings, when Nelly made her sit down in a tub and scrubbed her with a bunch of leaves, the water turned black. Razyé was even worse, and Nelly used to hold her nose when she picked up his clothes.

It must have been because of these differences that her children were so foreign to her. When the nursemaid brought them to her, their hair shining with brilliantine, wrapped in velvet and English embroidery, harnessed like parade horses, she hardly dared touch them. The colour of their skin, the blond down on their heads and the blue of their eyes fascinated her. Was it really her who had made these little dribbling darlings with porcelain cheeks? Frightened by her reticence, the children did not dare approach her. Their papa got all the attention. They ran to him as soon as he was within reach. They clung to his trousers and passed their hands with great delight over the bumps and hollows of his face. Yet, during the first months of her pregnancies, she had been so happy! The body that had wanted to die seemed to be reconciled with her since it was bringing back life. With a feeling of guilt she caressed Isidore's and Déodat's tiny hands. How soundly they slept! They didn't need her any more asleep than they did when awake.

She went over to the window. A thin crescent moon in its first quarter barely lit the drive of royal palms, the lawns, the flower-beds and in the distance the swell of sugar-cane that rippled as far as the horizon. The great house stood on top of its hill like an island in the middle of the ocean or a lighthouse on its rock. It was then, through the darkness, that she distinctly saw a black horseman as straight as an I on his black horse.

It was Razyé! It was him!

Her first reaction was to rush out and join him as she used to do so that they could gallop the whole night through to the end of their desires. In the sky, the moon would have given way to the sun before they had quenched themselves. Then her common sense prevailed. How could she just get up and leave her husband to his cold feet and cotton nightshirt in the conjugal bed? Well might we ask how he would receive her on her return and what excuse she would give to justify her absence. As if he reproached her for pondering and hesitating, the horseman disappeared as quickly as he had come.

Cathy was shivering and she decided to return to her

room. Suddenly she was gripped with apprehension. Why had Razyé come back? Why was he living at l'Engoulvent? Something told her that all this was a bad omen and that he had not come as a Christian to turn the other cheek to those who had offended him.

On the landing, a white shape almost made her shriek, then she recognized her little sister-in-law, a braid down her back, in her boarding-school nightdress.

'Irmine!' she exclaimed. 'You gave me such a fright!'

'I can't sleep,' Irmine murmured. 'Cathy, tell me about Razyé.'

'Razyé?' Cathy scoffed. 'It's difficult to talk about attachments formed when you are children. But don't go by his looks or fancy French. He's a person without education or culture. A kind of *soubarou*, a wild man of the forest, a runaway slave. I'm sure he's never opened a book in his entire life, and though he knows how to count, he can hardly sign his name.'

Irmine shrugged her shoulders.

'What's that to me? Do you think my French is so good or that I've read a lot of books in my life? He's not like any of those wimps they want us to fall in love with . . . I bet he . . . '

Thereupon, she bent over and whispered into Cathy's ear. By way of an answer Cathy sent her flying down the stairs. She got up, furious, but at that moment the lamp downstairs went out, and the stairway was plunged into darkness.

8   A Forest Sojourn

Every year during the second two weeks of August, on the recommendation of Doctor Louisor, Aymeric took Cathy to Dolé-les-Bains to take the waters. The old doctor, who had taken care of her since her wedding, was worried about a persistent cough that plagued her every evening at dusk and heartbeats that the slightest distress quickened or on the contrary slowed down. Usually Cathy looked forward to this forest sojourn. She loved the hotel at Dolé-les-Bains, slumbering amidst its thick vegetation like the castle of Sleeping Beauty. She adored the same old suite she occupied with her husband on the first floor. The front windows looked out onto the islands of Les Saintes, prettily arranged in a semicircle on the silky blue sea. The back windows almost touched a dark green tangle of trees, creepers and vines. Way up above, the formidable volcano stood watch, a pipe between her teeth like a shrew. Breathing an air so different from that of Grande-Terre, cooler, damper and softer, Cathy always felt like another person, no longer estranged or tormented, but in harmony with herself, almost happy. That year, however, she could not bear the thought of being separated from Razyé, having just found him again. Without even consulting Aymeric, she invited Razyé to accompany them.

They set off at first light in a rented carriage with Irmine, Lucinda Lucius, two other servant girls, the children and their *mabo*.

Inside the carriage the atmosphere was tense. Ever since the incident on the landing, the two sisters-in-law no longer spoke to each other unless they had to. As for Aymeric, he was turning the same questions over and over in his mind. Should he have stopped Razyé coming with them? Shouldn't he have put his foot down as a husband? Only Razyé watched the landscape go by, hiding behind the smoke of his Havana cigar, as if nothing was the matter.

Once past the River Salée, the scenery undergoes a sudden transformation. The traveller enters the actual island of Guadeloupe, still named Basse-Terre, and he leaves behind him the arid landscape of limestone bluffs spiked with prickly pears, the salt-coloured sandy coves and the white madreporic cliffs. The air is heavy with the taste and smell of rain. The damp sky lowers and darkens. Then the outline of the mountains becomes apparent, now grey, now dark green, lying across the horizon like a herd of lazy cows. The first banana groves appear and the vegetation becomes thicker and thicker. Soon, it is the realm of the candlewood, the mastwood, the red mahoe and the mastic trees that soar to the clouds.

The journey took almost the entire day. They rumbled over rivers hiding under shaky bridges, and at bends in the road, villages loomed up, wedged between sea and mountain. They arrived at Dolé-les-Bains when the light was fading and the fireflies had started to glow. As usual, however, Cathy had not given enough thought to what she was doing. Never at Dolé-les-Bains had they received a negro guest, and it required much persuasion by Aymeric for the hotel management to accept a man of colour. Finally they carried his bags to a storage room under the roof.

In order to make up for this humiliation, which he accepted with his usual impassiveness, Cathy threw herself around his neck, without even waiting for her trunks to be carried up.

'Come, let me show you the forest. I come here so often I know the name of every plant, every tree and every creeper by heart. I can tell you the name of the candlewood and mastwood tree or the oilcloth flower, the goosefoot creeper and the morning glory.'

Then she dragged him away in a fit of laughter.

When she returned to the hotel, the stars were hanging in their usual spot in a crêpe de Chine sky. The air reverberated with all sorts of sounds: the croaking of frogs and toads forever thirsting after the soft rain-water, the song of the hot springs as they flowed under the vegetation, and the lament of the gullies as they furrowed the belly of the earth in every direction. Was it as late as that?

She took fright. Picking up her skirts, she dashed up the stairs leading to the first floor. On entering the salon only Irmine was to be found, melancholically drinking lemon-grass tea in the company of Lucinda Lucius.

'Where's Monsieur?' she asked the servant girl, out of breath.

But before the latter could answer, Irmine wailed: 'I would like to be out walking in the forest too.'

'I'd like to see you,' Cathy jibed. 'You who can't put one foot in front of the other, you'd be falling and stumbling over the roots.'

Irmine started to cry.

'Is the whole stay going to be like this? Will you go on keeping Razyé to yourself like you did this evening?'

Cathy sat down in front of her.

'Now listen to me,' she said in a serious tone of voice. 'I've already told you to get Razyé out of your head.'

'Why?' the other shouted. 'Because you want him all to yourself?'

It was Cathy's turn to shout.

'What do you want? A child in your belly? Is that what you want?'

Irmine shook her head with disgust.

'You say he's your friend, and that's how you speak of him? It shows the sort of person you are. You're nothing but a hypocrite, a viper's tongue.'

Cathy threw herself onto her, clawing her, and they both rolled on the ground like two slave-girls fighting over the same man. On hearing such a commotion Aymeric came out of the bedroom, pale and haggard, so distressed had he been by Cathy's behaviour.

'What on earth is going on?' he thundered.

Cathy got up and grudgingly had to explain to him what had happened. He then turned to Irmine and said roughly: 'For one of you to be crazy about him is quite enough. I'm not talking about his colour. The Lord knows that in my eyes a negro is no different from a white or a mulatto. But he's an individual without a name, without an education and without any virtue whatsoever. We don't know what he does or how he earns his living. I no longer want to hear his name mentioned in my presence.'

Cathy, who had never seen her husband in a temper, was stunned.

As a result of this incident, the stay went wretchedly, and only the children profited from the change of air. Aymeric read in his room from morning to night and thus devoured the complete works of Victor Hugo in two weeks. Cathy no longer dared leave the salon and embroidered an entire table-runner in cross-stitch under the watchful eye of Lucinda Lucius. As for Razyé, he carefully oiled his rifle every day and went off to slaughter the thrushes, partridges and woodpigeons that abounded on the upper slopes. He would return to his room mid-afternoon and emerge an hour later for a long walk in the forest. When finally he got back to the hotel, the oil-lamps had been lit and the guests were eating in the dining-room. Everyone looked up to watch as he sat down alone at a secluded table and noisily lapped up his soup. After the meal he went and joined a crowd of no-good individuals who played cards for money in the dives at Trois-Rivières, and pocketed the money he won from beating them all hollow.

Lucinda Lucius, however, could see with her own two eyes that Irmine, at first in a foul mood, grew increasingly cheerful as the days went by. She would get up humming the tune to various biguines, and it was a *Ban mwen an ti bo* here and a *Doudou ki jou? pa jodi la!* there. At lunch she nibbled at her food, had a short siesta, then at the end of the afternoon disappeared under the tulip-trees in the park. When she got back from her interminable walks her face was red and flushed. Lucinda Lucius decided to get to the bottom of things.

9   Lucinda Lucius' Tale

The great house of Belles-Feuilles is the jail of my life. That's where I was born, where Estella, my maman, was born before me, and Fanotte, the maman of my maman, as far back as Fankora, my Bambara ancestor, who was captured by some 'mad dogs in the bush' outside the walls of Segu while she was returning from washing her clothes as white as cotton in the waters of the Joliba. Her wedding with a nobleman from the house of Diarra was to be held three moons later. Instead of which she found herself captive, a wooden collar around her neck, being forced to march to the tip of Cap-Vert.

On the slave ship that carried her to the land of her degradation a sailor took his pleasure with her, and when she got to Guadeloupe she gave birth to a little girl the colour of curdled milk whom her new master, Amédée de Linsseuil, christened 'Snow' as a joke. I don't know much about my ancestors except that they toiled, suffered and died on this plantation where I myself am toiling, suffering, and where I shall die when the Good Lord calls me to Him. For my generation the end of slavery means nothing. It's the same sadness, the same wretchedness we've been chewing on for as long as we can remember.

I'm sure I'd have suffered less if I had found a man to pull me up, even a very black man, 'kongo' or 'blue' as we say. But men don't even give me a second look. They say I'm too tall, that I've got nothing up front and nothing behind and making love to me would be like a dish without salt or hot pepper. That hasn't stopped several of them from taking me by force on the ground in the savanna, but afterwards, when I wanted to see them again, they laughed in my face.

'Yellow girl, who do you think you are? Have you looked at yourself?'

To tell the truth, since maman died, I walk alone through the potholes of life.

I didn't want to look after Cathy Gagneur or rather Cathy de Linsseuil (although everyone called her jokingly Mam Razyé behind her back), for I knew she was capricious, brazen, with no education and no manners, the very image of her papa, a mulatto who thought the world of himself and died like the dog he was. But I was the one the master chose. Ever since I was little, the master has been good to me. He likes the way I walk with my eyes lowered, the way I never raise my voice and the fact I don't have any friends or family to gossip with. He knows it won't be me who'll go prattling about whether there was any blood on the white embroidered linen sheets on his wedding night.

A few days before the wedding he called me in. I lowered my eyes out of respect. Even so, deep down, I couldn't help noticing he didn't have that contented and assured look of a man about to take possession of the woman he desired. Quite the opposite. He seemed worried, tormented, like a cat on a hot tin roof. He was pacing up and down his study, wringing his hands. A Bible lay open on his table, with its pages crumpled and dog-eared, as if he were constantly searching for consolation in the words of the Lord, the only ones you can count on not to lie.

'Listen to me,' he advised me. 'Ever since she was ill, her health has remained fragile and her temperament whiny.

But through gentleness and love we'll work wonders with her, you'll see.'

I assured him of my devoted services.

In early April, Cathy de Linsseuil entered the house of Belles-Feuilles in her princess's gown, under her veil pinned by a diadem of orange blossom, without even a glance at the servants lined up on the front steps. As if she had forgotten that in times long ago, her ancestors had climbed out of the same boat as ours and toiled under the same sun before catching the master's eye and earning the bitter favour of carrying his illegitimate children. She passed in front of us without so much as a look and went straight up to her room. I went and introduced myself and helped her get ready for the ball. I perfumed her and made up her face, for she had the colour of a corpse.

As early as the next day I saw that what people said about her was no exaggeration. She swore like a heathen and flew into fits of rage I had never seen in anyone. More than once, in her anger, she raised her hand against me. But the master was right, there were moments when she chattered away and was as touching as a little girl. I'm not quite sure how, but my heart quickly grew fond of her.

I listened to her while she talked about her maman, who died when she was three; that's why she was like she was, as hard as a breadnut. She also talked about her papa and her brother, but never mentioned Razyé, as if she didn't have the strength to pronounce his name. She only mentioned the master's name to praise his goodness and generosity. Tears filled her eyes when she murmured: 'No other man comes near him.'

But I knew that her heart and her body lied and that he didn't give her what she needed. In the morning when I entered her bedroom I would find her already awake, propped up against her pillows, brooding and dissatisfied. I would lay down the breakfast tray in front of her on which I had arranged the cassava cakes, litchi jelly and a tall glass of coconut milk. I tried to get her to laugh by searching for the key to her dreams.

'You dreamed of a fishing-boat? A journey! Perhaps you'll leave for France with Monsieur.'

'Pregnancy? You'll be granted everything you wish! What would you like in your secret heart?'

She became even more melancholic.

So I would stop and untangle her silky locks, so long, so different from my picky-picky hair. At siesta time I told her stories until she dropped off to sleep and I watched her slumber with pearls of sweat around her mouth. In the evening, before going to bed, when I gave her her bath, I let the perfumed water run down her shoulders and her breasts with large aubergine-coloured nipples that bore the mark of her black blood, to the soft folds of her belly. She spread her thighs and my hand delved into the most secret spot of her body. Cathy was my mistress, but she was also my lover, she was also my child. She was the woman I wanted to be. I worshipped her and sometimes I hated her. That's why I told her what Razyé was doing behind her back. Out of compassion, I wanted her to know the truth, but I also wanted to hurt her and remind her she was nothing but a woman like the others, like all the others: cheated and deceived by the man she loved.

It was one late afternoon. The day had been overcast and blustery as it often was at this altitude. The clouds hung low and heavy like a lid. That's why I don't like Basse-Terre. Its climate is not suited to my melancholy nature. I need the laughter of the sun and its sparkle to warm my heart and body.

Everyone thought that Irmine was taking a siesta in her room, whereas in fact I had seen her tiptoe up to the attic.

The master was reading or sleeping, one or the other. Cathy was sticking her needle into her tapestry with her head down. Poor Cathy! Ever since her jaunt the day we arrived she had tried to be well-behaved, reading, embroidering or playing with the children. Darkness had stolen down from the mountain slopes and crept over the carpet in the living-room in a layer of black. Soon I would have to light the lamp and dress Cathy for dinner. When I made up my mind to tell her what I knew, she listened to me open-mouthed, her eyes wide with astonishment and already a trace of pain.

'Are you sure?' she stammered.

I nodded.

'Sure as can be. No later than yesterday I was walking behind them and saw them rubbing up against each other like dogs in heat behind a turpentine-tree. After that they went deeper into the woods and I couldn't follow them. A short while ago I saw Irmine creep up the stairs to Razyé's room.'

'He can't be in love with her,' she breathed. 'It's impossible! Even if I heard it from his own mouth, I would know he was lying. So why is he doing this?'

'Perhaps he wants to marry her for her money?' I proposed.

She shrugged her shoulders.

'Marry her? Are you out of your mind? The Linsseuils would never accept a negro. They'd throw her out, they'd disinherit her, as simple as that, and that wouldn't get him very far!'

Then she went silent, furrowed her brow, looked up and staring right through me, added: 'Perhaps he wants to take his revenge on Aymeric? Drag his sister into the mud out of pure spite? But what has Aymeric done to him? I'm the guilty one!'

Suddenly, she jumped up.

'Are they upstairs?'

And as quick as ever, she dropped her tapestry and ran out of the living-room.

What was going on in that room in the garret? I waited, trembling and praying to the Good Lord for over an hour. Then I heard cries and shouts. Finally the door opened and Cathy entered dragging in Irmine, flushed, dishevelled and in tears.

'I haven't done anything!' she groaned. 'I swear!'

But Cathy wasn't listening and repeated: 'I'm going to tell your brother. I'm going to tell him. Aymeric!'

At all this commotion, Monsieur de Linsseuil finally came out of the bedroom, already dressed for dinner in his dove-grey suit and stiff high-collared shirt, more of a heavenly Cherub than ever, only whiter and blonder.

'What is going on now?' he asked irritably.

At the same moment Razyé made an appearance. How can I describe the contrast between the two men? Never had I noticed how the master's nickname suited him so well. He looked like a choirboy who serves at high mass on Sundays, or else a lamb that sucks his maman's teat, or a red-eyed, twitchy-nosed rabbit in its hutch. As for Razyé, he was a volcano, a hurricane, an earthquake, a nigger stud with his iron spike pointing between his legs.

'Aymeric!' Cathy cried like a fury. 'I've just caught your sister in Razyé's room and she is incapable of telling me what she was doing there. Ask her! Ask her!'

But instead of interrogating his sister, Aymeric turned on her, shouting: 'All this is your fault! You're the one who imposed on us the company of a good-for-nothing, a scoundrel!'

Beside himself with anger, he walked over to her and apparently was about to lay his hands on her when Razyé stopped him.

'Well, this lamb now threatens like a bull. Lay one finger on her! Lay one finger on her, do you hear, and I'll cut you to pieces.'

Thereupon with a single prod he sent my master sprawling on the carpet and, taking Irmine by the arm, marched calmly towards the door. At that moment it was as if Cathy went mad. She threw herself onto him and hammered her fists against his chest. Getting no reaction, she ran to the door and put her arms out to bar the way.

'Where are you going with her?'

He pushed her gently but firmly aside, and she shouted to her husband,

'Do something instead of lying there like a wimp. Oh! I always knew you weren't a man!'

Aymeric de Linsseuil lay prostrate on the floor, oblivious to what she said, and Razyé walked out with Irmine clinging to his arm.

It was around midnight when Cathy fell ill with the fever. The moon was high and round in the sky when the sweat came gushing out of her body and soaked the bedsheets. She sat up, erect, took off her nightgown and tried to tear it to pieces. Then she suddenly fell back on her pillows, sat up again, fell back, all the time talking off the top of her head, repeating over and over again: 'Lucinda, don't go. Don't leave me.'

Finally I got scared of her senseless chatter and decided to call the master. I thought he was locked in his room, but however hard I knocked and hammered on the wooden door, there was no answer. How could he be sleeping at such a time? As I was walking back across the living-room, a voice came out of the dark and made me jump.

'What do you want?'

I lit the lamp and took fright. All dressed and as pale as Lazarus stepping out of the grave, the master was sitting in an armchair. Suddenly he looked like an old bag of bones, lugging on his back all the suffering and weariness of the world.

'She,' I panted, 'Cathy . . . Madame . . . is unwell.'

He looked me up and down.

'And me, do you think I'm well? I'm more than unwell, I am dead.'

'In the name of God,' I insisted, 'who created us creatures on this earth, come and see her.'

He made as if to get up and then slumped back down in his armchair.

'No, I bet there's nothing the matter with her and she's simply playing the spoilt child. If she sees I'm not running to her like her dog Pompom, she'll get over it.'

Beside myself with anger, I returned to the bedroom.

Cathy had thrown her nightgown on the floor and was standing in front of the wide open window. At this late hour of the night, a cold breeze was blowing in from the mountain and wrapping her in its chill. In the moonlight her body appeared as lovely as a miracle, but her face was that of a madwoman. Her hair floated around her head like strands of seaweed. I picked up the blanket she had thrown to the floor and tried to wrap it around her. She burst into tears in my arms.

'If he leaves again, I'll never get over it. Never, I tell you.'

Monsieur de Linsseuil was finally convinced that his wife was in a serious condition, beyond hope perhaps, and he brought her back to the Belles-Feuilles plantation.

Even if the Good Lord is cruel enough to keep me alive until the age of a hundred and seven, I shall never forget that journey in a closed carriage which lasted a whole day and a part of the night. Because of Cathy the horses ambled at a walking pace, and I had the feeling I was inside a hearse, holding the icy cold hands of a corpse in mine. With eyes closed, Cathy remained motionless. Sometimes she was silent and the only sign of life was her heavy breathing. At other times she started to ramble again. Between her bouts of tears, the master dampened her temples with bay-rum, had her inhale tinctures of benzoin and asafoetida or else spooned drops of orange-blossom water between her lips.

Around ten in the evening the carriage trundled over the bridge crossing the Salée River and I recognized the harbour in La Pointe from the smell of mud and saltfish. From there on the horses quickened their pace and we were soon home.

As we rumbled up the drive, I saw with amazement that all the lamps on the ground floor were lit. It was because a family meeting was being held. Madame de Linsseuil, the mother, had just received a letter from Irmine that was being passed round. Some of the Linsseuils were offended. Some were crying. Others talked of going to fetch the guilty party so that her fate might serve as an example to all those who were tempted to imitate her and soil the whiteness of their sheets with a nigger.

Postmarked from Dominica, Irmine's letter went as follows:

I know you will never give your consent to our marriage and I am not asking you for it. Besides, what's the use of marrying? There's no need for a priest and his blessing to unite two beings who desire each other. The man you so slandered and denigrated is better than the best of you. His soul is whiter than yours. You are not worthy to tie his shoelaces.

I hate you, you and your society, who had nothing better to do than invent bondage, the bondage of blacks and the bondage of women.

It wasn't my business. I had my patient to look after. With the help of two servants, I carried my treasure up to her room.

Cathy's cerebral fever lasted two months. Once again it wasn't Doctor Louisor with his white folks' medicine that saved her. It's no use at all, white folks' medicine. You need the science and power of our gods from Africa. Aymeric went to fetch Mama Victoire in her cabin behind the church in Le Moule and brought her back to the house – a small, black woman dressed in mourning, vested with powers from places even she did not know of. Mama Victoire refused to live in the great house and set herself up in the servants' quarters. Every morning she was up before first light and was bent in prayer under one of the man-jack trees in the park. She didn't eat the food of ordinary humans but cooked *migans*, country stews, that she seasoned with magic words. I did everything she bade me do. I went to search for plants in the savanna or by the seashore, I put them out to dry, I ground their roots, I made decoctions, I prepared poultices and potions. With our combined forces Cathy got better, together with the child she was carrying, for she was pregnant. But merciful Lord, the sickness carried off her senses. When she regained consciousness, she seemed to have forgotten everything that had happened at Dolé-les-Bains. She had become a little child again, living her life from one minute to the next, and the big belly that stuck out in front of her seemed shockingly absurd.

It was about this time that a rumour started to spread around the neighbourhood. Razyé and Irmine had returned from Dominica, where Razyé had increased his wealth by gambling, and they were living with Justin and his son Justin-Marie at l'Engoulvent. Those who claimed to have seen them said that Irmine was a sorry sight when she came to church. Looking like a poor wretch in rags, her skin had blackened under the sun and her hair no longer saw a comb. She took care of Justin-Marie like a nursemaid, and what's more, waited hand and foot on the two men. Other malicious gossips went so far as to assert that these two souls of the damned put her in their bed and took their pleasure with her. As a result, she would be incapable of naming the papa of the child peeping through in her belly, for she too was pregnant.

I have never wasted my time listening to the malicious gossip of niggers, who only know how to bad-mouth, and I certainly would never have paid attention to such wicked lies if one Sunday in October a little boy smelling of ylang-ylang hadn't handed me a letter that a person had given him for me after mass.

'A person! What person?'

The boy fled without a word, his dry flaky heels touching the seat of his patched trousers.

Like all the servants at the house I had learnt to read and write, since the master never stopped repeating that only education would make us forget Africa and set us on the road to improvement. So I locked myself in my room under the roof and unfolded the thin sheet of paper.

L'Engoulvent, 13th October, 189—

Dear Lucinda,

How many wrongdoings we commit during our time on this earth! When we are faced with death we shall only have the Good Lord's mercy to count on! I have greatly offended my brother and all my family. I refused to listen to Cathy and called her all sorts of names. Now I'm in agony. I'm burning with a question that I turn over and over in my mind without finding an answer. Is Razyé a man? Did he come out of a woman like you, like me? Is it blood that flows in his veins? Or is it pus like the devil in the Ti-Marie story? Does the milk of human feeling water his heart? Sometimes I tell myself he's a fiend from Africa, as evil as a bloodsucker, eager to destroy the happiness around him.

We stayed two months in Roseau on Dominica. What a lovely little town it is! So different from the dirt and crowds of La Pointe. The houses are built of pink brick with flowers on the balconies. On Sundays the men, all dressed in white, play cricket, a game their masters, the English, taught them. For everyone's English, though they also speak Creole, like in Guadeloupe. Absolutely nothing happens. Time and life itself with its trail of misfortune seem to have come to a standstill and the inhabitants appear perfectly happy. As for me, however, my life was a living hell. We stayed at a hotel by the sea called the Kiskadee, frequented by *dames-gabrielles*, those women of easy virtue recognizable by their silks and necklaces made of chrysocolla. I never left my room for fear of meeting them with the men they took in. Razyé was always out and only came home around two or three in the morning, swearing and drunk. At first he was always on top of me. He tore me, showered me with kisses and drenched me with his frothy white seed. Then, for some unknown reason, he stopped altogether. He no longer touched me and turned his back on me in bed. Oh, Lucinda, you will never believe me, but I suffered more from this indifference than his repeated rapes. I had become like a dog who needs her master to give her a kick and then asks for more. One day he suddenly announced we were returning to Guadeloupe the very next morning. I didn't even have time to protest. In the small hours of the morning we set sail on the *Southampton*. What a boat! A walnut-shell daubed with tar that the waves seemed to swallow up at every instant. You know how bad the channel is between Dominica and Guadeloupe! We had hardly left the coast when people started to vomit left and right. I was as sick as a dog but Razyé didn't take a scrap of notice.

Now I am burning in a worse hell. Razyé has 'given' me to Justin and profits from the indecent passion the latter feels for me to strip him of his property. L'Engoulvent is already heavily mortgaged. Every evening Razyé plays cards with Justin and encourages him to drink rum, or worse still, absinthe. Justin never has a thought for his child, poor Justin-Marie. I am at the mercy of a man I loathe, and despised by a man whom, despite everything, I have never stopped loving.

I dare not write either to my mother or to my brother, for I know they will not read my letter, and rightly so. I cry for my lost youth. Ask Cathy to forgive me.

Irmine

I did not take the trouble to mention this letter to Cathy. Could she still remember who Irmine was?

10   *Lucinda Lucius' Tale (continued)*

One afternoon in November I settled Cathy on the veranda.
Her pregnancy was now in its seventh month and all that
could be seen was the mound of her belly, for all the con-
tours of her body had melted. She was nothing but a bag of
bones. Her hair had fallen out in great lumps; her withered
skin had yellowed. In short, her beauty was nothing more
than a memory. Nevertheless I cherished her like a maman
cherishes her sickly child, misshapen by Nature, unlucky in
life. As for the master, he had left for the factory and was not
about to reappear. He remained absent like that for the
entire day. It was as if, in spite of his love, he could not bear
being with his wife and seeing the contrast between what
she had been and what she had become.

That afternoon the sky was leaden and the winds were
laden with salt and water. We had just celebrated All Souls'
Day in memory of the dead. From one end of Grande-Terre
to the other the graves were covered with candles and
flowers, and every graveyard looked like a huge tray loaded
with offerings for the invisible spirits. I helped Cathy stretch
out in a comfortable chair and was about to tell her a story,
something that would occupy her mind, when she asked me
calmly and solemnly, as if all her senses had returned:

'Lucinda, do you believe that after we die we meet up
with those we loved on earth and we spend eternity
together?'

'Don't you hear the priest promise us that every Sunday from his pulpit?' I answered in as soothing a voice as I could.

She shook her head.

'He's talking about Heaven. But I couldn't care less about Heaven. That's not where I want to go, to find myself in the company of saints and angels. Heaven is not for me. I dream of an after-life where we can express all the emotions and desires we have had to stifle during our lifetime. An after-life where we would be free at last to be ourselves.'

'If people could hear you!' I scolded her. 'It's not Christian to speak like that.'

'I know, I know,' she murmured. 'You see, ever since I was little I've wondered whether the Christian religion is not a white folks' religion made for white folks; whether it's right for us who have African blood in our veins. Shouldn't there be a religion for every race, every people on this earth?'

It must have been the first time I heard her claim her African heritage. I was stupefied. And then something in the way she spoke frightened me. It was almost as if she was already on the other side of the world.

'The religion we are taught in church forbids us everything that makes life exciting,' she whispered. 'Because of that the needs of our body are transformed into a curse.'

In my dismay I ran to the kitchen to fetch the tea-tray. In the parlour I bumped into someone hiding behind a dresser, the last person I wanted to see – Razyé! I could only look at him with hatred and terror. Wasn't his treachery responsible for the state of my mistress? He grasped my arm in a claw-like grip and growled:

'I want to see her!'

'Never, never on my life, do you hear! Do you want to kill her?'

'I want to see her,' he repeated, as if my words had meant nothing.

'She remembers nothing,' I pleaded. 'I'm not even sure she would know you.'

He laughed bitterly.

'Do you really think she can forget me?'

When we came out onto the veranda, with him walking behind me, Cathy looked up and stared at him, intrigued, as if she were trying to picture him back in her mind. Then all at once the colour returned to her cheeks. She became flustered and chattered disjointedly. He fell at her feet, pressed his face against the woollen blanket over her knees while she caressed his curly hair, reproaching him in her little girl's voice: 'Heartless! You see what you did to me when you left! Are you happy now?'

By the shudder of his shoulders, I realized he was crying, but I didn't pity him any the more. Cathy went on, in the same childlike voice:

'I'm going to die, and you're the one who's killed me!'

He quickly got up and with eyes full of tears protested wildly:

'It's not me. It's you. It's your fault. You were ashamed of all the happiness we had together when as little heathens we roamed wild and free. You began to despise me. To prefer those with white skin, who read books and speak fancy French. You didn't realize it was yourself that you were despising, that you were repudiating. And in the end it was your ruin, because you can't lie to your own blood. You can't.'

Cathy began to cry. Unmoved by her distress he went on, even more savagely:

'Have you thought of the life I'm going to lead once you're gone? Have you seen people live without their soul?'

She cried even louder and he took her in his arms and

showered her with kisses which she returned with great passion, frail as she was. I was horrified at their shamelessness. They seemed to have forgotten they were on a veranda in full sight, that I was there and that the servants could come in at any minute. What they must do when they were all alone!

And then I heard a horse galloping over the stones in the drive. The great mastiffs we kept around the house to protect us started to shake their stubby tails and bark like crazy. It was the master, back earlier than usual, as if he had sensed there was danger. I thought I would lose my mind and rushed to separate them.

'Here's Monsieur de Linsseuil! He mustn't find you here.'

But he pushed me away.

'So let him try and make me go!'

It was that night that Cathy, Cathy Gagneur, Cathy de Linsseuil, whom everyone called Mam Razyé behind her back, passed away. It was that night her daughter was born, a motherless child her papa christened Cathy, like the woman who had just left us.

11   The Wake and Cathy's Story

Dressed in her wedding-gown, with her diadem of orange-blossom clasping the dark velvet of her hair, Cathy lay on a bed placed in the middle of the hydrangea drawing-room that opened out onto the veranda. A pearl crucifix hung around her neck and a silver rosary was rolled around her fingers, while Barbados lilies and crumpled corollated tuberoses were strewn over the bed. By the magic of death, in a single stroke she had regained her lost beauty and youth and looked like the girl she used to be before wanting to be admitted at any price to polite society.

But despite the religious objects and her hands crossed in prayer, nobody could have mistaken her for a real lady. First of all the colour of her skin was not white. It was as if her black blood could no longer be contained and was taking its revenge. Victorious, it was flooding through her. It thickened her facial features, distended her mouth, giving a mauve touch to her lips, and with the stroke of a pencil redefined the arch of her eyebrows. It did wonders for her figure. What was this girl of African descent doing here, you might well have asked, and how did she get laid out on a sheet surrounded by all these white Creoles trying to put on an appropriate face for the occasion?

In the glow of the many candles a nun was leading the prayers, Sister Léa, a Linsseuil who had been relegated to the convent of Saint-Joseph de Cluny at the age of twenty-two because there were too many girls in the family and not enough husbands to go round. Ever since she had taken her vows, her cheeks and upper lip were covered in bristly hairs, her voice had become as deep as a man's and you could hear her thundering out the Our Father and Hail Mary as far as the kitchen, where the servants were busying themselves around the pots of thick soup, the baskets of bread-rolls, the bottles of rum and corked wine, and coffee-pots filled with coffee black enough to keep everyone awake until morning. None of them really felt any grief at seeing Cathy leave for her final resting-place, but they were all struck by the circumstances surrounding her death. All were filled with pity for the new-born baby.

'Po pitit'à manman,' repeated the women, sobbing into their aprons.

And the men shook their heads.

Sister Léa had brought with her the school choir of teen-age girls who whispered and occasionally giggled amongst themselves when they were not singing the *Libera* in their high-pitched voices. However many angry glances she threw them they took no notice, and the hubbub continued. At the head of the bed Madame de Linsseuil, huge and decrepit, sat beside her son. While her head gently nodded she softly caressed his limp, lifeless hand. Despite her gown of deep mourning her face betrayed the almost jubi-lant way she was scheming: Aymeric was barely twenty-seven. His youth would inevitably prevail over his grief. In one or two years he would at least be resigned, if not con-soled, once again good for marriage, and this time there would be no mistakes! They'd choose a wife for him, a good Christian, who'd raise the children from his first marriage. She was not the only one to think this way. In fact, among the crowd surrounding the funeral bed, apart from Aymeric nobody was really grieving, except for Justin and Huberte de Linsseuil, who had been sincerely fond of her sister-in-law.

Aymeric had lost his strength and colour. With vacant eyes and stuffed with calmatives prescribed by Doctor Louisor, he could not get out of his head the events of the previous day. He had spent the whole morning at court in Petit-Canal as a witness in the trial of one of his workers unjustly accused of rape. Neither the judge nor the jury – all white Creoles – could accept the idea of a black man's being innocent, and the lawyer, whom he had to pay out of his own pocket, had his work cut out for him. On the way home, his ears still buzzing with the racist words he had heard, he let his horse roam where it liked on the stones of the road bordered with sugar-cane fields, as he turned one thought over and over in his mind. When would the world be like a garden where every race on earth could walk together in harmony? When would this island cast off its demons? Tortured and disheartened, he had arrived home to find his wife in the arms of another man. He knew he would never forget this picture of Cathy confronting him, rejecting him, utterly transformed by a burning passion she had never shown towards him.

She had never been very active in her love-making, letting herself be taken with passiveness, even indifference. Recently she had tried to conceal a genuine repulsion. Because of this, he was ashamed of his never-ending desire. Night after night, ashamed of himself, he suppressed the eternal question and the name of Razyé.

'Why do you prefer him to me? Is a man's qualities measured by the lustiness of his member? Isn't my heart bigger and warmer than his? My mind more cultivated?'

Recalling the sweetness of those moments when he had made her burst into tears on reading to her passages from *Uncle Tom's Cabin* or playing for her little capriccios on his

86

violin, Aymeric's eyes suddenly filled with tears, like his brother-in-law sitting erect on his left. What was Justin weeping for? For the small affection he had shown his sister and his share in the blame for her death, since he had only been interested in selling her to the highest bidder? For bringing ruin on himself? Razyé had just won l'Engoulvent from him at cards. His child no longer had a roof over his head. Not an inch of land to his name. Nothing. Those who watched him out of the corner of their eye noted how his complexion had turned brick red, how his hair had turned prematurely white, in short, how vice and rum were finishing him off. He had brought with him his son, the little Justin-Marie, and the child, impressed by all the paraphernalia of death, stared without blinking at this aunt he had virtually never known. The other mourners yawned furtively, rushed through the prayers to the dead, yearning deep down for the daylight to filter through the louvred shutters so that they could go home after the chore of the funeral, which would probably last two full hours under the blazing sun. Once home, they would wash down the bitter taste this marriage and its premature end had left them with a carafe of Bordeaux chilled with ice. To their great surprise, they learned that Aymeric would not open the family vault at Petit-Canal. He preferred to lay his beloved Cathy to rest in the little graveyard at l'Engoulvent, as if he were giving her back to the world he had never managed to wipe from her memory.

On the first floor, Lucinda laid in her cradle the little girl gurgling with milk, who would never see with her own two eyes her namesake in the flesh. As tiny as she was, it was plain to see that the new Cathy had nothing in common with the rest of the family. Unlike her brothers, her skin had already darkened, as if she had gone back in time in search of a lost family-tree. This forbode a fine future for her! They would make faces and comparisons and declare: 'How dark she is!'

How pitiful a society where qualities are defined according to skin colour!

Lucinda went over to the window to close it. What had become of Razyé? Where was he holing up? Shouldn't he be downstairs, sitting with those watching over the body?

The messenger they had dispatched to l'Engoulvent after Cathy had died could only find Irmine, Justin and the little Justin-Marie. Lucinda wouldn't have been surprised if he had committed some act beyond repair. Thrown himself over the cliff. Drunk himself to death. Or else set sail on the first boat for an unknown destination. Lucinda pressed her forehead against the shutters. How could you tell who had hurt the other the most? Who had been destroyed by whom? When the body and the heart are grappling with egoism and ostentation, the self-inflicted wounds are more than either can take.

There was then a knock at the door and a little maidservant entered, holding a letter in her hand. It was unsigned and merely ordered: *Meet me under the great manjack-tree.*

Lucinda did not need a signature. She went down the stairs buzzing with the hum of voices. A procession of servants was crossing the hall, carrying at arm's length huge trays clattering with Limoges porcelain plates. The glasses of Baccarat crystal were also tinkling cheerfully. Outside, farewells were being exchanged. You could hear the wheels of the tilburies grating on the flagstones in the drive as they carried off those in a hurry to get away, those who could no longer bear to stay and keep up pretences. No, this wasn't the wake Cathy deserved. Hypocritical expressions, mouths pinched halfheartedly in prayer and self-righteous litanies. Where was Maroudé, the storyteller? Where were the drummers? Where was the rum? The dances, the laughter and the hearty jokes that were not afraid of drawing lessons from life?

'Ladies and Gentlemen,

'Come and hear what happened to the toad who wanted to be king, to the heifer who thought she was a young girl, to the hot-blooded mulatto girl who married a white Creole with nothing between his legs . . . Come and see how you die when you turn your back on your culture. . . .'

Lucinda wiped the tears that were streaming down her cheeks and went out. In the night daubed with Indian ink the din of the frogs calling for rain was deafening. By the dampness in the air you could sense their prayers would be answered and the sky would soon burst open. A wind filled with as many tears as a mourning handkerchief was already flattening the tops of the bushes and shaking the branches of the trees. Shivering, she made for the great manjack-tree. A shape emerged from its shadow and walked briskly towards her.

'Don't give me any nonsense. That she died like a saint, that she looks like an angel and so on and so on. I want to know one thing. Did she ask for me before she died? Did she mention my name?'

Lucinda started crying even louder.

'She mentioned nobody's name. Nobody, you hear? . . . All this is your fault, and you haven't even come and prayed for her soul to rest in peace.'

'As long as I live,' Razyé sneered, 'she will never rest in peace. She will always be beside me. She'll cling to me like the murdered haunt their murderers. Because you and all the rest of you think I'm the one who killed her, isn't that right?'

Lucinda did not answer, and after a while, Razyé went on, imploring her.

89

'Can't you get me a picture, a lock of her hair, a dress she wore, anything!'

This seemed a legitimate request, yet Lucinda was suspicious. You can do so many things with a dress, a lock of hair or a portrait! She looked up.

'What for? I don't trust you.'

'What a stupid question!' he answered impatiently. 'You're truly a heartless creature. I have nothing left of hers. Don't I deserve something to remember her by?'

She hesitated, then nodded, murmuring: 'It's agreed. I'll give you a locket and a lock of hair of hers I've kept. Now come and pray for her soul!'

But Razyé shook his head violently.

'That's not her in there!'

Shrugging her shoulders she turned her back on him and returned to the house. In the funeral chamber the scent of tuberoses, lilies and candles, whose tallow dripped down the silver candelabra, mingled with a bitter, captivating and intimate smell, as if the secret humours of the dead girl's body were starting to warm up under her skin. This was the first sign of the decomposition her figure, at one time so coveted and admired, could expect once it was in the shadow of the earth. Lucinda made the sign of the cross, slipped into the place Madame de Linsseuil had just vacated and tried to repeat the prayers Sister Léa was singing at the top of her voice. Propped up against her pillows, Cathy gently moved her lips and spoke to those who had ears to hear her.

I am gone.

At last I have finished with life and all those who loathed me are here, hypocrites, pretending to mourn me. Even Madame de Linsseuil, taking out her handkerchief and looking for water in the desert of her eyes.

90

What does it matter! Loved by some. Hated by others. All that is no longer my concern.

I'm frightened. I don't know what is waiting for me on the other side of this door that I must push open to slip into the other world and begin my eternity. But I already know that what awaits me will be no more painful than what I experienced in my lifetime, through my own fault, through my very own fault.

Where are you?

I don't see you in the crowd. Don't you love me enough to forgive me the evil I have done to you? You must realize we shall never see each other again, for death is nothing but the night. It is a migration of no return. You see, I was right.

When we were little and we played our games in the graveyard beside maman's tomb, you promised never to leave me. You told me that if you were the first to go, you would not leave for the other world, but stay on earth and circle me for ever. You would be in the tree that trembles, in the wood that creaks, in the rushing streams, in the stagnant pools, in the vault, in the crowd. You would never leave.

I claimed it was impossible. But you said that all you had to do was learn the secrets of the *kimbwazè*, those sorcerers in perpetual contact with the invisible world, and you prowled around the places where they lived. Once, when he had gone out, you dragged me inside old Carnot's cabin. We stared, fascinated at the jumble of nails, the crucifixes, the pictures of saints hanging on the wooden walls, the pieces of bone, the skulls and the jars full of roots soaking in murky water. Unfortunately old Carnot returned earlier than usual and he gave us more blows than we could take. Impenitent, you tried to approach other sorcerers. In vain! They always rejected you. You frightened them. They sensed that with you, their secrets would be in the wrong hands.

While I was on earth, I had the feeling you were inside me, always there, in my head, in my heart and in my body. I even got the impression I was you. It was often painful, because you were not a very agreeable companion. No more was I; richer in failings than in virtues. But now I am gone and I have lost you. For ever. And this emptiness is suffocating me.

If I think back, my happiest years stopped at the age of fifteen, when I was invited to the Belles-Feuilles plantation. Justin took this invitation to be a great honour. In great excitement he drove me to La Pointe to buy me clothes, at least enough to fill a small wicker basket, for I couldn't visit a respectable house with the rags I had on my back. Up till then I had only left l'Engoulvent to go to mass at Petit-Canal with Nelly Raboteur, unbeknown to papa, because he thought all this business with the Good Lord a waste of time. If the Good Lord existed He would never have tolerated slavery, wars and all the vile deeds in the world. I had therefore never set foot in a town before and I remember my amazement at discovering the straight streets hemmed in between the tall façades of the houses squeezed one against the other. In some neighbourhoods, everything was peaceful. Sandbox-trees lined a square that on one side opened out onto the sea, the ships and the bluish zigzag of a chain of mountains. On the other side, however, it was chaos. Crowds thronged the pavements and blackened the streets, and at every instant horses almost trampled on unwary pedestrians. Rowdy individuals auctioned off pieces of richly-coloured cotton and silk in front of shops, mysterious as caves, overflowing with all sorts of cheap goods, while big-bottomed women, with their faces covered in sweat under wide straw hats, sat on small benches, steps away from piles of dung, reaching out for the legs of passers-by and trying to get them to buy blood pudding, coconut milk, cakes and candy such as *nèg an sak* and *kilibibi*, with a litany of sugary words: *Coco, chéri-doudou, bel pitite an mwen, choubouloute à manman!*

Justin bought me a glass of cane-juice at the corner of the rue Frébault then entered the store, Au Bon Marché. He purchased some panties, a petticoat and a dress in blue silk with grey flowers. Then he bargained for the price of a corset. A corset! I had never seen anything of the sort! I pulled him by the sleeve and whispered: 'What's that for?'

'All the girls in high society wear them,' he replied, importantly. 'It gives you what they call a wasp waist.'

A wasp waist! I remembered the mason-wasp nests I used to wreck with Razyé and gave up trying to understand. To get a better look at this strange object, I took hold of it and fingered its whalebones and iron rods. I had no idea that for me, this was the beginning of the end. That everything I had been was about to die in me.

After that, I didn't have one minute of happiness. I lived in opulence. I possessed what I had never possessed before. Yet when I looked at my painted face in the mirror, with rings on my ears and heavy necklaces around my neck, the night of a ball, I knew that behind this mask lay solitude and regret.

I made every man who loved me suffer. Razyé. Aymeric. Razyé could face the suffering. But not poor Aymeric. He tried to change me with the power of love. An impossible task! Love has to be drunk in sips with the milk from your mother's breast, otherwise it's useless. When I was little, nobody really loved me. Nobody took the trouble to teach me anything at all. Good. Evil. Beauty. Ugliness. Justice. Injustice. I grew up like a wild coolie-plum in the savanna. My papa was no good and an ignoramus. He turned Razyé into his plaything before Justin turned him into an animal. As for Justin, when he finally knew how to read and write,

93

he kept it all to himself. Like the miser he is. Aymeric, however, guided the pen in my hand. He bought me books. He corrected my mistakes and explained the difficulties of language. He read me poems that I could understand.

> Reed that ripens in the plain,
> Making a hedge along the dusty road,
> I shall pick your proud stems,
> And bend them blade by blade.
> I shall weave them with my hands.

He taught me the proper name of flowers, plants and animals. He would laugh.

'Don't say *kongolio*. Say myriapod. Don't say *manzè Marie*. Say sensitive plant or mimosa pudica.'

He spun a globe and showed me the green of the forests in Africa and the Americas, the white of the polar ice-fields and the deep blue of the oceans just about everywhere on the surface of the earth. He talked to me of God in whose image all men are created, even the blacks, he said. Their sins had burnt and cracked their skin, but they could, if they walked straight, be redeemed, so great was the torrent of God's love for his Creation. During those moments tears filled my eyes because I couldn't help thinking of Razyé. Nobody had loved him either. Except for me, who in the end betrayed him.

What's the use of lying! I desperately regret leaving this life, however bitter it has been for me. Will I miss my children? They'll have enough loving care without me. They say that daughters only ever belong to their maman. So perhaps Cathy will rummage for my image in the dresser drawers where the sepia-coloured portraits slumber, with the faded velvet ribbons and the empty perfume sprays.

'What was she like?' she will ask those who knew me. 'Do I look like her? Tell me I'm the living image of her.'

Yet what could I have given her, a no-good person like myself?

Above all I shall miss the intangible things. The taste of blood, as it flowed warm and salty from my wounds when I fell on the rocks, the sear of the sun, the burn of the sea when it opened its belly for me, the spray of the waves and the bitterness of the coco-plum snatched from over the hedge. I shall regret the heat from Toussine, my mare, and the ridge of her back as we galloped together over the savanna. Above all I shall miss my body and Razyé's, a marvel of flesh and blood created for my satisfaction. The first time we made love it was by accident. We didn't know what we were doing. Our hands and mouths simply followed an untrodden path, and at the end the red flash of pleasure blinded us. We started over and over again, each time more skilful and more passionate. Call it vice if you want to. I know it was innocence.

I heard that Aymeric wants to bury my body in the little graveyard at l'Engoulvent beside maman. Only a living person could think that such a belated reunion would be of some use. We never knew each other, our hearts didn't have time to love one another. Now is not the time. Our bones will crumble into dust beside each other. That's all there is to it.

Life is past. Eternity ahead. Eternity. Infinite time on my hands. Infinite.

12 Life Repeats Itself

Cloaked in the blackness of the night, Razyé left the park and strode off along a sunken lane that cut across the cane-fields. The pain and the revolt had in a way diluted into his blood and now irrigated every particle of his being. The rain beat down on his back, but he couldn't feel it. He knew he would carry this fever with him as long as he lived, mixed with the vital fluids of his body. It would only abate with death.

The man he was searching for lived on the Linsseuil estate, for when he was not conversing with the invisible spirits, Ciléas, a Nago negro, son of Ciléas Ciléas, the Ancestor, known from the Pointe-des-Châteaux to Matouba, put on a pair of drill *konoko* and crushed cane-juice at the factory. He had even lost two or three fingers doing it. But since everyone on the plantation feared him, Aymeric had allotted him a secluded place, remote from the other black shacks, near an abandoned mill overgrown with thistles. Yet the women complained that, as soon as darkness fell, they bumped up against all sorts of terrifying shapes in the sunken lanes, probably spirits in disguise, on the prowl for wicked deeds; shapes like Ti-Sapoti, *jan gajé* in league with the devil, running to find their skin, and *soukougnans*, drinkers of fresh blood. Because of this they lived in fear and kept their little ones under their skirts, frightened that they would catch a fatal sickness. A hurricane-lamp lit up the outside of Ciléas' cabin, which resembled any other until you looked up at the ridge of the roof. A row of birds of prey, with wings drooping, mounted guard night and day, and you realized that the man who lived under this roof was no ordinary mortal. A yellow-eyed creole dog started barking furiously as Razyé approached, then suddenly crawled in front of him as servile as a slave. At the commotion the door was opened by a very young woman, an infant clinging to her breast. Razyé brusquely pushed her aside.

'Listen, I've got no time for you. It's your man I've come to see.'

Ciléas was a short, slender little black man of about thirty, whom you wouldn't notice if it hadn't been for the void in his eyes that stopped you dead in your tracks. The depths of time swirled beneath his swollen eyelids. Since his return from Cuba, Razyé had had frequent dealings with him. They had met one evening over a glass of rum in the shadows of Childéric's bar, when Ciléas had slipped beside Razyé to ask him about Melchior. When Razyé jumped: 'How come you know Melchior?' Ciléas had smiled mysteriously. 'Why does that surprise you? Don't we all come from the same place? Don't we all share the same thankless earth under our feet?'

Ever since that day the two men had become inseparable, one showing the other the colour of his gold, the other in exchange revealing his secret knowledge.

'I've got what you asked me to get,' Razyé murmured in an urgent tone of voice. 'Can you snatch her spirit, the way you told me you could, and seal it at the bottom of a jar before it embarks on its journey?'

For a moment, Ciléas said nothing, then tipped his head backwards.

'What do you want me to do with it? Hide it in the body

97

of a new-born infant? A household animal? Or release it among the living to haunt their sleep and peace of mind?'

Razyé shook his head.

'Deliver her to me as a prisoner. So that she never leaves me. So that she's with me for the rest of my days. So that she haunts me like the murdered haunt their murderers . . .' He completed his sentence with a bitter, triumphant laugh, '. . . since I'm the one who killed her!'

Used to Razyé's manner, Ciléas was not taken aback by such an outburst and merely said: 'Good, now let me get to work! The night is going to be long.'

The next morning they found Ciléas lying in the tall clumps of eddoe. No sign of a wound could be found on his body. No blood either. He was simply as cold as marble. As stiff and heavy as a log of lignum vitae.

The police made no investigation, merely asked his tearful wife with a child in her arms a few hasty questions. It was clear from the start that this was no ordinary case. What mortal in his right senses would dare attack a *kimbwazè*, especially if he had Ciléas' reputation? It was without a doubt a combat of the giants, between spirits squabbling at a higher level than the world we mortals tramp daily.

So, without taking the trouble to organize a wake, they hurriedly buried Ciléas, and that is how his funeral cortège passed Cathy's as she came out of the church at Petit-Canal. Well, 'cortège' is an exaggeration! A few motley men and women, shivering under a steady rain, doffed their *bakoua* hats at the procession of Linsseuils and their friends who in their pomp and silks didn't even give them a glance. In the meantime Papa Legba, sitting at the crossroads with his pipe between his teeth, was nodding his head: Weren't Cathy and Ciléas both going to the same place, a place where there were no whites, no blacks, no mulattos, no rich, no poor, no misbegotten, no wellbegotten?

Half hidden behind an almond-tree on the church square, Razyé watched those following Ciléas drift into the fading light and recalled another, more imposing, procession – Melchior's. So life was repeating itself. For the second time, the invisible spirits were scorning him. Twice they had let him rub his face against the murky window of death, only to snatch away its secret at the last minute. The great dream he had cherished would never come true. The girl he loved was now out of his reach. How could he live without Cathy? Can a human being live without his soul?

13   Irmine de Linsseuil's Tale

He's coming.

He has just spent another day sitting motionless for hours on the barren tombstone of Cathy's grave, looking out to sea, at the island of La Désirade outlined against the horizon. All that remains of her is there. What goes on in his heart? Not a word is spoken. Not a prayer murmured. Not a tear fills his eyes.

As stiff as a poker, he's crossing the savanna, a black shadow in the approaching darkness. The last rays of the setting sun burn his neck. But he cannot feel them. All he can feel is the thistle of pain scratching his heart. I have no pity for him. Now it's his turn to suffer, after having made my life so unbearable. How could Catherine's heart stoop so low as to love such a monster? But perhaps his mouth, that only has insults and curses for me, was less hard on her? Perhaps his embrace, that has been nothing but defilement and humiliation for me, was laden with tenderness for her?

Five days ago, at the same moment as poor Cathy, my womb opened and I was taken with the pains of labour. There was nobody to go and fetch the midwife. God knows where Razyé was. Justin was snoring in the kitchen. Zébulos, the handyman, had disappeared. So I pushed out the foetus in a torrent of blood; I cut the umbilical cord with a knife and washed the new-born baby in a bucket of lukewarm water. Any doubts about who its papa was were dispelled immediately. The baby was the very image of Razyé, but a lighter skinned version. The same fiery eyes, the same forehead. It was as if all my white blood had been to no avail. Logically I should have hated him, this son sown in my flesh by a man I had ended up loathing. Yet from the moment I clasped him to my breast I experienced feelings I had never felt before. Nothing is so cunning as motherly love. It slips in through the fissures of the heart like bats squeezing in through the narrowest cracks in the roof. I kissed his eyelids and his rosebud mouth, promising myself to teach him a whole different language from his father's. When he stuffed my breast into his toothless mouth, my heart finally melted.

He is the reason I have made up my mind not to stay a day longer in this house, a home only to grief. I'll go and seek the rays of happiness elsewhere. When I was little, only one person understood me: my nursemaid, *mabo* Julie. She was my real maman. Black as the bottom of a cauldron, with her hair straggling out from under her madras headtie, and the smell of sweat hidden in the folds of her loose-fitting dresses. Everyone found me too argumentative, inquisitive and insolent. Except for her. She answered my questions and helped me as best she could to decipher the world.

'It's true, they say the earth is round like a ball, flat at each end, and if you start at one point and keep walking you'll eventually arrive back where you began.'

I suppose the Good Lord had something in mind when He created the Blacks, the Whites, the Yellows and even the Reds. He wanted to show that some colours have all the misfortune imaginable, while others are his favourites. To get to the school we had to ford the Ravine-Blanche. When it rained the stepping-stones would be well under water and sometimes the gully overflowed. So *mabo* Julie would perch me on her shoulders and take me across. When she heard of all my misadventures – my elopement, my pregnancy and my nameless child – she tried to find out where I was, to get a letter to me. When I returned from Dominica she came over to see me at l'Engoulvent, and without bothering to take me to task she offered me her help and assured me of her affection. I shall go to her house to hide before leaving for some secret corner of this earth where nobody, nobody will find my baby and me.

Here he comes, as stiff as a poker, cutting across the savanna. His strides are mechanical and he looks like a zombie. Cathy was the salt of his life and he has lost her. He no longer eats nor sleeps. At night I can hear him ranting and raving in front of his window wide open on the spongy, barren darkness.

'Where are you? Tell me where you are. Are you hiding in the shooting star that has just fallen in the sea? Or in the firefly that glows all on its own? In the mason-wasp that sharpens its sting? Or in the frog that rasps in vain for water?'

In the hour before dawn he throws himself exhausted on his bed and tosses and turns till morning. Sometimes in the middle of the night he goes and joins Justin, who is drowning his sorrows in rum, and the two souls of the damned down one bottle after the other in a torrent of most dreadful abuse. At times I can hear them singing 'Faro dans les bois'.

No, I'll not stay one minute longer in this house. I have already folded the few wretched clothes my child and I possess in a small wicker basket. When the eye can no longer distinguish a white thread from a red one, I shall slip away and leave all this shame and mourning behind me.

Razyé is standing in the middle of the paved yard, looking up. You'd think he was looking at me, and yet I'm quite sure he doesn't even see me. He peers at the shape of the clouds in the sky and measures the void of his remaining days. Another thirty, another forty years left. What is he going to do with all those remaining years? He finally enters the house and I can hear him shout sharply at Justin.

'What are you waiting for? I've already told you I don't want to see you in my house any more! Take your child, pack up and go! Get the hell out of here!'

Where can the wretched Justin go? He no longer has a cent to his name. I would have pity on him if I didn't loathe him so much. His hands groping my body! His breath laden with rum! One night he suggested I break with Razyé and begin a new life with him. I threatened to tell the police and he never repeated his offer again.

Razyé mounts the stairs and passes my bedroom door. Not an evening passes without my heart beating in the senseless hope that perhaps he will stop, look in on the child he hardly remembers, and who knows, life will start all over again. He never loved me. Yet there was a time when the longing for his body gave me the illusion. That is all I miss. He enters his bedroom, opens the window, and I can hear him moan as he does every night: 'Cathy, Cathy!'

Deep down I despise him. How can he fall into the depths of despair for a woman! After all, what did this Cathy have that we didn't have?

Mabo Julie lives in Petit-Canal, a featureless little town that people pass through without noticing. Her cabin stands at the entrance to a *lakou*, a tenants' yard, that opens out just steps away from the cathedral. Her two rooms are neat and clean, piously decorated with pictures of the saints. Now that she is too old to find an employer for her services, she has set herself up in business with her five daughters, all with children of their own. Together they wash and iron the clothes of the white Creoles and society mulattos from all over the district. As nobody wields a tallowed iron better than they do, people have nicknamed them 'miracle hands', and they have countless customers.

In a way, living at *mabo* Julie's might look like a fate worse than living at l'Engoulvent. Here I rely on the kindness of a servant. I live off her entirely among our former slaves. But I have never taken pride in my colour.

Before I knew Razyé and brought his child into this world, I took an interest in the negroes. I was born well after slavery was abolished, and *mabo* Julie always described it as hell on earth. Yet it is difficult to imagine how the conditions of slaves could have been worse than they are now. I saw the negroes coming and going through the house like subordinate, inferior shadows, satisfying our slightest whims. My father maintained that they should not be trusted; my mother recalled the duties of a Christian towards them. In fact, nobody took the trouble to know precisely who they were. I believe their passions to be more heated than ours and the dreams inside their heads wilder. I believe them to be unruly. Because they have truly suffered, they are susceptible, aggressive and slow to confide and tell the truth. In their minds, nothing will ever free them from life's wickedness.

When the rumour of my presence at *mabo* Julie's spread, people popped out from everywhere to stare at me as if at a strange animal. It wasn't every day that a white woman falls so low. The house never emptied, and I was surrounded by a buzz of words and exclamations in Creole. The village gossips stopped to stare on their way to market or on their way back from the chore of fetching water from the standpipe with their buckets on their head. The children had nothing better to do than play at touching me. The girls tirelessly combed my hair. The boys caressed my arms and my neck. I myself looked at them out of curiosity. At that time the island was going through a difficult period. Black politicians were covering the country on horseback, hollering out speeches on equality and racial justice. Blacks were now mayors, assemblymen and senators. But this did not change things very much for their brothers of colour. After they headed for the towns where they thought life would have a sweeter taste, the men had quickly returned home to become yet another mouth for their women to feed. Monsieur Victor Schoelcher's workshops were not working, and those who did not want to return to a slow death from the scabies of the sugar-cane had no other solution but to die of hunger. It was rumoured that gangs of looters ransomed travellers in broad daylight, and the short distance between Petit-Canal and Anse-Bertrand was filled with dangers. Since the prisons were overflowing, the police executed all those they caught in front of the cathedral, and the thieves died with a defiant smile on their lips. Another scourge was the threat of arson. Every night the plantations went up in flames. The fire was lit at different places in the same cane-field and nobody could ever lay hands on the culprits. In the meantime the French Republic had declared education compulsory and a school was opened somewhere in town. But nobody ever went. I don't even know whether there was a teacher.

I made use of my time in Petit-Canal to have my child christened. I called him Aymeric, like my brother whom I had so offended, in the hope that this saint's name would triumph over the bad blood that blackened his veins. The priest deliberately humiliated me by making me have Aymeric christened on a Saturday, the day reserved for children born out of wedlock and of adultery. I meekly took my place in the long line of derided women carrying babies of every colour as it stretched out under the palms and almond-trees around the square. Those who hadn't yet seen him twisted their necks to catch a glimpse of Razyé's child, sleeping in his humble cambric blouse. My plan, as I said, was to stay a few weeks in Petit-Canal, then look for a place to live in another corner of the island, perhaps even on another island. Many were leaving for Haiti, which apparently was governed by negroes, very intelligent though, like the whites, and where there was plenty of work. But the day after the christening I heard a resonant step on the pavement that I could recognize in a thousand. My whole body turned to ice. Razyé entered, blacker, more handsome and yet more terrifying than the man I remembered. His eyes were flashing. His hair coiled around his head like snakes. Without uttering a word, he gave me two slaps that knocked me to the ground. Then he knelt down beside me, and while I sobbed he pounded into my ear: 'You dared give my child the name of the man I hate most on this earth? Did you think I'd finished with you? You and your child are my instruments of revenge. For I shall take my revenge, a devastating revenge, on what Heaven, in league with the white Creoles like yourself, has done to me. And my story will go down in the history of this country.'

Then he forced me to get up and follow him.

I returned to l'Engoulvent.

On 1 January 1900, the day this century was born, I married Razyé at the town hall in Petit-Canal. Don't judge me. I loved this man, my executioner.

Since I was under age, Razyé had to write to my parents to get their permission, and my mother answered in her withered, shaky hand: *For us, Irmine is already dead. Do what you will with her.*

The man who married us was a fat jowly negro, a cabinetmaker by trade, who had angered the white Creoles and also the mulattos by winning the municipality under a new political party ticket: the Socialist Party. Refusing to speak simply in Creole, he gave a short homily in bad French, describing a future when the notion of colour would lose its meaning. But his eyes contradicted the words in his mouth, and it was as clear as crystal that he hated me because I was white and despised me for marrying a black man. Justin and Zébulos were our witnesses, and since the latter did not know how to write, Justin held his hand for him to draw a cross on the big marriage-register.

When the ceremony was over, Razyé mounted his horse and galloped off along the main street without bothering about us, while Justin and I set off on foot for l'Engoulvent. The sun's knife scored the face of noon above our heads. The road was covered in dust between the fields of cane and I longed for death. When we arrived in sight of the little graveyard where the tombs of the Gagneur family were dotted among the scrub, Justin, who up till then had not said a word, took my arm and whispered: 'Thank the Lord I haven't got much longer to drag my body around. All I ask you, when I am gone, is to continue to watch over my poor Justin-Marie. You're the only person he's got!'

I was at a loss for words.

It's true I had grown as fond of Justin-Marie as my own son, little Aymeric. He was going on four and really a handsome child. He looked exactly like his Aunt Cathy. He had her eyes, her smile, her despondent pout. Nevertheless, you sensed that the sensuality that had been her downfall would be tempered in him by intelligence and sound judgement. Because of this resemblance, Razyé could not help showing him some feeling. The father who wouldn't look at his own son would bring Justin-Marie back a fleshy white guava, a black coco-plum or a honey-sweet Bourbon orange, clasped between his shirt and skin, and I could see that often he had to keep himself from showering him with kisses. Yet this love that was speaking over and over again to another through the child had something perverse and formidable about it.

A few days later Justin passed on.

That morning I was awoken by shouting. Gertrude, the scullery maid whom Razyé had hired to help me about the house, had gone into Justin's room and found him tangled up in his rags, long cold, with a look of liberation on his face. Since there wasn't a single pair of good sheets in the house, I had to borrow some from *mabo* Julie, and Zébulos laid the body out in the living-room. To my surprise, out of pity or curiosity, a few people came over from the surrounding villages, and around midnight there were about twenty of us mumbling the words from Ecclesiastes amidst the smell of coffee and melting candle wax.

'All the rivers run into the sea, yet the sea is not full; unto the place whither the rivers go, thither they go again. All things are full of weariness; man cannot utter it: the eye is not satisfied with seeing nor the ear filled with hearing.'

That night Razyé did not show up. He couldn't care less about Justin's death, for which he bore full responsibility. I went out into the yard and under the full moon I could see him striding over the savanna, head up towards the sky, like a dog barking at the moon. He was still wailing for his Cathy. In that murky white light around four in the morning, he came home dishevelled and haggard. He walked across the living-room, without even making the sign of the cross, oblivious to everything and everyone, and went up to his room. He did not show up at the funeral the next morning either. Since all three priests from the neighbouring parishes had refused to set foot inside l'Engoulvent, Zébulos unceremoniously slid the rough wooden coffin he had made himself into the grave that had been gouged out of the stony ground. Whereupon we threw in a few lilies. That evening Razyé came into my room. Ever since my return I had prayed for and feared this moment. How should I greet him? How should I react? I took pleasure imagining myself wildly refusing his advances. Yet that night, no more than the following nights, did I have the strength to refuse him. He took me with his usual savageness, without even bothering to remove his clothes. While I was catching my breath, he hurled at me on his way out: 'Pack your things and get the children ready. Tomorrow we're leaving l'Engoulvent.'

I thought I had misheard and stammered: 'We're leaving l'Engoulvent? Just like that?'

He kicked open the door.

'We're going to live in La Pointe.'

In La Pointe? In the end I had become attached to l'Engoulvent as a prisoner, I imagine, becomes attached to her jail. The world outside frightens her and she huddles up in her captivity. And what's more I was born in this region of Grande-Terre. I'm used to the rustle of the sugar-cane, the droughts, the scarcity of rain and the unexpected, violent gusts of wind. I only left it once for four or five years to go and study Latin, Greek, geography, arithmetic and above all hypocrisy at the convent boarding-school of Saint-Joseph de Cluny at Versailles. Before I lived with Razyé, I always thought those years were the unhappiest of my life.

I spent the night praying and weeping. What would I do in a town? What did tomorrow have in store for me?

14 Mabo Julie's Tale

I am seventy-two today. For fifty years of my life I have served white folks. I have said: 'Yes, right away.' I have lowered my eyes. I have scrubbed the floors, done the cooking. I have satisfied desires, the master's as well as his friends' and visitors'. Sometimes standing up on the stairs. Sometimes lying down in the attic. I have soothed the stomach of my illegitimate children with oregano and arrowroot, and I have kept the nourishing, frothy milk from my breasts for the children of the house. I have cared for their fevers, their worms and their diarrhoea. I have sung our folk songs to them. Several times the priest has mentioned my name from the pulpit to congratulate me, and in the end one of the governor's men came over from Basse-Terre to pin a silver medal on my breast. I have kept it with other treasures – a picture of the Sacred Heart blessed by the bishop, a lock of Julie-Marthe de Linsseuil's hair, an angel whom the good Lord called to Him as soon as she was born, and Irminette's milk-teeth.

And despite all that there is only mourning, hatred and resentment in me for the fate that has inflicted my colour on me and condemned me to hell. Of the two men I loved, Bois d'en Bois had his spleen burst by a head punch from a foreman and died. The other, Cyrany the Mulatto, was hanged. In front of my very eyes. I watched his body swing from the lower branches of a silk-cotton tree, then I received him in my arms, lifeless, lacerated with red stripes and as heavy as a trunk of mahogany. All that happened during the turmoil that preceded the abolition of slavery, during the days of frenzy and hope, before the country slumped back into its rut of wretchedness and despair. The only spot of tenderness in my heart is for Irmine – Minette, as I used to call her when she was little. Why? Because from the very moment she started to think and speak I saw she was not like the rest of the family, except for Monsieur Aymeric. Those two have their hearts filled with genuine goodness and compassion. But the world is unjust. Those two are the ones suffering, victims of their naïveté.

When I learned that the Demon – in my opinion he doesn't deserve a better name, after having done what he did to her – wanted to take her to La Pointe, I went and offered her my services, old and bent as I am. My daughters reminded me of my old age and called me all sorts of names. Oh no, slavery isn't over for someone like me. I suppose I'll always remain a slave to white folks.

We left for La Pointe at the break of dawn, Razyé galloping in front, the sun behind us like a jailer who never loses sight of his prisoners. The church bells in Petit-Canal, Anse-Bertrand, Morne-à-l'Eau, Le Moule, and even Saint-François and Port Louis, were pealing, for the canefields were going up in flames. Over a thousand acres went up in black smoke. This time they arrested a certain Siriapin, off the boat from Calcutta a month earlier, and the Indians were running all over the place in their fear of the police. They hid in their temples whose red flags you could see fluttering under the mango-trees.

Around four in the afternoon we arrived on the outskirts of La Pointe, swarming with people, which didn't surprise me since it seems that La Pointe has twenty thousand inhabitants, three churches, including a cathedral made of stone, and two hospitals with doctors who have studied in France.

Without me and without the charm of the children, those two innocent children who have not yet realized in what wretched cradle fate has had them born, how would Irmine have endured her new life? No. 2 on the Place de la Victoire where we settled was a house daubed in pink and white with a yard in the back and a garden in front that had once belonged to the Romilly family. Razyé had bought it for next to nothing two months earlier, when its owners had auctioned it off to pay their debts. Then the family, completely ruined like so many white Creoles in present times, returned to Arles where they had relatives. If, from the outside, the house might just have deceived passers-by, as soon as you stepped inside there was a string of rooms with sagging floors. Almost no furniture. The wallpaper was blistered and the murky mirrors reflected nothing but poverty and filth. In actual fact it didn't matter, since poor miserable Irmine did not receive a single visit. Our neighbours, all white folks born on the island, needless to say, directors of chambers of commerce and owners of import-export businesses on the wharf, looked at me like a pile of rubbish when in the evening I sat on a bench with the other *mabos* together with the children, looking so adorable you'd think the Virgin Mary herself had made them. During the day, except for the market women from the outlying districts with their loads of vegetables and tubers on their heads, the only person who crossed the doorstep was a priest, older and more dilapidated than I was. Razyé had hired him to teach Justin-Marie his alphabet, on the condition he never mentioned the name of God in his presence. Razyé remained locked up in the attic all day long. Once I glued my eye to the keyhole and saw him kneeling on both knees in front of a table. On this table, scattered around an enlarged photo of the late Cathy de Linsseuil, was an assortment of jugs, bottles of wine or liqueurs, carafes, stones soaking in oil and playing cards. Two 'perpetual lamps' gave a little light to the room. A few chromos were pinned to the wall. A cutlass with a curved blade was stuck upright in the floor. Unfortunately, I was unable to spy for very long, since Razyé turned towards the door and shouted: 'Va ki là?'

In the evening Razyé would go out and not come home until two or three in the morning, accompanied by *dames-gabrielles*, black-skinned or mulatto girls smelling of vice under their perfume and make-up whom he probably picked up in the Bas-de-la-Voute or Cayes districts where that sort of person lived. This lot drank, shouted and made merry till the small hours of the morning. Irmine never discusses her relationship with Razyé, and I never ask questions. Some wounds can never be lanced and dressed. The pus and purulence build up inside the flesh and gangrene the whole body. I noticed she was with child again. From the look of her, I guessed she hated herself for having given in to her torturer. But let those who have never wavered cast the first stone. I know I won't.

One morning I had just scrubbed our pavement when two strapping men placed their muddy boots on it. Two well-to-do men, dressed in the latest fashion, jacket, stiff collar, neck-tie, patent leather shoes, top hat, but with skin as black as mine.

'I thought they didn't make them as ugly as this since the abolition of slavery,' one of them sneered at me coarsely.

'Go and fetch your master, and quicker than that,' the other ordered.

I stood up to him.

'And what name shall I give?'

'Monsieur Jean-Hilaire Endomius, assemblyman and mayor of La Pointe!'

Assemblyman and mayor of La Pointe? What could he be wanting with Razyé?

15 The Past Recaptured

Sitting in his office in the town hall, Jean-Hilaire Endomius looked Razyé up and down. The individual corresponded exactly to his description. Tall as a tree from the rain forest, a muscular athletic build, dressed like a dandy with a skin as black as a moonless night. Pleased with his inspection, he put on his winning smile.

'Sit down, sit down. And let's have a drink. True alliances are sealed in rum.'

The two men clinked glasses and let the rum trickle down their throats. Then Jean-Hilaire asked: 'They tell me you bought the house of a white family? And that you got another family's daughter pregnant before marrying her?'

At a nod from Razyé he said approvingly: 'That's what we all should do. Ruin them and humiliate them.'

After a silence he went on.

'I have created a party. You must have heard of it?'

Razyé made a face.

'I'm not interested in politics.'

This did not please Jean-Hilaire.

'You should be,' he said severely. 'Two things will save us and send us from the bottom rung of the social ladder to the top: education and politics. You can read and write, I assume?'

'Yes,' Razyé growled. 'I learned when I was in Cuba.'

Jean-Hilaire looked at him with curiosity.

'Tell me about your life in Cuba.'

Razyé shrugged his shoulders.

'What do you want me to tell you? I didn't choose Cuba; Cuba chose me. I was blinded by my grief, weeping endlessly for the girl who had betrayed me when, one morning, the ship docked on that island which like ours hides its wounds under the gold and purple of its Nature. Ruthless judges descended on the hold where I was wallowing under the vermin and offered me a deal: "Choose! Either you die in prison or else you save your skin by killing other men."

'Illogically, I chose the second solution. They gave me a uniform that was too small for me, a gun too heavy, a bag full of ammunition and I climbed up to the forest, the *manigua*, to hunt down the rebels and their supporters. In other words, all the peasant folk. For the people had had more than enough of the Spanish. I didn't have a minute's rest. Every day, even the day of the Lord, I set fire to villages, I tortured women and children, I slaughtered cattle. Sometimes, under the acanas and mahoganys I came face to face with men, hiding naked in the forest, not knowing that slavery was over. They could no longer speak Spanish and had returned to the languages of Africa. I killed them even so, but felt bad about it. I was in the plain of Boca de Dos Rios when they shot José Martí, who had just been named Major General of the Liberation Army. I saw him jump from his horse and covered in blood roll towards our lines. After that, the rebellion lost its soul and the rebels dragged their feet. So me and the mercenaries finished them all off. Then, with my hands red with blood, I went down to the city to claim my freedom.

'If you hadn't seen Havana with your own eyes in 1895 you hadn't seen anything. They talk of Paris. Bordeaux. Nantes. I haven't seen any of them, but I know there's no comparison. Contained within its city walls, Havana lies on a headland that extends to the north as far as the Castillo de la Punta. In the harbour, between the remains of the rusty wrecks lying in the ocean deep and the little isle of Luz, just five or six fathoms of greenish water laps the shore.

'The Atares and San Carlos del Principe castles defend its western flank. Between their massive ramparts lie the districts of Horcon, Jesus Maria and Salud, inappropriately named because in any season you can be carried off by the *vomito negro*. In the cool of the late afternoon the women are no longer afraid of darkening their skin. They come out to walk along the Alameda, and the men throw them bunches of mariposas and frangipani with impassioned overtures.

'Fairly quickly, I found a shabby room for rent in the calle Soroa, that stunk of salt beef, the *tasajo*. I led the carefree life of Havana's free men of colour, the blacks, the mulattos and the Chinese, who live in paradise on earth. They sleep all day and wake up only at night for their drunken trips to the gambling dens. I cheated unashamedly and accumulated a small fortune. I was afraid, however, of being picked up by the police again and sent back to where I came from. So I looked for a semblance of work. I found it in the *tabaqueria*, Señor de Fonseca's cigar factory. I had got to know Señor de Fonseca, a pure blue-blooded Spaniard of dubious nature, through meeting him in the same gambling houses and the same bordellos. And then one night when some Chinese in a fury were after his gold, I deflected the blade of their knife. Afterwards, between two glasses of *aguardiente*, I told him my story. He wanted to show me his gratitude, and in exchange for a little contraband, he registered me as one of his employees.

'Ah, tobacco! You think sugar-cane is worse? Or even cotton? Wherever the nigger toils, he is bound to perish! I spent a few months in that hell and I know what I'm talking about. Despite my connections with Señor de Fonseca I could not be hired as a skilled worker. I was therefore assigned to preparing the tobacco leaves. Each leaf was over a foot long and arrived in rough, reddish bundles of five from the rich black soil of Pinar de Rio. We carefully dampened them one by one and left them hanging to absorb the moisture for two to three hours. Then we placed them to dry on bamboo racks inside wooden hangars with palm-frond roofs. Sometimes we had to wrap them in muslin for protection. Lying side by side in the semi-darkness, looking like gigantic, misshapen infants, they almost scared us. Then we sorted them by size, colour and strength before sending them on to the workers who have to grind them with a machine to make pipe tobacco or else hand-roll them to make cigars.

'That's where I heard them talk of *santeria* for the first time. Through Carlo, a comrade from the *tabaqueria*, a Nago, assigned to making cigar-boxes.

'Until then, as far as I was concerned, all this business about God was nothing but a trap fabricated by the whites the better to enslave us with. When we were little, Cathy and I invented a prayer to our liking. At bedtime we would yell it in the ears of poor Nelly Raboteur who was at her wit's end and ran after us shouting: "Hush, you little heathens!": "We hate you, sitting invisible up there in Heaven. There is no justice the way you share out colour, plantations and land. We shall never call you our father, cos you're not."

'But this was something quite different. The *santeria* religion came from Africa. Olorun-Olofi had created the earth, the water, the plants and the animals for the good of his black-skinned children. One Saturday, Carlo took me to see Melchior. The white-haired *babalawo* hung a necklace of six red and six white beads around my neck and began my education. I returned every evening between five and seven. During one of his lessons, he taught me that separation and the final stage we call death are meaningless. Provided my eyes learned to see, I would never be far from this Cathy I was eating my heart out for. I would know what she was doing at every minute. What she was feeling. What she was thinking. Whether she was happy or unhappy. If she was thinking about me. Hearing this I jumped for joy. "Is this true what you say, master? Then teach me now, now!"

'But he gruffly ordered me to calm down. The moment had not yet come. When it did, he would take care of matters. Alas! Melchior died before my initiation was complete, and I have remained in the dark, with two eyes and nothing to see.'

Although it was he who had started Razyé off, Jean-Hilaire had paid little attention to this rambling speech. He was obsessed by something else. A series of numbers were constantly swirling through his head: the price of a ton of sugar-cane, the sugar content of the molasses, the daily wage, the price of a pound of fertilizer, and even when he made love to his mistresses on the Morne-à-Cayes they would not leave him alone. When Razyé fell silent, he got up and began to pace back and forwards in his office, assuming the tone of a political speech.

'You are no doubt aware that our island is undergoing a profound change. The factories have gradually replaced the old sugar-mills. These factories process the cane from a co-operative of planters who are under contract to them. From the owners' point of view, this means increased productivity and lower costs. In fact for the workers it simply means widespread impoverishment. You know that the white Creole Aymeric de Linsseuil. . . .'

Razyé jumped at the hated name. But Jean-Hilaire did not even notice and went on:

'. . . has established the Compagnie Sucrière de la Pointe as a joint venture with the Savilor company from Paris and has built the Dargent factory in the new district of La Carène, which he boasts is the biggest sugar factory in the French West Indies. Only last month, as mayor, I had to give an inauguration speech that still leaves a nasty taste in my mouth. It went something like this: "Honour to all those of you who worked on this edifice. You are a worthy example to your country. Your memory will be blessed by every generation who comes after you." At the same time twenty per cent of Grande-Terre is his land. He is the real master of the island. Razyé, I'm out to get him.'

Razyé's heart echoed: 'That makes two of us. But my reasons are different from yours.'

'What do you expect me to do against an individual like that?' he said out loud. 'I'm less than nobody around here.'

Jean-Hilaire sat down again behind his desk. He took a pencil and a sheet of paper.

'I have arranged everything.'

When Razyé stepped outside the town hall, La Pointe was living its last few moments of daylight. Soon lights would go on in all the houses and the cabins would flicker with candle-light. There had just been a heavy shower, making the streets muddy, but at last making the air a little cooler.

Razyé was shivering with excitement. Cathy's death had left him helpless, as if he had been emptied of his vital organs. Life had been dragging him along by the scruff of the neck ever since. Jean-Hilaire had infused him with new energy. He would do everything possible to ruin Aymeric de Linsseuil with the help and on behalf of the Socialists. He had left l'Engoulvent on a sudden impulse, little knowing what he was doing, merely that he had to get out of Grande-

Terre if he wanted to write revenge in capital letters in the sky of Guadeloupe. But since he arrived in La Pointe, all he had been doing was weep for his beloved, drink, fill his pockets in the gambling dens or make love without even looking at the face of the woman who was moaning with pleasure beneath him. Now his life had found a new direction.

He headed up the rue de la Voûte towards the new Carène district that spread along the eastern side of the town, struck by the sickly smell of cane-juice that immediately brought back all his memories of childhood with Cathy. Firmly he shut them out. Despite the late hour the wheels of ox-carts loaded with cane echoed over the unevenly paved streets, while barges with similar loads loomed up flat and grey in the dusk from the sea. He heard someone cry out.

'But isn't that Razyé?'

Two young boys in rags were driving a muddy ox-team with great lashes of their whips, while a third was perched on top of the load, peeling a kongo-cane with his teeth. They were three workers from the Espérance plantation in Anse-Bertrand that belonged to the Linsseuils. The sugar-mill had closed its doors and they had been on the road since dawn. Ah, times were not good! And even more poverty was on the way. Before, you started at seven in the morning and finished at five in the afternoon, with a well-deserved rest between eleven and one to stoke up the stomach. Wasn't that so, José? Now they were talking of replacing day-labouring by job-labouring. And what would happen? Those overseer swines would see to it that no job could be done in one day and you'd have to continue over to the next.

Razyé did not miss the opportunity.

'When can we get together so that I can come and speak to you?' he said in a whisper.

The boys looked at each other. From Anse-Bertrand to Le Moule, the name of Razyé was synonymous with tales of drunkenness and pregnant women. He had never been mixed up with politics; that was the realm of Monsieur Légitimus and his supporters.

Razyé smiled and assured them haughtily: 'Things are going to change around here, believe me. From now on, you're going to see quite a bit of me.'

Then he pushed open the door of a rum-shop oddly named Le Tricolore, to celebrate his new vocation. Le Tricolore was crowded with people: the usual collection of brawling rum guzzlers, rolling dice or slamming down dominoes on the wooden tables. He sat down in a fairly quiet corner and ordered a bottle of Belle-Plaine rum. He always sipped the same quantity of alcohol, about three-quarters of a litre, no more, for he had no intention of drifting into unconsciousness. He wanted merely to numb the old pain that had sunk its teeth into him like a Cuban bloodhound. At times it hurt so badly he was bent in two, shuffling like an old bag of bones, never getting anywhere, never finishing a sentence or a movement. He had got to the stage when he desired a little comforting: a gentle touch or word. He had only Justin-Marie.

He had always hid a tender spot in his heart for the boy because of his resemblance to Cathy. As he grew up, this resemblance had become quite simply amazing. At first he hadn't really noticed it. Then one Sunday he had entered the little metal-sided cabin where the men of the family took their weekly bath. Justin-Marie was stepping out of the tub of soapy water, clutching the bunch of leaves he used to scrub his skin, when the graceful vision of this hardly virile body had blinded Razyé like the sun. An insane idea gripped him. Wasn't this the girl he had been seeking in vain, returning to him travestied in some perverted play?

She was quite capable of it! Ever since that day, Razyé, who as a rule took no notice of anyone in the house, never missed an opportunity to study Justin-Marie, to ply him with questions and draw him close under some pretext or other. More than one night he had entered his room and watched him, hidden behind the folds of his mosquito net, without daring to wake him, deeply moved by his resemblance. Tears would stream from his eyes that he thought had dried up for ever, while words of tenderness softened his mouth.

> You were my north, my south, my season of drought,
>   my season of rain,
> My sun, my rain, my hurricane.
> My noon, my midnight, my talk, my song,
> Beloved, your cruel games are wrong![1]

The man who never wanted to spend a cent on anyone was planning to send Justin-Marie to study law in Bordeaux to become the spearhead of his revenge. The boy was doing well at school, despite hostility from students and teachers alike.

Razyé had half emptied his bottle of rum and was beginning to float ever so gently over reality. The memories of his love for Cathy, their jokes and games flashed in front of him, arousing little else but a limp sense of revolt. What! Was that all the happiness he had been allotted? Fate stuffs some and famishes others. How many more years did he have to get through? Despite the constant checks on himself, there were no signs of his body weakening. His eyes could still distinguish a black ant from a red ant in the dark. He could still swallow all his breadfruit and fish. Every morning, in the pre-dawn hours, his member stiffened with

[1] Inspired by W. H. Auden

the same force. Oh no, his death was nowhere to be seen on the horizon. And after all, would they be reunited? He ended up doubting it. He would have to resign himself to the fact that death perhaps is no remedy.

At that moment a man asked him if he could sit at his table: a man of uncertain age, reddish, lanky, lost in his oversize overalls, but with a knowledgable look. As he sat down, Razyé noticed the dog that slinked against his leg; a bitch, nothing but skin and bones with black and yellow spots, her teats trailing the ground.

'Since when do animals drink in the company of men?' he asked irritatedly.

The stranger stared at him with eyes as old as the earth.

'You say she's an animal? Yes, that's what she looks like. But her two ears can hear what you don't. Her two eyes can see what you wouldn't even dare dream of.'

Razyé then realized whom he was dealing with and said in an apologetic tone: 'I'm sorry. I didn't recognize you.'

Throughout the years, in the hope of seeing Cathy again, he had never given up frequenting the *kimbwazè*, the *gadèdzafè*, and all sorts of genuine or fake masters of the invisible world. At one point, mistress Pulchérie, a healer from Morne-la-Loge, had made him take potions and decoctions that twisted him inside out with vomiting and diarrhoea then left him emptied and panting like a small child. He realized too late that she was only after his money. Another time, master Mano from Marbial had recited for him all the *loas* in the voodoo pantheon and had promised to place him under the special protection of Azaka-médé who left Guinea in the colours of the rainbow. Three days later, a stab in the back almost got the better of him. After so many disappointments Razyé was suspicious. Yet something in this man's expression restored his confidence.

He drew up his chair.

PART TWO

Guadeloupe

1   A Meeting Fraught with Consequences

The day he was seventeen, Justin-Marie had another fit. Seated around the birthday table to eat the brown, red and yellow marble-cake and drink the thick vanilla-flavoured chocolate were his 'brothers and sisters', as he liked to call the Razyé children, and Irmine cradling the newly-born Cassandre who, in spite of her name, looked as innocent as the Infant of Prague in her blue blouse. Justin-Marie collapsed on the arm of his chair then slipped to the floor, legs limp, eyelids fluttering, his veins coiling in his forehead like ropes. He only came to after thirty interminable minutes, when Hosannah, the servant who had replaced *mabo* Julie, called to the Good Lord the previous rainy season, rubbed his temples with tincture of arnica. After that it took him some time to regain his senses and he chose to go and lie down.

The adolescent climbed up to his room in the garret and laid down on his mattress stuffed with corn leaves. Every evening the Indian Curibamgo would stretch himself over his stomach and tell him stories of times long ago. Before Christopher Columbus and his bunch of ruffians had looted the island, then a paradise of parrots, macaws and crested cranes. When gilded fish with streaming strands of hair swam in the rivers and laid their scales to dry on the rocks of the river bank. Above the bamboo groves rainbows lassoed the clouds. Sometimes his favourite 'little brother'

127

Zoulou came to play with him, and shouting 'the Whites are coming, the Whites are coming', they re-enacted the battles of old. They were always victorious and rewrote history back to front. Zoulou was twelve. As a baby he had remained forgotten for days on end, wailing at the bottom of his cradle, until Razyé found him this name. He didn't want Irmine to play the same trick on him as she had done with Aymeric. After Zoulou came Gengis and then finally Cassandre. Only Aymeric was baptized with a Christian name. This was probably why Razyé beat him more than the other children, even though he was his spitting image. Nobody was allowed to call him Aymeric, and everyone, even his schoolmistress, called him Razyé II out of fear of offending the cruel father.

This new fit by Justin-Marie, which had lasted so much longer than usual, together with the memory of his burning fever all through the rainy season, so terrified Irmine that she made up her mind to take him to the hospital where, Hosannah had told her, the consultation would be free.

Irmine never went out, not even to go to mass or confession, so it had been a very long time since she had been to church, which was only just around the corner. The reason was that she had nothing decent to wear. She had only one dress, quilted from constant mending, like the ones worn by the women bundling sugar-cane, cut from a piece of taffeta a Lebanese peddlar had sold her on credit. At times she trembled at the idea of hell, then told herself that the Good Lord in his understanding would surely forgive her. Outside, the melted gold of the sun shimmering over the harbour dazzled her. Large butterflies danced in front of her eyes, then tiny insects. Finally she could clearly make out the sandbox and almond-trees on the Place de la Victoire as well as the coloured façades of the houses. Red and white steamers crowded the wharf and the sea was laughing in a never-ending ripple of laughter.

In the morning, once the sanitary tubs had been picked up and their foul smells hastily washed away by the refuse collectors, La Pointe resembled a dancer about to prepare for her entrechats. Spinning, whirling and pirouetting, she sang with the trills of her Indians, sellers of water who for a few cents filled buckets, barrels and basins, yelped with the cries of her market women selling whelks and black pudding, and whistled through the throats of a thousand ragamuffins offering their services from house to house and ready to pilfer anything that fell into their hands. In the meantime, the boxes of bougainvillaea flashed red on the balconies. Irmine crossed herself ostentatiously as she passed in front of the cathedral of Saint-Pierre-et-Saint-Paul, as if she hoped this would appease the tall stone saints sheltering in their niches.

The general hospital, which La Pointe had just been endowed with, was the pride of the colony and had been inaugurated in great pomp by the governor, as if it were a palace of fun. Standing at the top of a hill, in the midst of a verdant park planted with all types of trees, it was a wooden building several storeys high, girded with verandas that fluttered with the white cornets of the nuns. A crowd thronged the ground floor reserved for out patients, and Irmine had a lot of trouble finding her way through all these people, along these unending corridors that wound round and round and then suddenly backtracked. Doctor Bellisle was a dark-skinned mulatto with languishing eyes and delicate slender hands. He found Justin-Marie to be too thin, too puny, short of breath and the inside of his eyelids anaemic.

'He doesn't eat,' Irmine made an attempt at explaining.

But the doctor wasn't listening. He examined Justin-Marie's narrow torso again and again and appeared worried. He put his stethoscope back on, listened, tapped here, tapped there, had the boy cough and repeat 'ah' dozens of times.

'Now get dressed,' he finally ordered him. 'And go and wait for your maman on the veranda.'

Alone with Irmine, he looked her straight in the eye, but couldn't hide his aggressiveness. He knew these white Creoles like the back of his hand, not a cent to their name, despising anyone with a darker skin, but forced into making pretences given their new state of affairs. This one hadn't even been able to pay for her consultation and had registered with the destitute.

'Is there a history of lung disease in your family or your husband's?' he asked her abruptly.

Irmine started by swearing to the gods on high there was none. When they didn't die by accident, the Linsseuils lived to be ninety. As for Razyé, well, he was as solid as a rock, as eternal as Satan. Irmine had clean forgotten that Justin-Marie was not a child of her womb. Suddenly she remembered. He was in fact the son of Marie-France de La Rinardière, descendant of a family who for generations never stayed very long on this earth. Seeing her hesitate, the doctor asked her in an even rougher fashion: 'Madame, think yourself in a confessional. Don't hide anything from me.'

She told him the story. When she had finished he said in an even more serious tone of voice: 'We shall continue with the examinations, but I'm afraid it could be tuberculosis.'

Tuberculosis? It was Irmine's turn to faint. Doctor Bellisle was used to this sort of incident. After having dampened her forehead and temples with assafoetida, he gave her a thimbleful of Port mixed with an egg yolk that he had beaten himself. When he thought she had sufficiently recovered, he accompanied her to an adjoining room where his next patient, Aymeric de Linsseuil, was waiting for him.

Aymeric had not crossed his sister's path for almost ten years and seeing her so changed made his heart bleed. What! This is what that smart, sassy girl in the flower of her youth had turned into? She had a tragic expression on her face that was scored with wrinkles: crow's-feet at the corner of her eyes, furrows around her mouth. Wisps of hair straggled from her grey and white-streaked chignon. Her awkward body was crammed into a dress not even the poorest would want. And her eyes were red and swollen from the tears she had just cried. He felt guilty and almost asked her forgiveness for what the family had done to her. As for Irmine, she looked in dismay at what was left of the handsome heavenly Cherub: he had started to go bald, his cheeks were flabby, he was as thin as a rake and yet he was growing a pot belly. After a moment's hesitation, brother and sister embraced. Then Irmine began to cry again into her handkerchief.

'I heard that maman passed away last Christmas.'

'Like a true Christian,' Aymeric murmured, with an even sharper feeling of remorse. 'The name of our Lord Jesus Christ on her lips.'

He thought of adding that she had asked for her daughter before dying, but could not bring himself to lie. At that moment Justin-Marie, who had been bored on the veranda, entered the waiting-room and made Aymeric gasp. Was this his Cathy he was getting back, younger than ever, as radiant as the first days of their marriage? She had cut her shoulder-length black hair into a fringe, and although her cheeks were more hollow than he remembered, her greenish blue eyes were brimming with a life-like sparkle. He was about to run towards her, take her in his arms and embrace her when, pricking the illusion, Irmine affectionately ordered: 'Justin-Marie, come and embrace your uncle.'

The adolescent frowned, and in his breaking voice asked: 'Monsieur de Linsseuil?'

The tone was clearly hostile. Although Justin-Marie knew nothing of the old rivalry between Razyé and Aymeric, he nevertheless considered the latter to be a symbol of a hated class that had to be eradicated. Moreover, hadn't he forced Irmine to live in solitude and destitution, the woman whom Justin-Marie loved like his very own maman, and the woman he could not help pitying like all the rest?

Aymeric far from suspected what was going through Justin-Marie's mind.

'You're her very image!' he murmured in an uncontrollable outburst of emotion.

Irmine blushed. She had never spoken of Cathy to Justin-Marie, for she did not know what attitude to take. She had never forgiven her for coming between Razyé and herself. Even dead, her memory haunted her all day and turned up in her bed at night.

So without understanding why, Justin-Marie found himself embraced and caressed by a complete stranger.

On leaving the hospital, Justin-Marie ran to school, the lycée Carnot. He had already missed two hours of French and one hour of natural science. He had no intention of missing the geography class, his favourite, and dreamed of seeing one day with his own eyes those far-off lands of Africa, India and China whose maps were drawn in the pages of his atlas. Monsieur Oriol, the teacher from France, described them so well. He was sorry he had not shown more dislike for Aymeric and that he had let himself be treated like a little boy. It was because Aymeric was not at all like he had pictured him and what he expected of someone of his sort. He looked shy, preoccupied and unsure of himself.

As he reached the corner of the rue Schoelcher and the rue Sadi-Carnot, the school bell rang for classes to resume. He ran as fast as he could, but arrived at the bottom of the monumental flight of steps that led to the classrooms just in time to faint again. His head banged on the flagstones, and he only regained consciousness in the infirmary amidst the smell of bay-rum. The janitor's wife, who also served as a nurse, advised him to go home.

Justin-Marie felt worn out.

Retracing his steps along the rue Sadi-Carnot, for the first time he felt worried. What was happening to his body? For months he had a burning fever at night. Every morning he woke up wet through, wrapped in the smell of his sweat-soaked sheets. The slightest effort, such as climbing the stairs, playing ball with the little ones or carrying Cassandre in his arms, made his legs give out. Sometimes he coughed so much he lost his breath. He was not scared of death, provided she didn't come for him too early, before he could prove to all those neglecting him who he was. It must be his mother who had left him her tainted blood together with her colour. He knew he was the child of an adolescent, hardly older than himself, who had not stayed long on this earth. One morning, which must have been All Saints' Day, Irmine had given him her portrait in a locket, begging him in a melodramatic tone never to part with it. He had looked at her pale cheeks, her colourless eyes and her strands of lifeless hair, then he had thrown it in the bottom of a drawer. When he thought about it, he had no feelings for this dead girl. Nothing but bitterness, for she had cared little about him, turning her back on him when he was just seven months old.

Suddenly a procession of men in rags, armed with cutlasses, with a determined look under their *bakoua* hats, cut across the rue Frébault and headed for the seat of government yelling slogans. The sight had become so commonplace that passers-by did not even slow down to watch. Only Justin-Marie stood on the edge of the pavement to admire them. Everyone had had enough. For over a year it had been one strike after another, accounted for in every detail in *Le Peuple, La Cravache, Le Libéral* and *Le Nouvelliste*, but always with differing viewpoints, as if their reporters had not witnessed the same events. The previous week in Morne-à-l'Eau, the workers from the Dubost factory had held their boss hostage for two days and two nights. In Belle-Plaine, the gendarmes had had to use their clubs and left three men as good as dead on the distillery flagstones. Justin-Marie carefully cut out all the articles that dragged Razyé in the mud, calling him the henchman of Jean-Hilaire Endomius and Monsieur Légitimus's Socialists, and likening him quite simply to the Devil himself. This hatred the rich of the island bore Razyé warmed him like a bonfire. He too, when he grew up to be bigger than Razyé, he would unleash this same hatred, and everyone would know what sort of a person the little boy nobody had taken any notice of had grown into. Standing in the sun, Justin-Marie in his elation did not tire of looking at this cortège of shadowy faces, chiselled and remodelled by the hand of poverty. Yes, perhaps he would become a lawyer in order to avenge them and punish the well-to-do.

Irmine was waiting for him in the room that had the best of their unpresentable furniture, the one they used as a drawing-room. He suddenly noticed in slight disgust that she was pregnant again. In spite of this, she appeared to be in an unusually joyful mood. She took his hands, kneaded them in hers and announced in that excited little girl's voice she sometimes assumed: 'Just imagine! Your uncle . . . your uncle has invited you to stay at Belles-Feuilles.'

Justin-Marie looked down to hide his thoughts and said sullenly: 'And what about school?'

Irmine burst out laughing.

'In a week's time it'll be carnival. You'll be able to rest in the fresh air and the doctor says that's just what you need.'

Thereupon she threw herself on him and showered him with kisses. He wriggled free in irritation. Couldn't she understand he was a man? That a weapon whose power he hadn't yet tested, but whose lethal nature he knew, was lodged against his thigh? He was wondering how to teach her a lesson when Razyé, whom they never saw home before nightfall, appeared. Although Razyé had put on weight, although fat had softened the fibres of his muscles, his appearance, despite the passage of time, remained striking. Always erect in carriage and immaculately dressed in black, his mop of grey and white hair now formed a wild crown over his head. The journalists called his expression diabolical because they were unable to read what lay at the back of his eyes that so attracted women, every woman, from the *dame-gabrielle* to the ladies of society. Irmine literally threw herself around his neck, and he pushed her away, exclaiming: 'What's got into the woman? Are you crazy or what?'

Without losing countenance, Irmine told him what had happened at the hospital.

'And so the great reconciliation has been made!' he said ironically. 'For years he's not interested in knowing whether you're dead or alive or whether I've bullied you to death. You meet him by chance and suddenly all is forgotten.'

At the same time his restless mind was making a rapid calculation. Wouldn't it be nice to have a spy on the inside? Justin-Marie never hid a thing from him. If he stayed at Belles-Feuilles he would know how to get him to tell

135

everything that went on there. He walked towards the stairs and said hypocritically: 'Do what you like! Do you think I'm interested in your doings?'

Astonished by this unhoped-for victory, Irmine turned once again to hug the disconcerted Justin-Marie.

2   Return to the Belles-Feuilles Plantation

For three years Aymeric de Linsseuil had suffered from a duodenal ulcer. Doctor Bellisle diagnosed the ulcer as psychosomatic. Aymeric first noticed it when his financial troubles began. The Dargent factory was losing money. It had become a money pit. Expert at sniffing which way the wind blew, the Savilor company had very quickly withdrawn, while Aymeric bought up their shares in a blind borrowing spree. Because of the unending sugar crisis and the ever higher taxes, he had been forced to ask his workers to make the heavy sacrifice of a cut in wages. They had not understood, and this had been the start of the strikes, kindled by the Socialists and that henchman of theirs. But the wage cut had not been enough, and with a heavy heart he had had to sell bit by bit his rich sugar-cane fields at Calvaire, Blanchelande and L'Espérance to the colonial Crédit Foncier. The estate was now amputated, reduced to a third of its original size. He was virtually stripped of his liquid assets and he would wake in the middle of the night, dreaming that he had been expropriated by the banks.

Yet on the surface nothing had changed at the Belles-Feuilles plantation, where the family had just moved in for the Easter holidays: the green of the foliage against the fierce blue sky, the yellow splashes of the matalpa-trees, the flame of the flamboyants and bougainvillaea. It was the same harmony, the same serenity, whereas all around things were falling apart. Soon the former owners of the sugar plantations would wander over their land like lost souls, while their former slaves would lay down the law. After all, it was only right. He himself had wished for such a time; now that it loomed large, why did he feel so much anger and bitterness? And against whom?

With a feeling of remorse, Aymeric watched his daughter Cathy dunk her cassava cake into her bowl of chocolate. What future was he building for her? In two or three years he would have to marry her off. What dowry could he offer to her suitor? Cathy was a serious girl for her fifteen years and a half, sombre even, subject to fits of exuberance that made everyone dizzy. The nuns at the Saint-Joseph de Cluny boarding-school wrote in red ink on her quarterly reports: 'Capricious'. In appearance she seemed to have expelled all the whiteness of the Linsseuils and her mother in favour of her distant black heritage. In the dry season, when the sun roasts creatures and objects alike, she became as dark and juicy as a *capresse* with her black braid coiled like a snake down her back. You couldn't help envying the man who would one day relish undressing her. On Sundays when they saw her walk up to the altar with her papa and brothers – all three pink, blond and white – the white Creoles jumped in their pews. Since when was it fashionable to bring one's illegitimate children into the house of the Good Lord? Then they remembered that sad story of passion, denial and, to end it all, premature death. Malicious tongues started to wag. They well recalled the first Cathy de Linsseuil, née Cathy Gagneur, whom everyone called derisively Mam Razyé – may she rest in peace. She would have set a baptism font on fire. She alone knew what had been brewing in her belly, and nobody would have been surprised if Razyé hadn't slipped in a drop of his semen.

Aymeric had never let such thoughts cross his mind. He

did his best to keep his faith in Cathy, his Cathy. As the years passed he even began to revere her and forgot her caprices, her sulking fits, her tears brought on for the slightest reason, and considered her relationship with Razyé as an error of youth for which she had sincerely repented. When he described her to Marie, the wife he had been obliged to take to keep his house and bring up his children, she was pure perfection. The only picture he wanted to keep of her was that last portrait, when she lay like a saint on a bed strewn with flowers, her hands joined together, all dressed in white. As for the colour of their daughter, he put it down to the mysteries of hybridization.

Cathy finished eating her hard-boiled egg and laid her spoon down on the edge of her saucer. Then she stared at her papa.

'Why did you invite him?'

Aymeric hesitated. How could she understand, at her age? Seeing his sister so old and devastated, a remorse as violent as a squall had swept away the painful memories, the hatred of Razyé and any other consideration. Moreover, poor Justin-Marie was sick, Irmine had confided. Aymeric did not want to confess that his heart had missed a beat on seeing the boy who looked like another version of the first Cathy.

'All of us children,' she went on, 'we're very surprised that you've invited the child of this Razyé who is doing you so much harm.'

Aymeric thought he had misheard. He had never revealed to her anything about the past. What did she know exactly?

Seeing his amazement she said scornfully: 'You think we don't read the newspapers? We know you had to sell all your land because of him and that you're now virtually penniless.'

To a certain degree, Aymeric felt reassured. She only knew of the present.

'You mustn't exaggerate!' he joked. 'I'm not finished yet. The man who'll tailor my shroud is not yet out of his mother's womb.'

The joke did not make her laugh.

'I read that our workers have agreed to stop the strike?' she resumed with a frown.

Yes, Monsieur Légitimus had a new slogan. He claimed to be in favour of an agreement between capital and labour. What lay hidden behind his words? Wasn't it a stratagem to win the local council for himself? All the planters had almost convinced Aymeric to run for the next local elections.

'Justin-Marie,' he said, rather severely, 'is not responsible for the evil deeds of his papa. Besides, Razyé is not his real papa!'

'Tell me about maman,' Cathy asked suddenly. 'Don't tell me all those silly things I've already heard: that she was as lovely as an angel, gentle and as good as gold. I want to know the truth.'

Terrified, Aymeric stammered: 'The truth about what?'

'About everything,' Cathy gesticulated. 'What she liked. What she didn't like. What she said. What she did. What she wanted. What she thought. Whether I look like her, even just a little bit . . . Blacker, of course!'

She uttered the last words in a tiny little voice, because there were any number of people, including members of her own family, who were quick to remark on her colour. The nuns at the boarding-school, who could not afford to lose Aymeric's generous donations, treated it as a trial the Good Lord had sent Cathy in His mysterious way. She herself did not quite know what to make of it. *Mabo* Sandrine would tell her over and over again, while showering her with kisses, that it did not prevent her from being the loveliest of little fairytale princesses. And Aymeric confirmed it. Yet she had doubts.

Aymeric looked at the features of the pretty face turned towards him. A low, rounded forehead. Black eyes slit like an almond. Full-bodied lips. Dark brown complexion. What Bambara ancestress did she hail from?

'No,' he said with regret. 'You don't take after her.'

At that moment a rumble of wheels on the gravel in the drive interrupted them and a ramshackle carriage could be seen drawing up to the front steps. Its coachman was badly dressed. The horse was foaming at the mouth and seemed about to give up the ghost. A young man in a threadbare jacket climbed out, then shuffled up the steps rather awkwardly, probably out of bashfulness. Aymeric jumped up then dashed down the steps, exclaiming: 'Justin-Marie! How wonderful to see you!'

Indeed it was a long time since he had appeared so happy and had bounded like a young man. Justin-Marie looked around him and remarked: 'This is a beautiful place!'

He said it in a tone of reproach, as if he were comparing this splendour to the poverty of the villages and hamlets he had just passed through. For the road from La Pointe was a sorry sight, except for Nature's background. Cabins made of corrugated iron or patched up with wood. Children with bloated bellies capped with a tumbler of flesh, wallowing in filth. Women giving their dried-up breasts to infants as skinny as themselves.

Aymeric seemed oblivious to everything.

'You haven't seen anything yet. People usually prefer the Basse-Terre side of the island because of the parasols of its tree-ferns, the tall trees and cooler climate. But for me nothing beats our Grande-Terre.'

He took him by the arm and led him towards the house

where, alerted by the sound of the carriage, the servants had surged out in a crowd. Cathy remained alone and forgotten at the breakfast table. Her eyes filled with tears.

'He's the very image of a girl!' she scorned.

She went up to her room and sat down in a seat near the window where she liked to sulk and dream. Through the muslin curtains dotted with tiny flowers she could see a part of the balcony and below, a great expanse of the terrace whitened by the glare of the sun. Despite her affection for her family, she felt separated from them by an invisible wall that prevented her from partaking in their games and their company. When she heard her favourite uncle curse the blacks and advocate the return of slavery it was as though he had her in mind. When her father talked about 'my niggers', she felt like reprimanding him, even though his voice was filled with affection. Sometimes she dreamed of living in a country where neither class nor colour existed.

When *mabo* Sandrine came looking for her, she found her slumped in a rocking-chair. What was she doing there, when they were looking all over for her to go for a swim at Saint-François?

Cathy did not move.

'Have you seen the new cousin?' she asked.

Mabo Sandrine's mouth curled up in contempt.

'A great nincompoop, if you want my opinion, who hasn't even got a bathing-suit to wear. Monsieur is too good to invite little rascals of that kind into his house.'

'*Mabo* Sandrine,' Cathy begged. 'You knew maman, didn't you?'

Did she know Cathy de Linsseuil, née Cathy Gagneur, whom everyone called Mam Razyé behind her back? On Sundays Madame used to accompany her husband to the plantation chapel and after the *Ite, missa est*, with eyes lowered, she would hand out coins. You would have taken her for the Good Lord in person, whereas in fact she was a shameless hussy. But can you say such things to a child?

'Hurry up now,' *Mabo* Sandrine said softly. 'Everyone's waiting for you.'

Doctor Vercors, who had been the family doctor since Doctor Louisor retired, was wearing his face for sad occasions.

'Our climate doesn't suit him at all,' he explained. 'With his sickness, he needs some mountain air. Saint-Claude, Matouba . . .'

Taking stock of the situation, Aymeric kept his spirits up and began to make arrangements. His cousin, Marguerite de Linsseuil, owned a coffee plantation in Papaye. Since coffee was no longer a going concern, the place had been practically abandoned. She herself no longer set foot there and had entrusted the upkeep to Sanjita and Apu, a pair of Indian servants whose parents had been in the family service. She would be only too willing to lend it to him. They would drive Justin-Marie there as soon as possible and the Good Lord would see to it that he recovered his good health. If Irmine had Justin-Marie's health at heart, she would not object to the arrangement and would manage to persuade her husband.

He let the doctor see himself out down the stairs and returned to Justin-Marie's room. The boy was lying in a sweat – despite the coolness of the room – as white as the linen of the canopied bed but with cheeks oddly splashed in red. He looked at Aymeric, terrified, as he tried to catch his breath.

'What is the matter with me?'

Aymeric did not have the heart to answer his question directly.

'We're going to take you to Papaye,' he said firmly.

Weak as he was, Justin-Marie sat up abruptly, propping his hollow torso against the pillows.

'Papaye? But I have to go back to school!' he protested.

Aymeric sat down on the edge of the bed and took his hand that lay palm up on the sheet, like a dead fish drifting on water.

'Forget about school.'

It was blunt. But that's how he was: ever since he was little, he had hated lying. He was incapable of covering up or, in the face of tragedy, inventing those insipid yet encouraging words that soothe away worries and anguish. Justin-Marie fell back under the shock and panicked.

'I'm as sick as that?'

In his crumpled cotton nightshirt he looked so much like Cathy when her illness had started to set in, before it destroyed her beauty, that Aymeric felt he was reliving the past, as if she had been given a second chance at life for an extra dose of suffering. He clasped Justin-Marie to him, and quite naturally his lips found the damp spot at the nape of his neck that cherished the memory of kisses long ago. Justin-Marie let himself be kissed without realizing. He was too preoccupied. He was watching his life shrivel and fall away under his feet like a mountain path that suddenly comes up against a precipice. Was that all he was destined to be? An anonymous adolescent poorly raised in a cheerless home? A mere name on the class register at school for the morning roll-call: 'Gagneur, Justin-Marie? – Present.'?

He felt bitter towards those who had been unable to protect him against fate: his teachers, Irmine, Razyé, especially Razyé. He had admired him. He had believed in him. He had listened to his diatribes against injustice, and here he was leaving him to the worst injustice of all – death at sixteen! The man who spoke of defending and protecting the workers of the island could not even defend and protect the boy he called his son! He was nothing but a monument to weakness and hypocrisy. He clutched Aymeric as if he were going to drown and whispered in his ear, begging: 'You'll cure me, won't you, uncle?'

His eyes brimming with tears, Aymeric swore he would.

Thereupon he got up and quickly left the room. Without wasting any more time, he would send a letter to Irmine. Marie, his second wife, was waiting for him on the landing. She was entering her eighth month of pregnancy and he wondered in surprise who was sowing all these children in her womb.

'It's serious isn't it?' she asked anxiously.

Two days after he arrived at the Belles-Feuilles plantation, right in the middle of lunch on the veranda, a coughing fit had made Justin-Marie double over, terrifying everyone present, especially Elodie and Clémentine, the twins from the second marriage. Two days later he had fainted when coming back from the sea. Several times he had had to excuse himself, leave the guests and lean on the arm of one of the servants to climb up to his room. Marie de Linsseuil, who was a member of the Bon-Pasteur association, knew all the faces of sickness and had persuaded Aymeric to call the doctor.

At a nod from him, she stammered: 'But we can't keep him here.'

And since he neither seemed to hear her nor notice her she insisted: 'The contagion. With all the children in the house . . . '

He swept her objection aside with the sweep of a hand and went and locked himself up in his study.

For Marie, these ten years at the Belles-Feuilles plantation had not been pleasant. She had begun by struggling with the ghost of a dead wife to make room for herself in the house during the day and in the conjugal bed at night. Finally she had given up and reached a state of resignation. She would never be anyone but the woman who carried the keys to the pantry and handed out the wages to the household servants on Saturdays. Her three children would never be anything but illegitimate children, with none of the rights to affection of the legitimate heirs. The arrival of Justin-Marie had brought her a new load of worries. All the children, one after the other, except for Cathy, who was always so cold to her, had come crying on her shoulder that their papa preferred an intruder, a stranger, not even a white boy, who had nothing to his name. She herself could see full well that Aymeric, who was a good papa and a doting papa, had neither eyes nor time for anyone else. In the early hours of the morning he would saddle Justin-Marie between his knees and ride off over the plantation. With the excuse that the boy had never seen how rum was made, he galloped with him as far as l'Arjenac, an old sugar plantation converted into a distillery, or to the *platine*, where they made cassava cakes. The servants came and told her how shocked the workers were. The master would put a wooden rake in Justin-Marie's hands, and amidst the heat of the burning charcoal, the boy would jump for joy like a small child as he stirred the paste on the cast-iron slabs. And then there were the presents of books and clothes. It's true the boy had nothing to wear. He had arrived at the house with a cardboard case full of rags. On wash days the servant doubled up with laughter as she held up his clothes. Now he was dressed in a worsted suit and patent-leather shoes. Aymeric let him work the gramophone he had ordered at great expense from metropolitan France that nobody else had the right to touch. Having supposedly discovered in him an ear for music, he had him take classes from the twins' music-teacher. All this would have been laughable if it hadn't been so pathetic. It would have been acceptable if Justin-Marie had been a fascinating individual. Far from it! He was nothing but a sly, arrogant little person who always had to be the centre of attention. He was all sugary words and smiles with his uncle and Cathy, who, moreover, did not fall for all this sweetness. But he treated the servants like dirt, declaring they were 'unworthy of their freedom'. One day she heard him threaten Isidore and Déodat.

'Soon the white Creoles will be penniless on this island. And us mulattos we'll have everything. Together with the blacks.'

What's more, he had no manners. He belched noisily and yawned with his mouth wide open on his thirty-two teeth.

Marie descended the stairs heavily, avoiding the gaze of the Linsseuils, crucified one after the other against the wall, prisoners of their over-elaborate frames. At that moment it seemed she despised this family, from the first of the line who had settled in Guadeloupe to the last, her own son, Eugène, aged two. If she had had a say in the matter, if her place in the house meant anything to anybody, she would have wasted no time shoving Justin-Marie and his well-stocked suitcase into a carriage in the direction of La Pointe.

Farewell! Good riddance!

Then she would have purified the miasmas from his room by burning leaves of sarsaparilla mixed with a pinch of marjoram and cooking salt. But Aymeric just did exactly as he pleased.

In the kitchen a small servant girl was plucking a fowl with a broken neck. The blood was dripping into an enamel basin while the down, like the flock from a silk-cotton tree, was fluttering under the vaulted ceiling and flying everywhere.

Happiness, oh happiness, catch it while you can!

3 *Losers Will Be Losers*

The writing paper was elegant and cream-coloured, the stroke of the pen already assured. The childish signature curled in a pompous flourish.

> The Belles-Feuilles Plantation   2 April 19—
> Dear parents,
> My uncle is very good to me. His Great House is magnificent and I like it very much here. The doctor has discovered I am seriously ill. If I'm not careful I might even die. But uncle has promised to cure me. He is taking me to Papaye to care for me. I am sure you will agree it is in my best interest.
> Your loving son,
> Justin-Marie

Razyé read the short letter over and over again. It inscribed his defeat in writing. Once again he was beaten. Why had he let Justin-Marie leave for Belles-Feuilles? He could blame nobody but himself. Aymeric had only to turn up with his pompous air, his great house, what was left of his land, the portraits of his ancestors on the walls and his Limoges porcelain dinner-plates engraved with a cipher, to turn the tables and seduce Justin-Marie. The boy was turning his back on him without a moment's hesitation, without one look behind, forgetting all about the affection and plans he had for him. Once again he was left with his heart and his hands empty. Looted. Vandalized.

He looked up at Irmine, standing in front of him with her bloated belly, four months pregnant, and asked her calmly and collectedly: 'Tell me! What have you got that we haven't got? You're no better looking, no stronger, no more intelligent and yet you win every time.'

Irmine, who was used to her husband's enigmatic words, did not try to understand. She quickly crossed herself and exclaimed rather sadly, for she was struck by Justin-Marie's ingratitude – not a word for her: 'How lucky he is to have found in his misfortune someone like Aymeric!'

That was the last straw! Razyé stood up and silenced her with the back of his hand. Then, so as not hear her whimpering, he walked out. In the yard the children were flying the orangey triangle of their kite over the roof. They quickly stifled their shrieks and ran to a safe distance. He caught sight of Razyé II, the child he hated most even as a baby, and called him over. When the boy was level with him, he interrogated him, at first quite calmly, but then as his anger mounted, his voice grew louder.

'Why are you here on this earth? To put tears in our eyes? To make us crazy? Quite simply crazy! As God is my witness, I'll send you back where you came from!'

Razyé II looked him straight in the eye, without a blink of defiance or fright. At the back of his black eyes lapped a lake of tranquillity. Razyé was so struck by this that he took stock of his first-born: sculptured out of locust-wood like himself, almost as tall, black, perhaps a shade less black, with finely chiselled features. There was a silence, then the young boy quietly asked: 'Justin-Marie's not coming back?'

Without a moment's hesitation, Razyé slapped him aside.

Outside, La Pointe was daubed in red. The façades of the

houses, the walls and the balconies were bleeding, and the burst sky dripped scarlet rivulets on the passers-by, who cowered on the pavements. The sun was burning and crackling like a bonfire in the dry season and heat waves shimmered in the air. The sea was restless and swelled up, flaunting its painted canvas. Razyé arrived at the town hall and went up to his office on the first floor, just behind Jean-Hilaire Endomius's. Idling on a bench, his henchmen were waiting for him, unscrupulous individuals whom he paid to stir up the cane-workers and, when need be, to help them set fire to the plantations. The newspapers claimed they had a number of assassinations, political and otherwise, on their conscience. But there had never been any proof. Razyé gave orders to Nelson, a one-eyed braggart, who was looked on as the head of the gang.

'Get the horses ready and take a few men. We're leaving for Petit Canal. I want all that's left of Aymeric de Linsseuil's land to go up in flames this very evening.'

Nelson looked surprised.

'That's not what the boss told us. With the capital-labour agreement he ordered us to lie low.'

'Yeah, yeah!' Razyé said angrily. 'The capital-labour agreement is a load of rubbish. The Socialists are quarrelling about it amongst themselves . . . Everything must go up in smoke tonight, I'm telling you.'

Nelson said not another word, and together with his associates ran to saddle the horses tied up in the town-hall yard.

The men left La Pointe by the Vatable canal district, Razyé leading the pack, wrapped in a red fury, and the passers-by and the children coming home from school wondered where this wild, galloping cavalcade could be headed, led by a man all dressed in black. Frightened, some made the sign of the cross and took the precaution of murmuring a prayer. Others recognized Jean-Hilaire Endomius's gang and crossed themselves even faster.

Leaving the town of Les Abymes, the traveller immediately enters the sugar-cane basin. In some places the cane had just been harvested and in the bare fields the stumps were waiting to bud again. In others, nothing had been cut and the cane stood straight and strong, as tall as a grown man. Balancing their horns, oxen grazed the grass on the sides of the road, while their Indian herdsmen, sprawled under the mango-trees, kept an eye on them. Donkeys tied to their stakes brayed the hour of noon. In spite of himself, Razyé felt his heart melt. The dry smell of the earth baked by the sun and the blistering air brought back memories of his younger days. Many years back he had stumbled along this same road, half crazed with pain, almost falling into every rut. At that time a rum-shop stood beside the calabash-tree at these crossroads. He had gone in, collapsed on a table and the die-hard drinkers had gathered round to laugh at him. A nigger like him crying? It was the first time they'd seen that. But it was here that a servant girl had taken pity on him and taken him home. A mangy dog guarded her cabin where two or three fatherless children slept. He had eaten his *diriémori* and laid down beside her on the corn-stuffed mattress. But he hadn't thanked her or given her what she expected. So in the yellowish light of the pre-dawn hours she had put him out and he had set off again, straight ahead along the unending road. The dogs had yelped as he passed by and doors opened a crack in suspicion.

After two hours at full gallop they reached Morne-à-l'Eau with its splendid houses of the dead guarding the gates. On the black and white marble tombs the archangel St Michael tirelessly brandished his sword and the crosses made of pearls never came unthreaded. The men stopped their mounts in front of the entrance to let a hearse through, and received smack in the face the stares of a handful of mourners, whose curiosity got the better of their grief. Judging by the expression of the mourners, it must have been a miserable wretch they were burying under the hot two o'clock sun without a flower or a wreath. Barely a squeak of music. Life hadn't been kind to him, keeping its sweetness for others. No matter! He had been laid to rest. Razyé envied him, as he envied all those who had done their time. He didn't expect much from death now, even though he stubbornly sought the key. He had been a frequent visitor to Madhi, the *kimbwazè* encountered by chance in the Carénage district, who had dug up some things from the past but had not yet ventured into the future or the after-life. He took his money and filled his head with mysterious prophecies that could be interpreted in many ways.

Razyé whipped his horse then set off again at a gallop. Morne-à-l'Eau, with its string of cabins like so many cowpats strung out on a savanna after the rain, was quickly swallowed up by the sugar-cane fields. This was the former land of the Linsseuils, sold to the Crédit Foncier some years before. Their remaining estates covered a loosely drawn square around Port-Louis. They were not more than an hour and a half away. As the sun was still too high in the sky for what they had to do, Razyé led the men in the direction of l'Engoulvent, left in the care of Zébulos, where he hadn't set foot in months.

The vegetable garden, which the Indians had taken so much trouble over in the past, was now abandoned. Nothing grew there any more – just a few cabbages gone to seed and some pepper plants. The old house, however, was still standing, staring through the louvred shutters of its attic windows at the yellowish savanna bristling with columnar cacti and the scrub of *razyés*. In the distance the waves still took out their rage on the rocks strewn haphazardly in the ocean and on the geometrically walled silhouettte of La Désirade. A fishing-boat pitched its sails. Letting the men continue on up to the house, Razyé galloped over to the little graveyard on the edge of the cliff, a few yards from the void. He dismounted in front of Cathy's tomb. Unlike the other graves of the Gagneur family, whose bare, grey stones were flaking, Cathy's tomb stood white and adorned with bunches of fresh, sweet-smelling flowers. Taken with a fit of rage, he knocked over the vases of lilies and arums, and stamped on them. He knew that Cathy was not under this slab, otherwise he would have gone to join her. But these painstaking efforts to rob him of her over and over again exasperated him. Once his fit of anger had passed, he stood standing helpless, at a loss what to do, feeling the sun drilling nails into his head. It was as if he were losing Cathy a second time in this new version she had devised for herself.

At midnight, a wall of orange hue loomed up in the sky. Clusters of sparks exploded in the darkness and drew cabalistic signs in gold. The heat was so great that it reached outlying villages and drew people from their beds. Wrapped in the rags of sleep they ran to their doorsteps and saw the glow of the fires. A single cry went up.

'Kann-la ka brilé!'

The sight was a common one. Yet it roused the same terror. Sugar-cane is the mother of every Guadeloupean. A fatal blow, and what would be left?

The fires had been lit in numerous places at the same time and flames leapt up everywhere. Powerless in their efforts to put them out, the men, women and children of the plantation, armed with buckets, cans and even pitchers, formed a human chain from the ponds scattered around the savanna, while waiting for the municipal water-pumps. As they passed along the water, they lost themselves in conjectures. Some claimed to have seen a pack of black horsemen, the spitting image of Jean-Hilaire Endomius's henchmen. Others swore that they had seen with their own two eyes a ball of fire fall from the sky around ten in the evening that set the cane-fields alight in a single blaze. There was something unnatural about this fire. While the crowd argued, their efforts proved useless. The fire played havoc with them and leapt under their noses, devouring one patch of cane after the other. Aymeric galloped around on horseback like a madman. Whereas these Bengal lights, as they were nicknamed throughout the island, had ruined all the planters, one after the other, his estates had always been spared. At the Chamber of Agriculture meetings he was even a little proud of it and put it down to the respect his workers had for him, even when they were goaded to strike. Now he galloped in circles, humiliated and exasperated. Where were the municipal fire-pumps? Except for Anse-Bertrand and Saint-François, all the municipalities were in the hands of the Socialists, and they must have been only too pleased at what was happening to him. The harder he yelled, shouting words of encouragement at the rescuers, the more his voice got lost amidst the crackling and the hot hissing of the flames.

At four thirty in the morning, when the first water-pumps finally arrived from Anse-Bertrand, there was practically nothing left to save. Almost ten thousand acres had gone up in smoke, and Aymeric de Linsseuil was penniless.

4   Sanjita the Housekeeper's Tale

On 21 December 1867, the *Allahabad* set sail from the port of Calcutta for the island of Guadeloupe with Shashi, my father, aboard. My father was the son of a fishwife seduced by a Brahmin, who hid his noble birth under his traveller's rags. Such stories are common in India, the land we come from. You might even say they can be heard in every lane, in every street. The poorest Indian can see through the disguise of the destitute traveller standing on his doorstep and recognize the wise man underneath. He opens wide the door to his house and offers him drink and his finest food. When night falls, he lays his most beautiful daughter in the bed prepared by his wife. However, things did not quite happen like that for my father. His mother was scaling fish on the banks of the Ganges, our holy river, when she saw the Brahmin's boat drifting downstream. Before she had time to realize what was happening, he had sprung into the river with a great splash and rapidly swum in her direction. Then he had dragged her behind a curtain of trees and gallantly mounted her. My father's mother was sixteen and a virgin. Rape? No, when the ardour of God manifests itself, this word is unbecoming.

'I am Parashar and a saint,' the wise man had said suavely as he withdrew. 'A son will be born from our union.'

As he had predicted, the belly of my father's mother soon began to swell. Her father, who was also a fisherman eking out a living, noticed it and was about to disown her when she told him the story of her visitation. So he accepted the fact and nine months later Shashi, my father, was born.

At least that's the story my parents used to tell us, and I am sure they ended up believing it. They never answered our questions. So they could never explain how this fairy-tale beginning ended with my father's exile, his humiliation in the plantations of Guadeloupe and the poverty we, my seven brothers and sisters, now endured. I think their heads must have been full of dreams, and that every man has the right to dream, especially if his life is wretched. In actual fact, my mother and father were probably peasants from Bengal who grew jute and roamed around looking for work. A sirdar had no difficulty propositioning them on the edge of a marketplace.

My parents had always been in the service of the Linsseuil family, the branch from Basse-Terre, the one that owns land in the region of Gourbeyre and beyond. On his death Amédée de Linsseuil left my father almost fifteen acres at the bottom of his estate, La Solitude, in Plaisir. It was in fact a poisoned gift. The land was covered in scrub and tall trees. Despite his unremitting work, my father could never get anything to grow there. I saw his hair turn white, completely white, for a few cabbages, carrots, turnips and lettuce, not even enough to sell on Sundays outside the cathedral. Up to the day he died, the only pleasure I saw him take was an afternoon here and there at the pit. He was too poor to bet. He was merely content to watch the cocks fight each other.

Neither my mother nor my father had ever set foot inside a school. They could neither read nor write, and on pay-days my father would trace a large cross on the overseer's register. When they opened up school for everyone in Guadeloupe, he enrolled us. But the other children made fun of us; they would hold their noses saying we smelled; when they hit us for no reason at all, the mistress sided with them. So after a few years I dropped out and began hiring my services to the white Creoles in the area. That's how I met Apu, who was breaking his back as a gardener on a neighbouring plantation. Oh, our marriage wasn't easy. My parents were from Calcutta, almost as white as the white folks we served. Apu's family came from the South of India. They all had skins as black as black folks and the same coarse features. So my father began by saying no. He brought out all his Parashar stories and went to great lengths explaining his mysterious birth. How his mother stunk of fish, but this did not stop the saint who hid a real shaft under his dhoti. How he had conjured up a kind of cloud that hid them from the eyes of all those who crowd the banks of the Ganges every morning. (There was never any mention of my mother's origin; I suppose she didn't count.) But we held firm and finally we were married in church because our parents had become good Catholics who prayed to the Good Lord.

Now coffee-growing is dead in Guadeloupe, or almost. The coffee plantations have fallen into ruin, one after the other. So you can't imagine how wonderful they were. When Madame Marguerite offered us the job of guarding the estate for her, I knew I was going to be in paradise. A paved road, two or three miles long, lined with palm-trees and giant ferns, led up to the house, itself somewhat rustic. To the left was a vast, tiled terrace which was once used for drying coffee. A hedge of white roses separated the garden from the roasting pans, once piled high with sacks of coffee, and from the plantations terraced in four tiers up the sides of the mountain. When we arrived in Papaye the tightly-knit rows of coffee-trees were covered in a veil of star-like flowers, and their perfume mingled with the hedge of roses.

In the surrounding park grew the most beautiful trees I had ever seen, not the common trees around here such as candlewood, mapoo or guinep, but trees from French France such as pines, thujas, oaks and especially a peach-tree that Alphonse de Linsseuil, Madame Marguerite's late husband, had taken pleasure in planting. He was fond of saying: 'This is my orchard, my little corner of France,' and when he died, that's where they buried him.

We settled into the quarters built to accommodate the twenty or so servants in the old days; used to our cabin, we would get lost. Everywhere you looked you could see the volcano that never slept, day in day out, and quietly rumbled. Occasionally, it would puff out rings of smoke like an old person puffing on his pipe. In Papaye the soil is blessed. It gives everything man's heart desires to feed his stomach. With Madame Marguerite's permission we staked out a part of the coffee plantations that were no longer any use to anyone and dug four trenches thirty feet by three where we planted vegetables: cabbages, carrots, turnips and runner beans.

We would get up before first light and go to bed in the dark. We would carry water from the gully, stumbling along the paths that wound along the sides of the mountain. We would go looking for cow-pats and spread them over the soil. In the evening our bodies were so *krazé* we collapsed on our beds without a thought of making love. But after a few months, what rewards for all our trouble! We were able to supply the table of every Linsseuil, from Basse-Terre to Grande-Terre, and there was even enough left over to sell in the market at Saint-Claude. Three times a week I went down, carrying my produce on my head, only too happy to show everybody that we were not like those good-for-nothing Indians who roam the roads, fill the jails and whom everyone wants to send back to where they came from. I had many customers who came for my looks and I took pleasure in their praises: 'Fanm Zindien bel tou bònnman!'

At the end of the day I would climb back up with my empty basket and in my pockets a little tobacco for Apu, some sweets for the children and a yard of madras cloth for myself.

Alas, this happiness did not last!

We had been in Papaye for about four years when one day our good fortune turned like the wind. All my boys died. First Eugène, the eldest at fourteen, my favourite, the handsomest, the whitest; then Ernest and Etienne, all three within a few days of each other. My eyes had no sooner dried than salt water came and soaked them again. That year, the year 19—, Guadeloupe suffered a terrible calamity. Typhoid fever landed off the boats with the oxen from Puerto Rico, those colossal animals driven to the slaughterhouse, whose quarters, blackened by flies, can be seen hanging by the feet in the meat booths in the market. In three months the typhoid fever laid out 3,265 people. Five hundred survived with nothing but skin on their bones; the rest went to fill the places reserved for them in the cemeteries. Very quickly, the general hospital in La Pointe and the Camp-Jacob hospital in Saint-Claude became too small to handle all the sick, and the governor had to erect tarpaulins on the Place de la Victoire and the Champ d'Arbaud. Military doctors in khaki uniforms arrived from Guyana, where they had been hard at work on leprosy, yaws and all the diseases of that country. In the churches unending novenas were said, and the priests from their pulpits begged the blacks and the mulattos to repent. Why were they persecuting the white Creoles? Why did they steal their cattle and set fire to their cane-fields? For this reason the Good Lord was no longer good, and his wrath was burning the island. My sons were dead. All three of them. One after the other. I saw their stomachs release a stinking excrement. I saw the blood spurt from their nostrils, flared like animals, and their whole bodies become as hard as rocks. Why was it happening to me? Was it because I had turned my back on the gods of India, the real country we come from, and was worshipping the god of the white Creoles? In my fear I tore up the pictures of the Good Shepherd, the Sacred Heart of Jesus and the Holy Mother pasted on the walls of my bedroom and replaced them with images of Kali, Vinayagar, the elephant-head god, and Hanuman, the monkey god. Then these idols disgusted me. I was even more frightened and hurriedly took them down. Even today I have no answer to my questions, and sometimes I think I am going mad. The only child I have left is Etiennise, the youngest. A daughter is of very little value. My mother told me that in India they are killed at birth and thrown out at the crossroads where they are trampled on by our sacred cows. In spite of everything, that child has become the apple of my eye, but I don't show it for fear fate takes her from me.

Etiennise was all I had. And work. Nothing was ever the same again. Both Apu and I lost the joy of harvesting the fruits of the earth, and everything could have gone to seed or rotted for all we cared.

It was then that Apu started to become one of the regulars down at the rum-shop. That's another of the heavy crosses I have to bear.

One morning, Etiennise had just left for school, Apu was snoring off his rum in the bedroom, I was drinking my coffee in the early morning light, when Madame Marguerite arrived, saddled on Penelope. The mare was all in a sweat. She had whipped her along a winding, mountainous path from her plantation at Plaisir. In the family they called Madame Marguerite, the Grand Creole, because she is tall, carved like a man, and with a voice that booms for miles around. She frightens her children's children when she goes to kiss them.

'Sanjita,' she ordered. 'You're to open up the house and make everything clean. My nephew Aymeric is coming to stay. I'm counting on you and Apu to make sure he has everything he needs.'

She looked worried.

'From his letter I didn't quite understand who is sick. I hope it's not one of his children, with all the misfortune he's having at the moment.'

'What misfortune?' I asked.

'Goodness,' she sighed. 'You haven't heard what's happened to him? All his cane-fields went up in smoke like cigarette-paper. He had delayed harvesting, and for him it's a complete disaster. It seems he can't even pay his workers. This time he'll have to take out a mortgage on the factory, which is already in debt. It's not only the end for Aymeric, it's the end for all of us. Sometimes, Sanjita, I wonder whether it was the Good Lord who created the niggers. He can't have, because they're a heathen race. Yet in the old days they weren't like they are now. Do you remember Adélia, that black woman, who took care of Mathilde when I weaned her? She worshipped the child, just worshipped her. Even now, whenever she sees me she asks after Mathilde and kisses my hands. But they won't get off lightly – their day of judgment will come.'

Without waiting for an answer, Madame Marguerite turned her back and I could hear the hoofs of her horse clatter over the stones in the drive. She was returning as fast as she could to Plaisir. I toiled all that day. I opened the windows, I scrubbed, I scoured and I swept. Then I went down to the gully, where the giant heliconias bloom, and brought back a fine bunch. Two days later, towards the end of the afternoon, I heard a carriage bell. I ran out and saw a closed carriage drawn by four horses that looked like a hearse. Monsieur Aymeric climbed out first, then tenderly helped out a pale-faced person with untidy hair. I say person because boy or girl, it was anybody's guess. The person, wrapped in a cloak that trailed on the ground, looked like a package. Monsieur Aymeric greeted me with his usual kindness. He asked after my health, Apu's and Etiennise's, whom he had known since she was little, but I could see he had other things on his mind. Then he turned to the person.

'Look how lovely it is here, Justin-Marie. Breathe in the good air. In a few weeks' time you'll be trotting and leaping around like a foal.'

Justin-Marie . . . It was on hearing the name that I realized the person was a boy. He cast a glance around him and in an angry whine like a small child, he said somewhat unpleasantly: 'I hope to God you're telling the truth.'

I took the luggage and preceded them into the house. I was proud of myself for the flowers looked splendid in their vases, the plants in their jars, and everything was in order. Yet nobody paid me any compliments. While Monsieur Aymeric was making himself comfortable in Madame Marguerite's room, the one we call 'the cornflower room' because of its wallpaper, I led Justin-Marie into the room next door that looked directly out onto the coffee plantations. At that time of the year they are veiled in white, sweet-smelling flowers. Anybody who has occupied this room has never failed to utter cries of admiration. Justin-Marie never even took the trouble to look at the view and sat down on the bed, worn out by the short walk he had just undertaken. I was studying him with an air of compassion, when he shouted brutally: 'What are you doing standing there, looking at me with the eyes of a sacred cow? Help me get undressed!'

I quickly did what I was told. As I gradually took his clothes off, my heart took pity on his skinny body. I don't know why, it was as if I was seeing the twisted bodies of my poor children again, my Eugène. His thighs were as spindly as his arms. His shirt opened onto a double row of ribs that seemed about to pierce his skin. His neck measured no more than a child's hand, was no bigger than a chicken's and just as flabby. It was especially sad since he had a handsome face that was not the slightest bit ravaged. Yet it gave you the shivers with its staring eyes, gleaming with fever, its cheeks flushed with red and its thick African mouth. You could see full well that death was hovering over him, eager to carry off what was left of his life. What relation was he to Monsieur Aymeric? Was he his illegitimate son? I didn't know he had one. But you never know with men!

My close attention annoyed him and once again he shouted: 'What are you waiting for? Get out!'

I returned to the kitchen. Apu had lit the lamp and was filling the firewood box with branches he had just cut. Without looking at me, for we no longer look at each other now, him being lost in his rum, and me in the memory of my boys, he said: 'Be careful, he's got tuberculosis. He's already spitting blood. He won't last six months. Madame Marie didn't want to keep him at home, so Monsieur Aymeric brought him here.'

'How do you know all that?' I asked, stupefied.

He poured a little water into a basin to wash his hands and went on explaining: 'It was Joseph, the coachman, who told me. I had a drink with him before he set off back.'

From then on my heart took pity on him. Eugène was almost the same age as Justin-Marie when the Good Lord took him from me. I understood now why he was so disagreeable. Inside himself he was in revolt. To die when he was merely an adolescent! When he wasn't even twenty! Some people are here stacking up month upon month, year upon year, dragging out their lives on this earth, frail, toothless bags of bones, gnarled with pain, and a burden for the family; others don't even have time to taste what's good in life! Had a woman had time to teach him about love? Poor wretch! Like my Eugène he was going to die knowing nothing. I made up my mind. For the remainder of his time I was going to surround him with love as if he were my child. I would lovingly cook the best stews, the best casseroles, the best broths, mash vegetables into purée and pick the choicest fruit – sapodillas, Otaheite apples and canary-yellow bananas.

In order to amuse him, I wasn't going to tell him the same old boring stories of silly Zamba and trickster Rabbit. Oh no! I would make him dream with the wonderful adventures of Rama and Sita. Shashi, my father, did not even know the letters of the alphabet and yet he told us these tales without changing a word as if he was reading from an invisible book open in front of him.

My beloved, my devoted Sita! Daughter of royal lineage,

We must now part, for now is the time when I must begin my wandering through the thick woods.

Before leaving you, my beloved, give me a final proof of your love.

Serve the king, my brother, with all the devotion you owe to me.[1]

The following day I put my resolutions into practice. I filled my basket with pink-shelled lichees that only come

[1] Taken from *The Ramayana*.

every seven years. I added Bourbon oranges, white guavas, strawberries and peaches picked in Monsieur Alphonse's orchard, as we still like to call it.

I arranged the fruit in the prettiest saucers I could find and placed them on a tray covered with an embroidered cloth. Then I hurried to take them to Justin-Marie. I thought he must still be asleep, for it was still very early and it would be a nice surprise. Once he had eaten I would help him wash and dress. I already had some water simmering. I knocked gently on the door and went in without waiting for an answer. Once inside, I froze, swinging back and forth like a gourd. I did not know whether I should go forward or step back. Whatever the case, I was nailed to the spot.

Monsieur Aymeric was sitting at the head of the bed in a rocking-chair. In one hand he was holding a book from which he was reading out loud.

"Fig trees were growing around the kitchen; a grove of sycamore trees extended as far as a tangle of green where pomegranates glowed among the white tufts of the cotton plants; vines, loaded with bunches of grapes, climbed among the branches of the pine trees; a field of roses bloomed under . . ."[1]

With the other he was caressing the hand of Justin-Marie who, with a bored look, floated on the huge bed as in a boat at sea. Around them, the darkened room with shutters closed and louvres lowered looked like a jail. Justin-Marie was the first to see me. He propped himself up against the pile of pillows and cried out: 'Is that you? What do you want now?'

Hearing him, Monsieur Aymeric stopped and leapt up. In a fury he walked over to me. I thought he was going to hit me or throw me to the ground. Then he pulled himself together and thanking me, took the tray from my hands.

[1] G. Flaubert, *Salammbô*.

5 Etiennise, Sanjita's Daughter's Tale

It's Thursday and there's no school today. Maman advised me not to disturb Monsieur Aymeric. As for his nephew, I mustn't go near him on any pretext. Doctor Sacripant says that if I breathe the air that comes out of his mouth, I'll catch his illness and die.

From where I am, I can see him. He is lying rigid on a chaise-longue out on the paved yard. He is wrapped in a blanket that makes a bump where his knees are. I wonder whether he's asleep or just pretending so that his uncle won't come and fill his head with his book reading. From the expression on his face, I can see that these readings are as dull as dishwater. As dull as the books at school, where we never do anything interesting. He's moving now, flings off his blanket and almost sits up. He coughs. He spits into his handkerchief. He looks carefully at what he's spat out. I wonder if it's blood. Doctor Sacripant says that people with a chest condition spit out all the blood in their body. That's how they drain themselves and die.

I move out a little from my hiding-place so that he can see me. Yesterday we managed to whisper a few words while Monsieur Aymeric was writing letters in his study and maman had gone down to market.

He looks around and sees me with my back against the white rose hedge. I wonder if he's older than I am. Not much, in any case. One or two years, no more. Finally he quickly motions to me to come over. I weigh up the situation. The windows of the kitchen where maman is clattering her pans do not look out onto the yard. I take the risk. Close up, he almost scares me. How thin he is! He may be as white as a sheet, but he's no white Creole. You can see that straightway: his mouth is too big and there's something in the shape of his cheekbones.

'What's your name?' he asks, inspecting me from head to toe.

'Satyavati,' I answer.

That's the name I call myself for I hate Etiennise, my real name.

'Are you the daughter of the housekeeper?' he asks. 'Your maman frightens me. She looks like a vampire.'

He can say all he wants, I don't at all feel like discussing my parents. I don't answer.

'What class are you in at school?' he continues.

I turn my back.

'Well, if that's all you have to say to me, I'm going.'

He half gets up from his chaise-longue, almost falls, catches my skirt and begs me:

'Don't go! I'm so bored . . . '

I turn back and he asks me, sulkily: 'What do you want me to tell you?'

I lean over. Under his lavender scent, he has a sick baby smell, like sour milk. It's slightly nauseating.

'They're saying a lot of things about you. In fact they say you're Monsieur Aymeric's illegitimate son. Since you have a bad sickness, he can't keep you at home. He has to hide you here . . . '

He angrily interrupts me.

'Rubbish! He's not my papa. He's taking care of me, he's going to cure me, that's all. Do you know who my real papa is? . . . Razyé!'

167

I'd never heard that name before and I tell him so. He looks disappointed, shocked, as if standing in front of the Archangel Michael or Christ on the cross, I was asking who they were.

'You don't know who Razyé is?' he exclaims.

Thereupon he launches into an endless explanation. According to him, Razyé's name is in every paper, without exception. He is terrorizing the whole of Guadeloupe. He works for the Socialists, but he is cleverer than they are. Cleverer than Monsieur Légitimus. Cleverer than Jean-Hilaire Endomius. He's the one who sets fire to all the cane-fields. He's going to kill the white folks down to the very last man. And the blacks and the mulattos will take their place and govern the island.

'If you don't like white folks, what are you doing here?' I ask.

He shrugs his shoulders.

'I'm convalescing, I tell you . . . '

He begins to cough. I think he'll never stop. A red froth appears at the corner of his lips. It's awful. He manages to get his breath back and sighs: 'It's funny, my uncle used to impress me at first. His great house was so magnificent. Rugs on the floor, tapestries on the walls, mahogany furniture and portraits hanging everywhere. I bet you've never been in a house like that. At table we ate things I had never eaten. Breast of chicken, vols-au-vent stuffed with mushrooms, and strawberries. In the evenings we listened to music. Not any old sort of music. Violin, piano. He played records on his gramophone: *The Magic Flute* and the Brandenburg Concertos. And then one day, I don't know why, it all began to get on my nerves. My uncle as well. Especially my uncle. Now I can't stand him. If I wasn't sick, I'd have left a long time ago.'

I don't like him speaking this way. Monsieur Aymeric is

kind. Every time I meet him, he bids me good day, and digs into his waistcoat pocket to find a coin. He's not like the other white Creoles, who order you around all the time and treat you as if you were at their service. I tell him what I think and he shrugs his shoulders.

'Yes, but he's too kind. It gets on my nerves. It's not natural. He's not a true person. He's not . . . he's not real.'

Now it's my turn to shrug my shoulders and scoff: 'What do you mean by a "true person"? What do you mean by "real"? People who speak gutter Creole, swear, drink rum and are at odds with everyone? Come and spend some time with my papa.'

Yet life did not always have the bitter taste it has today. I can remember the time when my brothers were alive. It's since they died that my papa drowns himself in rum and maman has become a different person. She has become a woman dressed in black for every season and her hair is pulled back into a chignon so tight that the skin on her forehead is wrinkled. I know what would make her young again. Having another three babies. This time I'll do it for her. But with whom? With the boys from Papaye? Black or Indian, they're all the same.

Deep in my thoughts I forget he's right beside me until I hear him speak.

'You know, at our house it wasn't very merry either. People claimed my papa was rich – as rich as Croesus. Yet nobody at home ever saw the colour of his money. We had nothing. Not even a candle to see by or a piece of soap to wash with. All we had to eat were tubers with meat or saltfish, like the poorest of niggers. Every day I wore the same clothes to school. The boys nicknamed me "My one and only". I never heard my papa say one kind word to my maman. He treated her like a maid. Even worse. When I was old enough to understand certain things I wondered what he did with her at night. He must have done something since she was pregnant all the time. In the evenings he would bring women into the house . . . '

I interrupt him.

'And that's the man you're so full of admiration for?'

He thinks for a moment and then declares: 'Yes, I do admire him. It's people who made him what he is, a girl he loved who rejected him because he was too black and didn't have a cent to his name, preferring a rich white Creole.'

I rather agree with the girl, I thought, but didn't dare tell him what I felt. He goes silent, looks me straight in the eye and murmurs: 'Can you keep a secret?'

What sort of secret? He is whispering so low that I have to lean over to hear what he says.

'I believe the rich white Creole who took his girl was my uncle Aymeric.'

What sort of cock and bull story was this? I burst out laughing.

'You're making it up! You don't know what you're saying! Your uncle is married to a Mademoiselle Le Dentu, everyone knows that. The Le Dentus have an estate not far away in Matouba.'

'That's his second wife,' he whispers. 'The one I saw at Belles-Feuilles. But what about his first?'

I shall remember that day as long as I live, for that's when it all began. That Thursday in March, a Thursday like any other. I was expecting to be bored, like I am all the time. The sun was just as hot and the Soufrière just as jagged, silhouetted against the sky. The wind sang the same old song in the trees, like a carnival beat that returns year after year, so familiar that you don't hear it anymore.

The stories about his family didn't interest me. But I took

pity on him. He looked so old, stretched out on his chaise-longue under his woollen blanket.

I wasn't going to waste my time interrogating maman, she wouldn't tell me anything even if she did know the name of Monsieur Aymeric's first wife. For her, white Creoles' business is the Good Lord's business. It's sacred. So in the late afternoon I went to see papa in the vegetable garden behind the coffee-trees. At this hour, he was sober, standing with his hands on his hips, breathing in the cool air. When he saw me he quickly hacked at the weeds with his cutlass as if he were busy working. From where we were, we could see the blue of the sea through a gap in the tangle of green.

'Bapu?' I asked.

I call him that. It's our little game.

'I heard that Monsieur Aymeric was married before, a first time. Do you know if it's true?'

He looked at me, feigning to be angry. His cheeks and chin are covered with a tangled grey beard. But his hair remains as black as ink, carefully greased and brushed back.

'What's it got to do with you? Since when do children pry into grown-up affairs?'

Then he began to laugh, as if he remembered something.

'She was one hell of a Miss! Perhaps if I'd have tried I'd have got lucky! The number of men she took in! A real baker's oven!'

'What was her name?' I asked.

He couldn't remember her name at all, and I realized he knew nothing about this first wife, merely repeating the nonsense he had heard from the mouths of bad-talkers. People are like that. No use wasting my time! I turned back towards the house. Abélard the hunter was standing near the kitchen, holding up the birds he had just killed in the forest and maman was bargaining.

171

'How much do you want for your thrushes? I want to make a pâté.'

She goes to so much trouble now, considering that ever since my brothers died she's done nothing but boil up salt meat, Congo peas and tubers in water. But I've noticed that neither Justin-Marie nor his uncle touch her cooking and the plates come back cold. I entered the warm smell of the kitchen, usually cold and cheerless, and as I went over to the kitchen range as if to look inside the cooking-pot, I asked: 'What are you cooking tonight?'

She bustled about importantly.

'Poor wretch! He's not eating anything!'

And there you go! All she needed was a boy in the house to give her back a taste for life, something I was never able to do! I'm only a girl, and my feelings for her don't count. I went out scuffing the soles of my sandals over the kitchen tiles, something she hates, but she didn't even notice, so busy chopping up herbs and shallots. Near the jasmine hedge Abélard was putting his birds back in his game-bag. The blood dribbled around his cigar-like fingers and he dried them on the grass. It made me think of the massacre of the innocents. I hope all hunters go to hell. Abélard winked at me and murmured: 'When are they going to marry you off? If you continue the way you are, one of these days I'll do it for you.'

I knew he was just talking. He has watched me grow up and wouldn't harm a hair on my head. Besides, people say his real gun, the one between his legs, can't fire. That's why he's got no wife. He lives all alone in an *ajoupa* in the depths of the forest. I went up there once with my brothers and we ate roasted bush-rat.

He delved into the pocket of his old drill *konoko* and showed me a few coins.

'Come on. I'll buy you a cornet of roasted peanuts.'

Maman doesn't like me to leave the estate, except to go to school, because she says the people in the village are an uneducated lot. According to her, they're only interested in one thing: putting a bun in my oven. At that instant I felt like disobeying her. So I clutched Abélard's hand and we crossed the garden. Once past the gate we found ourselves on the road that cut through the flesh of the trees like a wound. I sneaked a glance to see whether Justin-Marie was in the yard. But he had already gone inside. At this hour a chill descends from the mountain and the air is too damp for him. His uncle was probably sitting at the head of his bed reading him passages from *Salammbô*, the book he hates so much. He must be listening to him in boredom, prisoner of his sickness, incapable of shouting what he really thinks: 'Stop, stop! Go away! You're boring me to death!'

Abélard and I walked down to the village. Darkness was hanging over us, about to fall. For the moment it was still hesitating and hovering, spreading its great wings above the mountain. But at any moment it would swoop down upon us. In the cabins, the oil lamps and tallow candles were about to be lit and the forest would flicker with a thousand flecks of light from the fireflies. In the village, already empty and ready for night, the snow-cone sellers were leaving the only stretch of street, ringing their bells. The women were already laying out their piles of peanuts behind the smoke of their oil-lamps. They were spreading sheets of newspaper on the pavement to protect their behinds from the damp.

I ate my peanuts. Then, taking advantage of the last rays of sun, I went and knocked on Astrélise's door. Knowing how strict maman was, she was surprised to see me. Astrélise is my best friend at school. I could say my only friend. Yet she's not an Indian. She's of African descent. She boasts that the ancestor of her maman's family was Nago and could read the future from oil-palm kernels. She also boasts that her papa's grandfather ran away and hid in the Deux Mamelles mountains, that General Richepance could never catch him, despite all his massacres, and that he sailed away to Haiti alive and well in a hollowed-out tree trunk with a whole gang of Maroons. It really is the first time I've heard someone get satisfaction from such a lineage. The blackest individuals boast of having white parents. But Astrélise is no ordinary individual. Nor is her family. Her papa, her maman and her brothers walk tall and proud. Of course, the people in Papaye can't stand them. They call them *nèg-Kongo* and pour tar in front of their door.

'Have you ever heard the name Razyé?' I asked.

She laughed.

'Of course! Who hasn't? Are you interested in politics now?'

Then without further explanation she dragged me into the yard behind the cabin. It was filled with people. One of her brothers was beating the *gwoka*; another accompanied him on the *ti-bwa*, and still another on the harmonica. In the flicker of the *chaltounés* the entire family was dancing, from the infants learning to walk to those on the edge of the grave. Bonne-maman, as everyone calls her, who is almost a hundred and two and hasn't one whole tooth to her mouth, was holding the edges of her *golle* dress and jumping in the air like a goat. After a while I felt my whole body burning. It started with my hands and I couldn't stop clapping. Then a shiver went through my thighs and my knees started knocking. When the beat reached my feet I couldn't control myself any longer and I entered into the dance. I could not control myself, but I was ashamed. I wanted to silence all those around me who clapped and

174

shouted: 'Now we've seen everything! Mi Zindien ka dansé léwoz!'

It seemed to last as disturbingly long as those dreams when you do all sorts of forbidden things. Finally the music stopped, and I fell into the arms of Florimond, Astrélise's elder brother, the one who is always pleased to see me. He took advantage of the situation to kiss me on the neck.

I rejoined Astrélise while basins of food started to go the rounds. Blood pudding. Rice and beans. Breadfruit stew with salt pork. Tripe and plantains. Astrélise and I shared the same *kwi*, and while I was filling my belly, I thought of Justin-Marie. What would he have thought of these people around me? Would he have said they were real because they drank rum and beat the *gwoka*? Because they sang and danced, uninhibitedly shaking their *bondas*? Is that what it is to be real? Did he mean the white man's ways are an obstacle to being real? In that case I don't want their 'reality'. Oh no, I don't! Yet this 'reality' was hidden somewhere inside me, ready to come out without asking my permission.

Sometimes my heart is too big for my breast. I can feel it beating and beating, and perching on the edge of my mouth. How it would like to fly away. Leave this speck of land manhandled by all sorts of devils, volcanoes, hurricanes, fires and earthquakes. I wish I could close my eyes, go to sleep and wake up in another country in another colour. Not mine, that's a curse and a shroud.

Alas, I know all too well they are nothing but dreams in my head, and I'll never be anything else. When I got home my maman was standing at the gate, watching for me with a worried look.

'What are you doing roaming around at this hour?' she cried. 'What do you think you're doing, eh?'

175

I didn't even take the trouble to answer her and watched her close the gate like a prison door. And the great house, too, made me think of a jail. Shutters closed, louvres lowered, not a sound or a light filtered through. The whole night long, lying on my straw mattress, I dreamed that Justin-Marie was holding me in his arms and was taking me away. Far away.

6   Back To Earth

Aymeric read over again the letter he had just received.

> My dearest,
> God has sent us another ordeal. He did not want us
> to have our little Angèle and called her to Him the day
> after she was born. You cannot be with us for the wake.
> But we shall wait for you to lay her to rest. Be brave,
> my dear, as I am trying to be myself.
> Your affectionate,
> Marie

It was an annoying disruption, but he felt no real emotion. It wasn't the first time that he and Marie had laid a
baby to rest. Over these twelve years together they must
have lost three or four infants carried off by worms, fever,
pernicious anaemia or some other childhood sickness.
Though Marie seemed so distressed each time that one
wondered whether it wouldn't be her turn next to be laid to
rest, Aymeric, however, grew hardened. His sojourn at
Papaye had turned him into another man, younger and
now indifferent to life's tribulations. Gone were his pre-
occupations with his family, the firing of his cane-fields, the
factory, his unpaid workers and his urgent debts. What's
more, he had almost stopped torturing himself over the loss
of Cathy whom he had constantly mourned. He was too
busy watching Justin-Marie convalesce. The boy slept better

at night. His temperature was down. He ate more and had gained a little weight. Although he coughed just as much, there was never any blood at the corner of his lips. Recently, well wrapped up, he had been taking a daily walk under the trees in the park without a stumble. Doctor Sacripant, who came up from Saint-Claude twice a week, declared one should never lose hope with young people. The best, he repeated, was yet to come. While reluctant to leave at this stage, Aymeric was too much a man of duty to think of ignoring his wife's call and he quickly made plans. If he set off immediately he could reach Capesterre before nightfall. There he could stay on the Bois-Baril plantation with his cousins, the Saint-Esprit, and change horses.

He got up and walked over to the window. In the garden he caught sight of Sanjita's black back, like a giant spider flattened against the greenery. She was walking up and down in her graceless way, cutting roses and wisteria blooms. The watchful presence of this woman hovering around Justin-Marie at every hour of the day exasperated him, for he was jealous enough to want his patient all to himself. A vague sense of anguish gripped him. If he left what would happen behind his back? Then he came to his senses. What was he afraid of? Sanjita was simply yearning for motherhood.

He called her over, and when she was up close he examined her angular face with its tapering, elusive eyes below her hair that was tightly brushed back.

'I have to go away for a few days,' he explained brusquely. 'I'm counting on you to take great care of Justin-Marie.'

She did not betray her real feelings.

'Yes, of course,' she merely said submissively. 'You can count on me, master.'

And yet Aymeric could have sworn he saw a flicker of contentment around her mouth. While Apu got the carriage

178

ready, he entered the room where Justin-Marie, sprawled in the middle of his bed, was sulkily contemplating his breakfast, although Sanjita had put all her goodwill into it, even going so far as to arrange for him three different-coloured fruit juices. He sat down next to Justin-Marie and felt him shrink away – just as Cathy used to do when she furtively refused his embraces. What had he done to antagonize both of them? He noticed Justin-Marie's impatience when he read to him, his boredom on hearing him talk and his weariness at constantly having him by his side. Sometimes, he knew full well Justin-Marie pretended to sleep to escape his company, as Cathy used to do. Nevertheless he could not help hugging his shoulders, distressed at feeling his bones through his skin, and then announced the bad news he had just received. Justin-Marie squirmed free and stared at him wide-eyed.

'Does that mean you will have to leave for Belles-Feuilles?'

In response to this unconcealed joy, Aymeric could not help asking him bitterly: 'What do you think you'll do when I'm not here?'

Justin-Marie burst into forced laughter, and without further ado, Aymeric walked out of the room.

The countryside around Papaye is as resonant as a guitar. The hollows in the earth, the gullies and the deep woods reverberate with echoes that merge in the air like music. The twitter of the carouge birds mingles with the rustle of banana leaves tickled by the wind and the hoarse braying of the donkeys hitched to the mountain slopes by their four hoofs. In the distance, the sea never winks. With eyelids wide open it glares at the volcano. Sometimes a cloud bursts and soaks the mass of greenery, but never for long. A burning sun quickly reappears through the shroud of mist and everything is dry again.

Aymeric made a detour through Basse-Terre to check the axle on one of his wheels. The capital city was very different from La Pointe. As different as the nonchalant wife of a planter is from the valiant woman working in the cane-fields. She sprawls around her bay, her back to the volcano, staring at the ocean through louvred shutters like a coquette sheltering behind her fan. Even at this hour her streets were almost deserted. Market women were walking down the slopes, their knees bent under their load of vegetables balanced on their heads; while uniformly light-skinned children, their hair slicked down with water, were making their way to school, hand in hand with their *mabos*. The wheelwright's shop was located in the Carmel district, in the shadow of the cathedral's grey stones. Aymeric remained standing on the pavement while two apprentices busied themselves around the carriage. After a while he went up to the man standing at the street corner selling *La Vérité*, the newspaper owned by the mulattos that he never read. Headlines jostled each other on the front page. Another strike for more wages by the workers at the Grande-Anse factory on Marie-Galante had spread to Guadeloupe. The strikers had again taken the planters hostage and, tired of such outlandish behaviour, the governor had appointed a former magistrate known for his uprightness to conduct an enquiry. All this had been decided without once thinking of informing him, as if his peers had already forgotten him. Aymeric felt sad and exhausted.

It was four o'clock in the afternoon when he came in sight of the vertical trunks of the royal palms bordering the allée Dumanoir. He then set off along the path leading to Bois-Baril. The sun swayed low in the sky. Low-lying and squat, the plantation house was not much to look at. Its iron roof had been messily patched up, and the façade could have done with a coat of paint. Yet its owners, the Saint-Esprit, had not lost a cent since the day slavery was abolished. On the contrary. People even said they had managed to increase their profits, thanks to smuggling. They succeeded in hiding most of their rum production from the authorities, and their white rum flowed to the shopkeepers in Basse-Terre in forty- and fifty-litre copper drums, duty free. Jean de Saint-Esprit was a lout. He had a wife, Alicia, born a de Linsseuil. But everyone knew he hadn't touched her for years and gave child upon child to a black woman from Grands-Fonds-Cacao. He removed his *bakoua* hat, which stuck to his straw-coloured hair with sweat, in order to embrace Aymeric.

'Our condolences! We learned of the sad news. Alicia left yesterday for Belles-Feuilles.'

Then he added,

'It's not as if it were your only child.'

Aymeric sat down on the veranda in a rickety wooden chair and murmured, despite himself: 'No, I've got six others.'

He was unable to think of his dead child. All he could think of was Justin-Marie. What was he doing at this moment? On whose arm was he leaning to cross the park? Had he managed to eat something? He had just remembered that Sanjita and Apu had a daughter the same age as Justin-Marie. Once, returning unexpectedly from a ride, he had caught her deep in conversation with Justin-Marie. Who knows if she won't go prowling around him again? Trying to get control of himself, he asked his cousin: 'What's his story about a commission of enquiry I read about in the paper?'

But Jean shrugged his shoulders and answered laconically,

'A load of nonsense.'

Darkness found them drinking one glass of rum after another while the crickets sizzled against the glass of the lamp on the veranda. Jean, more than half drunk, was now ready to talk his head off. He ranted on about the white planters from Martinique who, in his opinion, took advantage of the misfortunes of those in Guadeloupe to buy up their land for next to nothing. He carried on about the colonial authorities who, under the pretext of helping the landowners in difficulty, in fact stripped them of their assets. He then slipped into his own secrets.

'The only white you see in me is the colour of my skin. I eat like a nigger; I swig my rum like a nigger; I swear and I fight like a nigger; as for fucking, I fuck like a nigger, and that's why Alicia can't stand me. For her, love's all quadrilles and waltzes with a violin.'

It was not the first time Aymeric had heard such boasting in the mouth of a white planter. On the contrary, it was a never-ending topic of conversation. He had always found such inane behaviour pathetic. Yet that evening it aroused in him a strange feeling of anger mixed with suffering. Is that all women were? Flesh for taking one's pleasure? Tenderness, respect and constant attention, didn't that mean anything to them? If he had mounted her as roughly as Razyé, he would have won Cathy over. At the same time something told him it was not as simple as that. Illogically, his bitterness spread to Justin-Marie. He had done everything for him, and it had been to no good. Once more he had been duped. Around two in the morning he left Jean to sleep off his rum and went up to his room on the second floor. As he walked along the corridor his eyes, blurred with sleep and alcohol, thought they could make out a white form skipping and backing away from him, as elusive as smoke. Cathy? Shortly after her death he thought he saw and heard her everywhere. In the shape of a cloud stretched across the sky. In the icy-cold water of the gully running over the rocks. In the sunlight. In the wind. And then one day she disappeared, and all his prayers had not brought her back. Was it she who had come back that night? It was surely only to mock him.

What was she trying to tell him?

7   Barbaric Nuptials

Justin-Marie stared at her, his eyes shining with malice, and hissed: 'Your name's not Satyavati. It's Etiennise. I heard your papa call you yesterday evening. Another lie, you lie all the time.'

Hurt, she could think of nothing to say. What lies was he accusing her of? She had told him the story of Shashi, her grandfather, to amuse him. She herself didn't believe a word. Anymore than she believed in the tales of Rabbit and Zamba or Ti-Jean. As for her name . . . Our misfortune is to go through life with the names our parents chose for us, inappropriate names that we have to drag with us right to the very end. Etiennise sighed. She attributed Justin-Marie's cantankerousness to his condition and did her best not to hold a grudge against him.

Poor wretch! She knew he was seriously ill. Yet, until then, she hadn't realized the infinite extent of his weakness. His nostrils often became pinched, as if he were about to suffocate. Several times he had been gripped by interminable coughing fits and she had seen the handkerchief he pressed to his lips grow purple. Could it be blood? The day before, against her recommendations, he got it into his head to climb down into the gully. Going down had been easy enough, apart from a few slips on the roots. Once at the bottom he joked and laughed with the exuberance of a child grown up in town who suddenly discovers the countryside.

He struggled onto a big rock and dipped his hands into the icy water, sharp as a razor-blade. He had even tried to lift up the crayfish traps the boys hid under the leaves of the wild lily. But climbing back up, what martyrdom! She had to hold him up and almost drag him along the path, gasping for breath, bent double, whimpering and cussing as he was so good at doing. Several times he had stopped to catch his breath, and each time she thought he was going to have a fit. The next morning he was unable to stand, and they had to lay him out on his chaise-longue all bundled up like a parcel. He hadn't been able to swallow a thing all day and left his tray virtually untouched. In spite of all that, those few days were filled with happiness. The Good Lord works in mysterious ways! Hardly had Aymeric turned his back than a fit of malaria nailed Sanjita to her bed. The attack came quite unexpectedly. One evening she lay down as on the day before and the day before that, her hair smoothed with bay-rum, encased in her long, brushed cotton nightgown after three Our Father's and three Hail Mary's, chanted head down in front of a picture of the Sacred Heart of Jesus. The next day she couldn't get up. Her head spun. Shivering, her teeth chattering, she lay in her sheets soaked with a sickly sweat. Since Apu was still snoring, Etiennise gave her two spoonfuls of calomel, then ran to the village to ask for help from Dorisca who, when she was not besotted with rum, was unsurpassed in the kitchen.

For Justin-Marie and Etiennise there was now no longer any need to hide. As soon as the chore of school was over, Etiennise would throw off her school satchel and join Justin-Marie who was soaking up the last rays of the sun in the yard. As soon as he saw her he asked: 'Let me see your books. Tell me all about it. What did you study today? Didn't you have geography class? It was my favourite. And French composition. I always had the best marks and

Monsieur Taranne, our teacher, read out my homework in front of the class.'

She made a face, for she did not feel like talking about school and lingering over the memories of a place that was as gloomy as a prison. The one-classroom school that had just opened in Papaye was the last building outside the village, a square of corrugated iron sitting glumly in the middle of a field of cassava and pumpkins that the older students weeded on their afternoons outside. The school-mistress, a skinny, sharp-tongued mulatto woman, had a look of boredom about her. Since she never asked Etiennise any questions, sitting at the back next to Astrélise, the girl whiled away her time dreaming or playing noughts and crosses. In the playground having nothing better to do, she watched the boys fight over a ball, like all the other girls, secretly contemplating the promising bulge of their male members under their drill *konokos*. What was there to say about all that? Consequently, annoyed at her silence, Justin-Marie refused to speak to her and began to sulk. He would sulk for any old reason. Just like he complained about everything. About the chill from the mountain. About the heady smell of the roses and the jasmine. About the treacherous rays of the sun. About too much sugar in the lemonade. About too much grease in the soup.

Sometimes he asked for the newspaper and she had to sneak into the kitchen to fetch the paper Dorisca had used to wrap the fish or the meat. He would smooth it out fever-ishly and only return to a good mood if he read accounts of Legitimus, Jean-Hilaire Endomius or Razyé in particular – stories that bored her to death. He would read things out to her.

'Listen to this, listen to this! A strike at Les Mineurs factory. The strikers beat up the mayor and two town councilmen. And what about this! More cane-fields have gone up in smoke at Beauport.'

As her expression betrayed her feelings, he began to insult her.

'You girls, one wonders what you've got in your head instead of a brain. Caca, liquid caca, and that's all!'

In spite of this she did not tire of his company. All day long she waited for the moment when she would join him again. He seemed to her a most singular person. He was different from everyone else she had known and kneaded from rarer stuff. As in the fairytale, the words that came out of the mouth of other humans were vipers and toads compared to his precious emeralds, rubies and carbuncles.

Suddenly, as was often the case, his mood seemed to change. He became angelic. Two dimples hollowed his cheeks. He nestled his head against her shoulder and murmured in his winning tone: 'Why don't you come and join me after dinner? I'm afraid, all alone in this big house.'

She could not help caressing his hair that his sickness made slightly damp.

'All alone?' she remarked. 'Doesn't Dorisca sleep in one of the rooms in the attic?'

He made a face, like a malicious little child, and murmured: 'That's what she wants you to think. In actual fact, as soon as I'm in bed she runs as fast as she can to meet an admirer or drink her rum, who knows. Come! You can tell me some stories. Stories about the country your parents' ancestors came from.'

Etiennise hesitated. At the same time she was ashamed of being so timid. What was she afraid of? If she went up to his room at night, nobody would know. Sanjita drank cup after cup of worm-bush tea and was shivering and sweating badly under three woollen blankets. As soon as Apu had swallowed his root vegetables and saltfish for dinner, he set off for the rum-shop. He would only head back home around three or four in the morning. She lowered her voice so that Dorisca arriving with the tea-tray could not hear.

'First, say you're sorry for having called me a liar.'

By way of an answer he burst out laughing, which made Dorisca jump.

If she had not wreaked havoc on herself, as was now the case, Dorisca would have been a handsome woman. People said she began to drown herself in rum the day the man she treated like the holy of holies in the hope he would end up slipping a ring on her finger left for La Désirade, after having stolen all her gold from her wicker basket. The police caught up with him in mid-crossing. But from that moment on, life for her had lost all its salt and spice, so much so that she decided to shorten it with doses of delirium tremens. Her reputation as a cook was legendary, but because of her fits and ensuing absences she could never keep her job. She placed in front of Justin-Marie a tray decorated with a lace place mat on which stood a dish of granadilla water-ice and a slice of marble cake. His only thanks was a groan.

'Water ice? It's too cold for me.'

Accustomed to his whining, she walked off. She had no time for spoilt children, the never-content sort. As for taking offence at Etiennise's presence, that wasn't her business. The Lord is great. She did not have a daughter. She had only herself to worry about!

Etiennise laid her hand on Sanjita's burning, lifeless forehead. Sanjita moved her head from left to right, but did not wake up. Reassured, Etiennise tiptoed out of the room. But once she pushed open the door of the house, she almost went back inside so indiscreet was the night.

Not a cloud. A circle of orange-coloured moon, that

looked as if it had been drawn by a compass, gleamed in the sky and drenched in light the rose-bushes, the jasmine hedge, the clumps of white rayo, the silhouette of the great house and the tall trees that danced around it. The earth seemed to be covered with a similar orange-coloured fabric, as luxurious as a long-pile carpet, unrolled as far as the eye could see. This nocturnal light, almost as harsh as day's, but curiously artificial, gave Nature an evil, threatening appearance. You expected the great house to open its mouth and swallow everything up, the branches of the trees to change into whips and the rose-bushes to grow giant thorns like crab claws.

Etiennise plucked up courage and crossed the lawn, but could not help running when her feet sank in as if it were wax. The terrifying silence wailed to infinity. She knew the jar where they hid the kitchen key, and she had no trouble slipping inside the house. Once inside, however, she got another scare. The big hurricane-lamp they left burning at night drew twisted shapes on the walls and floor, and she thought she was surrounded by a throng of sinister, toothless hags like carnival masks. Once again she began to run, the floorboards squeaking like mice under her feet. When she knocked on Justin-Marie's door she was out of breath. On opening it, she stood dumbfounded. He was waiting for her on his bed, propped up by a pile of pillows. The entire room was illuminated by the glow of candles. They were everywhere: in candelabras, in flower-pots, in vases, in glasses and even in a porcelain chamber-pot. All this glow was reflected in the mirrors that were glazed by an opaque yellow veil. So her first reaction was that she had stumbled into a funeral chamber and was about to attend a wake, as if Justin-Marie was already dead. She was almost expecting to hear the drone of the women mourners, chanting mechanically the words from the Holy Bible. Then she noticed he had carefully brushed his hair and was wearing in her honour a white cotton nightshirt with a wide ruffle. Dressed the way he was, under the canopy of this four-poster bed drifting like a raft in the middle of the ocean, he looked more than ever like a giant doll painted red and white, whose face was half attractive, half repulsive, maybe male, maybe female, or both. He smiled at her and by way of invitation tapped the bed beside him.

'Come sit next to me.'

She hesitated. He shrugged his shoulders and asked in annoyance: 'What are you afraid of? Did you come all this way just to show off?'

He was right. She obeyed, sidled awkwardly over to him and perched herself stiffly on the edge of the bed. That evening he didn't smell of sickness, sweat or sour milk as he often did. He must have drenched himself in bay-rum or eau de Cologne in the hope of smelling like a bunch of flowers. He grabbed her wrist. She had never noticed before how big and strong his hands were at the end of his slender wrists. He drew her near to him, and at such close quarters she could make out the blotches on his skin. She could also smell his mouthwash that not only attracted her but also repulsed her somewhat.

'Have you ever kissed a boy?' he whispered. 'On the mouth?'

What a question! It had happened a number of times. At school behind the shack that sheltered the latrines. And at the village fête, behind the booths made of woven coconut fronds. She had also kissed Florimond, Astrélise's brother, who was always glad to see her. She had even let him slip his hand inside her knickers. But she shook her head, because she knew that's what he wanted to hear.

'Do you want us to try?' he whispered.

She hesitated again. But before she could word an answer,

in the negative or affirmative, he had brutally grabbed her face, turning it towards him, almost scratching her chin, and had glued his mouth to hers. She wanted to push him away. He clasped her tighter. Then everything happened very quickly. So quickly, that years later, at the end of her adult life, she could never reconstruct exactly what had happened that night, despite torturing her imagination day after day, constantly patching fleeting images together in anguish and remorse, and asking herself questions over and over again. At one point she found herself underneath him, suffocating under the frail and resolute weight of his body. With a firm hand he forced her legs open. She had the vision of a perfectly robust male member in erection that filled her with panic. And all the time he was panting and groaning.

The more she struggled, the more violent he became. Then what did she do exactly? Did she hammer his chest with her fists? Did she scar him with her nails? Did she clutch him by the throat like a villain in a back alley? Did she hug him closer and closer in all her fear and revolt? Whatever the case, he suddenly withdrew and collapsed limp beside her on the embroidered pillow-cases. Silence. A gurgle. Then the blood rose up to his colourless mouth. First it bubbled out in a reddish foam. Then in a frothy stream. His eyelids fluttered like two wings of a woodpigeon. His eyes closed.

In her life Dorisca had had to deal with a number of complicated situations. White Creoles, respectable negroes, as proper as they come, and even priests who had passed on in the arms of their mistresses. But situations like this one, never! The room was lit up as bright as day. Candles burning everywhere and their wax dripping in thick puddles over the furniture. Bunches of flowers withered by the heat.

191

Etiennise dishevelled, screaming uncontrollably and as pale as the colour of her skin allowed. Justin-Marie, his eyes closed and his chest covered in blood, like the sheets and pillow-cases under his head. She wasted no time asking questions that nobody would ever answer. Besides, she had a good idea what had happened. Did those two sly ones think she didn't know what they were up to? Always interrupting their private whispering whenever she approached. She glanced at Justin-Marie and did not need the services of a doctor to come to a conclusion. No need to call on death, she was already well on the way.

She walked over to Etiennise who, thank goodness, had stopped screaming, but stood standing like a zombie, and shook her like a sweet plum-tree in season.

'Go home to your maman immediately.'

The girl did not move. Dorisca gave her an almighty slap. First of all because she deserved it. Secondly to bring her back to her senses. Etiennise reeled from the shock, recovered her wits and as a result started to cry silently.

'Go home, I'm telling you,' Dorisca said in a softer voice. 'And keep your mouth shut. You were in your bed all night. I'll say that around eleven in the evening I came up to bring his medication as usual and found him the way he was.'

'Is he . . . ?' Etiennise groaned.

Dorisca nodded.

'Not far off, anyway.'

On hearing this, Etiennise cried even harder. Dorisca pushed her firmly out the door. Now that she was alone she wasted no time. She quickly blew out the candles that had almost entirely melted, and scraped the hardened wax off the mahogany furniture. She put away the objects used as candle-holders, whisked away the flowers drooping in their vases and straightened out the sheets on the bed, witness to an unfortunate struggle. In short, she tried to return the room to its innocuous appearance as a sick-room. When she had done her best she went over to Justin-Marie, and for the first time felt her heart moved. So young! So handsome! Here was another one who could have had everything he wanted, if life had let him. Some are calling out for death, who merely turns a deaf ear, while for others she is in too much of a hurry to come. What a shame the green fruit falls to the ground before it is ripe!

8 Mabo Sandrine's Tale

The great house was still asleep and us servants were drinking our coffee in the kitchen when Madame Marie came in to announce the news: Justin-Marie had died suddenly at Papaye. Her eyes were all watery when she announced it, because just the name of the dead person makes some people cry. Perhaps too she was thinking of her little Angèle whom the Good Lord had called to Him the other week and her heart was all upset. The others around me started to whimper in order to please her and pretend they felt compassion. It was quite a cacophany of sighs and 'Jesus, Mary and Joseph'. As for me, my eyes stayed dry. I cannot pretend I felt sorry, for ever since he turned up here with his superior airs and his old clothes in a battered suitcase there was no love lost between Justin-Marie and me. When he tried to order me around like he ordered everyone around, I told him: 'Enough of that, slavery's over' and turned my back on him.

So I shrugged my shoulders and remarked to Madame Marie: 'You've got a lot of salt water to waste on almost a stranger.'

She knew my ways. Yet she looked at me sorrowfully and exclaimed: 'Almost a stranger? The child of the brother of my husband's first wife? You ought to say your rosary ten times for what you've just said.'

Then she added sadly: 'Poor unhappy Aymeric has

fallen ill, he torments himself so. He thinks he is the guilty one.'

Guilty of what! Of having inflicted on his family a boy who could neither say Good Morning, Please nor Thank You to anybody and looked at you like a horse that has thrown its rider? He started out being all sweet with my Cathy. But she soon put him in his place.

I was born the month they announced the abolition of slavery. That very month. For weeks the news had been whispered around the cane-fields and at the sugar factory. By the river where the women washed their laundry. Even in the cabins where they shelled their Congo peas. But the old people on the plantation, who had already heard such stories before, shook their heads. They recalled what had happened before to those who had taken it at face value and thought themselves equal to other men. One fine day fleets of ships had sailed into every port, then Bonaparte's soldiers had hung clusters of blacks and mulattos from every available tree. Those they did not hang they stuck their bayonets through and left them to rot in the fields with their guts hanging out. So their advice was to remain low and carry on as if nothing had happened. Carry on as if nothing had happened? No way! The smell of freedom had gone to their heads! The most apathetic turned furious. As for those who were already boiling over like milk in a pan, they went crazy. There was no counting the number of blacks who were whipped or thrown into jail.

Finally, one morning, Monsieur de Linsseuil together with Monsieur Alix, his father, accompanied by the steward holding a big open register and two overseers, assembled all the blacks in the factory yard. He then told them the great news and gave every one of them a name. That's how Isaumar, my papa, came to be called Saturne. Isaumar Saturne. That's about all I know of him: his name. And that he wasn't very black, he was tall, as tall as a coconut-tree, with fine hair that he got from some grandfather planter. So as soon as he heard the words *A pwézen nèg lib*, the words of freedom, he rolled his few belongings into a bundle, picked up his guitar and disappeared in the direction of La Pointe. Maman never saw him again with her own two eyes. And yet she was pregnant, on the verge of giving birth. And she had four other children, all of them his. But men are like that, there's no understanding them. Maman cried her heart out. But she had no choice but to stay where she was on the Belles-Feuilles plantation with my brothers and sisters and me, who arrived before I was due because of all the grief my papa had caused her. Only too pleased because Monsieur de Linsseuil took pity on her and kept her on as laundrywoman. Only too pleased because twice a year, instead of a wage, he bought new clothes for her children. Only too pleased because we always had a slice of breadfruit at mid-day.

At the age of five I staggered around carrying wood. At seven I was beating the laundry on the rocks of the River Blanche. At ten I was fanning the fire for the cook and stirring the sauces. At eighteen, my knees in soapy water, I was scrubbing the miles of floor in the great house. Then when they noticed I had a calming effect on the children, even the most mischievous among them, they put me in the service of Monsieur Aymeric to take care of little Cathy.

Monsieur Aymeric has been very good to me. He had me taught how to read and write as he does for everyone who works for him. At the beginning of each month he deposits my wages in the bank to see me through my old age. But a master is a master. You can't love him. Sometimes the hatred I have for him stirs in my stomach and surges up to my mouth, fetid like the spit of a toad. It flows out in fiery abuse like lava from a volcano, as sharp as the blade of a knife. People who hear me are shocked.

196

'Sandrine, ka ki pasé?' they ask.

An animal is inside me and won't let go. That's how one evening I sneaked out with a group of workers on the plantation to listen to Jean-Hilaire Endomius at Petit-Canal. It was the year before the Socialists won almost all the local elections on Grande-Terre, much to the anger of the white Creoles. The meeting was being held in the school run by the monks in a room decorated with the flag of the Republic. There were people everywhere. Those who couldn't find a place inside were perched in the branches of the mango-trees. Posters on the wall shouted slogans that I managed to decipher without too much difficulty, much to my satisfaction. 'Education is Our Children's Future' or else 'Forward to Honour, Glory and Wealth like the Others'. Jean-Hilaire Endomius looked like one of those bulls from Puerto Rico that clear the streets and wharves when they lumber down off the boats and gallop tail up, mooing and storming to the slaughterhouse. He was so black he was blue, all dressed in white, which made him look even blacker. It was as if he dressed like that on purpose to show that the time when the black man was ashamed of his colour was over. He was surrounded by several men whom you didn't even notice. All you could see was him, and Razyé sitting on his left with his eyes half-closed. If you asked me what Jean-Hilaire Endomius said exactly, I couldn't tell you. All I know is that his speech went into my ears and then spread through my body like a guildive rum. I could feel my heart throbbing, my muscles relaxing and my blood rushing. I shouted, stamped my feet and clapped my hands like a young girl. Lord, why must I already be sixty? I shan't be here to see the sun rise on that new world where finally the blacks shall be the first and the whites the last like the poor and the rich in the Kingdom of Heaven. Why is it I have to be a woman? There's no age for a man. If I was a man, I'd be up and

197

following these Socialists. They say they set fire to the cane-fields. Well, I would have lit the fires with them. While the room rollicked and roared, Razyé did not say a word. I was told that at political meetings he always behaved like that. He didn't speak, he didn't shake hands, he gave no embraces, contemptuously considering all this a waste of time. As a result, women pressed around him like flies around a honeypot. He took his pleasure with them without even looking at them.

I went upstairs to wake my Cathy, whom the death of her little sister had brought home for a few days. When she's here it's as if dew was watering the dryness of my heart. That child, who is not of my womb, though I have watched over her since she could only crawl, since she held my hand to stand up, whom I have bathed, combed and coddled, that child is all I possess. I wish her a good life. And yet when I think about it, I see her situation as hopeless. I see her alone, for ever alone in life. What boy of her class would ever want to marry her? She's no longer got a dowry and as a result, she'd never find anybody even in the lower classes to make her his wife. She can only desire those who will never want her.

On the first step of the stairs I bumped into Doctor Vercors coming down, two furrows across his forehead, looking concerned. After having greeted him, I asked him laughingly: 'Madame Marie says the master's sick?'

His sickness is a constant joke. Ever since I've worked for the family I've always seen Monsieur Aymeric laid out sick for no reason at all. If it's not a cold that somebody else wouldn't even notice, he comes over hot and cold without a temperature or a sweat, goes down with the colic or a headache. In the kitchen there's always a goat-weed or worm-bush tea simmering on the stove.

Doctor Vercors stopped and looked me in the eyes.

'There's no beating about the bush with you, Sandrine. Get Madame Marie to understand that Monsieur de Linsseuil's condition is serious.'

'Serious?' I repeated, astonished. 'What do you mean by serious?'

'I told him to take precautions,' Doctor Vercors murmured, in an even lower voice. 'Apparently he ignored them, and he's been in prolonged contact with that tubercular boy.'

All in a fluster, I went into Cathy's room where she was sitting on the bed. She turned her head towards me as I came in and said coldly: 'I already know the news. The twins came and woke me up. Justin-Marie is dead.'

'It sounds as if you don't care at all,' I remarked, opening the curtains.

She too didn't beat about the bush.

'I hated him,' she declared.

I went and sat down next to her on the bed and began to undo her thick, black hair, damp as the undergrowth, that's becoming curlier and curlier, even frizzy, as she grows out of puberty.

'What's he done to you? You never told me,' I asked.

She thought for a moment.

'Everything he did was calculated. He told me I was beautiful and asked to kiss me on the mouth. But it wasn't me he was looking at. It was my class, my background. While his papa was burning the cane-fields of the white Creoles, he was trying to seduce their daughters. That's all it was. It was even more ludicrous because he only had to take one look at me to see that I'm not a real Linsseuil.'

I was speechless.

'What are you talking about?' I stammered. 'Have you gone completely crazy?'

She shook herself free and begged me once again: 'Tell me about maman.'

Once again I could find no answer. Besides, what did I know, except the stories and gossip? The one who did know was Lucinda Lucius, who left for the cemetery last year. There was nothing but gossip and rumour. After a long silence, she resumed vehemently, as if angry.

'Well, I'm going to tell you what I know, what I've guessed from piecing together your embarrassed looks, your meaningless words and your smothered laughter. She was a mulatto girl as poor as a church mouse who was madly in love with a black boy even poorer than herself. She sacrificed all this love to call herself Madame de . . . , to own acres of cane-fields, a sugar plantation, a bank account and horses in a stable. I'm not going to reproach her, because she punished herself. It was the death of her. But I don't want to end up like her. Two or three years more and I shall leave here. This is not my real place. Where? I don't know yet. But far, far away. Do you hear me Sandrine? Far away.'

Suddenly she started to cry. I took her in my arms. But I felt that from that moment on I could do nothing for her ever again. Nothing. Gone was the time when I could run with an arnica compress every time she had a bruise on her forehead or a scratch on her knee. She was now a grown-up person and life was waiting for her with its load of suffering. Life's not a masked ball or a *léwòz*, you know. Far from it.

After a while she quietened down. Like a child she sniffled, dried her eyes on the sheets, then declared as if she were taking an oath: 'I shall never try and find the name of my true papa. It's not my business. It was my maman's secret and I respect that. And after all, I don't want anybody else except the man who has loved me since I was a child.'

'But what makes you think . . . ,' I protested.

She interrupted me.

'I have two eyes to see what nobody wants to see. Now come and bathe me.'

We went into the washroom without saying another word. The servants had already filled a tub with warm water, and with a bundle of scented leaves I rubbed this body I had known since childhood. It's true that deep down her colour had always surprised me. But I put it down quite simply to her mother's family. African blood is treacherous. It's deep-rooted. It circulates in secret, then reappears one day at the moment when you least expect it. Out of the blue, her Bambara ancestress had decided to take her revenge.

'I suppose the wake will be at Razyé's?' she asked, while I wrapped a towel around her. 'Will we have to go to that individual's?'

I shook my head.

'I don't think so. It seems your papa is laid out sick.'

She smiled and I didn't dare worry her further. But I remembered the creases on Doctor Vercors' forehead. Good Lord, may he be mistaken. Don't add to the list of our misfortunes!

9   The Farewell Ceremony

Since the body had been transported from Papaye to La Pointe in a torrid heat, it had begun to decompose. On its arrival at the Place de la Victoire the stench was such that Irmine had to give orders to nail down the coffin as quickly as possible. The undertaker had arranged to cut out a glass square in the coffin lid that permitted a last look at a face that was seriously decomposing. Blisters were swelling on his forehead, his lips seemed swollen and his eyeballs seethed with a thousand shapes of emerging life.

Lilies drooped their heads in bottles wrapped in coloured paper. A few white roses were strewn over the funeral couch, and Irmine had brought down her picture of the Infant of Prague. Apart from her, Hosannah, the children, and two or three neighbours who came to pay their respects for a few minutes out of pure politeness, nobody attended the wake. Even the vultures, the name given to those who adored death, its smell of candles and *De Profundis*, were conspicuous by their absence. It was better that way. For Razyé, who was always such a miser, had agreed only to a third-class funeral without organ, harmonium or choir, and had refused to pay one cent more. In his words, Justin-Marie had betrayed them. You'd think he'd gone and died at the Linsseuils'on purpose.

Curiously enough, Irmine wasn't far from thinking the same, but she couldn't bring herself to let a boy whom she had cherished leave without a glass of rum, a bowl of thick soup or even a vegetable broth. So she felt obliged to accept Hosannah's offer and borrow from her meagre savings, a humiliation that added to her grief. She stood in her patched dress, head down and hands joined, her hair combed any old how, her body deformed by her recent pregnancy, and it looked as though it wouldn't be long before she was under the earth herself. As for the children, especially the youngest, they had that self-conscious behaviour those of their age adopt in the presence of death. Although frightened, they couldn't help giggling at a shadow, at a large cricket sizzling its wings in the candle or a lizard wriggling and drawing its knife as it perched on the coffin.

Only Razyé II, looking down from his fifteen years, had an expression appropriate for the circumstances. He held the open Bible level with his face and in a deep voice recited the Psalms that Hosannah drawled after him. He did not read very well, for his education was far from over when his father's miserliness had taken him out of school and apprenticed him to a blacksmith in Les Abymes. It had condemned him to wearing a pair of trousers and shirt in coarse blue drill like the ones worn by country folk – too short, too tight and so worn out by constant washing you could see through them. Yet his strength and beauty burst out from his clothes like the sun breaking through grey clouds. He was not really sad, for he had never liked Justin-Marie very much. It was not simply a mundane question of rivalry between brothers of the same age. It went deeper than that. He resented this orphan, taken in out of charity, for having claimed all of Irmine's affection as well as everything Razyé seemed capable of feeling as a father. But now that Justin-Marie was leaving them after such a short, unfulfilled stay on this earth, he realized that love and hatred are never far from each other and one can even be mistaken for the other. Moreover, since he was alive and the other dead, cramped in a coffin, he was avenged and felt ready to forgive him for all the snubs inflicted on him. He, on the other hand, had come on earth to stay – hot-blooded, thick-haired, heart throbbing and his member erect. The other week, because of his handsome face, a prostitute on the Morne-à-Cayes had taken his virginity free of charge and he had felt like God Almighty. So there were moments, despite the sadness of the occasion, when his voice resounded triumphant and Irmine in her grief looked up at him. Her feelings for Razyé II were not easy to decipher. He was her first son. He looked too much like his father for her heart to mistake one for the other. She never knew whether she felt like insulting him or embracing him, rejecting him or holding him in her arms. She was constantly aware of his growing virility. Watching him grow up, as strong as a tree, she imagined that one day or another he would end up making love, and that tormented her no end. In short, for many reasons, she was always impatient with him and had a firm hand.

Hosannah came and whispered that Fréda, her last-born, was crying to be fed. She had to get up and pass behind Razyé II, breathing in his smell that she would recognize anywhere. It was also Razyé's, whose cologne, pumice-stone and shaving-cream he stole unashamedly. She made her way up the ill-lit staircase, covered with a threadbare chintz carpet, and on the second-floor landing bumped into Razyé. Ever since they had brought Justin-Marie's body into the house, Razyé had locked himself in his room in the attic. At regular intervals he sent one of the children to buy a bottle of rum or absinthe. Noises could be heard, but you couldn't tell whether it was sobbing or swearing. You don't live for almost twenty years with a man without knowing him. Irmine knew he was suffering. But she could not understand a suffering that was unflinching, that made him hard of heart and arrogant of mind. Because of his grief, he would incite more workers to go on strike, set fire to more cane-fields and sequester their owners. He would sow even more evil around him instead of deciding to mend his ways.

She stopped in front of him and murmured: 'Won't you come and spend a last moment with him?'

He stumbled and held onto the wall. Then he looked at her pityingly.

'Aren't you tired of conceiving nonsense? Nonsense and babies, that's all you're capable of conceiving. That's not him down there, and wherever he is, he doesn't care a damn about those at his wake.'

'What do you know?' she retorted.

He pushed her aside and then swaggered down the stairs, lurching left and right. Once at the bottom, he found his balance and turned towards her.

'I know one thing and that's for twenty years I've been looking for her everywhere and never found her.'

So there they were, back to Cathy!

Disheartened, Irmine swept into her room. Nothing, ever, was going to cure Razyé of his obsession. Of his sickness. But what, for goodness sake, did this Cathy have that other women didn't have? Three breasts? A belly-button covered with mother of pearl? A golden pudendum that oozed benzoin instead of salty water? Irmine recalled she had no conversation, always looked as though she was bored, danced the waltz as if in a frenzy, and when she wasn't paying attention spoke terrible French. Even so, twenty years after her death she was holding two men at her mercy: Aymeric and Razyé. Life is unjust.

Irmine's room had the most rudimentary furnishings: a table next to a window draped with a calico curtain, a chair, a rocking-chair and a chest of drawers with a metal pitcher and basin. Fréda's cradle was placed next to her bed and under the mosquito netting the baby was screaming her lungs out. She was a strong little girl who already looked like her papa, dark-skinned as well, with very black, slit, almond-shaped eyes. Irmine took her in her arms and showered her with kisses, while the infant greedily ran its mouth over her cheeks looking for her breast. Why had she brought her into this world from which there was no escape, which she would leave feet first after having been dealt so many of life's blows? The inevitable suffering allotted to this innocent child made her head spin, and such a vision together with her grief set her crying again. She was still crying when Razyé II pushed open the door. In great agitation he had come to announce that Aymeric was downstairs with Marie, his wife.

'Aymeric?' she repeated, as if she had trouble believing it.

Then she pulled herself together. After all, there was nothing surprising about it. He had come to pay the respects that death requires of us all.

'Did you ask Hosannah to serve them something?' she asked, flustered. 'You know how she is!'

Instead of replying, he shut the door behind him and enquired: 'It seems Papa has made him lose all his money. They even say he will have to sell the Dargent factory to the colonial authorities. What's going on between them?'

'What a silly question!' she said nervously. 'You know full well your papa works for the Socialists. They're out for the planters!'

He shook his head.

'It's not just that. There is something more personal. I want to know what.'

She looked up at him and like a seer she knew he would never have anyone to comfort him or avenge him for so

206

many hurtful words, senseless beatings, spankings, unjust punishments and for a childhood devoid of warmth and light. She felt guilty and her tears fell twice as fast. He came and knelt down at her feet and laid his cheek on her breast that Fréda had abandoned. It was as if he had become an infant again, suckling her breast to start over a new life with her.

'You never thought much of me,' he murmured tenderly. 'You always preferred Justin-Marie who wasn't even your son. Why? Because he was fairer than me? Almost white? What do the whites have that we don't? They're no better-looking nor stronger. Their hearts are no warmer and their love no better.'

Razyé had said the very same words, she recalled. She was ashamed of herself.

As he repeated his question: 'Why?' she clasped his face between her palms and gave him his first mother's kiss.

They had brought bunches of white lilies and anthuriums that Hosannah did not know where to put. Finally, one of the children thought of using the ewers filled with water, and everyone was greatly relieved. Yet neither Aymeric nor Marie realized the embarrassment they caused with their flowers and elegant clothes. Marie had followed her husband to the wake because it seemed the right thing to do and because he looked so ill that she did not have the heart to leave him. Despite her dutiful words to the family, she was very close to hating Justin-Marie for having contaminated Aymeric and she cursed the day he had turned up on the estate. Now she looked around her in horror. Razyé, as everyone knew, was one of the richest men on the island. He bought the plantations from the white planters in difficulty, divided them up and sold the parcels of land at a profit to the black farmers greedy for land. He also lent money with interest and was accumulating a fortune in the gambling dens of Morne-la-Loge. Yet here was his house as bare and wretched as the humblest of cabins and here were his children all skin and bone and badly dressed. She felt she was in the den of some fiend whom she feared would loom up at any moment.

As for Aymeric, he had eyes only for Justin-Marie's coffin, a Mount of Olives to him. He had not dared look at the face behind the glass pane, convinced he would read reproach, for he was certain that he was to blame for everything that had happened. If he had not returned home, Justin-Marie would still be alive. But he had abandoned him, and behind his back the enemy had triumphed. Consequently he felt his sickness to be a well-deserved punishment and welcomed his dizzy spells, fainting fits and constant fever with satisfaction. He had categorically refused Doctor Vercors' recommendation to travel to St Moritz or the Swiss Alps for the air. Besides, how could he pay for such a trip? Once his workers had been paid off, he would be left with practically nothing. He would have to sell off the factory and think of working elsewhere. Try his hand at the saltfish and lard business, like so many others of his class. The thought revolted and exhausted him, as if his time was up and all he had to do was disappear gracefully. Farewell, one and all! Leave this world. Slide gradually into the earth's womb. Meet up with those who had left before him: his *mabo*, his mother, his father and some of his children. Cathy and Justin-Marie. Justin-Marie and Cathy. Strange how he associated Cathy and Justin-Marie in the same sorrow and grief, as if they were the same person. As if she had lain down a woman, slept and woken up a few years later, with all the grace of an adolescent, to seduce him again.

While getting up to greet his sister he almost fell, his head was spinning so much. He noticed the children were giggling at him. He didn't care!

Let them laugh, let them go on laughing. They did not know what lay ahead for them. They would see when they were his age and life in its wickedness had dealt them the blows of which she alone had the secret.

10 The Farewell Ceremony (continued)

Razyé was in bed with Mona, his favourite prostitute for the past ten years. But that night she had had to give up trying to arouse him and his member lay limp and wrinkled like a turkey's neck. Unashamed and oblivious, his thoughts were far away, far from this naked woman, from this bed with its crumpled sheets, this wooden cabin and this ill-famed neighbourhood of La Pointe. Could he be dreaming? He seemed to be lost in an unknown land where everything took on the colour of night. Although his eyes could distinguish nothing through a wall of darkness, his ears could hear. And they heard her laugh. And they heard her jeer.

She rejoiced no end at the trick she had just played on him. She had disappeared, reappeared, only to disappear again before he had time to understand what was happening. Now she was leaving him with a broken heart again, with a second body to watch over, mourn and bury. What had he done to deserve her anger? To his knowledge, he was beyond reproach. Not a single moment of a single day went by without his flowering her grave in his memory. Since she had left him, nothing mattered anymore. Neither women. Nor children. Nor material gain. He had lost all interest in the wealth he accumulated from his evil calculations. He could have gone without it and remained like Job, sitting among the ashes, empty-handed. But the dead are probably more vindictive than the living and take umbrage at trifling peccadillos.

On the other side of the bed Mona looked at him with concern, mistaking his gloom for anger. She had never seen him like this. What was he hiding from her? Did he know that last week she had made love to his son? She had met Razyé II at the bar Au Rendez-vous des Amis, where every day at sunset she came to drink one or two glasses of absinthe with her best friends. A regular gossip column was this Rendez-vous des Amis. Everything got discussed. The contract on capital and labour. Police beatings. The destruction of the printing presses at *La Vérité* and *Le Libéral*. Boisneuf's imprisonment. Réache's defeat. But especially gossip as mouthwatering as crab pâtés, such as: Mademoiselle Lherminier got married in white while everyone knew she had a bun in the oven or, the Larivière's baby looks awfully black and the Fourneaux' awfully white. Marriage is a real merry-go-round! The boy was prowling around the tables with his hands in his pockets, so like his papa that people jumped and looked round, thinking they'd gone back twenty years. He didn't have a cent to his name and Boisdur, the owner, who didn't like people coming into his bar to drink the air, was wondering how to get rid of him when she intervened. She had gone up to him, as if to reason with him.

'If your papa found you here,' she whispered. 'I bet he wouldn't be too happy.'

He laughed and his teeth gleamed as white as porcelain.

'I'm not crazy,' he answered. 'He left for Marie-Galante yesterday. Didn't you hear things are heating up over there?'

She invited him to sit down and without knowing quite how, one thing led to another and she ended up with him in her bed. She had laughed at him a little.

'What? A big boy like you, and you've never done it before?'

Afterwards, she hadn't thought any more about it, realizing how much her affluent clientèle of fifty- and sixty-year-olds, wheezing, pot-bellied and often balding, had made her forget the real taste of love. Even Razyé was no longer what he used to be and sometimes stalled in full throttle! She had tried in vain to get him to talk about himself, his childhood, his poor unfortunate maman and his brothers and sisters. All he could find to say was that he was dying of hunger. So to calm his craving she had given him the remains of some *fig é twip* and while he was wolfing it down in the kitchen, she murmured somewhat ashamedly, with a lump in her throat: 'Will you come back and see me?'

Too busy licking his fingers to speak he nodded but never came back. All week long she had waited in vain. In her impulsiveness she thought of going down to the forge where he worked. Then she thought otherwise, sure the little urchins would follow her from the bottom of the Morne-à-Caye to Les Abymes shouting their usual jibes: *Zouelle! Mi an danm gabwiel!* Besides, she had no idea how the boy would react. You need good reasons to lose your self-respect. The following days, the absinthe and the rum at the Rendez-vous des Amis had got the better of her lovesickness.

In actual fact, Razyé was miles from suspecting any of this. If he had had the slightest inkling of what had gone on in his absence, nobody could have predicted the violence of his reactions. He could very well have knocked Mona senseless just as he could have strangled his son with his own hands. Like the time when he found Mona in bed with a mulatto deputy and he had gone to fetch a cutlass to hack them to pieces. He had been like a wild animal and it had taken all the males of the neighbourhood to bring him under control.

He got up and without saying a word began to slip on his clothes.

'Where are you going at this hour of the night?' she murmured, growing more and more worried. 'You'd be better off staying put and resting your body next to mine.'

He did not take the trouble to reply, grabbed a bottle from the bedside table and swigged down the remainder of the rum. After that he seemed better, more focused, as if he had found his inner self. He delved into his pocket, threw her a few banknotes, the usual pittance with which he rewarded all her trouble, and headed for the door in more or less a straight line.

Outside, the jaws of darkness swallowed him up, and he began to walk down the hill.

It was that time of the month when the moon is a pale sliver floating in and out of the clouds. Nothing was visible. Only the rasp of the sea could be heard, for everything seemed to be coloured with Indian ink: the sky, the trees, the house-fronts, the stray dogs and the cunning cats. As in the dream he had just had, Razyé groped his way along, guided by the sounds of the night. The rum swiggers lurching out of the rum-shops did not recognize him. They took him for a spirit in search of wicked deeds and crossed themselves. When he passed by the cathedral, St Peter jangled his keys and huddled up in his alcove, while there was a great rustling of wings up above from the bats who had been disturbed in the gutters. In the Canal district, lights gleamed through the shutters of the Saint-Jules hospice, for suffering and death know no peace. The sisters were comforting the dying with lighted candles under the shadow of their cornets.

Razyé turned into the dead-end known as the Impasse Gaget, where Madhi lived with his wife and sons in a cabin that had nothing extraordinary about it, except for a few wicker baskets hanging in the branches of a mango-tree for the spirits. He knew from experience that on a night such as this the *kimbwazè* would not be asleep. For on such a night, he who uses his ears can hear. He can hear the words of all the departed who inhabit the other side of existence, coming and going, bumping into each other, fidgeting in the invisible world, squabbling, yearning for the earth, cursing over and over the infidelities of the living. It is on such a night you can call out to them and trick them into telling you their secrets. Razyé had not been mistaken. Hardly had he tapped on the door than Madhi came to open it. He was holding a candle whose straight steady flame lit his face from below, leaving his eyes and the top of his head in darkness.

'Did you manage to speak to her?' Razyé enquired in an urgent voice. 'What did she tell you? Tell me.'

But Madhi, like all those of his kind, did not like to be rushed. He closed the door behind him and silently led Razyé into the little windowless room, its walls decorated with chromos and spirals of coloured strips, where he performed his devotions. He blew out the candle and only the light of an altar lamp was left to confront the darkness.

11   Madhi's Tale

I know I've lived ten lives, I've lived a hundred lives before I came to live this one. I have been a toad in the mud, a slug on the rotten wood of the trees, I have been wild pine growing in the armpit of the candle-wood tree and quetzal bird feeding off fruit redder than my crest. I have been a dairy cow, I have been a goat, I have even been a woman and had two children.

Two sons, I think.

I have lived in many countries. In China. In Japan. In Belarus. Sometimes I remember all these lives, these loves and misfortunes, and there is a great commotion in my head and I have to stand still, without breathing a word, until it's over. I came into this life one day when the sky was black with all the evil the Good Lord is capable of. A great wind was blowing the cabins to pieces and with one hand lifting up the sullen oxen, left tied to their stakes in the savanna. My maman went into labour while she was trying to patch up the tin roof and I dropped to the ground in a torrent of dirty water and filth of all sorts. I was wearing a tight grey membrane around my forehead and my new-born eyes could already see all the suffering stored up for our race. When the wind had quietened down and people had put back up what had been blown down, my maman took me one Saturday to church. They sang a *Te Deum* and then the priest baptised me. My maman wanted to give me the two first names of Dieudonné-Bienvenu since she had laid to rest yet another daughter, Azuela, the Lent before. All she had was me. But I never wanted those names. Ever since I was little I knew I was Madhi, which means the Chosen One, the One Chosen by the Invisible.

At the age of three I heard voices. Lying in bed beside my maman, I watched a magnificent ballet above my head. Baron Samedi, all dressed up in a black frock-coat and tails, black glasses and top hat, was leading the dance. At six I was conversing with Baka M——, who knew all the workings of heaven and earth. One hot and sunny day I went for a swim in the River Rose and found him floating naked, his sex as long as a donkey lash wrapped around his waist. He was waiting for me. After the swim he took me back to his cabin and made me drink a calabash of manchineel tea that gives clairvoyance. I studied with him for eight years. At fifteen my spirit flew to a deep cavern in the plain of Castaneda, among the round huts of the Indians, where the pigs and the dogs are as black as the men. There were assembled the greatest masters of the invisible from every corner of the earth, in front of whom the world bows like a scythe: Melchior, who worked in Cuba and had not yet committed the sin for which there is no remission, Ciléus Ciléas, the Elder, who worked here on Grande-Terre, Déméter the Wise from Fonds-Saint-Jacques in Haiti, Escubando the First from Santo Domingo, and many others. In the morning the mist festooned the jagged edges of the cavern and the dawn shone bright as the sun. We spent seven days and seven nights in palavering, asking any question that came to mind. How far can you walk behind a soul once it has left its body? The soul must cross seven rivers, that's for sure. Which one is the point of no return? Is the deceased present at the ceremony nine days after his death, or is he too far along the road to the other world?

Who really eats the sticky rice, the ground corn and the rum for the sacrifices: the living or the dead? We exchanged recipes for magic baths, the names of plants, cabalistic signs and words. And then each of us returned home the way we had come. I left the cordillera of the Andes and their slopes of steel. Carried by the wind, I roamed on the crest of the clouds and I saw the Caribbean, island after island, lying beneath me like a willing female with its hills and lush valleys green with sugar-cane. The whites were idling on their verandas in panama hats. The blacks were wielding their cutlasses, their chests shiny with sweat. The loaded ox-carts jolted over the rocks while the factories spat out their venom, black as smoke. I knew it wouldn't last, that the pendulum would swing the other way for the whites. Yet I still couldn't see any happiness lighting up our lives. Once the whites were finished, the blacks would trade their accounts with the drivers and overseers for un-employment benefits.

It was a few years later, at the age of eighteen, when I performed what people called my first miracle. In the village of Goyave. I had continued my initiation with Désiré Pulchérie, the man with three balls, and I had started to acquire a name for myself. They came to fetch me in the middle of the night. Pitch dark. Not a single star in the sky. Dogs howling everywhere. You could feel the spirits flying above the white rayo in flower. To say the woman was sick was an understatement. Death was already clutching her throat and nobody could mistake the rattle she made. The wretched white doctor had given her an injection of camphor-oil in her left buttock and fled without even ask-ing for payment. When I placed my hand on her forehead it was already cold. Quite casually, I started to parley with death who was filing her claws near the window.

'Now let's have a little talk, you and me! You win every

time. Nobody ends up alive. So can't you wait just a little bit longer? Come back in a few months or even a few years? Her youngest son is only two. She's still feeding him. For pity's sake.'

For some reason the bitch listened to me and buggered off elsewhere. The blood returned to the woman's cheeks. Her face trembled, warm and pliant under my fingers. Her man kissed both my hands.

When I had reached the peak of my reputation, Razyé came to see me. Like everyone else in Guadeloupe, I had heard he was like a hurricane and an earthquake combined and worse than both of them put together. I knew that he had gone through every *gadèzafè* and *kimbwazè* on the island like a rider exhausting his mount. But he had the same obsession as me. Despite all I knew, I never stopped asking myself questions. How long does the passage of Death last? What is the space that separates two reincarnations? Why is it that we always come up against a threshold? Can we meet again those who have walked away from us and can they come back and remain with us? I could only catch a fleeting glimpse of Délia, the wife I lost, like the tail of Halley's comet in the sky. I have never been able to hold her in my arms, even less make love to her. Every time I've tried to touch her, she has escaped me. And that's why I took Razyé's money and worked tirelessly for him with so little result. The people who say I stole it are liars.

That evening, when I saw him arrive, I knew what was bringing him. But once again I had no answer for him. At a loss, I had consulted other seers who had all shaken their heads in a quandary. I tested the realm of probability, calculated the hours of birth and death. The fact that Aquarius and Pisces crossed in the sky at equidistant angles opened up a host of possibilities. I didn't know what to conclude. Was one the same as the other? Was the other the same as one?

I was about to give Razyé a good shot of rum to sweeten the pill when I noticed that he had had enough to drink. His eyes were small and red like two hog-plums. His breath smelled of bile. So I had him sit down under the picture of Petro, with his three necklaces, next to three lighted candles, one above the other, and sheepishly, I confessed my ignorance.

'I don't know. I can't tell you whether it's her or isn't her come back to drink the waters of wretchedness on our earth.'

Without a word, he got up and disappeared into the night.

I never saw him again.

PART THREE

Marie-Galante

1 O! Island in the Sun

Situated about twenty miles from La Pointe, the island of Marie-Galante, christened thus by the Genoan with the name of one of his three caravels, was first nothing but the haunt of giant lizards who during the day lazed in the sun and once night had fallen, crept down into the clayey hollows. The Amerindians used it to grow crops but never stayed long, just long enough for a season of howing, sowing and harvesting. Once this was over they quickly returned to Guadeloupe in their outriggers hollowed from the trunks of trees. You can still find mixed in with the sand and soil a host of ploughing instruments, pestles, mortars, flints, axes and whetstones. For a long time the history of Marie-Galante could be summed up as a series of killings and massacres by the Carib Indians, attacks by the English and revolts by the slaves together with all kinds of natural disasters – hurricanes, earthquakes and fires – reducing man's efforts to nothing. On this piece of limestone, as flat as your hand, shakily secured to a volcanic platform, criss-crossed with faults and gashes, edged by steep cliffs, many nationalities have clashed, from the French and the British to the Dutch hounded out of Brazil. But all of them linked hands to enslave the African and grow rich at the expense of his sweat in the fields of indigo, cotton, coffee and tobacco. For sugar-cane was a latecomer to Marie-Galante.

In 19—, at the time when our story takes place,

Marie-Galante began to merit the name it has been known by ever since: 'the island that's dying'.

One or two miles from Saint-Louis, behind the Massicot mill, on the land of an abandoned great house, the Republic had installed a one-room schoolhouse where reading, writing and arithmetic were taught together with a little French history and geography. For a number of years no child had crossed its threshold and nobody could remember when the last teacher, a former student of the Ploermel Brothers, had left on a boat for La Pointe with no hope of return. Everything was in a state of neglect.

Between the great, cracked limestone flags in the old playground, yuccas with their clusters of white flowers, prickly pears and columnar cacti grew undisturbed as tall as a man over the top of the *razyé* scrub and the Dominican acacias that had quickly become a scourge for the planters. This state of affairs had come about because the region bristled with charcoal ovens and when they were not at sea or in the cane-fields, the inhabitants of Saint-Louis had only their precious logwood in mind. A cart of seven hundred kilos of logwood could produce up to six or seven bags of charcoal that were loaded onto the barges in Saint-Louis or the creeks of Vieux-Fort and sold at a high price in all the markets of Grande-Terre. In a time of sugar crisis, it was at least a way of making a living.

So it came as something of a surprise when, as the last clouds of the rainy season scurried over to Dominica, the people of Saint-Louis heard it noised about that the school was to reopen its doors after such a long time, and that all the children of school age were to be enrolled or else the gendarmes would come knocking at their door. The thought of having to cut out shirts and trousers from jute-flour bags and above all of doing without the help of their offspring during the cane harvest did not exactly please the parents. So they scowled at a group of workers from the town hall who were busy whitewashing the three-room, wattle cabin, pompously called 'the schoolmaster's house', and scrubbing and filling the jar for rain-water that leaned up against one wall.

On the morning of 28 September, exactly four days before classes were to begin, an ox-cart drew up in front of the schoolmaster's place, driven by a fellow from Grand-Bourg nicknamed Romero, because of his female conquests, and out stepped a slim young girl all dressed in black, carrying a kind of cage housing a cat whose fur was as black as her clothes. (It was Romero who took charge of her two heavy wicker baskets.) A young girl! Could she be the schoolteacher? Since when were girls capable of reading and writing and teaching children? The inhabitants of Saint-Louise would not have been more flabbergasted if they had seen Lucifer himself settle down among them. A few hours after she arrived in the village, the young girl wedged a conch shell in her door and went into Ma Tètèche's shop to introduce herself and ask gracefully if there was someone to cook her meals and do her washing, since she could do neither. She tried to speak Creole, but those present could hear it was not her mother tongue and that it was proper French that was used to coming out of her mouth and was desperately trying to gain the upper hand. Ma Tètèche looked her up and down. What sort of a girl was this? A girl who could neither cook nor wash. Where did she come from? Who had brought her up?

She was very, very young, they remarked, not too light-skinned, but just a little too pretty, with a mass of unruly black hair brushed into a chignon. Around her neck hung a locket on a black velvet ribbon. Those who could read were able to decipher the initials C.L. intertwined, with a small 'de' between them. Once Ma Tètèche had grudgingly given her the name of a certain Romaine who was looking to hire her services to feed the illegitimate child she had brought back from La Pointe, she set off without wasting any more time. The two women must have come to an agreement, for shortly afterwards they could be seen crossing the village again, one behind the other in the direction of the market. Good Lord, a nice pair they made! One fruit already fallen and the other not far behind!

During the days that followed, everyone was dying to ask Romaine about her new mistress. But she kept mum and did not breathe a word. Nobody even knew the name of the baby's father. So they spied.

They did not see very much.

The young girl hardly left home. At most she appeared at the door to call her cat: 'Minou, Minou', when it strayed a little too far into the *razyé* undergrowth, tail in the air. Or else she came out to water a clump of hibiscus and a red rose-bush she had planted on the left and right side of her front door. Sometimes, but not very often, she walked as far as the old Desmarais factory and stared at the ruins, as if they brought back memories. Every evening she left her candle burning until late into the night and, remarking on the glow behind her shutters, the night-owls wondered what she could be up to. On the third day Romaine put out her first wash to dry and what pretty undergarments she proudly hung on the line! Scalloped, lace pantalets and petticoats, the likes of which had never been seen on Marie-Galante! Embroidered camisoles and loose blouses! Fine cambric handkerchiefs! In short, a whole wash that smelled very much of a noble birth! General curiosity was at its height. Where did this girl come from? What was her name?

The day before classes were due to begin, she instructed Romaine to sweep the school, dust the benches and desks while she hung pictures on the walls. First of all, there was a lovely lithograph by Evremond de Bérard depicting an old sugar plantation and its windmill. In the foreground, the pond and the vats, a big heap of cane-trash, and the gutter for the molasses. In the background, the mill and the black shack alleys. In the second picture men and women were working in a cane-field. A woman was bending over to tie up a sheaf and the ends of her headtie reached down to her neck like two wings. Finally, in the third picture, a girl and two boys were stripping stalks of sugar-cane with their teeth. The next morning, dressed and ready at seven, the new schoolmistress was standing at the door to greet her pupils. She separated them, lining up on her right the youngest with tearful eyes on their first day at school, and on her left those who were already droning into their reading books. At noon, both groups went home starry-eyed and told their inquisitive parents her name was Mademoiselle Cathy.

Cathy could never get over the death of Aymeric.

She could hear his voice. He was always in her thoughts. She saw him at every moment of the day. It was as if a painted canvas was being waved by invisible hands in front of her eyes. Her heart, a stranger to ill-feeling, hardened with hatred when she thought of Justin-Marie who had contaminated him with his sickness, and of Razyé, who had ruined him, then cast a shadow over his last days.

Everything had happened so quickly.

In October he had felt too weak to face up to his responsibilities and no longer left his bed. In November he had experienced his first haemorrhage, bleeding through the mouth and nostrils. In December he was dead. Like a saint, asking forgiveness from his children and praying. The sickness had melted the flesh off his bones and he was thinner than a young boy. In a way he had found his youth again. He had asked to be buried beside his Cathy in the tomb that stood on the headland at L'Engoulvent. But Marie, who had always respected his wishes, had rebelled for the first time. To her mind, this unjust request erased the ten years they had lived together, especially during his sickness when she had watched over him and taken care of him with unselfish devotion. So she had refused to grant him his wish, and Aymeric had been laid to rest in the Linsseuil vault in Petit-Canal, beside his father, his mother and his grandparents. The ceremony had been simple and moving and the choir of pupils from the Catholic school of Saint-Joseph de Cluny had sung the *Requiem aeternam*, the *Dies Irae*, the *Lacrimosa* and the *Pie Jesu* from the Requiem by Dvořák, a Czech composer whom Aymeric adored and listened to over and over again on his gramophone. The day after the funeral, the tears had not yet dried on the family's cheeks when the notary informed them that Aymeric had left virtually nothing in his will. Honest and conscientious, he had sold the Dargent factory as well as almost all his estate in order to pay off his debts and provide a pension for his workers and house-servants. All he had managed to save was the great house, minus the land, like an island in the middle of its park. While the Linsseuils procrastinated, appalled by this sudden encounter with poverty, Cathy quickly made up her mind. In a way, her father's death gave her the chance to achieve what she really wanted. While he was alive she would never have had the courage to break his heart and leave Belles-Feuilles to lead the life she desired. As for the other members of the clan, she was liberating them; she was relieving them of the burden of her presence, for, except for the twins, nobody knew exactly how to treat her, especially now that puberty had darkened her skin unacceptably. The family was constantly in a quandary, divided between the remnants of their affection and the horror she represented.

For some years a teachers' school for young women had been annexed to the girls' college in La Pointe. Thanks to the Linsseuils' connections, she had obtained a scholarship from the local authorities. Then, without too many regrets, she had kissed *mabo* Sandrine, her little brothers and sisters, especially her god-daughter, Elodie, goodbye and spent two years behind barred windows learning how to teach French, History, Geography, Mathematics, Science and how to sing to keep up your spirits.

> En avant, jeunes filles,
> Aux dernières bastilles!
> Il y a trop longtemps que les hommes
> Occupent les premiers rangs.
> Nous voulons prouver que nous sommes
> Les égales de ces tyrans.[1]

Saint-Louis on Marie-Galante was her first position, and she was not unhappy to see the sea unfurl behind her to separate her completely from her life as a spoilt child. Her older brothers, Déodat and Isidore, had nevertheless accompanied her to the boat. They both bore a grudge against Aymeric. They criticized him for not having stood up enough to Razyé and the Socialists, and in the end caring more about his negroes than his own children. He had guaranteed a pension for his workers. Bravo! But what about his sons, now that they didn't have a cent to their name? They had no inclination to study for years and years to become civil servants. So what was left? Marry some richly endowed

---

[1] Forward girls, To the last bastions! It's been too long, Since men have taken the fore. We want to prove, We are the equal of these tyrants.

mulatto girl, prepared to do anything to whiten her blood? Many of the white Creoles were now indulging in that little game, and the priests working as go-betweens had their surplices full of the right addresses. Listening to them whine and wail, Cathy believed that girls have more self-esteem and endure better the whims of fortune.

Yet Cathy thought she was braver than she was, she who had never really seen the face of poverty. When, after an endless crossing, she landed on this scorching hot, rocky plateau, she couldn't believe her eyes. The island was recovering from a killer cholera epidémic while a plague of swine-fever was raging through the pig population. Men, women and children were covering their scrawny bodies as best they could with rags made of jute or, for the luckier ones, canvas flour-sacks. The markets were empty except for piles of charcoal, weevilled cassava-flour and Congo peas as hard as stones. Razyé, who was a regular visitor to the island, had left a wake of mischief. Because of him, gangs of thugs, drunk on alcohol, had plundered the plantations. Many of the white Creoles had been scared into selling their land to the Crédit Foncier. Since the three factories that had replaced the sugar houses were constantly disrupted by strikes and social unrest, their owners threatened to close them down and leave for France, which would have put a good many heads of family out of work. In short, poverty loomed up everywhere: in the feverish eyes of the children, in the emaciated cheeks of the mothers and in the toothless gums of the fathers. With their little lice-infested, scabby heads leaning on their wooden desks the children slept, mouths open. They slept from hunger and only awoke if a juicy piece of meat came within reach in their dreams. Their arms and legs, as spindly as guava twigs, swelled up with boils and carbuncles that burst in a foul-smelling pus. Cathy was not the daughter of

Aymeric de Linsseuil for nothing. She had spent her entire childhood amidst the odour of charity and good deeds. First of all she thought of setting up an infirmary like the one at Belles-Feuilles and healing all this suffering with tincture of arnica, methylene blue or a glass of milk. Then she quickly realized that it would take more than her entire pay. Despite the mighty declarations from the local authorities who praised them for being 'soldiers of progress, distributing the bread of intelligence', the primary schoolteachers of Guadeloupe were paid a pittance. They had been waiting for years for the wage increase voted by the colonial authorities. So she decided to use another remedy that this time would cost nothing. Since she could not fill the bellies of her pupils with food, she would fill their ears with words of affection and their hearts with love.

Never were children more cherished, more admired and encouraged to work harder and behave better. She pinned up their drawings of blue seas, orange suns and red-roof cabins under the boughs of a mango-tree and invited the astonished parents to come and admire these masterpieces. The carnival in Marie-Galante was usually an uncouth affair, three days of disorder when *mass à kònn, gwo siwo* and *bwa-bwa,* carried on poles, ran through the streets shouting and gesticulating. Cathy dressed up her little negro boys and girls as marquises and princesses complete with cotton wigs and fans. She got together a choir that performed for the mayor of Saint-Louis and town councillors who could not believe their ears. Although, under her management, the school garden produced nothing, neither cassava nor Congo peas, the older pupils were capable of reciting poems in French-French to whoever liked to listen. One of them had his poem published a few years later in *La Cravache* and made a name for himself locally.

Des Antilles, nous sommes la phalange
Du grand Parti de tous les travailleurs
Qui vont bientôt retirer de la fange
La Guadeloupe aux mains des exploiteurs.[1]

Consequently, after only one year of teaching, ninety-five per cent of Cathy's pupils received scholarships and six fishermen's children were admitted to the lycée Carnot in La Pointe.

[1] Antilleans, we are the phalanx, Of the great Party of all the workers, Who will soon pluck Guadeloupe from the mire, Out of the hands of the exploiters.

2   *The School Mistress and Razyé II*

He was a good foot taller than she was. So she had to raise her head to figure out his face in the deep shadow of his *bakoua* hat.

She hesitated.

'I have never prepared anyone for the school diploma. I don't know whether I can.'

'You can change grandsons of slaves into marquises,' he said. 'So you are capable of doing anything you want.'

She felt he was poking fun at her and replied on the defensive: 'That was for fun. The carnival is an amusement.'

He shrugged his shoulders.

'You could have played at other things. Dressing them up as Mandingo ancestors or Maroons, for example.'

She stood dumbfounded, wondering whether he was joking. No, he seemed serious, even earnest.

'Do you know the history of this piece of land?' he continued. 'And of these people who seem so harmless to you?'

She did not say a word, but, despite herself, she felt tears rushing to her eyes. His voice became softer.

'I'll take you to the Punchbowl Pond or else Tartenson Heights, where a few years back the crowd stood up to the gendarmes. And you'll see who the people of Marie-Galante really are, the people you think are as tame as turtles.'

She caught her breath again.

'If you've got nothing but stories of killings and massacres to tell, I've got better things to do.'

'Go on,' he said, mockingly. 'Cover your eyes and ears. Convince yourself that everything is for the best and that our island is a real paradise.'

She looked out at the languid sea which, under a dull sky, was turning grey and sombre, like the young man in front of her.

'That's not what I'm saying. I know we're going through difficult times. All Monsieur Schoelcher's fine work has led to nothing. The former slaves respect neither God nor work.'

On hearing these words, he flew into a temper.

'You talk like the slave-owners,' he cried. 'And stop going on about Monsieur Schoelcher, Monsieur Schoelcher. You'd think the slaves did nothing to win their freedom.'

There was silence.

'Having given it thought,' she said drily, 'I don't think I'd be able to teach you anything.'

With no further comment, he shrugged his shoulders. As he turned round and headed for the classroom door, she felt ashamed of herself. What did she blame him for, in fact? For having mocked her endeavours at carnival time, that was all. All at once she realized how ridiculous her behaviour had been. What had got into her to powder the peppercorn heads of her little children like hoar frost? She called to him as he stepped outside.

'Why are you so keen on this school diploma?'

He stopped, barring the entrance, blocking the daylight with his well-built body.

'To make your dear Monsieur Schoelcher happy,' he answered ironically. "Educate yourselves, savage Africans, and shame your detractors." Isn't that what he said?'

She had to laugh.

'I don't even know your name!' she declared, as if they had made peace.

He hesitated, then hurriedly let out as if he was reciting a lesson: 'First-Born. That's how my papa christened me. After me came a string of children. Six in all: girls as well as boys. My mother's womb waited seven years for me and my parents were only too pleased when I turned up.'

In actual fact, Razyé II had had to put the sea between him and La Pointe in order to save his life. One evening Mona had finally confessed to his father what had happened. Puzzled, Razyé II had never stopped asking himself what her motive had been. Was she tortured by her conscience or was she toying with the impossible hope of making him jealous? How can you ever tell with women? The fact is that Razyé took it very badly and around midnight returned to the Place de la Victoire in a rage, bent on flaying the hide off his son. Razyé II had fled to Les Abymes, to his employer's house, a good fellow, who referred him the next day to his younger brother, Tonin, a blacksmith in Saint-Louis on Marie-Galante in need of an assistant, for he was overloaded with work: oxen and horses to shoe, cartwheels to ring, and picks, shovels, hoes and tools of all sort to repair and weld.

With no questions asked, Tonin had offered Razyé II a place in the wattle cabin he shared with his wife and litter of children. They ate root vegetables from a *kwi*. They slept on the ground on pieces of jute. They relieved themselves wherever they could, here and there, in the mud of the swamps. They washed when the skies deigned to let a cloud burst. As a meagre consolation Asturias, Tonin's eldest daughter, let him take his pleasure with her whenever he liked. So, one night, while everyone was snoring all around him, he looked the life that lay in store for him straight in the eyes and got scared. The remnants of his education were fast fading and nothing distinguished him from an animal. His body had become increasingly ungainly. His intelligence had degenerated. He spent days on end without speaking, blinded by the sparks of the forge, deadened from toiling like a brute. His sleep was dreamless. Was it for this that his African ancestors had revolted and gained their freedom by drenching the earth of the plains and the hills with blood? He recalled Jean-Hilaire Endomius's inflammatory speeches on the dishes served up at the banquet of education and he had a vision of the path he had to take. Unfortunately, unlike Justin-Marie, he had not paid much attention at school in La Pointe and had not really suffered when his father had taken him away. He had been content to see his body grow stronger, his shoulders grow wider and feel his gaze soar higher and higher above the heads of those who spoke to him.

He had long hesitated before going to see Cathy. She belonged to a family that was hateful to him, not only because of what Razyé and the Socialists repeated about the whites and the mulattos, but because it had been an example of racism and caste prejudice by condemning his mother to a life of poverty and suffering. Yet when he came face to face with her – tiny, fragile and, of all things, almost as black as he was – he quickly understood that she was a de Linsseuil in name only. Good Lord, she had come out the wrong colour, like himself! Could she be the illegitimate fruit of a rape? Who was her maman?

He stepped outside into the dusk, under a sky now soiled with long black streaks. Night had almost fallen. A breeze was swaying the tops of the almond-trees on the square in front of the new church that had replaced the one smashed by a hurricane. On a corner, street criers announced a political meeting for next Sunday. On hearing them shout the name of Razyé, people came out on their doorsteps to know

236

more. They could expect some disturbances, perhaps even a brawl and some blood. Whatever the case, the white Creoles would be in for it. At first Razyé II shivered. Then he realized that his father would have difficulty finding him under his borrowed name, First-Born, to which he had added Sabrimol, a name he had devised just like that out of his head.

Now that he was far away he had almost forgotten the ill-treatment of his childhood and was at a loss as to whether to hate his father or pity him, look upon him as a victim or a torturer. He had got a muddled picture of his past and knew just enough to deduce that in his youth, Razyé had felt terribly ill-treated and made everything an accessory to his revenge. Because of a tragic passion, he had rejected the joys of a second union and considered wife and children an unbearable burden. No woman deserves to be mourned for the rest of a man's life. What men call love is in fact nothing but a sickness of the mind.

Razyé II, or First-Born as he had chosen to be called, had made up his mind to lead quite a different life.

Left all alone, Cathy pensively placed the wooden bars on the heavy classroom doors. The more she thought about it, the more the conversation she had just had opened up old wounds. She realized she was not at the end of her troubles. It wasn't enough to turn her back on the Linsseuils with the excuse she was not of their blood. She had to discover who she really was. Mandingos, Maroons, she had certainly heard of them, but always in a negative fashion. The most terrible stories were rumoured about them. Stories of rape and robbery, massacres and murder. So it would never have occurred to her to revive their memory for a carnival procession.

Likewise, the late Aymeric professed a boundless admiration for Monsieur Victor Schoelcher, all of whose works he possessed. He had dog-eared one of them in particular through reading it over and over again: *De l'esclavage des Noirs et de la législation coloniale* (On the Enslavement of the Negroes and Colonial Legislation). For him, Schoelcher was the greatest benefactor of the black race.

She set off along the stony path leading into the village. At this time of day, the great slabs of limestone floated in the shadows and she had the feeling she was fording a river in leaps and bounds. Soon she entered Saint-Louis, politely greeting folk as she went. Yet, despite her smiles and agreeable manners, the villagers had little fondness for her. They found her too headstrong and too rational for their liking. Despite all her achievements with the school they did not appreciate what she was doing. Didn't she forbid the children to speak Creole? Creole was our mother tongue, they grumbled. Anyone who prevented its natural expression silenced a child for life.

Cathy was oblivious to the looks she got. Her thoughts were far away. In all her life she had never looked at another man except her beloved papa, her brothers or perhaps a favourite cousin. Now the desire to see First-Born again swept over her like an infection. She knew he spoke French badly and smelled of sweat. She could see he had never held a book in his hands. But he was unlike the usual country bumpkin. He was strong and tall! His voice was beautifully resonant! She tortured herself with countless questions, trying to guess who he really was.

She went into Ma Tétèche's shop, supposedly to buy some tallow candles, but in fact to find someone who could inform her. Inside there was a rum-shop filled at every hour of the day with rum guzzlers and wastrels, never at a loss for hawking gossip. But when she stepped over the doorstep she bumped into a young black woman with a pleasant face dressed in one of those wide shapeless dresses worn by pregnant women, who gave her such a look that she turned round and ran home. In her panic she was oblivious to what was going on in the village. And yet there was a great disturbance in the street. At the announcement of Razyé's visit, the women party members of Legitimus's Socialists, the 'True Daughters of Schoelcher', as they called themselves, were standing outside their cabins screaming their famous war chant.

> La socyal, la socyal,
> Moun la lévé, lévé!
> An Razyé, An Razyé menn!

Already half a dozen thugs were on patrol, brandishing their sticks or swirling their lassos with which they boasted they would catch light-skinned people.

At home Romaine had already lit the hurricane-lamp and the insects were starting to swarm around it. Large crickets were roasting their legs against the glass, as they did every evening. Cathy sat down in the rocking-chair, swaying herself in silence for a few moments, then she turned her head towards Romaine.

'What do you know about a certain First-Born who works, so it seems, for Tonin, the blackmith . . . ?' she asked, trying to hide the impatience in her voice.

Romaine did not even let her finish her question.

'First-Born?' she said hurriedly. 'Everyone knows it's not the name his mother gave him. What's behind it, only the Good Lord knows! Some say he must be a bastard son whose family was ashamed of his colour . . . '

Like me. Just like me, thought Cathy in ecstasy.

'. . . Others think he came here to hide from some mischief he committed in La Pointe.'

'That's not possible,' Cathy protested, recalling his openly earnest face.

She would have walked though fire to defend this boy she had seen so briefly. Romaine was too sharp not to notice her mistress's feelings and wanted to caution her. She hesitated, then said in a firm voice, for she did not want Cathy to go through what so many women have gone through:

'Everybody knows, except Tonin himself, of course, since the family is always the last to know, that he's put a bun in his daughter's oven.'

Cathy started.

'That's not true. It's a lie. Don't ever say that again, do you hear?'

Whereupon she ran and locked herself in her room. But that evening she had not the slightest inclination to read or correct the homework of her darling pupils. She did not feel like sleeping either.

If her father had been alive she would have plied him with questions. She knew how he felt about her mother and how he had never ceased to mourn her long, long after she died. She would have liked to ask him what love is and why it is born. When she was a child she had read a tale where the hero was suddenly swept away on a flying carpet. From his vantage point the earth appeared more beautiful than he had ever seen it, with its valleys, its hills, its beds of flowers and tangle of trees. The feelings aroused in her heart were sweeping her onto this magic carpet and she felt a strange ecstasy inside her. Yes, she had been born to conquer and to spread happiness. Yes, she had come to accomplish great things. For others. For herself. She did not know exactly what. For a moment she recalled the face of that woman who had given her such a mean look at Ma Tètèche's, but she no longer felt frightened and she was silly to have been so scared.

She pressed her forehead against the shutters and caught sight of the moon, lounging on a cushion of clouds. It seemed to smile at her and she got the feeling it was a friend come to enquire the colour of her thoughts.

3   Romaine the Servant's Tale

I was born on this raft of land anchored in the sea whose
mast the fury of the ocean winds has not yet broken. Our
cabin stood high on a plateau scored by gullies. As far as the
eye could see there was nothing but *razyé*, heath and sugar-
cane, more often than not yellowed and scorched by the
sun. So ever since I was small I had wanted to cross the line
of the horizon, to go beyond that thick blue line that marked
the unknown. At home we lived off poverty. Papa, as black
as the logwood charcoal he burnt, looked out at life through
the two red gaps of his eyes. He had lost his forearm at the
factory and could no longer work. So he tried to earn a little
money with his charcoal and his fighting cocks, Zyé wouj
and Fésé pyé. As for my maman, who was still only thirty,
she looked like an old woman with empty udders hanging
down her front. With many a sacrifice, she did manage,
however, to fatten up a hog that we killed at Christmas. It
was the only time we ever saw any meat. I forgot to say I
was the oldest of eight children. That meant there was never
a Sunday or a day of rest. So every night, to escape my
reality, I journeyed in my dreams. I saw La Pointe. The
people who were lucky enough to live there never stopped
talking about its upstairs-downstairs houses, so pleased
with themselves under the red kerchiefs of their roofs, with
bougainvillaea of every colour on their balconies, its straight
streets running between the legs of the almond and sand-box

trees and its four-wheel carriages that outnumber the goats around here. So as soon as the blood flowed out between my legs, as soon as I became a woman, I tucked my meagre sugar-cane money between my brand new breasts and set off to get a life.

I arrived in La Pointe one New Year's Day, late in the afternoon, after taking a whole day for the crossing. I wasn't tired, though. I looked around at all the lights glowing like suns in every house. Except that people had not told me in their descriptions that there were two La Pointes, one for the rich and one for the penniless. Penniless like myself. Although I easily found a job at a bar, Au Soleil Levant, all I could get with my pay for a roof over my head was one room in the Carénage, in a tenants' yard flanked by a lean-to that housed an earthenware pot, a basin and a pitcher for nature's needs and washing. Behind a sheet of cretonne sat the imposing, earthenware *toma*, the thunderbox, in all its majesty. The Dargent factory ruled the neighbourhood. Well before the sun half opened an eye, ox-carts loaded with cane lined up in front of its gates. Day and night, a thick smoke belched out from its chimneys, and you could hear its machines throbbing and throbbing like a heart that never tires. What revolted me was the sight of the workers. For me they were little better than the slaves of long ago, responding to the strident call of a siren, with no time to catch their breath, their bodies scarcely covered in rags. The oldest had their arms and legs scarred with festering ulcers under their plaster of leaves.

It wasn't long before I struck up a love relationship with one of them, a certain Déodat Déodatus, who, every evening, once the factory had closed its gates, came and wet his whistle at the Soleil Levant, but never ever lost his dignity in rum. He wasn't any old sort of man. I might say he had class. But he weighed no heavier than a cane peel. He wasn't taller than a tuft of Guinea grass. When he lay on top of me, I didn't feel his weight and it was like clutching a tiny child, my child. Only his voice sounded raspy and low like a conch-shell when he spoke.

The first time he came over to whisper in my ear, I almost laughed, because I couldn't understand what was going on. Since when did a brat dare look a grown-up in the eye? But he persevered. He was born on a plantation at Grands-Fonds-du-Moule, but even as a youngster he refused to live like an animal. He would go into the cabins and say to the astonished inhabitants: 'Get up, get up! I have a dream', and people didn't know whether to laugh or shove him out like a madman. One day when Jean-Hilaire Endomius came to Le Moule campaigning, he started to walk behind him just like that and Jean-Hilaire fell under the spell of his amazing voice. As the years went by, he became one of his most loyal henchmen, like other men, like Razyé for instance. They say that when he spoke, everyone went silent. When he finished, even the most docile of men brandished their cutlasses and were prepared to ransack everything.

And that's why they took his life from me.

One day they found his body lying in a cane path, navigating the red sea of his blood. The gendarmes didn't even pretend to find the person who had beaten him to death.

But I don't want to relive that agony. For weeks, I wanted to die, but I couldn't. Sad, tender-faced women behind their handkerchiefs leaned over my bed and murmured: 'Be brave! You've got your child, your son, to keep you anchored to life. What can you expect! There's no happiness on this earth. Not for us negroes, there isn't.'

At Déodat's wake, Razyé brought me a purse full of money on behalf of the Socialists. That man, whom everyone says is so wicked, wickeder than a rabid dog, had his eyes filled with tears. He clutched my hands.

'I too have gone through what you're going through today, and every time I see a corpse or attend a wake, my grief returns and comes galloping back. They say that sorrow heals with time. It's not true. The more the years go by, the sharper it gets, and it leaves no room for any other feeling. Years ago, you see, it left me free to prepare my revenge. Day after day I sharpened it like a blade, like a double-sided knife. I told myself: "Not only will I lay in the dust the man who has wronged me, but I'll destroy everyone like him, all those of his colour, all those of his class." Now, I don't even feel like doing that. I'm tired of dragging myself around. All I want is to lie down and die so that at last I can find her. But I'm not even sure about that. All the *kimbwazè* and *gadèdzafè* from here and elsewhere have pocketed my money with a bunch of promises that have brought me nothing. I only saw her once, shortly after she died. And perhaps that was just a figment of my imagination. One afternoon, lacking the strength to live, I was lying flat on my back in a field with the sun in my eyes. An arabesque unfurled a little way off and she emerged, as resolute and bossy as she always was, her black braid bouncing behind her back. "Come on! Catch me if you can!" she shouted at me. And I began to run after her as fast as I could, without ever catching her of course. Ever since that day, however hard I cry or pray even she has never come back. Sometimes I stay all night long in front of my wide open window watching for her. I breathe in the wind and the salt of the harbour. Exhausted, my eyes blur over. I see nothing but the bats that flit from sandbox-tree to sandbox-tree.'

That man's grief only plunged me even further into despair.

Once my Déodat was gone, I could no longer bear La Pointe or the Carénage district that I had loved so much, or the Dargent factory. Besides, the Dargent factory was no longer the Dargent factory. Before he died, Aymeric de Linsseuil had sold it to the Crédit Foncier to pay his debts, and you could sense the end was near, even though there were still lines of ox-carts clanging their wheels in front of the gates and yells from cane-cutters sitting on piles of sugar-cane. So with my child, my little Déodat clutching my headtie, I sailed back on the *Notre-Dame-des-Victoires* to Marie-Galante.

We were in the month of November. What a rainy season it was! The sky was drilled with holes that water poured through like a sieve. There was no telling the sky from the sea. When we got close to land it loomed up like a darker line against the surrounding grey. My family wanted nothing to do with me, because of the shame I had brought on them. So I looked for a room in the town of Saint-Louis and I tried to hire my services for housework. But jobs were hard to come by and, more often than not, me and my child we stopped up our bellies with cassava flour and sugared milk. Men would come up to me, sniff me over, drag their boots over my floor, but had nothing good to offer me and I sent them packing. In a word, my life was nothing but solitude and boredom. Until the day Cathy de Linsseuil comes knocking on my door.

I didn't know her, but I knew what family she came from. For the people of Grande-Terre and Basse-Terre, except for the Socialists, Aymeric de Linsseuil was the model of the good white man and good plantation owner. When he passed on, the whole island went into mourning. As I stood in front of the cathedral of St-Pierre-et-St-Paul among the crowd of other people who had never seen him with their own two eyes, who didn't know him from Adam, but had heard of him as the Good Lord Himself, I watched the funeral as it filed past. The procession stretched out like ants dressed in deep mourning from the far end of the rue du

246

Père Labat, almost as far as the Hill of Massabielle. The music marched up front: Monsieur Démonin with his entire band was playing dirges that made you want to lie down and die, if you hadn't done so already. Behind him came dozens of little boys and girls carrying wreaths of white flowers, little white Creoles, children of his friends and relatives. But there were also little black children, children of his workers or from the plantation school as well as little mulattos. So there was no distinction of colour. The bier was pulled along by four horses dressed in black hoods embroidered in silver. You couldn't even see the coffin under the roses, the lilies and arums that gave off such a scent. In the same way you couldn't see his wife, wrapped under the miles and miles of black veil, or his daughters and sisters bundled up the same way, and all that grief gripped you and made your heart grieve. Standing on the pavement people started to cry hot tears as if it was their father, a brother or a cousin that was being carried along to his last resting place.

When I found myself face to face with her I was all surprised, quite astonished, at the colour of Cathy, and the more I looked at her the more something in her bright, staring eyes, the curve of her eyebrows and the bulge of her mouth made me think of someone I'd already met. But who? I couldn't quite place it.

She hired me straightaway and we became friends.

How happy women would be if, at some time in their life, they didn't have to give in to the whims of their heart!

From one day to the next, I saw Cathy change. When I started working for her, she had few things on her mind. Always the same. The memory of her beloved papa; Razyé whom she claimed was the cause of her papa's death and whom she hated like poison; her forty pupils, their education and amusement. When she talked about her papa, she never stopped. A real carnival rattle. How her papa loved Guadeloupe, how he loved the negroes, though he was white, how he loved the poor, though he was rich, and so on and so forth. Sometimes I was tired of hearing her ramble on, but I had to put up with it for a long, long time. Talking about her papa would get her on the subject of Razyé.

'Oh, if I were a man, I'd take my revenge on him!' she moaned.

'But how would you do that?' I said, poking fun at her, all casual like.

That shut her up because she'd never thought how to go about it. Then she said: 'I'd go and see his wife and children and set them against him. I'd get them to hate him as much as I do.'

I shrugged my shoulders.

'His own family? That would be the first time! Even the devil in hell has people who love him. The bonds of blood and heart know no reason.'

She began to cry and I tried to comfort her.

'A Christian like yourself must learn to forgive. Didn't they teach you that in catechism?'

On hearing me she flew into one of her tempers.

'Forgive? Never! Never!'

When she wasn't talking of her papa or Razyé, she kept herself busy with the school. For hours on end, with tongue between her teeth, she would bury her head, correcting the pupils' homework and preparing for classes, and sometimes it was past midnight and I could still hear her Sergeant-Major pen scratching away in red ink. On Saturday afternoons she put on a battered wide-brimmed hat that she tied around her neck with two velvet ribbons, and took the pupils under the blazing sun for their walk outdoors. Sometimes she took them on visits to the distilleries, the factories and the windmills, her favourite she told them, and showed them the cartouches, the rubble of limestone masonry, and the remains of the old grinding-stones. Other times, marching her litter of children like rows of soldiers, singing at the top of their voices 'J'aime la France, c'est mon pays,' she went down to the mudflats and mangrove swamps. There she explained to them the different types of mangrove – red, black, white and grey, and what's more, their names in Latin: *Avicennia germinans, Conocarpus erectus.* When the pupils in their amazement plucked up courage to ask her how she knew all these things, she sighed: 'My papa taught me.' She began to cry in front of the children, who took no notice since they had seen her cry a hundred times before for the same reason.

From the moment she met First-Born, as he wants to be called, things were very different. At the beginning, it was all moans and groans.

'He smokes like a sugar-cane train. His breath smells.'

'He'll never pass his exams. Every time I give him an exercise in French he has to look up every word in the dictionary.'

'Romaine, I don't think he's very intelligent. He never says anything of interest.'

'I wonder if he dreams at night, if he travels in his imagination.'

And then suddenly she sang another song.

'He's a good fellow, you know.'

'People say – and you do too – that he's the one who gave Asturias a belly. He would never do a thing like that, never, do you hear?'

Good fellow or not, First-Born arrived every afternoon, once classes were over, on the stroke of four thirty, his face hidden in a cloud of smoke. It's true he did smoke a lot. He helped Cathy in her garden, watering, weeding and pretending to like flowers, sometimes bringing her cuttings of red ginger, torch ginger or blue allamanda wrapped in newspaper he'd found somewhere or other. They worked in silence as dusk fell. Then they entered the house for his lesson, still without saying a word.

I was waiting for fate to make her move.

4   Political Meeting at Grand-Anse

Seated on the upper deck, Razyé was watching the line of waves and thinking what a wonderful shroud these flecks of mourning would make as they rolled as far as the eye could see. The rain was soaking his black wide-brimmed, felt hat, his black cloth riding-habit and black hand-made cow-hide boots. He himself did not feel a thing.

The *Josephine*, which had replaced the *Notre-Dame-des-Victoires* after it almost sank with all on board in the very middle of the channel, was bravely ploughing through the bad weather that had blown over from Dominica these last two days and would soon change into a hurricane, according to the doomsayers. The boat groaned, wheezed and seemed about to break in two at every new wave. Passengers were vomiting left and right. Those who had the presence of mind to bring lemons pressed the pulp to their colourless lips, but this did not prevent them from joining the numbers of the sick. Even the infants and babies, usually unaffected by seasickness, were not spared.

This political meeting had been decided at the last minute, since a violent quarrel had broken out between the partisans of Jean-Hilaire Endomius, defenders of the capital-labour agreement, and those of Boisneuf, who rejected it. At that time tempers flared easily on Marie-Galante (they still do). There had been bloodshed and one of Boisneuf's followers had been laid in a coffin, his body shredded by a cutlass.

Razyé had been sent to restore unity in the Socialist camp, a job he had accomplished very well at the troublespots of Marquisat, Sainte-Amélie and Pointe d'Or, but this time he was none too pleased. Moreover, nothing pleased him very much nowadays. Walking. Dressing. Drinking rum. Making love. He had lost his taste for everything. He had trouble remembering he had to drink a cup of coffee when he woke up, that he had to sit down for lunch or quite simply drink goblets of water when he was hot. Never very talkative, he could spend a whole week without voicing a word or even communicating in gestures, like he used to do. Since Aymeric had passed on, the revenge he had hankered after was meaningless and he no longer saw a reason for living.

In fact Razyé had agreed to travel to Marie-Galante for quite another reason, a very personal reason. He had learned through his spies that Razyé II was hiding in the vicinity of Saint-Louis, under some ridiculous name. What would he do to him once he laid hands on him? He did not know and in actual fact had not given it a thought. It was as if a part of him was so used to savagery it continued to act behind his back.

The curtain of rain frayed at the edges and the corrugated iron fronts of the hovels in Grand-Anse and the egg-yellow dome of its church appeared. Standing in the puddles, five or six men were waiting for Razyé on the wharf. People made way for them, for they were notorious, ferocious-looking, club-wielding thugs. The group set off for the Inn of the Forbidden Fruit, a grand-sounding name for a building that wasn't much to look at and could only accommodate a few travellers at a time. Before showing Razyé to his room, a dank, stifling rat-hole, Padéole, the innkeeper, thought it best to offer a round of drinks. Razyé was about to refuse, now that alcohol merely burned his throat and provided no pleasure whatsoever, when he thought of the effect this might have. Who would ever be mad enough to refuse a neat rum? So he let his glass be filled with Paul Rameau 90% proof rum. Then he coughed, which surprised nobody given the weather, and declared: 'Politics will have to wait until tomorrow. This afternoon I have a personal matter to settle. I'm after my son. Has anyone seen him?'

The thugs looked at each other cautiously. Finally, one of them made up his mind to speak.

'He works for Tonin. But if you want to find him, you'll have to look elsewhere, if you want my opinion.'

'At the schoolteacher's, I bet,' added another.

Laughter broke out.

'What schoolteacher?' Razyé asked drily. 'What are you talking about?'

There was a silence. Then speaking all at once, the men told the story, one of them summing it up with the words: 'It seems he wants to put a bun in *her* oven as well. He's some fellow, your son!'

Amid the chuckling, Razyé remained speechless. He had a poor opinion of his son and wondered what any woman could see in him. Had he been mistaken? So he had taken up with Aymeric de Linsseuil's daughter? Well! Well! Here was the revenge he had virtually given up on. What the sick or weak-natured Justin-Marie had been incapable of doing was now within arm's reach. He was now in a position to graft his own rotten, wretched offspring onto this respected family-tree.

He stood up and yelled.

'Padéole, a horse!'

A voice tried to stop him.

'Where are you thinking of going in this weather? Outside the lightning's as bright as daylight!'

Razyé didn't hear. He was already leaping onto a stallion in the yard.

Those who saw Razyé that day as he galloped through the rain, the lightning and the thunder were of the firm opinion that the occupant of the Devil's Hole had emerged from his lair, a few yards from the morne de la Treille. In order to ride faster than the wind, Razyé lay flat along his mount. He clung to the long hair of its mane, digging his heels into its sides. The road from Grand-Anse to Saint-Louis at that time was pitted with potholes and water spurted up in a muddy spray under the horse's hoofs. Those made homeless by the previous hurricane, who had taken refuge in the old Roussel-Trianon plantation house, came out in the pouring rain to try and understand what manner of creature was this. Too late! They were unable to identify the meteor that shot past towards the mangrove. All they could do was cross themselves and haphazardly recite two or three Hail Mary's.

Saint-Louis was already flooded, its streets stood in three feet of water and its inhabitants perched on beds and tables in their cabins. Most of the trees had been blown down and branches and leaves were strewn over the land. Razyé entered Ma Tètèche's where come hell or high water the regular rum guzzlers were drowning their sorrows in neat rum. He did not even take the trouble to wish them good day, but yelled: 'Where does she live, that schoolteacher?'

They recognized him and immediately twenty mouths stammered directions and forty hands shot out to point the way. He dashed out as quickly as he had entered.

Cathy's house was at the far end of the village, the last of a jumble of cabins made of straw. Since she moved in she had put all her efforts into making the garden as pretty as she could, distinguishing it by a bed of flowers, roses that were now flattened, heads drooping under the deluge, sadly dripping petals. Razyé was oblivious to these details and almost knocked down the door with a shove of his shoulder. He had not counted on the bad weather playing havoc with his plans. There were no lessons that day, and only Cathy and Romaine cradling her little Déodat appeared in front of him. A stream was lapping across the floor of beaten earth. The two women had opened an umbrella over their heads and were perched on an oleander-wood chest of drawers inlaid with magnolia, one of the remaining pieces from her childhood bedroom that she hadn't the heart to part with. What Razyé had not counted on either was the effect that Cathy would have on him.

He had never seen her before. He had never been curious to see her.

Suddenly, the rumour he had heard, the rumour he had never paid attention to, first of all because he was not a man to listen to rumour, but mainly because his head was too filled with mourning, engulfed his memory in a flood of conviction. This was no wicked slander. In this face in front of him he saw his own eyes, his forehead and his mouth. How could this be possible? During her final days she had been so fragile he no longer touched her, however much he had wanted to. And were the people around so blind that they suspected nothing? Had Aymeric been really such a dolt? And yet he was taken with regret, a regret tinged with bitterness and a kind of fury. The daughter looked nothing like the mother. Nothing at all. Once again, she had cruelly slipped between his fingers and left him empty-handed.

Cathy jumped down from her chest of drawers and stood facing him.

'What are you doing in my home?' she shouted at him.

Razyé got control of himself and used the first excuse that came to mind.

'I've come . . . I've come to see my good friend Romaine. I didn't know she worked for you.'

Cathy spun round and in stupefaction asked the servant: 'What? You mean you know him?'

'That's a fine trick you played on me,' said Romaine, gloomily. 'Now I'm out of a job, with a baby on my hands!'

It was as if the infant realized its misfortune for it started to squeal like a piglet. Razyé drew a wallet out of his pocket.

'How much did she give you each month?' he asked.

Romaine, looking woeful, did not answer and he placed a wad of banknotes on the table in front of her. At the sight of so much money, her face lit up. However, when she looked up to thank him she had a sudden illumination. The resemblance she couldn't place ever since she had worked for Cathy was his! Him! It was the same burning eyes, the same slightly heavy lips and the same wilful chin. After a moment she took a grip on herself, telling herself she was losing her senses. Whatever could she be thinking of? Aymeric de Linsseuil's daughter looking like Razyé? It was pure madness. And yet the more she looked at him through the dim candlelight, the more she saw another face take shape beside his. It was the expression that was different and deceiving. One was young, glowing and tender, the other ageing, bitter and aggressive. One belonged to the soft light of dawn, the other to the black night of a hurricane. It was simply their expression that was different. As she couldn't help gaping at him, he barked in his usual manner:

'What are you looking at me for like a horse that has thrown its rider?'

She grabbed his hand, not knowing exactly what she was going to say to him. He shook himself free.

The regulars in the bar were watching and the diabolical wagging of tongues began. Who would ever have thought that someone like Razyé would have dealings with a good-for-nothing like Romaine? You never can tell with men! They must have met when she was living in La Pointe. That's right, it was rumoured she was often seen with the Socialists. It didn't take much to jump to the conclusion that her illegitimate son was his. Some denied it categorically. No, no! The child was as black as midnight with tight peppercorn hair. If he'd had Razyé as a father, he'd have come out better than that.

Oblivious to the stir he was causing, Razyé made for the door and opened it, letting in a blast of wind laden with whirling leaves and branches. Bending over, he grabbed the bridle of his horse who was dejectedly soaking up the fury of the rain under a flamboyant-tree. Then he began to walk along beside it at an uncontrollable pace. He was plunged into a state of utter confusion. This Cathy, so different as to be a traitor to the first, disgusted him, and he had no inclination to claim her as his own. A daughter who does not look like her mother is a monster. Yet, to claim her would be a revenge more cruel than any he had ever imagined. No more secrets. Everyone would know what had happened in the past. The name of Linsseuil would be tarnished. His offshoot would replace the master stock.

Suddenly he was deafened by a terrible noise. It sounded as if two sugar-cane trains had collided at full speed and been derailed. At the same time the fronts of the houses flashed as bright as day, while a tree splintered halfway down its trunk and fell across the road. Razyé was forced to seek refuge in one of the few cabins still standing. The dying flame of a hurricane-lamp was flickering. In the shadows, a large woman and three young children were holding up part of the roof with all their might and never stopped calling on the name of the Good Lord. At the other end of the room, serene and almost smiling on his mattress, a man appeared to be meditating. By his bearing and the secret, sagacious expression in his eyes, Razyé, who had seen a fair number of them, recognized a seer. Without further ado, he sat down beside him and offered him a little of the chewing tobacco that for years he had been sent from Cuba. The man willingly helped himself and spoke as if he were talking into space.

'What's good about life is that whether we are twenty, forty or sixty, it always has a surprise in store for us.'

Razyé sighed.

'Yes, but sometimes you'd like it to be pleasant.'

The man shrugged his shoulders.

'Hey! What are you complaining about? In my opinion, you should just let things happen now. You win. Every time.'

Razyé was about to press him with questions when the remaining sheets of corrugated iron on the roof lifted away from the helpless hands and blew off with the wind. The woman screamed. A torrent of water poured inside and he found himself wriggling in the middle of an icy flood. Silently, the bodies of his companions slipped into the night. Fortunately, he had learned how to swim.

When he returned to Grand-Anse at the end of the day, he was being mourned as one of the missing.

The sky was suddenly washed clean. Anonymous (at this time hurricanes were not given names), the tropical storm continued on its course towards other islands, leaving a trail of ruin and hundreds of homeless behind it. At the inn, Razyé emptied half a litre of rum, had his chest rubbed with camphor then set off for the church, the only building

258

still standing, where, despite protests from the priest, the political meeting was to be held. Those who accompanied him realized full well he was not to be approached, he looked so sombre and withdrawn. In fact, though there was a large turn-out, nobody was in a mood to discuss the squabbles between Socialists that evening. They had had a close call with desolation and death and people felt united. They were black and unfortunate, wasn't that right? There was a general outcry against the smallholding contracts granted by the white factory owners – the favourite topic of conversation. The smallholders cleared the ground and prepared the soil. Though half the artificial fertilizer was paid for, it was up to them to provide the manure, cut and carry the cane. What profit, they wondered, would be left for them? As for the Indians remaining on Marie-Galante, the last of them had taken the boat for La Pointe the day before, with no hope of return, because the black workers got two francs a job, whereas they were only getting one franc twenty-five.

Exploitation, disrespect!

Suddenly Razyé was fed up with the same old slogans. To everyone's surprise he left the church, cut a path through the rubbish and amidst the salty breath of the wind slowly walked to the end of the jetty.

All around him, the listless immensity of the sea. Above him, the black sailcloth of the sky.

He remained standing for a long while, then sat down on the rough stones, his feet dangling in the void a few feet above the water. Strange that for almost twenty years he had never thought of putting an end to his life. It was not as if he were frightened of displeasing the Good Lord and finding himself in hell. His hell was inside him, where his heart lay. He was a coward, that's all. He hadn't the courage to leave ahead of his time. Or else he was a hypocrite. Though he had never admitted it, something had made him cling to life all this time. He had remained attached to life's little pleasures. The flesh of a lady of easy virtue, the scent of iodine and salt from the sea, the sear of the sun, the burn of rum and the smell of sweat of men playing cards or dominoes. But now he had lost his taste for everything.

So what was he waiting for?

He would do better to swim out with a calm stroke to the swell of the open sea, and once there, with eyes closed and fists clenched, rolled up in a ball like a foetus in its element, he would lower himself further and further to the very bottom of the body of the ocean.

The flabbergasted fish would welcome him with a serenade. Far away the world would continue its crooked course; but that would no longer be his business.

5   A Well-Kept Secret

Saint Theresa of the Infant Jesus, Saint Anthony of Padua and the Archangel Michael looked on with contrite expressions, for admittedly the sight was a sorry one. The pews that hadn't been washed out to sea were scattered here and there in the aisles; leaves, branches and even tree-trunks littered the nave; a layer of mud covered the floor, to the great satisfaction of the fowl who pecked around with cluckings of joy. A group of homeless had spent the last three nights in the chapel of the Virgin Mary to the left of the main altar and had hung their rags to dry on the edge of the font. Unlike the saints in their niches, however, the inhabitants of Saint-Louis were not really sorry for the state of their church, parishioners who for years had never attended mass without an umbrella open over their heads to catch the leaks through the roof. Noisy and unruly, the children waited in front of the confessional for their catechism. They were all to take communion the following day for a mass of thanksgiving. Father Dupuytren wondered whether he should get them to shut up with a kick as he usually did, then decided to stay where he was. Through the mesh he could see Cathy, who took confession every Saturday, for every Sunday she received communion and offered her prayers to the memory of her papa. He could have recited her sins by heart. Venial. Always the same, week after week. A few fits of temper, for she was choleric and flared up at her pupils. A little greed. She was fond of the crab patties and calalu her servant Romaine cooked for her. Stale stuff, in other words. Nothing juicy. Nevertheless, if he had been observant, as any man of his calling should be, he would have noted that her familiar, pretty face was unusually careworn. Head lowered, striking her breast with her hand, she whispered: 'Father, forgive me, for I have sinned. Seriously.'

'I am listening,' the priest answered, routinely.

Cathy took on an inspired air as if what she was about to confess frightened her. Then she leaned forward, her forehead glued to the wood of the confessional. Her cheeks were flushed, the colour of a freshly sliced sapodilla. A mixture of dark brown and red. She seemed beside herself and murmured: 'Father, I wanted to kill someone.'

The priest looked at her in amazement.

'You?'

She nodded and told her story. How a few days earlier, vomited up by the fury of the storm, Razyé had had the nerve to show up at her house and how, face to face with the man who had murdered her father through a series of strikes and riots, who had stripped him of his land and his factory, she had only one desire: to grab the kitchen knife and stick it in his back. Like a woman of the Maroons hacking with a cutlass at the master who had raped her. As she spoke, she relived the events of that night with growing passion. She interrupted herself to catch her breath then resumed with an even greater violence.

'At one point I had a kind of dream, more frightening than reality. I found myself in a room whose window was wide open to the rain and the chaos of the wind. Somewhere I could hear a shutter banging. He was lying on the ground, his clothes soaked, not dripping with water but with blood. His horrible black eyes were staring blindly seeing nothing but the blackness of death. And I had killed him. I leaned over him. I pushed his body outside and the water carried him off to hell.'

'My dear Cathy!' the priest protested, aghast.

He had not expected anything of the sort and realized that the paltry number of rosaries he was going to precribe would be a small penance. As if she still had a lot on her conscience, she started off again.

'That night I turned Romaine out with her child, the poor little Déodat. But this time it was not in a dream. It was for real. She who had always been so good to me, even more than *mabo* Sandrine at papa's. I wanted to hit her. I took a stick . . . yes, a stick!'

She began to cry.

'Romaine? Why? Why?' the priest could only stammer.

She looked up in agony.

'I got it into my head that she had had dealings with Razyé and that she had hired herself out to spy on me.'

What was there to say?

Father Dupuytren searched his memory for the seminary lessons, then stammered, realizing as he spoke the pitiful nature of his homily.

'One does not pay back evil with evil. This is not what the Good Lord wants. Even if Razyé is a devil, and that everyone knows, you must have compassion in your heart for him. Like your brother or even your papa, whom he so wronged. We are all the children of the Good Lord. He created us. It's for us that His son Jesus Christ died on the cross. What is going to happen to this poor Romaine and her child? Though she is unmarried, she's not a bad person. You know that. You must ask her forgiveness and take her back.'

Cathy lowered her head and groaned: 'Will she accept?'

'Go and ask her,' the priest ordered. 'As for your unholy houghts . . . '

Thereupon he began to mumble again. When he stopped, Cathy, still in tears, made the sign of the cross. Then she went and kneeled in front of Saint Anthony of Padua whose blue eyes and plump, bearded cheeks she had liked since she was a child. With one hand on her heart, she recited her five dozen rosaries, which calmed her a little bit. Prayer has that effect on those who believe in its virtues.

When she came out of the church, the sun was wistfully hesitating on the horizon. Was he going to take his daily dip?

One day is never like the next. You would never have thought that less than a week earlier Nature had unleashed its forces. Now the sea, picture perfect, was caressing the sand along the beaches and the fishermen's nets drying beside their boats. The flock of the silk-cotton tree fluttered on the evening breeze and the air seemed to be floating with butterfly wings as white as cotton.

She recalled that Romaine used to live just round the corner from the prison in a *lakou*, a tenements' yard called the Luttrel *lakou* after the landlord, Siméon Luttrel, one of the town's most respectable merchants. The yard was connected to the street by a stinking passageway squeezed between two cabins. On account of the recent weather, wooden planks had been thrown over the mud and Cathy had great difficulty keeping her balance. Since it was mainly occupied by single women, some with children, malicious gossip claimed it was a den of women of easy virtue that the town hall would do well to look into. The tropical storm had had fun tossing away the sheets of corrugated iron and planks that made up the yard's two-storey buildings, and the unfortunate women, who had lost everything in the way of clothes, furniture and crockery, were trying to shelter their nakedness.

They looked at Cathy menacingly, insulted by her youth

her percale dress, the large velvet bow in her hair and her tiny embroidered slippers, now covered in mud.

After clearly hesitating, one of the tenants decided to answer her questions and told her they hadn't seen Romaine or the little Déodat since the storm. They had probably been swept away by the sea that had flooded the town. She said this in a matter-of-fact tone of voice that made the information even more horrible. Cathy was appalled.

'Disappeared? But it can't be true!'

Another woman, who was sweeping up heaps of rubbish, shrugged her shoulders.

'It seems there are hundreds missing on Marie-Galante and there's no counting the numbers in La Pointe.'

Cathy, shattered, found herself back on the street. The realization of her sin broke her soul. She was the one who had sent Romaine to her death. It was as if she had killed them, mother and child. From whom did she inherit this hot temper that led her to take actions she would regret? Not Aymeric, of course, who only had one answer for evil. Once again she thought of her mother, whose real nature nobody had ever wanted to reveal to her, and she caught herself hating her. It was from her she inherited this violent temperament she could not get rid of. They said there was no physical resemblance. But the resemblance was inside her, invisible and all powerful under her skin. She started to run, as if to escape an assailant who would catch up with her whatever she did.

Out of breath, she arrived in front of Ma Tètèche's shop just as Asturias was coming out.

The shape of her belly, as round as a calabash under the folds of her dress, left no doubt as to her condition. Her face bore the faded, worn-out mask of pregnancy. Cathy slowed down to a walk. She and First-Born had kept their distance until now. Evening after evening they sat on the same bench

265

and solemnly acted out being mistress and pupil, their heads bent over the same maths problems and the same natural science lessons. At the end of the month, by way of payment, he would bring her a basket of fresh eggs, a skewer of tench or goatfish or else a bundle of *pakala* yams that melted in the mouth. Their eyes never met. Their hands never touched. Sometimes the words trembled on their lips, but they held them back, convinced the rest of the world shared their conviction that they were made for each other, as if the same blood flowed in their veins, that they were as close as brother and sister separated at birth and there was nothing they could do but calmly wait for the inevitable moment when they would be one.

Asturias was not one of those brazen hussies who take offence and scornfully eye their rival or cast aspersions. She knew full well she was no match for such a pretty and educated *demoiselle* who, to the surprise of everyone in Saint-Louis, honoured First-Born with her favours. Girls of her status were born to be seduced, taken and abandoned with a belly. That's how it's been ever since the world began spinning like a top. So she merely addressed a reluctant greeting to Cathy and flashed her a look of hatred and pain that alone was worth all the attestations of paternity.

That look sank into the heart of Cathy, who started to run again without knowing exactly where she was going, and those who saw her run like the wind past their doors came out to see what was happening. The last person to have run like that was Eudora on the afternoon that Gelbrant, her husband, fell from the top of the coconut-tree and broke his back. Nobody had been able to stop her and they found her smashed to smithereens on the rocks.

Cathy left the town and took the same direction as Eudora. But arriving at the Fort, she stopped. They called the 'Fort' the blackened remnants of an edifice on a cliff-top built perhaps by the first settlers to trade with the Carib Indians. From here there was a view over the immense circle of the sea and the islands of Les Saintes sparkling in the glow of the setting sun. Cathy dropped to the ground, oblivious to the thorns sticking into her calves and buttocks. The sight of this hypocritical sea that had rolled so many men, women and children in its folds, filled her with terror. How like herself it was. One day as calm as could be, the next in a raging fury. She had wanted to kill Razyé. She had killed Romaine. She was on the point of committing a third crime; because of her an innocent, fatherless child was going to enter this world and a poor wretch was going to find herself all alone with just her two eyes to cry with. Wherever he was, Aymeric must be ashamed of her. For his sake, she tried to make some serious resolutions. When First-Born came for his lesson, she would not let him in or sit down. She would make him understand where his duty lay. He would listen to her, standing in front of her, head lowered, in that somewhat awkward manner of his. Then one day, amidst the din of church bells, she would attend his wedding. At the same time she wept even harder, for she knew that all that was a trick of her imagination. Nothing could undo the knot that tied her to First-Born, body to body and heart to heart.

When she stood up, the beast of the night had swallowed her surroundings. She groped her way back to the town, guiding herself by the great cross on the church that stood out blacker than the night. Behind the cabin doors, nightmares had begun to torment the little children. Crouching under leaves, toads and insects took heart from their own concert of shrieks.

6   Death of the Wolf

Hosannah opened the living-room door, carrying level with her face the large lamp she lit at the very last minute to save paraffin. The night was now as black as it could be. Dinner would soon have to be served – *dasheen* and a few cheap cuts of goat-meat she had cooked in a colombo curry. But hardly had she entered the room that always had a musty smell about it, even when aired, than the sight of Razyé sitting erect and motionless in the dark red armchair, with his hands spread on his knees, made her jump and almost fall over. What terrified her was an expression she had never seen during the ten years or so she had worked for the family. He was smiling in the dark and this smile, or rictus rather, was more frightening than a grimace. She laid her hand on her heart and said in a whisper: 'Good Lord, why are you sitting like that in the dark?'

He did not seem to hear her. First of all, what was he doing in the house at such an hour? Usually he was up on the Morne-à-Cayes with one of his mistresses, drinking rum, playing cards or doing goodness knows what else. Good Lord! The more she looked at him, the more he looked to her like a *soukougnan*, a bloodsucker. Was he human like the rest of us? Hosannah turned on her heels and scrambled up the stairs to alert her mistress. Irmine had at last got Fréda off to sleep and settled down to her regular evening read of a few pages of *David Copperfield* that one of the children had borrowed for her from the school library. The story of this unfortunate little boy, scarcely more unfortunate than her own children, engrossed her. Yet she turned the pages very slowly, half a dozen each evening, for too many sad thoughts clouded over the print in the book. Her mind was in torment. What had become of Razyé II? She did not know what had gone on between father and son. One day the boy had disappeared and Razyé had simply forbidden his name to be mentioned. A few days later, Razyé II had sent her a badly written, incoherent letter that provided no explanation. He reiterated his affection for her, yet blamed her for not having loved him in return and assured her she would soon hear of him in Guadeloupe. Since then, not a word. Hosannah had heard that he was hiding either in Dominica or on Marie-Galante. It was also rumoured he was quietly making a fortune from smuggling rum in the region of Basse-Terre, and owned a great house and seventy-five acres.

Irmine listened to Hosannah and was not surprised at what she heard. For some time she had found Razyé changed, especially since his return from Marie-Galante with a bronchitis that he refused to treat. He no longer went out, and stayed for days on end silently locked in the attic without drinking or eating. Only the thick smoke from his pipe curling under the door proved he was still alive. Sometimes, however, she heard him talking to himself in a loud voice. At other times he would grind his teeth so violently the noise could be heard all over the house. He would clamber downstairs, making a great din, then immediately go back up again. A few nights earlier she had been terrified by a dream. He had passed on. She had been entrusted with the inscription on his grave, but knowing neither his age nor his birthplace, she had been unable to come up with anything. What's more, 'Razyé' was his only name and he had no Christian name or family name entered on the civil registers like other human-beings. She had opened her eyes in the pre-dawn hours and found him lying full-length up against her, as if he needed her warmth. Yet when she timidly placed her hand on his shoulder, he had jumped up and gone back to his room.

She ran to the living-room.

Razyé was still sitting enthroned in the dark red armchair, staring at the colourless paper on the wall opposite him. It was as if he had seen something underneath the tawdry reproduction of a *Vue du Moule* by Clémence Genelès de Sourville that she had pinned up. She went over to him and took his hand, which for once he did not snatch away.

'Would you like to eat something?' she proposed.

He did not answer.

'A little coffee or hot tea?' she insisted. 'How many days has it been since you've not taken anything?'

After a while he turned his head towards her and asked, almost distraught: 'Are we alone here, just the two of us?'

The strangeness of the question made her shiver. She looked around her and stammered: 'Of course we are. Except for our loyal Hosannah.'

The 'loyal Hosannah' stood huddled up and seemed on the verge of fainting. He went back to contemplating the wall, moving his eyes from right to left as if he were following the movements of an invisible ray, then suddenly he stood up to his full height and without another word left the room. The heels of his boots could be heard pounding the flagstones in the yard and then the pavement.

Irmine's dinner was a sad affair. Could Razyé be sick? Could he be losing his head?

Seated around the table, the children were making their usual din, behaving badly, smearing themselves with food, fighting and laughing at the top of their voices. Gengis was whispering in Cassandre's ear that a snake was waiting for her, coiled under the sheets of her bed, and the little girl was screaming in anticipation. Irmine looked at them. Their egoism amazed her. They seemed to have clean forgotten their elder brother, who had been gone for three months. Yet they had seemed genuinely fond of him and always returned the affection he deserved. He was loving and protective. Cassandre, in particular, had a soft spot for him. She would roll up like a cat at his feet when he played the clarinet and shower him with kisses to show her appreciation. When finally the children went up to their bedrooms, she did the same. Yet it was almost eleven and she could not get to sleep. Nightmares kept her awake. She would walk into a room and there would be her own wake or one of her children's. She would stroll in the countryside and the earth would open up under her feet and swallow her.

At midnight, the rain that had let up since the storm began to pour down again. It hammered on the roofs, lashed the house-fronts and seeped through the louvred windows. Soon the wind joined in and there was a great commotion as it broke the branches of the sandbox-trees on the Place de la Victoire. Then it began to roar through the streets and shake the houses.

Razyé returned home around three in the morning, much to her relief. Usually, he stumbled on every stair, but that night he was not drunk and he climbed with a steady step. After a while, however, she heard him utter such deep sighs and call out the name of Cathy in such a way that her anxiety returned. She quietly climbed up to his room. The door was open and dozens of candles burning on an altar with gaudy, pagan images, flasks, calabashes, nails and tin objects lit up the room like daylight. In the heat they emitted, Razyé's face was covered in sweat. He seemed out of breath and beside himself. His bloodshot eyes shone with an unbearable fever.

'What time is it?' he asked in a strange, nasal voice.

Recalling the stories of her *mabo* in which the spirits all spoke though their nose, she stammered in fright: 'Almost four in the morning.'

Deep down, she told herself she was wrong to be afraid. She had made love with this man in front of her, had borne his children. She knew he was only a human being, a little more desperate, a little more lonely than the rest. He looked straight at her.

'I haven't written my will yet,' he declared. 'All these possessions I've wrongly acquired, I want to get rid of them.'

She had the courage to look up and protest.

'Get rid of them? Think of our children. They've never done you any harm. Our boys must study, our girls must have dowries for a suitable marriage.'

He paid her no attention and continued.

'The priest won't come, that's one good thing. But I don't want any wake. No flowers, no candles, no wreaths. I want only one thing: to be buried next to her in the graveyard at l'Engoulvent. You, Hosannah and the children can come with me if you like. But I don't want anyone else. Certainly not the Socialists.'

All this was said in a measured tone, almost with a smile, and this gentleness was more terrifying than his usual savagery. It was as if he were already dead and his ghost were dictating his last wishes. Irmine told herself she ought to send for a doctor, and at the first break in the clouds she dispatched Hosannah to fetch Doctor Bellisle, the only doctor she knew who would accept credit. He was not long in coming, languid-eyed, with a carefully trimmed beard and small black leather case. But however hard he knocked on Razyé's door, the latter wouldn't open. He apologized very politely from inside in his new manner, repeating: 'I assure you I don't need you. My body is not suffering from any sickness.'

The doctor went back down the stairs. He took the opportunity to examine Cassandre and Fréda who were playing hopscotch in the yard, found them well-developed for their age, blooming and in good health. He found Irmine, thin and anaemic, however, gave her a prescription for iron and recommended she eat fried ox-blood. Around ten o'clock the rain started up again, drumming even harder on the tin roofs. Once again the storm channels overflowed and streamed around the slope of the Morne de Massabielle while the waves soaked the sacks of sugar in the warehouses on the wharf. The shutters in Razyé's room creaked on their hinges and at each gust of wind let out a dismal sound.

At noon, Hosannah and Irmine could no longer put up with the noise. They climbed up to the attic, stuck their ears to the door and, hearing not a sound, managed to break the lock by shoving their shoulders against the door.

The rain had extinguished the candles and soaked the altar. Razyé was lying on the floor in the middle of the room, his shirt unbuttoned on his hairy chest. No trace of a wound could be found on his body. Irmine leaned over him, sobbing. She pushed back the hair over his forehead, and under the long black strands he was staring, wide-eyed, as if he had really tried to discern the indiscernible.

Death has the privilege of being a great leveller.

When the news of Razyé's death had gone the rounds of La Pointe, people saw that he was as mortal as they were and they began to denigrate him. Nobody knew the name of his papa. Nobody knew the name of his maman. He hadn't spent one day at school. Reading and writing meant nothing to him. He was a miser and a womanizer. The women who had made love to him now claimed he never changed his linen and that they were bothered by his smell. Everyone remarked that, despite his diatribes against the white Creoles, he had taken one of their women as his wife, whom he hid from prying eyes. And lastly, he had been a servant to the Socialists, their slave and nigger. When they ordered him to cut, he cut. To axe, he axed. To burn, he burned, full stop. When he accompanied them on their political rallies, his mouth opened no wider than a blowfish. He had never been heard to improvise in French-French one of those hypnotic speeches à la Jean-Hilaire Endomius.

All night long, tongues wagged disrespectfully in the Company rum-shops and bars where the bone of the dice and the domino is struck against the wood of the tables. In the early morning, Razyé, who had been over six feet tall while alive, had now been cut down to a few inches.

You only get one maman and one papa. So Irmine hoped that the announcement of Razyé's death would bring Razyé II out of his hiding-place and that he would turn up at the house on the Place de la Victoire in tears, his heart filled with grief and remorse. But the clouds of the night turned white, the sun warmed the schooners and barges in the harbour, and darkness returned and still there was no Razyé II. They couldn't wait any longer. With a heavy heart she sent Hosannah down to the two employees from the undertaker's who were biding their time in the yard. They brought the coffin down and placed it in the first carriage,while the family squeezed into the one behind. Irmine had not dared disobey her husband, even dead, and had bought neither rum nor candles. She had left the coffin in the attic and intended to spend the night with him in tears and prayers, in the sole company of Hosannah and her eldest boy. She had reckoned without the Socialists, who insisted on saying farewell to the man who had done so much for their cause, and between the street and the garden, the ground floor and the top floor there was a constant stream of men in buttoned morning coats, their faces sweating under their top hats. Jean-Hilaire Endomius, detained, sent a wreath of gardenias and white frangipanis she could not refuse, like all the others they brought her. Finally, the attic was turned into a temporary morgue and throughout the night she found herself crying on the shoulders of strangers who, head bared, repeated: 'Ah, he was one hell of a man. One hell of a man, I'm telling you. We won't see one like him for a long time to come.'

At eight o'clock the next morning the procession set off.

They hadn't jolted along more than a few yards than the horses released a golden, sweet-smelling heap of dung that made the children burst out laughing. Despite their mourning attire, they had not known quite how to behave since the death of Razyé. Now, spared his scornful remarks and his constant savagery, they had the feeling of being liberated. Hosannah had told them they would now wear patent-leather shoes, dress in silk poplin and eat, like white folk, the choicest morsels, chicken every day off Limoges porcelain plates. And yet the red eyes and grief-stricken expression of their mother affected them. And then this silent, sombre and brutal father had been part of their lives, like the alleys on the Place de la Victoire, the cathedral bell that woke them for mass at dawn and the big dilapidated house they were going to leave, according to Hosannah, where other children would come and play other games.

The coachman cracked his whip over the horses' backs,

but to little effect. They ambled down the rue Frébault. They crossed the Canal, swollen with muddy waters from the previous night's rain. They trundled past the almshouse and through the ever-open gates of the cemetery on the Morne-Miquel. The growing crowd of idle onlookers stopped, made the sign of the cross and wondered in surprise what sort of funeral this was, with no choirboys swinging incense, no priests chanting in Latin. Then they headed for Les Abymes on the road that wound in and out, white under the sun, between the pink cedars, the Santa Marias and the turpentine-trees.

It was a lovely morning.

7 Death of the Wolf (continued)

Irmine woke up with a start, as if an icy hand had touched her.

She was alone in the middle of the bed. The shutters she had closed herself before going to sleep were open, and the light from the full moon was like a stream of milk flooding the wardrobe, the rocking-chair and the locustwood bed that sailed over the crevices of the old floor. Nobody had lived at l'Engoulvent for ages and ages. So there was no room left for humans. Termites, caterpillars, bats, spiders and all sorts of insects, connoisseurs of silence and the shadows, had settled in. Disturbed by this intrusion, they showed their anger by a high-pitched, scarcely audible commotion, emitting a ticking and a tocking, a whooshing and a swishing. Irmine turned over on her side. It was in this very room, in this very bed, that back from Dominica she had laid beside Razyé, humiliated, ill-treated, two eyes not enough for her tears, but burning with a passion that years of insults had not managed to quell. Now that she had lost him, she had to admit that she loved him as much as that first day, when she had watched him climb down from his horse in front of the terrace at the Belles-Feuilles plantation. Yet could she say she had lost him, since she had never possessed him? He had gone to join the woman who possessed him, who led him like a bear-tamer. Well, that's what he hoped. And that was why he had accepted his death so calmly, almost with a smile.

She got up and ran to the window.

She looked out again with surprising pleasure at the landscape she'd never forgotten in her worst dreams. Guinea grass had pushed up through the flagstones in the yard and a flowerless, fruitless guava-tree grew gnarled and twisted in the middle. Beyond the ruins of the stables – a few brick walls, a few heaps of corrugated iron – nothing had changed. A few more thorn-bushes, a few more wild acacias, a few more columnar cactus and prickly pear, the savanna was the same arid wasteland stretching out under the white moonlight. The same trees were flattened by the fury of the wind and seemed on the verge of taking off in the direction of the sea to escape it. The sea, however, kept her freedom intact. Way down below, she dashed against the foot of the cliffs in her rage and swelled with waves as far as the shore of La Désirade.

Some twenty years earlier, as an innocent young thing convinced that she was right, she had followed Razyé's footsteps through this yard and of her own accord had locked up her youth in this rat-hole. How many tears had she shed on her pillow afterwards! How many escape plans had she drawn up during the day, only to have them undone during the night! When her memory took stock of the years gone by, she had trouble counting the moments of happiness: the birth of her children, their first suck on her breast, their first kisses and little words of affection. All the rest had been nothing but suffering and solitude. Yet now that she found herself free, free to 'start her life all over again', as the simple-minded say, she realized that she had lost her inclination for life, like a sick person who recuperates too late to recover her appetite. And she even realized that in a way she regretted none of it. If she were given the power to be born again, she would relive her life the same way. With the same man. In fact she regretted only one thing: not having been able to change Razyé. Perhaps she hadn't known how to love him, for then she would have cured him of Cathy. Love is a miracle. It works in magical ways. Her thoughts went out to him, solitary as he always had been, once again abandoned by the world in a narrow, uncomfortable space under a layer of stony ground at the edge of the cliff, and her eyes filled with tears. She had the feeling that she also had turned her back on him. She had been able to sleep like an innocent child while he was wasting away in exile. She slipped on her clothes and crept out of the room. Two bedrooms opened onto the landing on either side of the stairwell that was now as black as an oven. One of them had been the late Justin's. Perhaps if there was one thing she could reproach Razyé for, it was having forced her to share Justin's bed, that rum-soaked wreck drifting on a sea of regret for his beloved. Fortunately, his illusions had dampened his manhood. Night after night he vainly attempted to plant his flabby penis between her thighs. When he had died, she had thanked the Lord with all her heart. The other room had belonged to Razyé. Here she had put the little girls who after much crying had ended up falling asleep. L'Engoulvent, with its smell of a freshly-opened tomb, its spiders tangled in their webs in every nook and cranny, its bats hanging stiffly upside down in the window casements and the squeaking of its thousand invisible tenants amidst the dust, had woken all their fears – sure that spirits and werewolves were haunting the room, sure that under the bedcovers the people in league with the devil had folded up their skins and flown out through the attic windows with a great beating of wings. Hosannah had only been able to calm them down by chanting one of those old slave laments that the children of Africa used to sing in memory of everything they had lost. Irmine set foot on the first step of the stairs and the creak of the boards sent the rats scurrying between her legs, almost tripping her up. In the living-room, the candle lit by Hosannah had long wept its last drip of tallow, but the moon was driving its shards of light through the holes in the walls. Under the kitchen range a couple of mongooses were watching over their litter and hissed furiously as she went by.

Outside was the stillness of the night.

Irmine set off in the direction of the cliff. As might have been expected, the priest at Petit-Canal had refused to give his blessing to Razyé, a scoundrel, guilty of having stirred up social unrest and sown thoughts of revenge in the child-like souls of the former slaves. So she had taken her courage in both hands and recited all alone over the coffin the Twenty-Third Psalm.

The Lord is my shepherd; I shall not want.
He makes me to lie down in green pastures;
He leads me beside the still waters.
He restores my soul; He leads me in the paths of
  righteousness for His name's sake.
Yea, though I walk through the valley of the shadow
  of death, I will fear no evil.

Deep down she blamed herself for chanting these hollow words and paying homage to rites she no longer believed in. For there was no love lost between her and the Good Lord, so inaptly named, who spoiled some and destroyed others and shared out happiness and good fortune so unequally. What's more she hated all those priests, round-shouldered and simpering, whom she had known since she was a child and who now despised her because she had married beneath her colour. And yet she had a weak spot. She could not bear to bury the man she loved like a wretched animal. She arrived in sight of the graveyard, where the scrub grew among the rocks and pushed open what was left of the gate.

She had respected Razyé's wishes and the undertakers had lowered his coffin into Cathy's tomb, beside her remains. She moved the flowers to one side and sat down on the gravestone. It was now inscribed with two names, one below the other, united as if on a marriage register.

Yet she who had hated Cathy for all these years no longer felt jealous of this inscription. The two wooden coffins lay side by side, touching. In both of them there was nothing more than flesh and bones crumbling into dust. Her heart told her that Razyé was still forging on alone in his tunnel, his fists and hands bleeding from hammering against the wall that hemmed him in, more formidable than the Great Wall of China.

It would be too simple if death avenged us for all the failures we accumulate while on earth; if, once in the other world, we could possess everything we wanted. Losers we are when alive, losers we remain in eternity.

Suddenly she felt exhausted, tired to death, frightened at the thought of all those years she would have to live through, in even greater solitude. Without a man and his savagery to fill her days. Without those vague moments of tenderness that gave her hope for a brighter future. Her children would grow up. They would no longer need her. Even Fréda, who for the time being clung to her skirt and could only say her name. She would grow old. She was already old. She would die. She would set off for the cemetery and lie alone, alone as in life, for an eternity. She slid helplessly to the ground, feeling the scratch of the prickles and weeds through her clothes. She closed her eyes, swollen with water, and the night descended around her.

A moonbeam caressed Gengis's forehead so persistently that he opened his eyes. One of the window shutters was silhouetted against a large square of sky and the room was flooded with moonlight. Beside him Zoulou was snoring, his mouth open. He realized therefore that they had both ended up falling asleep in the foul-smelling room. After they had talked in whispers for some time to keep each other's spirits up, he had remained motionless, a heavy weight on his chest. However hard he squeezed his eyelids tight, sleep didn't come. On their black screen flickered the terrible events of these past days. The wake ceremony in the suffocating heat of the attic. All those strangers dressed up like Baron Samedi, with frock coats, canes, top hats, lugubrious expressions and appropriate words.

'Oh yes, he was one hell of a man!'

If that was the truth, why did everyone hate him like poison? Why did they say he was a devil?

The scent of the gardenias had been more pungent than all the other flowers. The following morning the undertakers' men, indifferent and almost grinning, jostled the enormous coffin down the stairs, banging it against the wall at every turn. The journey from La Pointe to Petit-Canal seemed endless in the sun and the dust, with the dogs barking and the children running behind the carriages. All the while, wrapped in her veil, Irmine acted the weeping widow, to such an extent that he felt like shaking her like a plum-tree. What was she crying for exactly? For the man who treated her as you wouldn't think of treating an animal? He could remember how almost every day the commiserating Hosannah had applied compresses of arnica to her swollen, smashed face. Like the other children, he could still hear the insults and the contempt Razyé showered her with as soon as he set foot in the yard. And all those women their father had no scruples bringing into the house and whom you could hear clucking away at some

282

ungodly hour. One night he had come face to face with Razyé and one of these women on the first-floor landing. Razyé was wearing one of his tight-lipped, taciturn expressions, but the woman was painted up like a carnival float and showed him all thirty-two teeth in a smile. Then she stroked him with her hand that stank of patchouli and cried: 'Mi bel ti moun, mi!' (What a lovely little boy!)

Razyé II had avenged them all when he made love to one of their father's mistresses. They never tired of hearing him embellish and embroider the story of how he had made her feel like a real woman and how, under his rule, she had called out for her papa, her maman and asked forgiveness from the Good Lord. Unfortunately, one fine day, Razyé had uncovered the secret and Razyé II had had to run for his life. He got a message through to them that he was hiding near Saint-Louis on Marie-Galante, and Gengis dreamed of going to join him.

Gengis hated his father. This was a constant subject of argument with Zoulou, who took his father's side and invented all kinds of reasons and circumstances to mitigate his guilt. It was because a woman had deserted him, it was because of the evil in black men's hearts, it was because of the racism of the white Creoles. It was one thing, then another that had turned him into Satan himself. As for Gengis, he felt none of this compassion. Every minute of his life he raged at the absurdity of his name. He had learned in an encyclopaedia that it was the name of a khan in Mongolia who had gone down in history for his massacres and fearsome character. He had read over and over again the all-to-succinct accounts of the rapes, murders, burning and looting his homonym had committed. Insidiously, this monstrous heritage his father had imposed on him while he was too small to fight back was seeping into his blood and turning him into a monster as well. That's why he was rebellious, violent and always up to mischief. He tortured blackbirds and wood pigeons in the yard. He terrorized his younger sisters, especially Cassandre with her irritatingly chubby cherub-like face. He wished he could have raped and tormented women, as Razyé had done before him. In his dreams he roamed the streets of La Pointe on busy market days and stationed himself at the crossroads. Not content with a few punches here and there, he brandished his cutlass, slashing everyone who didn't run fast enough. The storm channels grew red with blood. The heaps of corpses were piled sky high. He didn't attack just the white Creoles for the sake of justice, but the Indians, the mulattos and the blacks, especially the blacks who think they are untouchable victims and never stop harping on the evil that's been done to them. He burnt the great houses and the cabins; the cane-fields as well as the coffee and banana plantations. He put Guadeloupe to the fire and the sword. For whatever their colour, men do not deserve the life they are given.

At one point, seeing his mother's grief, Zoulou had started to cry as well. As for Cassandre, girls have no character of their own and always do what you expect them to do. He alone had remained dry-eyed. Even when the bearers had lowered the coffin to the very bottom of the grave, even when they had thrown in a few withered flowers at this late hour and shovelled in rocks, even when Irmine in a faint voice had recited the Twenty-Third Psalm.

He carefully got out of bed so as not to disturb Zoulou and went over to the window. He wondered if he could be really awake, seeing his surroundings transformed by the moonlight. The bleak landscape had turned into the fantasy land of a watercolour. The sky merged with the earth in a golden colour. The desolate savanna became a mysterious realm of blue where horsemen galloped, their soft scarves

284

wrapped around their heads. The shriek of the insects, the hissing of the mongooses and the barking of the stray dogs harmonized in unison with the voice of the sea.

On hearing this strange music he was flooded with an emotion he had never felt before. He leaned over and saw his mother hurriedly cross the yard, her greying hair floating down her back, her shapeless robe pulled tight over her portly figure. He realized how she had changed since the time when she used to lean over his cradle and take him in her arms to whisper sweet nothings. For the first time, perhaps, he felt pity for her. Where was she running as fast as she could? Was she going to meditate on the grave of her tormentor?

He could see all too easily how she was going to spend the rest of her life. She would padlock herself in the mourning of widowhood. She would offer up prayers to the Good Lord for the departed. By cleaning out her memory, she would convince herself he had not been such a bad husband.

He went down the stairs in turn, oblivious to the commotion his presence was causing. But when he walked out into the yard and looked left and right, Irmine had disappeared. Once again everything around him had been transformed. Suddenly, the moon had been snuffed from the sky and replaced by an ebony blackness. Crawling on its belly like a python, it had stealthily extinguished the stars and blotted out the space above the savanna and the sea. And yet Gengis could see as if it had been daylight. As if his senses had been stimulated, his sight sharpened and his hearing quickened, like the day he had smoked Indian hemp with Zoulou. He could make out every spike on the thistles, every thorn on the trees and every rock embedded in the earth. He could hear the slightest sound, from a procession of ants under the roots to the dry flap of the wings of a flight of chicken hawks over La Désirade in the distance. He hesitated, a little frightened, then ran as fast as his legs would carry him, his feet touching his behind, zigzagging across the scrubland.

Someone was sitting on one of the tombs.

Even at this distance he needed no one to tell him it was the silhouette of his father. Sitting motionless, Razyé was dressed in his funeral attire, his watch-chain hanging across his stomach and his white shirt contrasting with his frock-coat. His clothes were all crumpled as if he had slept in them, his shirt collar was open and his hair oddly tangled. Father and son looked at each other. Strangely, the sight of Razyé had not sent the usual little shiver of fear and hatred down Gengis's spine. He got the feeling that from now on there was nothing more to fear from him – neither his blows, nor his insults, nor his scorn. It was as if he had become his equal, even his superior, as if the roles between them were reversed, as if he were facing a child.

He walked up to him. Razyé turned his head and remarked: 'It's not you I'm waiting for!'

Gengis, who the moment before had felt grown up, was suddenly ashamed of standing there, barefoot in his too tight pyjamas and stammered: 'Who are you waiting for? Maman?'

Razyé laughed as if he had just heard a good joke and shook his head.

'No, it's not her either.'

He remained silent for a while and then continued (from the way he talked Gengis felt the words were not meant for him and he would have done better to leave).

'In fact I don't even know any longer why I'm waiting. I'm stuck here like a rock in a patch of ground. Soaked by the rain, dried by the heat. I watch the sun rise then go down behind the jagged line of mountains, then come up again. I see the clouds scurrying one behind the other in the sky, sometimes as white as spilt milk from an overturned calabash or the orange blossom in the hair of a young bride; at other times, as blue as the enamel of the sea below, then purple like a bishop's robe and finally black, a shade I know well since it colours every day of my life. One day, when I was at my wits' end, someone advised me to drink some rum. I listened to him, I drank some rum, but its fire turned to ice inside my body. Someone else told me to have children, they're the remedy for everything – mourning, solitude and even death. So I did. Four, five, six, I've lost count. But I felt nothing for these little heaps of flesh. Sometimes I couldn't even look at them, they made me so angry and disgusted. I also smoked herbs that make you talk off the top of your head, but nothing came out. I kept my head and all my grief that stuck in my throat like the bone of a red snapper. Now I'm here and I don't even know any longer why I'm waiting. I can see a path stretching out in front of me. I have to follow it, but I know it leads nowhere and in the end I shall be back where I started. I am tired. I wish it were over.

'What am I going to do with all this time on my hands?'

8   Roro the Fisherman's Tale

I haven't done anything wrong. I have nothing to reproach myself for. I took him to Dominica because he was my friend and he asked me to. When the winds blow in the right direction, from Saint-Louis to Roseau, it's a breeze. Half a day at the most. So I didn't even think of refusing.

The sea's my maman, my wife, my mistress, my child and my sister!

When I climb into my *Marie, Mère de Dieu*, my boat daubed in blue and white, the colours of the Virgin Mary, and I lean on my oars, I become another person. I'm no longer a nonentity mocked by the children and nicknamed Roro Rum because of what happened to my papa. I forget the rat-hole where I live just two steps from the seashore. I forget the rags I have for clothes. I forget I haven't got a wife or a child, I forget I've lost my maman and my papa. That I've got nothing to warm my heart or my body. Except for my boat, a few bamboo lobster-pots, a few nets I patch up as best I can. And the sea.

I prefer the bad weather days when it squalls, when the waves rise up to soak the dome of the sky, when a black bar shuts out the horizon and you can see neither Terre-de-Bas nor Terre-de-Haut, the islands of Les Saintes, and even less Dominica, usually lying close by on the other side of the channel. But I also like those days when, lapping over the sandbanks, the water takes on the colour of hope and

288

the sand sparkles white under the sun like the teeth of a handsome black woman.

Maman has gone where we'll all go one day or another, a few hours after I was born. Yet I didn't grieve as a small boy because I had my papa.

My father was a master seiner. His family, who supplied the fish for the Murats' table, had never really known slavery, so to speak. They were a proud and upstanding race.

At eighteen, papa had four boats under him and as many accompaniers, water-beaters, divers and look-out men who sailed off with him in the early morning to net the shoals of fish in the ocean depths. Most of the time his seine brought in loads of cavali, tarpons and tuna. Under their weight the net swelled like the belly of a pregnant woman and seemed on the verge of tearing. When he came home with a good catch like that, there was jubilation in Saint-Louis. People came dancing out of their cabins to help the men carry in the fish. The children played hammock in the nets and everyone hauled them up onto the shore. In the evening when we went to bed we had our stomachs full and hunger did not lie down beside us on our pillows.

Sometimes papa did not go far and was merely content to let his net drag in the creeks around Marie-Galante. On those days he brought back only silversides and bonefish, just for him and his crew.

Because of his fine catches, everybody in Saint-Louis looked up to him. When he walked by in the street, his *bakoua* hat firmly clapped on his hair scorched by the salt, people greeted him with respect.

'Good day, master Ben!'

He didn't even answer. On Sundays he recited the words of the mass louder than anyone else. He placed banknotes on the collection tray and was the first to walk to the altar to take communion. In the evenings he won against everyone at dice and dominoes at the rum-shop. On his way home, he had only to look at the woman he liked and she would follow him on the spot to warm him up in bed. And then from one day to the next he took to drinking rum, and that was the end of him. People say someone jealous cast a *kimbwa* on him on account of a woman, and this could be true. I don't know. When he was young he didn't gulp down any more rum than others of his age – a few neat white rums a day. Then it became a litre, a litre and a half and two litres. From that moment, he lost his way to the sea. He got up and went to bed in vomit. He slept on the path, on the beach, on the rocks, in the mud and on the sand, wherever sleep took him. He imagined rats, bats and centipedes crawling over his belly, his stomach and his face, and he would scream like a hog being slaughtered. One drizzly morning they found him lying stiff under a manchineel tree. Rain had fallen during the night and his entire body was burnt. He was unrecognizable. They threw him in a hole under the casuarinas in the cemetery and the priest did not even take the trouble to come out of his presbytery for him. I inherited his boat, his nets and his cabin made of planks next to a wild banyan-tree. Every All Saints' Day I go and light candles for him because to me papa was not a bad sort.

When First-Born Sabrimol arrived in Saint-Louis, he immediately became my friend. How did we meet? One day while I was minding my own business a brute tried to hit me out of pure spite in front of Ma Tètèche's shop and he stepped in between us. Yes, that's how our friendship began. When they saw we were inseparable, people made fun of us.

'Roro Rum and First-Born? Now we've seen everything!'

Nevertheless I've got a brain to understand and two eyes to see what's going on around me. I understood full well that First-Born was hiding something under his rags, his bare feet and that look of his; I realized that it was not his real name. I could see he was no ordinary fellow like us, no orphan abandoned under the sun. The fine features of his face, the way he spoke French, the way he walked erect and drank with moderation all told me that his placenta was not buried under any old tree; rather under a locustwood, a West Indian mahogany-tree or an ebony from Senegal.

On Saturdays and Sundays I went and fetched him before sunrise and we would set off to sea. I would row as far as the islands of Les Saintes, Petite-Terre, La Désirade and Dominica. Sometimes even further. The sea is not every-one's cup of tea. At first he would climb into my boat trembling, looking around him at the waves, the waves that rolled on for ever.

'I'm scared, Roro!' he would say in a tiny little voice.

I would laugh.

'What for, for goodness sake? If the sea hugs you in its arms, you'll forget all about Asturias. Believe me, it'll be the tenderest kiss you've ever had. What woman's body is as soft and vast as hers?'

While I rowed he sat motionless at the back of the boat and stared at the changing sails of the sky. I didn't ask any questions and he didn't tell me anything. One day, while we were coming back from Terre-de-Haut-des-Saintes, he suddenly asked me: 'Do you know my papa's name?'

'What a question!' I replied, shrugging my shoulders. 'How do you expect me to know it if you've never told me?'

He took on an inspired look, like someone about to sail on the high seas.

'Razyé!'

Hearing that name gave me such a start. It was as if he had said his father's name was Lucifer or his papa's called Beelzebub or any other name given to the spirit of Evil. He then told me the story of his family. While he talked, for the first time I noticed little details that hadn't struck me before. How thick his mop of hair was and how it grew into a widow's peak over his forehead. How his eyes stared, black and shining. How his mouth was red and sensual. Now that I think about it, his face was rather unsettling. He stared at me again.

'Do you know why I'm hiding here, in the filth of Tonin's cabin?'

'No, I don't,' I stammered, still under the shock.

'If there's one thing I take after him for,' he went on, 'it's my taste for women. Ever since I was small I've been like that, I can't help it. If Irmine, my maman, had cherished me, caressed me and taken me in her arms, things would have been very different. Like all other boys my thoughts would have lurked around her bed. Nothing more. Alas! maman couldn't bear me. So on Sundays when, unbeknownst to papa, *mabo* Julie took me to church with my brothers, I would stand behind the confessional and spy on the Virgin Mary suckling the Infant Jesus. My blood burned, thinking I could be in the place of this baby. Later I started to hang around the Morne-à-Cayes, behind the prison, around the hospice, in the districts where the women hang out. I went into their bars to get a smell of them, to try and make out the shape of their breasts under their loose-fitting dresses. And that's how all my misfortune began.'

He reeled off all this and lots more besides. How his papa found out he had taken his pleasure in the bed of one of his mistresses and how he had almost killed him. While he talked, I wondered whether he wasn't worrying himself for nothing. Blood is thicker than water. Who knows if his papa hadn't already forgotten all this nonsense! And yet I remembered what I had heard about Razyé and his tiger's heart, and I said to myself perhaps he was right.

And that's all I know.

When he started paying visits to Mademoiselle Cathy de Linsseuil, the schoolteacher, he had me believe it was to learn natural science, algebra and geometry. And I believed him.

Asturias' brothers broke open the door of my cabin and then they threw me on the floor and pummelled me with their fists and feet, shouting: 'Scoundrel! We'll teach you! Didn't you know what he put in our sister's belly? You deliberately helped him to escape.'

That's not true. I took him to Roseau because he was my friend and he asked me to. I know nothing else, nothing. And that's the truth.

After having almost beaten me to death, Asturias' brothers hacked at the wood of my cabin with their cutlasses and left. You would have thought a hurricane had gone through it.

When we pushed the boat into the water it was close to ten o'clock in the evening. You could count the stars in the sky. No need for the lantern to light the velvet of the sea. Sailing down towards Grand-Bourg we kept the shore in sight and all along we could see the oil-lamps in the cabins flickering like candles in a cemetery on All Souls' Day. Then the blackness blotted everything out. Not a sound could be heard except for the lapping of the water against the boat's hull and the wind whistling in the sails. Flying-fish, their bodies gleaming like knife-blades in the dark, jumped into the air as if they wanted to keep an eye on us. Flocks of seabirds flew over our heads, so low we could almost touch them. Here and there we caught sight of fishermen dragging their nets from their boats, looking to surprise the tuna-fish and sea-bream deep in their sleep.

Both of them were sitting at the back of the boat, with their wicker baskets between their legs. At first I had trouble recognizing her with the headtie pulled tight over her forehead like an old woman. They didn't say a word to each other. They didn't touch each other. You would have thought they didn't know each other. I was flabbergasted to see them sitting there side by side. I didn't understand what was going on, since he never told me anything about her. Except that she was his schoolteacher and was nice to him. Not superior at all. Sometimes I gave her a skewer of fish and he brought me her thanks. I had so many questions I wanted to ask him but couldn't because she was sitting there. Unanswered, they went swirling round and round in my head. Why had he left Saint-Louis? Had his terrible papa discovered where he was hiding and come to kill him? Why was he taking Mademoiselle Cathy with him? What was going on between them? About midnight, still without saying a word, he put his arm around her waist and made her lay her head on his knees. Then he sat rigid, without moving an inch, as if he was afraid he'd prevent her from sleeping. Around two o'clock in the morning there was a chill in the air, the wind got up and the sky blackened as if we were in for a squall. Fortunately, it didn't last. The clouds scudded away and the night sky cleared again. At sunrise the mountains of Dominica, crisscrossed by the silver threads of rivers, loomed up in front of us like a solid wall. He woke her up and all three of us watched as land drew near.

In spite of the early hour, what a commotion was going on in the harbour when we entered! Roseau is busier than Saint-Louis and even Grand-Bourg. Travellers say that only Fort-de-France in Martinique is busier. There was no counting the number of three-masters, schooners, barges and small fishing-boats rubbing against each other's hulls. The smoke from steamships blackened the air. First-Born took me by the arm and held out a letter murmuring: 'Count two times seven days and give it to someone you trust to deliver it personally to maman in La Pointe. Don't post it, please. You never know.'

He hugged me as if he would never see me again on this earth. It was then, with a grief-stricken heart, I had to ask him.

'But tell me why are you leaving? What is there in Roseau? How long are you going to stay here?'

His only answer was his finger on his lips.

'Shh!' he whispered.

He embraced me again. Then he took her by the arm and set off towards the town. I stood there, looking helpless, my feet in the sand, not knowing what I ought to do. And then, after a while, I got back in my boat and went back out to sea. I had lost my only friend.

That's all I know.

9 By Way of a First Epilogue

... He found my trail. So I had to flee even further to escape him. I wonder whether we shall ever see each other again in this world.

Your First-Born.

How could she get through to the young man who sent her these lines that the papa he so dreaded had passed on? Irmine turned the letter over and over in her hands but could find no indication where it came from. The paper was ordinary. The ink purple. The messenger had disappeared before Hosannah had had time to offer him a goblet of water. Grief seemed to blind her as she thought of her lonely, hapless son, exiled in a distant land.

It was bright daylight. All around her the air was filled with the smell of turpentine, the sound of hammers and the rasp of handsaws as the workers banged nails into the roof, replaced beams and repainted the walls. From one day to the next Irmine woke up to find herself one of the richest women on the island. But she had ignored the advice of the notary, and did not have the heart to leave La Pointe to which so many memories moored her. Monsieur Desfossés, who had untangled Razyé's succession, wasted his time telling her in all manners of ways that Guadeloupe was going to the dogs. Yesterday's propertied classes had become today's dispossessed. The white Creoles were rushing to buy berths on the steamships and sailing empty-handed for Pau, Bordeaux, anywhere they could hope to start a new life. Their country properties and their town houses were being auctioned off to the firstcomer. Matouba, Grippière, Sainte-Marthe, Le Moule, the great plantations were being parcelled off. For the price of a mortgage. There was no counting the number of mulattos who were moving into the ancestral homes and the blacks taking over good acres of sugar-cane. If she wanted to, she could have the biggest estate. She had stood firm and settled on repairing at great cost the house on the Place de la Victoire. She had spared no expense. The pink stone had come from Italy, the roof from a factory in Trois-Ilets in Martinique and the red cedar wood from the forests of Guyana. In the dining-room painters delicately drew their brushes over the tiles and brought to life an imaginary town with children, fountains, flower-sellers and horsemen seated erect on their mounts. Gardeners dug over the garden and planted the yard with hibiscus, lemon and pomegranate-trees. Irmine had also bought a horse and tilbury complete with coachman, and hired three servants, one to do the washing, one to do the housework and the third to serve at table. Since she did not go to church and never paid any visits, the only time the coachman got the horse out and put on his livery was once a week when he drove her to Razyé's grave. As for Hosannah, she had nothing else to do except spend her time chattering, tasting the sauces and criticizing the colour of the washing put out to bleach in the yard, the amount of starch or the heat of the flat-irons on the coals.

Finally, Irmine had found a meaning to her life.

With Razyé's death a chapter had closed and everything could have gone back to how it was when she was a child. But she could not accept that way of life any longer. Once her initial tears and despondency were over, she was seen to show a determination that perhaps she had never possessed. It was as if the deceased's temperament, of which she herself had been a victim, passed into her body and she was determined to carry out his revenge to the very end. It was for him and his memory that she restored the house on the Place de la Victoire to its former glory. She wanted the *mabos* cradling their infants under the sandbox-trees, the lovers strolling along the paths and even the good-for-nothings sitting on the benches to lift up their eyes at the balconies, the frieze and the dormer-windows and say to themselves, trembling with emotion: 'Ah yes! That's where Razyé once lived.' After the school holidays, she decided she would send Zoulou and Gengis to a boarding-school in France run by Jesuits. They were already rich. They would graduate with flying colours. For the time being, however, their life was hell. They had difficulty finding their way in their new life for the memory of their father floated around them like a bad smell. Both their money and their colour were unpardonable. At school the teachers showered them with poor marks. Students in the same class avoided them; the bigger ones beat them up. Every day they came home with their clothes torn. She would have to help them smash open the doors of La Pointe's polite society, locked against them, and burn down the hypocrisy. Her heart ached because one way or another she would lose all her boys. First it was Justin-Marie. Then Razyé II. Soon these two. Too bad. It had to be done.

She re-read the letter she had dropped in her lap.

'I wonder whether we shall ever see each other again in this world.'

In spite of herself, tears rolled down her cheeks.

At this moment a little hand gently pushed open the door and Cassandre entered. It was as if she had sensed her mother's grief, for without a word she ran towards her and buried her face in her lap. Irmine nestled her face against her soft, sweet-smelling body. Within a few weeks, Cassandre had been transformed. Like the other children she had exchanged the drab, shapeless clothes in which Razyé's miserliness had encased her for the most expensive attire. Over a honeycomb embroidered blouse she wore a blue silk velvet pinafore dotted with tiny bunches of pink flowers. The pinafore flared slightly above the knee, revealing her plump legs squeezed into immaculately white stockings, also embroidered with pink flowers. She was shod in patent-leather shoes with a buckle. She looked like one of those porcelain dolls little girls are given at Christmas. Not a trace of the Bambara ancestress in this one. With her light skin, so much lighter than the other children, and her hair carefully smoothed with brilliantine, everyone could easily forget she was not what she seemed. So the nuns at the Saint-Joseph de Cluny boarding-school, usually so finicky, adored her. Last 15 August, during the procession of the Virgin of Massabielle, she had been given the supreme honour of appearing as a white-robed angel, hands joined and muslin wings wide open on her back.

What never ceased to enchant Irmine was how every day she was struck by her daughter's growing resemblance to Aymeric, the beloved brother, in spite of everything the saint, the martyr, the master that everyone still mourned, the late heavenly cherub. Cassandre had his azure-coloured eyes, his delicately curled lips and, despite her young age, his serious, considerate expression. When she spoke, it was with the same sanctimonious tone of voice. Irmine could already see the time when her lovely face and her bank account would be coveted by the sons of the most aristocratic families on the island. They would fight over her and she would cast a look of disdain. Then she would walk to the altar wrapped in yards and yards of white tulle, and those who had spoken ill of her papa and jeered at her maman would be punished.

The little girl, who knew her powers over Irmine, caressed her cheek and asked tenderly: 'Why are you crying, Mamita?'

She had invented this pretty Spanish-sounding word all on her own, for she hadn't yet started learning this language at school. Irmine hesitated.

'I'm thinking about your big brother,' she simply said. 'Have you forgotten him? He used to love you so much.'

Cassandre shook her head violently.

'Last night I saw him in a dream,' she declared in a soothing voice.

She often announced dreams in order to comfort her maman. But unlike her illustrious precursor, the scenes she described were always joyful and happy: sarabands of pink clouds at sunset, farandoles of girls in brocaded bodices and concerts of crickets tuning up like violinists in the fading dusk. All this playfulness made everyone laugh. Irmine jumped.

'In a dream? And what was he doing?'

Cassandre put on a mysterious air.

'He looked happy. He was living in a big house with a garden all around it.'

PART FOUR

Roseau

1   Life in Roseau

The wind was shaking the shirt-tails of the sea in all directions and the waves were surging back towards the houses
in Roseau.

First-Born set down on the sand the cases of codfish from
Newfoundland whose weight was digging into his shoulder, and breathed in the peppery smell of the wind. For
weeks he had knocked on every door – from the warehouses, trading companies and stores to the churches and
prisons. He had applied to be driver on the Cabot Lodge
plantation, coachman for a family of white Creoles and
bodyguard for a politician. Everywhere he had been refused
and the only job he could find was unloading the ships from
every corner of the earth, their bellies filled with drums of
lard, demijohns of wine, jars of olive-oil and bolts and bolts
of calico cloth and silks. At the end of the week he took his
place in a line of wretches and received enough rice and
beans to fill his stomach. Cathy too had looked for work.
She had been refused for other reasons. She was too pretty,
too clean, too obviously well-educated. Where did she come
from with a face like that? So she learned to weave baskets
that she tried to sell in the market like the other women.
They lived in one bare, dirty room above Simmons Bros. All
day long, when she was not at St Mary's, she could hear
the rumble of handcarts and the employees swearing on the
ground floor. At first, the inhabitants of Roseau, spying on

Cathy and First-Born, took them for brother and sister they looked so much alike. But when Cathy's belly began to swell in such an unmistakable way, they realized they had been wrong.

Cathy never complained and never said one word louder than the next. But the harsh life she lived scored two vertical lines at the corners of her mouth and traced around her eyes two dark circles. Her legs no longer carried her. Only her belly grew round in her emaciated body. For First-Born, watching her lose her youth in solitude and poverty was the cross he bore every day the Good Lord made. Hundreds of times he had made up his mind to return to Guadeloupe. The more he thought about it, the more he told himself that Razyé could not be that much of a monster. If he saw him with a wife on his arm, surely he would forgive him the sins of his youth. He rejected such an idea, however, because he had never had the courage to confess to Cathy who he was. One day, when she was describing the final moments of her beloved papa for the hundredth time, her eyes brimming with tears, she suddenly shouted: 'You know who is responsible for his death? Razyé! It's Razyé who killed him!'

Thereupon she told him a story that he knew already, but from a different point of view. But he hadn't dreamed of contradicting her on the grounds that you don't get mixed up in people's personal affairs. Hadn't it been whispered, long ago, that Aymeric had stolen Razyé's woman in a dishonest way? A man whose woman has been stolen is perfectly entitled to take his revenge in every way possible and who could blame him under such circumstances? He had been too terrified by the hatred that had transformed Cathy. She was unrecognizable. It was as if she had turned into a witch. Her cheeks turned the colour of burning coals, her eyes flashed and her mouth twisted around the words that were falling over each other. It was some time before she got control of herself. Good Lord, what would she do if she found out that he was Razyé's son? She would probably kill him, for there was a hidden violence in her that sometimes surfaced. So he said nothing. Neither that day nor the following. But as time went by, his silence slowly strangled him. He could no longer bear the identity he had fabricated for himself that had started out in fun: the illegitimate orphan of a mother whose father, one of the merchants along the wharf, had never wanted anything to do with him. He burned with the longing to rid himself of these effects and recover his true identity.

Perhaps because of this inner tension, his love for Cathy diminished considerably. She weighed him down like a burden. Her body no longer aroused impatience, anguish or surges of passion. He forced himself to make love to her and each time he had the sacrilegious feeling of embracing a second self, curiously transformed into a woman. He came to look upon her as a sister – cherished perhaps in the bottom of his heart, but humdrum, boring, even painful to bear.

He picked up the cases of Newfoundland cod and balanced them again on his shoulder. Then, digging the soles of his feet in the sand, he set off for the Sherbett store.

Mr Sherbett was born in Roseau, but his family came from Liverpool. After having made their money from sugar-cane, they had recently sold their plantations at a profit and gone into trade. Mr Sherbett, who owned two of the biggest warehouses in town, was smoking a Cuban cigar. The size of his bank account could be measured from the quality of the English cloth he was dressed in and his huge pocket-watch. He motioned to First-Born to come closer, wrinkled his nose at the smell and said in Creole: 'I want to do my stock-taking this weekend. I pay a shilling a day.'

First-Born looked at the greasy hair and the white skinned face that was pink and shiny from the heat. It was men like this that his father had humiliated, ruined and forced into exile. And what was he doing? Bowing in front of them, saying 'Yes Sir!' accepting their money. What a downfall! He felt filled with a sudden rage and thought of calling the other labourers to his aid. Like a ringleader he would shout the order to break open the cases they were carrying, wreck the place, sprinkle the floor with kerosene and, as they used to do in the cane-fields, burn the warehouse. The flames would glow red and Mr Sherbett would flee like a frightened cockroach. Instead of which, he merely said: 'A pas asé!' (not enough).

A little surprised, but knowing he would find dozens of other volunteers, Mr Sherbett shrugged his shoulders.

'As you like.'

Then he calmly went back to studying his registers. Mad as hell, First-Born walked out onto the pavement. The streets of Roseau, in every traveller's opinion the smartest town in the Caribbean, crisscrossed at right angles between the trunks of the matalpas and jacarandas. The blue, green and pink façades of the tall houses interlocked together like some gigantic pieces of a child's puzzle. The green of the lawns in the parks, the brilliance of the flowers in the public gardens, the fashionable crowd, the elegant tilburys and the sharp clip of the horses struck the eye everywhere it looked. Usually, this sight delighted First-Born, who had suffered so much from the filth of Saint-Louis. But that day, he could only think of his shame. A coward! That's what he was. How much longer was he going to remain in servitude? Slavery had been abolished for over half a century. Back home, ebony-skinned politicians spoke out for the black man whereas he was subjected to the tyranny of a white man. He walked as far as the wharf and stopped in front of the *Elizabeth Regina*, the somewhat shabby-looking steamship that once a month sailed from Roseau to La Pointe.

It was a day of departure. On deck, sailors busied themselves importantly. Loaded with trunks, wicker baskets and all kinds of bundles, passengers were hurrying up the gangway. Relatives and friends were exchanging kisses or already crying for those leaving. Temptation seized him: all he had to do was slip into the crowd, bide his time hidden in the hold and secretly climb off at La Pointe. He would return home. He would hug his brothers and sisters whom he sorely missed, especially little Cassandre. He would dry Irmine's eyes.

'Maman, I know I've made you cry. It's over now. Your son has returned.'

At night, in the bed that he had outgrown, he would sleep the lost sleep of his childhood.

He quickly elbowed his way up the rope gangway when the thought of Cathy stopped him in his tracks. And what would become of her when he was gone? And with a belly as well? He hesitated, turned back, started up again and once again came to a stop.

Wasn't this the end he had often dreamed of? The thought of this soon-to-be-born child he had not wanted was torture to him. He had first of all hoped that Cathy would never reach the end of her nine months, so convinced was he that by perpetuating life they were transgressing a very ancient and formidable order. Alas! Male or female, the egg had clung on. Now that the time of delivery was approaching, he had nightmares of Cathy's thighs spread open in a stream of blood over a little monstrous being – born with a caul, clubfooted, goitrous, crippled and Mongol. He would wake up perspiring and watch her sleeping beside him, bathed in sweat, her head resting on her arm like a wounded child. As they dried, her tears left traces down her cheeks. Out of despair, he showered her with kisses. She would then wake up in turn and look at him with her sad eyes, the same enquiring eyes as his. What had they done to deserve such a life? What crime were they paying for? What nemesis was pursuing them?

No! He couldn't abandon her. They were bound until death. And perhaps beyond.

He was hurrying back down the gangway as quickly as he had gone up when a hand touched him on the shoulder. A mulatto woman, dressed to the nines and bedecked with jewels, flashed her green eyes at him and ordered: 'Hey, you there, carry my luggage!'

A Man Friday! A porter! That's all he was now!

For Cathy, her pregnancy was the last drop in an ocean of misfortune. During the first weeks she had prayed so hard that she had imagined her fruit would rot and drop of its own accord. But the Good Lord hears only what He wants to. Days had dragged on into months and her calvary had continued. What was this child she was carrying? As savage and violent as an Arab horse, kicking the sides of her womb with its hoofs, prancing as far as her stomach, preventing her from drinking, eating, sitting or lying down.

Seeing her rags hang loosely around her, seeing her spit bile into the storm channels, the women in the market told her it must be a girl. Only daughters take to hating their mothers. They cannot tolerate being kept prisoner for months and months in their womb, and fight tooth and nail to break open their jail. To tame her they suggested she take all kinds of herb teas, worm-bush tea, goat-weed and *koklaya*. Touching the mountain of truth, Ada, who had taken her under her wing, shook her head, perplexed.

'All I know is that your blood and your husband's blood

are not in agreement. Why? Don't ask me because I don't know. The spirit's not saying.'

In the end the prisoner had become more docile. Gradually, Cathy's breasts, arms and hollow cheeks gathered flesh again and she could sleep a few hours every night. Something told her she would not survive childbirth, something she had told no one, least of all First-Born. There was no room on this earth for both her and her child. The story that had already played itself out would repeat itself, and she would begin her migration at the very moment her child took its first breath. Strangely, even shockingly, she felt no grief for the unfortunate little baby she had created who would remain motherless here below. She could only think of herself. She would cease to be an orphan. With heart beating like a slave who sees the coast of Guinea on the horizon, she imagined the reunion with her mother. She would not reproach the woman who had never bothered about her. Too happy to be reunited with her, she would throw herself into her arms. She would have her fill of all the kisses she had been storing up since childhood. She would discover the smell of her skin and hair. Then suddenly she realized how naive she was. There would be nothing to smell but the smell of a corpse.

The market stood in the centre of town. All the produce of this patch of land blessed by the Good Lord was piled up here – clusters of plantains, root vegetables, tomatoes, okra and garden eggs. There were also heaps of fruit, from pomegranates, canary-yellow bananas and guavas to seedless pink grapefruit. Cathy stood up. It had been a good day. She had sold all her baskets to the very last one, and her purse was bursting with shillings. She stopped in front of the fishwives and haggled for a pink sea-bream on a banana leaf. The paltriness of her occupations frightened her. Cook. Eat to fill up her belly as best she could. Sleep. Cook and eat again. The time when she taught at school, prepared her lessons and tried to give men's hearts to those little country bumpkins had the flimsiness of a dream. It seemed that all she was left with now were coarse, mechanical thoughts. When she looked at herself in the mirror she saw that she had begun to look like the other women sitting around her in the market – dishevelled, soon to be toothless, rigged out in rags, her face severe and expressionless.

It was probably for these reasons that First-Born could no longer put up with her company and, rather than spend his evenings alone with her, preferred to waste his time at The Last Resort, the bar at the corner of the street where he didn't even drink rum; in bed he turned his back on her, and couldn't even look her in the eyes when he spoke to her. Admittedly she no longer desired him either. The smell of strong tobacco on his lips and any close contact with his body disgusted her. What is love? A bonfire of fluttering leaves that you light in the evening and in the morning is nothing more than a heap of ashes. That's it; that's it exactly. A catch, a *zatrap*. That's it; that's it exactly. You go to bed with a burning heart. You get up with both feet as cold as an old bag of bones. Only the departed remain handsome and desired for ever.

She shuffled up the High Street. Steamships from neighbouring ports must have docked for their crews were running in all directions. The street was filled with a foreign-looking crowd that strolled, window-shopped and stood to admire the monuments: the cathedral, the governor's palace, the courthouse and the brand new square block of Lloyds Bank with its liveried porter greeting customers. He was a former boxer, who in his days of glory they called Battling Joe. All these people were in a festive mood while her own heart was in mourning! Romaine was merciless and was ferociously taking her revenge. She was constantly reminded of the face of the servant-girl she had sent to her death with her son, and caught herself pleading with her as if she were in front of a jury. She hadn't been a bad mistress all the time. She had taught her to read and write. She had guided the strokes of her Sergeant-Major quill over the lines of her exercise book. She had doted on little Déodat. For the religious holiday on 15 August she had dressed him from head to toe in velvet and silk. She had him drink cod-liver oil, thinking he looked sickly. It wasn't her intention to unleash the storm. A storm is sent by the hand of God. Were there no extenuating circumstances?

While taking the air in front of St Mary's, Father Bishop, who was keeping an eye on his parishioners, waved to her sanctimoniously. She didn't like these English priests whom she thought most inferior to those of her childhood, even though they were Catholic. Their noses were as red as their ears and they had no scruples switching from the altar to the gaming dens and the cock-pits. If the cock-fight was not over in time they shamelessly held up mass. Yet in Roseau the church had been her refuge against solitude and many times Father Bishop had dried her tears. Out of respect she was about to climb up towards him when she was bent double with a searing pain. Then came another on the heels of the first. She made a quick calculation. She was not expecting to give birth before Christmas; that was a good four weeks away. But a third pain tore through her, so violent she doubled over and lost her breath. She went back down the steps and dragged herself as best she could towards Ada's house, where she knew she would find help. Since living in Roseau, unable to rely on First-Born, Cathy had learned to rely on the kindness of strangers, and Ada, with her tall, gawky body, her calloused hands and fish-wife's smell, had become her maman. When the time came, she would take her to the hospice run by the Sisters of the

Visitation. To keep her strength up she would bring her chicken-noodle soup or vegetable broth, for the hospice did not feed its patients. As she was about to cross the street swirling with carriages, another pain seared through her. She thought she would collapse there and then among the feet of the indifferent passers-by and the bright yellow dung of the horses.

Apparently the prisoner had awoken.

Standing high on the square in front of the church, Father Bishop was watching Cathy's back. Where could she be going in such an ungainly manner, swaying like a crab walking sideways?

Father Bishop was one of those who was not bothered by her resemblance to First-Born. It was a fact that they had the same staring, wistful eyes, the same thick, black hair, the same domed forehead and the same furtive smile over an uneven set of teeth. But if his twenty years of living in Roseau had taught him one thing, it was that the tropical humus produced a society whose roots and branches were so intertwined, so twisted and interlocked that falling in love and sharing a bed with a half-brother or an unknown first cousin was no surprise. What's more, African, European and Indian blood had mixed in almost equal proportions in every inhabitant. So nothing was really surprising.

He had tried to fathom out Cathy, but for the past year he had never heard her admit through the confessional curtain to anything but peccadilloes. If she had sinned, it was unknowingly. He had ended up seeing her as the very picture of a good soul, anxious and finicky. Once, out of curiosity, he had made enquiries about First-Born, who seemed a useless character, a real good-for-nothing. While he respected neither Sundays nor religious holidays and never set foot inside the church, every evening he could be seen darting into The Last Resort, that infamous place frequented by men like himself. Strangely enough, according to rumour, he drank neither absinth, rum nor even Guinness. He merely rambled on about his maman and especially his papa, drowning the glasses of the other customers with his tears. According to him, his papa was some big boss that all of Guadeloupe respected. He was a great leader of men and so on and so forth.

In the end Father Bishop had kept his suspicions to himself and shrugged his shoulders. In the most muddled situation, the Good Lord always recognizes his own.

2 Season of Migration

A caesarian?

First-Born looked at Cathy. A butterfly of the night had spread its wings over her forehead and cast a shadow over her features. Her eyelids were wrinkled, her nose pinched tight and a large mauve circle outlined her mouth. He knew, without the doctor saying one barbaric word more, that death was whispering at her ear and moving in. Their short life together, at first so gentle then so bitter, made his heart ache, and he began to cry like a child. He had given her nothing of what she had hoped for and now she was leaving.

He seized her warm, listless hand, and at the moment when he least expected it, thinking she was already far away, within reach only of her regrets, she opened her eyes wide, looked at him and smiled. This smile dealt a blow to his heart. It was like the one she gave him on their wedding morning, when she had finally handed over to him everything she possessed. First-Born, who believed neither in the Good Lord and his saints nor the devil in his hell, and whose only fear on this earth was his father, would have made love before they got married. But Cathy insisted that, wherever he was, Aymeric could see her and she could not inflict such a wound on him. She therefore waited before giving herself to him until they made their vows before the mayor and the priest. The memory of this little ceremony, during which he had inscribed a completely fabricated name in the marriage register and pretended to honour the Good Lord, had tortured First-Born for a long time. What a scoundrel he was! But suddenly he got the impression that Cathy's smile, as knowing as a mother's, also signified forgiveness. Forgiveness for what he had wanted to hide from her. Forgiveness for what he never had the courage to confess to her, but in the secret of her heart she had guessed all along. Relieved, he pressed his forehead to the rough canvas sheet and whispered in her ear.

'So you knew?'

It seemed to him that she brushed his shoulder.

'You knew I was his son, the first of his loins,' he continued. 'Don't hold it against me. You hated him so much I never had the strength to tell you the truth. Sometimes, the words trembled on the edge of my lips and almost escaped me. Every time, I stopped them, held them back and swallowed them because I thought of your anger. What words would you use to insult me? How could you look into the eyes of the son of your father's assassin? Yes, I am his first son. I bear his name: Razyé. Not that he ever loved me. He always preferred his white-skinned bastard, that tubercular hypocrite Justin-Marie. When I was little, I soaked my pillow every night. In his eyes I never existed. He came home, shoved us aside and never noticed what I had invented to please him. That's why I became what I am. The school dunce: every day, the dunce's cap and made to stand in the playground; later on, the animal and womanizer. There was a time when I hated him. I had in mind several ways of finishing him off. He had a gun he kept loaded in his study and I dreamed of lying in wait for him one evening in a corner and killing him as soon as he appeared in the yard. Parricide at midnight. Or else I burnt him like a rat in a sugar-cane field. Afterwards I would stow away on a boat and go into hiding somewhere. In Cuba, which they say is so white, or Jamaica, so black with Maroons, or Puerto Rico. Sometimes I even landed in the United States of America. I walked the streets of New York. I looked into the eyes of the Statue of Liberty before making my fortune on Wall Street ... Today I no longer bear him a grudge. I pity him rather. Nobody ever loved him. Except for Irmine, my poor maman, and us, his children. But that love didn't count for him. If in life you don't receive the love you dream of, you can't give any in return. That's how it is. It was your love that saved me from damnation. Your love, so sweet, so even-tempered. I often got the impression I was bored in your company. I didn't realize we were bound to each other beyond passion.'

At that moment one of the sisters came over, the wings of her cornet floating around her very white, worn face. She pulled out a screen around Cathy's bed and in a mealy-mouthed voice said: 'You should leave now, my son. The doctor will soon be here. At least he'll try to save the child.'

First-Born shivered, hearing his intuition confirmed. Soon he would be alone. He went out into the yard.

Under the canopy of tall mango and mammy-apple trees, the hospice of the Sisters of the Visitation was an old wooden building with a faded zinc roof. It was built in the years following the Discovery, when the frail sisters arriving from England forgot their fevers and the fire in their bellies to treat the wretched Indians for the sicknesses that had landed with the caravels. Since then, however hard they patched it up, however many wings they added, it remained too small to house those suffering from the new epidemics that wreaked havoc on black and white alike – yaws, dengue fever, tuberculosis and dysentery. To the left of the actual hospice was a small chapel built of logs, like the chapels you imagined in the Canadian Far North. They had never celebrated mass there, even though the sisters changed the water daily for the flowers on the high altar. Only the parents of the sick came to pray here and beg for divine mercy.

It now had a pitiful appearance. The tiles on the floor were broken. In the niches, the statues of the saints had crumbled – a headless Anthony of Padua stood with one hand in the air and the remains of a fresco peeped through the dirt on the walls. First-Born, who had practically never set foot inside a church, sat down in a pew behind one of the regulars, bent over in prayer. He asked himself why she was condemned. Surely Aymeric was punishing this guileless child for having loved the son of his executioner. At other times he told himself she was atoning for a more serious fault that she had committed without knowing. But his mind refused to take him in this direction. He tried in vain to recall the words of the Hail Mary and remained sitting there, his head between his hands, too wretched to measure his suffering. At some point a hand brushed his arm. It was Ada who, he knew, had become close friends with Cathy.

'Has the baby been born?' she asked.

He shook his head.

'No! One of the sisters told me they were going to have to do a caesarian.'

Ada's eyes grew round with fright.

'You mean they're going to cut her belly open? Cut it open with a knife like a pumpkin?'

He nodded and without saying another word she knelt down beside him, stinking of the fish she sold in the market. Soon he heard her crying.

Why was she condemned, his poor, gentle Cathy? Even if she was guilty of loving him, it wasn't her who had made the first move. She seemed only interested in explaining fractions and theorems to him when, one afternoon with her back to the blackboard, he had pressed up against her. She had accepted his kisses and pledges of love. Then, without too much enthusiasm, she had followed him to Dominica which, in his opinion, would have more opportunities to offer than Marie-Galante.

'In Saint-Louis,' he claimed, 'I'll never be anything more than the apprentice to Tonin, the blacksmith, whereas in Roseau . . . '

And all because he felt so good in her company. At peace. Never had he felt such well-being. No passion, no aggressiveness. No great desire even. He did not want to make love to her so much as to lose himself in a conversation that would last for the rest of their lives. After a while, Ada stirred beside him.

'Well, I have to be going now,' she said. 'Don't stay here all alone. Come with me.'

He followed her.

Ada lived at Three Estates, a group of motley cabins in the middle of a clearing recently hacked from the forest. They crossed through Roseau then set off on a road that zigzagged up the mountain. Through the fringes of the coconut-trees they could see the golden sand of the beaches, the sea wavering between blue and grey and the sparkling sails of the fishing-boats. The world was going about its daily business. Its beauty continued to shine and Cathy was going to lose her life. To die. Why?

Ada's children were playing around the cabin while keeping an eye on the heaps of fish smoking on the fires of bay-rum leaves. She called them over and proudly introduced them one by one.

'Five! I've got five!'

Five? He felt a pang of jealousy. Then they entered the cabin, clean but rough and bare, except for a few pieces of crude furniture. Ada began to boil some water for the tea.

As she was setting out the cups on the table she stopped in front of First-Born and suddenly said: 'If it's a girl we'll call her Anthuria. That's what she told me.'

First-Born sat down on the edge of his bed. Despite the chill of the night, sharpened by the breezes blowing in from the sea, he was in a sweat, and his cotton shirt stuck to his shoulder blades. A pain tore through his chest. It was as if a piece of him had been torn out, like the rib from Adam's side, and he was sitting there with a gaping hole. He almost suffocated.

To his left the sky was white. The curve of night stretched away and the birds in their rumpled feathers flew off into the arc of day.

Cathy had passed on, he was sure of it.

She was lovely! From the delicately curled shell of her ears you could see she would not be light-skinned, but dark like father and mother. Very dark. Her black hair already grew thickly over her perfectly round skull and hid her domed forehead. Her little face had none of those swellings and puffiness that usually disfigure the newly-born. On the contrary. Her skin was as velvety soft as a sapodilla, coco-plum or sweet-plum ripe for picking from the branch. He ventured to stroke her tiny hand that lay with clenched fingers on the sheet, like a flower bud, and her warmth flowed into him.

Behind her cradle, the bed stood empty.

Some mindless stretcher-bearers had just carried off Cathy's body to the basement, where carpenters were indifferently carving out her last dwelling-place in pinewood. Then, without wreaths or flowers, they would take her to church. Father Bishop would bless the coffin and they would make room for her in the graveyard next to St Mary's. It was a great favour they were doing this child of God for she wasn't just a foreigner, she was destitute and had never been seen to place a farthing in the collection plate.

To his great surprise, First-Born felt no longer desperate, but almost triumphant. It was like the havoc wreaked by a hurricane. His garden was ruined. His house smashed to pieces and his belongings scattered by the wind. But there remained a precious asset – the life of his daughter. The sister who had finished saying her rosary asked him: 'What name do you want to give her?'

When she heard his answer she made a face.

'What sort of a Christian name is that?'

He didn't answer and she walked away, putting his silence down to his grief or his stupidity.

'When can I take her with me?' he called out to her.

'It's the doctor who'll decide,' she said piously.

Outside, the morning was damp.

First-Born entered The Last Resort. Not to drink – he never drank and Cathy who had so many other things to reproach him for had never caught the smell of rum on his breath. All he had ever done was pick up a girl and follow her home to bed. The memory of these uncouth creatures, when he himself had a jewel at home, now made him ashamed. Yet even in those moments it was not vice he was after. It was the warmth of other human beings and the smell of their company. To begin with, the regulars at The Last Resort had given him a cool reception. They did not understand who this Guadeloupean was, too light-skinned to be black, too black to be a mulatto, and destitute into the bargain. Then they realized he spoke Creole and since he was never drunk, he never drew a knife on anyone. So they adopted him.

At this early hour there was nobody in the bar except for a few rum guzzlers for whom only the level of rum in their bottles counted. Sam, the owner, was taking advantage of the calm to do his accounts. He looked up from his slate and exclaimed: 'I heard about your wife! It's a real shame! How old was she?'

Twenty. But what was the meaning of that? That there's an age for dying? Sixty? Eighty? Ninety? We are always too young to die.

'Take heart!' Sam said with compassion.

Then, as he could find no other gesture of consolation, he placed a glass of rum on the counter. Without thinking, First-Born emptied it. But it had no more effect on his throat than a trickle of cold water. Around eleven the regulars started to arrive and on seeing the tragic figure, adopted appropriate expressions. The great Clay, who in his spare time was somewhat of a storyteller, began to improvise, half in sadness, half in mockery.

'I'm telling you ladies and gentlemen, life is not a bowl of arrowroot. In actual fact, she's a real bitch. Two lovebirds, one male and one female, flew over from Guadeloupe to take refuge with us here in Roseau. What had they done to fly as far as here? Nobody knows, I don't know and it's none of my business. All I know is that they made their nest in the branches of a silk-cotton tree, and all day long anyone who passed by could hear their cooing and warbling . . . '

Distracted for a moment, First-Born returned to his thoughts. He had failed Cathy. Of her own accord she had given up the silks, the luxury and the hordes of servants of her childhood in the hope of living a nobler life. But he had been incapable of giving her what she desired. Would he fail Anthuria as well? How could he give her the care she deserved if he was nothing but a pauper?

All his life First-Born had never been concerned with material things. He had grown up with a belly full of wind, without a decent shoe or shirt to his name in the house of a father hoarding millions. As a small boy, he had carved kites and carriages out of avocado stones. Later on he devoured the few dog-eared books in the school library. He was rich with the immensity of his dreams. Suddenly he realized that he was one of the wealthy. How much money, ill-gained, was Razyé hiding in the Banque de France et des Pays-Bas? How much land had he stolen and how many victims had he plundered?

It was then that First-Born made a resolution he had always refused to make. He had to go home. Claim his inheritance. Not for himself, who had nothing left of a life worthy of this name to live. For her. For Anthuria. In a flash, the terrible face of Razyé loomed up in front of him. He almost lost courage. Then he felt himself fortified with an unknown feeling. He felt strong enough to fight, to hit below the belt, to kill even, if need be.

Wasn't he a papa now?

The great Clay playfully continued.

'In the end all that cooing and warbling came to the ears of Death – Madame Death – and got her temper up. You know how she is? She can't stand people being happy. So she took her cutlass and wap, slashed our lovebirds in two.'

With the others, First-Born began to clap his hands in unison.

3   Ada the Fishwife's Tale

He didn't even say thank you.

I breastfed his child with the milk for my boy. It was thanks to me she didn't go the same way as her maman and isn't lying under the casuarinas at this very minute. Yet not a word of thanks came out of his mouth. Could I expect anything else from a fellow like that?

I've been selling fish in the market in Roseau for years. Its smell is all over me. In my clothes. In my hair. In my skin. In my bed. It's why men never stay long with me. They start out taking advantage of me. They play all sorts of games. And then, out of the blue, they start criticizing me and one after the other they leave, swearing: 'Oh no, I can't stand your smell any longer!'

But I don't need men. I've got enough on my hands with my strapping young rascals. Sometimes I tell myself I'm fortunate because, as I see it, real fortune is not a bulging purse. Real fortune is a virtue you acquire when you're a baby and even before that, when you're still in your mother's womb. That's what I used to tell Cathy, to stretch the corners of her mouth and smooth the creases on her forehead.

People had no great liking for her. Behind her back they gossiped that under her superior airs she was surely not First-Born's wife and that they must be living together like everybody else. Perhaps it was true, but it wasn't my business. I never liked poking my nose into other people's dirty linen. Why did I grow fond of her? Because she wasn't like anybody else I knew. The first time I met her was in the waiting-room at the hospice. She was wrapped in a flowery shawl and sitting with her hands together underneath the black wooden crucifix. At first I thought she was praying and then on a closer look I could see she was crying. The tears streamed silently down her cheeks and she was shaking like a leaf. It made my heart bleed: someone who wasn't from here – you could see that before she even opened her mouth and could tell from her poor English and shaky Creole – so pretty, so young. I went over to her and before I could even ask her she looked at me and murmured: 'I'm pregnant.'

I scolded her.

'And is that why you're crying? Don't you know that a child is a blessing from the Good Lord?'

She cried even harder. At that moment Doctor Richardson, a good fellow with a generous heart, though he is English, put his head round the door and asked: 'Ada, take her home will you?'

I clasped her hands as cold as ice and asked her: 'Where do you live?'

She looked at me in a daze.

'Where do you live?' I repeated.

Still not a word. So I put my arm under hers to support her and we went out into the yard.

Dusk is my favourite time of day, when the breeze gets up. The fishermen return to the shore with a good or bad catch, depending on the luck of the day. Above their heads the sky darkens once the sun has disappeared. Its heat has baked and baked the earth for hours, giving it the smell of a loaf hot from a wood-burning oven and making it into a crispy crust underfoot. I repeated my question. But the retched girl, leaning on my arm, was incapable of telling ₁e anything. So I set off for Three Estates where I have my ₁bin.

It's no palace, my cabin, under its roof of palm-fronds and erched on four stones. But I built it all by myself, with the ₁lp of my boys. At Christmas, the poinsettias in front of ₁e door are scarlet. At the end of the dry season the flame-ees cover it with patches of colour. Behind it grows a ₁agnolia-tree always pink with blossom. I made Cathy ₁me tea with leaves of soursop for serenity and dreamless eep, with citronella for strength, with lemon for its aroma, ₁d I added three peppercorns to warm her blood. While ₁e drank, a little colour flowed back to her cheeks. She ₁ally stopped crying and began to talk, or rather talk off ₁e top of her head in three languages, telling me stories I ₁uld make neither head nor tail of, mentioning the name of er papa, her *mabo*, her brothers and her servant, a certain ₁omaine, time and time again.

Since it made her cry again, I advised her: 'Forget all ₁out that. You mustn't keep harping on the past. What's ₁ne is done. Look ahead of you. Think of your child.'

What had I said in the hopes of comforting her! She ₁llapsed, stammering: 'I'm expecting a child. Good Lord, ₁ave mercy!'

That's how I came to know her.

Our age, our lives had nothing in common. Our paths ₁ere not meant to cross. But solitude pushed her towards ₁e. She came to see me every day at Three Estates and I ₁came like a maman to her. It was Patience, my eldest ₁aughter, who showed her how to weave baskets from ₁rata. It was me who took her to sit in the market and ₁ught her not to put customers off with her sad expression. ₁ut all my affection could not stop her from taking the road ₁ her final resting place. I never stopped working one single day when I was pregnant with my children. As soon as I gave birth, I bound my belly with a strip of cotton and went back to selling in the market. She was sick all the time with her pregnancy. I felt it wasn't normal. So one evening I drank a tea made with leaves of *elebiana* that grows in the dankness of the forest, and I saw that it was her child that was eating her up alive. It was her growing child that was draining her blood, her lymph and the fluids of her body. I would have liked to know more so that I could have helped her. Unfortunately, when I tried to take her to see Alice, who is in constant touch with the spirits and can find the answer to every problem, she refused. She told me she didn't believe in all that nonsense. I did what I could for her. Unfortunately, I couldn't do much. A little tea, a few massages and back-rubs. I knew full well it wasn't enough and that one day she would leave us and never return. While I parted her black hair with a comb she would say: 'I am the daughter of tainted blood. Maman? Better not speak of her. As for my real papa, Ada, I'm so frightened I'd rather not know.'

I shrugged my shoulders.

'And me? Do you think I know who my papa is? That's how our men are. They sow and they sow, but never bother about the plant that sprouts.'

Other times she would sigh: 'I wish I were your child. Out from the womb of a hardy, stout-hearted woman like yourself with both feet on the ground. My mother had her head stuffed with dreams and longings. Where did that get her?'

'What are you talking about?' I retorted. 'You think we black folks are better than other people? I can prove the opposite.'

She didn't answer, as if she didn't understand what I was saying.

When she first arrived at the house she would sit down in

326

a corner and write in a notebook with flowers on the cover and squared pages like a school exercise-book. How I would have liked to write like her! I think that if I knew how to read and write my life would have been different. Alas, I never set foot inside a school. My brothers went to classes at Bas-Thorton where we used to live when we were young. They can sign their names and read the pages of a newspaper. My sister and myself, we don't know anything. We helped maman sell in the market and do everything there was to do around the house. I watched admiringly over her shoulder the letters she drew and she told me: 'If I didn't have this, my diary, I think I'd be dead already. I write everything, everything down here.'

I made a face and teased her.

'Everything? I wonder what you can find to write. Not many things go on around here.'

'I mean everything that goes on inside me,' she murmured.

That set me thinking. What goes on inside me? I don't know. It's as if there's a forest I've never got to the bottom of. During the last months of her pregnancy she didn't write anything, as if she had spent all her strength. She left her diary lying around. It was lying on the floor when I picked it up and gave it to her husband with the few things she had. I shall see her sitting there until my dying day. She would swing to and fro in the rocking-chair, her great belly lying in her lap as if it weighed too much, her face melancholic and blank. Her hair was falling out in handfuls. Her youth and beauty were fading and I could do nothing for her. She who always had something to say sat in silence, her fingers mechanically weaving the *carata*, and then murmured: 'What lies at the end of this long corridor? No one can say . . . I'm not even sure I shall find her again.'

Hearing her I knew full well she was thinking more and

more of her maman. But I pretended not to understand and told her a silly story to make her laugh. At least smile. Because laughter, she didn't know what that was. I don't think she ever knew.

When she went into labour, it was to me she came for help. I was the one who took her to the sisters at the hospice, whispering words of comfort. But it was obvious she no longer wanted to go on living.

Some women complain all the time about their men and never spare you a fight, a scene or the cussing. She never mentioned First-Born once, but I knew that the wound was eating her heart out.

He's gone. He set off to sea with the child I had grown to love as much as I loved her, without even a thank-you for all my trouble. He left her behind, all alone among strangers; with nobody to weed her grave, to light candles and set flowers on it on All Souls' Day. It won't bring him happiness.

I don't need any *elebiana* to see that at his age his life is already over. He's going to spend the rest of his life in solitude, without a soul to warm his heart. Contrary to what he hopes, Anthuria will be no consolation. Just the opposite. That child will lead him a real song and dance. Besides, children never are a consolation. They come to live their lives, not to brighten up their parents'.

The way he left was the way he really was: a good-for-nothing.

She never stopped saying that the curse of God was on her for some terrible sin she had committed; for some person she had killed. I didn't even listen to her. For me, it was all nonsense, rambling, senseless words. What killed her was her husband's indifference, the nights he spent away from home and the number of women he took. Everyone can testify to that.

Despite all my pain and all my anger, today is a day like any other. The sun is already high in the sky. As Christmas approaches, the poinsettias are painted in a lovely scarlet colour and behind the house the scent of the magnolia in bloom hangs heavy in the air. It's time to go down to the seashore and take my load of fish from the hands of Ethelbert. Then I'll set off for the market. I'll take my usual place so that, mourning or no mourning, my customers will find me where they've always found me, year in and year out.

At six, darkness will fall upon us all at once, without warning, as it always does. The market will empty and the famished dogs will tear apart the meat carcasses lying forgotten in the butchers' booths. I'll set off for Three Estates. Slowly climbing up behind the royal palms, the moon will light the way. At home the children will have lit the oil-lamp. Patience will have put the root vegetables to boil with a piece of salt pork. Before we eat, we will make the sign of the cross and thank God for what He hasn't given us.

4   Farewell to the Beloved

The long strings of rain fell in tangles on the ground. In order to pay for his seat aboard the steamship *Elizabeth Regina*, First-Born had borrowed the price of a ticket from Sam, the owner of The Last Resort. Sam hadn't given much credit to his story of a millionaire papa and had little hope of seeing his money again. But he had taken pity on him and told himself that the Good Lord, who never forgets anything, would take into consideration this good deed when he got to Heaven.

On the wharf the weather added to the usual commotion. Sheltering under jute sacks, the coal-women were digging into piles of fuel and completing their job of filling the steamers' holds. Passengers climbing down from their carriages handed their baggage to the porters. Then, holding their umbrellas with both hands, they ran up the rope gangway that sagged like a liana. First-Born had been careful to look neither right nor left. He settled into a corner of the second-class saloon, determined not to engage in any conversation. But the passengers around him, intrigued by the bundle he was clutching to his heart, were scared off by his expression and clothes of deep mourning and had no intention of speaking to him. Through the port-holes the houses of Roseau looked like a child's toys.

Clasping his precious burden with one hand, First-Born drew out of his pocket with the other the object that Ada had handed over to him, together with an unfinished cross-stitch embroidery, some balls of wool and embroidery materials. It was an ordinary, squared-paper notebook, with a stiff, flowered cover, which Cathy must have bought for a few pennies at the shop opposite the church that was also a haberdasher's. She had written in her schoolteacher's handwriting, carefully respecting the down and the up strokes:

This diary belongs to Cathy de Linsseuil
Address: 14, Oaks Road,
Roseau.

On deciphering these lines, First-Born was first of all gripped with an irrational anger and jealousy. He held between his hands the proof of how little he counted in the life of his wife. She had not changed her name. Daughter of Aymeric de Linsseuil she was born. Daughter of Aymeric de Linsseuil she would remain. Daughter of a so-called good white man, the model master who in fact was nothing but a hypocrite and a common thief of women. After a while, however, his anger subsided. He recalled the knowing little smile on Cathy's lips before she died and another thought superimposed itself with a forceful certainty. She had not been fooled by his deceit. She had guessed all along that the name Sabrimol was a product of his imagination. Even more serious, she had guessed who was hiding behind it. Now it all became clear. All at once a series of incidents that in his cocksureness he had not noticed at the time flooded his memory and convinced him that Cathy was not the naïve person he thought she was. She used to take pleasure in having him recount his childhood memories, pretending to be interested but at the same time casually interrogating him. Very often his answers muddled up who he was supposed to be and who he really was. That was how one day when, feeling homesick, he had talked about Cassandre, her funny little faces and her chatter, and she had interrupted him right in the middle of his story.

'So you've got a sister! I thought you were an only child?'

Another time she looked him straight in the eyes and asked: 'Sabrimol? Where does that name come from?'

He had launched into a complicated explanation. It was a name from . . . La Désirade. Yes, La Désirade. His mother came from Marigot. And he had gone on to describe the island he had only ever seen from the windows of l'Engoulvent. She hadn't said anything, but he felt that he hadn't convinced her.

Suddenly the siren wailed and the ship swayed like a dancer about to launch onto the dance floor. It rolled to one side and then rolled to the other. Some passengers pressed up against the port-holes so as not to miss seeing the departure. Others, little heeding the bad weather, ran to the ladder that led on deck. First-Born was about to do the same when a hand held him back.

'You're not thinking of going outside in the rain with the baby?'

It was a woman of a certain age, soberly attired, without rings or a necklace, in a Creole dress with a black and blue leafy pattern. Only a *tranblant* pinned back the folds of her madras head-tie. As First-Born hesitated, she swept up Anthuria, who went on sleeping, and declared with authority: 'It so happens I was taking care of children before you were even jumping around on this earth. In my neighbourhood they called me *manman tou moun*, everybody's maman.'

Reluctantly, he let her have her way. He did not like to be separated from his daughter. She had become his obsession. He watched her sleep. He combed her hair. Twenty times a day he changed her nappies or put his hand under her infants' clothes to check her skin temperature.

Very quickly Roseau had disappeared from sight. Even the outline of the mountains was already fading to grey, and it seemed to First-Born that in a flash a chapter of his life had been blotted out and there was nothing he could do about it – the most painful chapter, the most memorable chapter, in a word, the most precious. Nothing was real any longer: neither Sam, Ada nor Cathy. All he had was Anthuria to remind him that he hadn't been dreaming. On his cheeks his tears mixed with the rain and the salt of the spray.

Enormous waves washed over the deck. As far as the eye could see, the ocean swelled with the mouths of monsters that seemed determined on swallowing the ship. In trying to escape them the vessel heaved, cavorted and flung its passengers now starboard, now portside. These sudden lurches brought much delight to a group of white school-children in blue and gold uniforms whose two masters had trouble keeping control. First-Born managed to keep his balance and wedged himself against a lifeboat.

What did she know? Had she guessed his true identity?

He took the diary out of his pocket again and gazed at it. The truth was there. Written in these few pages. All he had to do was turn them and he would know.

But when the time came to make this apparently simple gesture, he couldn't bring himself to do it. He felt uncomfortable, as if he were about to do something wrong. When he was little he used to creep along the landing of his mother's bedroom and through the keyhole watch Irmine undress. After having coveted this forbidden body he stood ashamed, swearing he would never do it again and convinced that he was a godless child. Cathy had divulged to this diary the emotions and feelings she did not want to share with him. She had not only mentioned him, but probably everything that was cause for distress. Her mother. Herself. Their exile. Perhaps she had revealed aspects of her character she preferred to hide, and who knows if another Cathy would not emerge as he turned the pages? If he read her diary, all the memories he kept of her might be drastically changed.

Holding the ship's rail with one hand, he walked to the bow of the *Elizabeth Regina*, to the point where the waves are torn apart and churn back against each other. The wind wrinkled his eyelids and the salt burned his lips. Crested cranes lifted off from the funnels and flew back to the shore, their yelping cries as sad as farewells. He looked one last time at the notebook and its childish warning.

This diary belongs to Cathy de Linsseuil.
Address: 14, Oaks Road,
Roseau.

Without hesitating, he threw it overboard. For a few minutes the diary floated on the surface of the water, wings spread like a bird, then it dived into the foam and vanished amidst the swirl of the waves.

Whatever Cathy's secrets might have been, he would never know their monstrosities.

PART FIVE

Guadeloupe

1 Return To My Native Land

To be back in your home town after a long absence. To be back in the places you played, bowled a hoop, rolled marbles in the storm channel. To be back in the streets you roamed coming home from school with a satchel strapped to your back. The place where a bully punched you in the ribs.

Leaving behind the harbour-lamps, First-Born walked along the wharf in La Pointe beneath the shiny-leaved Indian almond-trees. At such a late hour the warehouse shutters were lowered. Everywhere was deserted. Only the reek of salt-fish crept along the pavements. Only the rats squealed and feasted on the piles of rubbish that stood guard at every crossroad. Intrepid cats came to taunt them and there were some unholy fights, some unholy war-cries in the dark. Drifting over from the Saint-Antoine market, just two or three streets away, was the smell of rotting vegetables that he breathed in like a perfume, the scent of his long lost island. Owing to the squalls, the *Elizabeth Regina* had arrived late. It only bumped against the wharf in La Pointe at around two in the morning. The passengers, whom nobody was waiting to greet any longer, had jostled for the rare tilburies that were still hanging around. The less fortunate who were on foot set off at a quick pace, squinting fearfully into the night, for La Pointe had recently become a lair of brigands. The front pages of the newspapers were full of stories of robberies committed at all hours – sometimes even in broad daylight – by bands of blacks deserting the plantations. As usual, the police kept their arms folded. Only First-Born strolled along as if he were afraid of nothing and had all the time in the world. For him, to be back in La Pointe was nothing short of magic. All at once, fear had flown, the memory of Cathy weighed a little less on his conscience and he felt more refreshed than he had for three years. He felt like waking Anthuria, who had fallen asleep again, and whispering: 'Look! Look! We're home!'

Instead of branching off towards the Darse and the Place de la Victoire, he plunged into the labyrinth of shop-lined streets, as silent and black as an oven. He wanted to yell at all those asleep behind their heavy wooden doors and lowered shutters that he was back, and he should be fêted like a prodigal son. He arrived in front of the cathedral of Saint-Pierre-et-Saint-Paul, at anchor in the square. The great double wooden doors were closed. But he could hear the rustling of the bats nesting in the eyes of the stone saints. What a pity he had never been to church! He remembered having slipped in sometimes to spit in the font. It was a great cause of grief for Cathy that he had never made his First Communion or been confirmed, and didn't know a single word of the prayers. In the early days he took delight poking fun at her, with inflammatory talk against the Good Lord whom he held responsible for the enslavement of the black man, the arrogance of the white Creoles and for all of life's misfortunes. But she cried so much he had stopped his games. Yes, deep down she had remained the daughter of Aymeric de Linsseuil, born and bred on the Belles-Feuilles estate. She thought she had broken with her class, whereas in fact it was ingrained deep inside her. He remembered there was a juicy mango-tree that grew in the garden of the presbytery. How many plans he and his brothers had concocted to lay their hands on the mangoes and fill their half-empty bellies! Alas, they had never managed to outwit the priests,who kept watch while walking in the yard and pretending to read their Bibles. He went up to the iron gate, reliving the cravings of his childhood. It was then, looming up behind his back, that a carriage as sinister as a hearse lurched level with him. Not a sound came from the hoofs of the horse as it trotted, head lowered, its nostrils snorting over the cobblestones. The reins hung loosely from the hands of the coachman, who sat motionless, apparently in a deep sleep. The man and beast passed by and were silently swallowed up by the night under the sandbox-trees. He stood transfixed, then was gripped by a superstitious fear. He had just encountered the horse of death. *Lan-mo*. It was her. Death had snatched his Cathy from him. What else did she want from him? Years had gone by since he had news of his family. Was he going to find them as he left them? Was his maman alive? Or had she died from Razyé's abuse and blows? He had not forgotten how worn-out, pale and shattered she looked when he left. He clasped Anthuria closer to him and began to run. His footsteps echoed in the silence and sent cats, dogs and vermin scattering.

It came as a shock, for first of all he did not recognize the house on the Place de la Victoire and wondered if his eyes were not playing tricks on him. An architect, who had spared no cost, had transformed the dilapidated construction where he had revelled in his childhood games. He had replaced its lovable weatherbeaten wood with rectangular stones. He had driven a straight line of French windows through the ground floor. He had made it taller, adding a second floor girded by a pretentious balustraded gallery. In a final flourish he had topped it with a juvenile roof of pink tiles. Its colour, too, had been changed. An off-white paint, with a matching green on the frieze and the door and window casements, was daubed all over it from top to bottom. In the yard where he used to fly his kite with Gengis there was a profusion of plants. A vine and a passion-fruit twined over an arbour around a blue-tiled, ornamental pool. Cleaned and restored, the house looked like an old woman who wanted to make herself look young.

The first thing that occurred to First-Born was that his parents had sold it and moved. He had already started to walk away, without knowing exactly where to go, when a doubt made him turn back. His hand rang the bell and very quickly a light went on in a window on the first floor as if someone had been waiting for that sound night after night to jump out of bed and run to the front door. In a moment Irmine and Hosannah appeared in the yard, the latter holding a lighted torch above her head.

He believed his father to be indestructible, carved out of an iron wood that was imperishable. And now he was gone. He felt an immense void deep inside and realized that his only reason for coming home had been to find him. Throughout his life he had measured himself against his father's contempt. The fear of him and sometimes the idea of hating him had fashioned his inner self. To his surprise, he found himself dry-eyed. Perhaps Cathy had carried off all his tears. He turned to face his mother, amazed that she could have survived him, so exhausted it was obvious she wouldn't last much longer. Without sparing him any detail, she had described the wake and the funeral. It was, he suspected, her way of reproaching him. He, her first son, had left her all alone at such a time. Did he realize that for three years she had not known what sleep meant? She lay, eyes wide open, under her mosquito-net and imagined all the traps he might have fallen into. In her dreams she saw him dead, with no one to watch over him, and woke up with a start, wracked with grief. He was the reason she had started praying to God again, making novenas and pilgrimages, attending vespers and saying her rosary. At last her tears dried on her cheeks. Amid much excitement she gave him news of the family. His brothers attended a Jesuit school in Bordeaux. Cassandre was at the nuns' boarding-school in Versailles. She had played the piano for the governor and kissed the hand of His Grace the Bishop.

All this convinced him that there was no place for him in the life she was building for herself. He was too old to go back and wear his trousers out on a school-bench, too set in his ways to learn a trade and not naive enough to pretend he could start his life over again. He was not more than twenty and yet he was already older than an old bag of bones.

'If your father could see this,' she concluded, all excited. 'He would be so happy. Everything I do is for him.'

Would he be happy? She had already disguised him as a model father, fussing over his offspring. He who had been nothing but indifferent and savage. First-Born could not understand what he was feeling. Poor Irmine exasperated him. She appeared insignificant and petty to him. He could not help asking her reproachfully: 'Why have you turned the house inside out?'

She launched into an endless explanation of which he didn't understand a word. Suddenly she stopped and cried: 'But what about you? Tell me about yourself!'

Himself? What was there to say? Nothing. Three times nothing. No fortune gained. No marvellous discovery. No new lands opened up. He was no conquistador, no Hernan Cortes offering Mexico to the king of Spain. But she didn't wait for his answer and pointed to Anthuria, still snuggled in his arms.

'Who is her maman?'

Something told him to lie. He felt he should be careful not to mention Cathy's name.

'It's a woman,' he merely murmured, vaguely. 'An English woman I met in Roseau. She died, unfortunately, giving birth.'

Irmine put on an appropriate expression and parted the wraps around the infant. Suddenly she started to cry.

'It's his very image!' she stammered.

First-Born looked at his daughter's brown cheeks and was amazed. He had always thought Anthuria was the picture of Cathy.

'Give her to me,' she begged.

He obeyed reluctantly and she began to devour the child with kisses.

So Razyé was dead and the island was going cold-heartedly about its business. The Socialists clung on to the municipality of La Pointe and won the major towns. They also held the General Council. But the lot of the black folks was no sweeter. The cane-fields continued to go up in flames. The Lebanese hawkers were now making a fortune. Italians off the steamships were chiselling jewels at the back of their shops and the Indians were demanding the right to vote.

Good Lord! What next?

First-Born stared at the ceiling.

Beneath him the sheets were as soft as the mattress. Like the rest of the house, the bedroom had been entirely redone. The walls were painted pale green. Above a six-drawer mahogany chest there was a watercolour of La Darse and the Place de la Victoire. The golden trunks of the sandbox-trees stood out against the blue of the sea where boats with white sails raced. Children and dogs ran along the paths bordered with flowers, while in the foreground two lovers were walking arm in arm. Antimacassars festooned with lace were draped over the backs of two rocking-chairs. A cupid held up the pink globe of the lamp he had left alight. This sugary décor sickened him.

'I cannot stay here,' he said out loud.

He had not been able to stop Hosannah and Irmine competing with each other for Anthuria, and Irmine, considering herself more entitled than her rival, had laid the child to sleep in a cradle next to the head of her bed. It was the first night he had slept away from his daughter and he felt dispossessed. He resented the two women plotting like two old wives, reducing him to a male role and hence a nonentity. Hosannah and Irmine had prattled on about blouses to be embroidered, bootees to be knitted, arrowroot pap and rice-water to be perfumed with orange-blossom. Even more serious, they had plotted to take Anthuria to see Father Angebert to get his blessing before the christening ceremony.

First-Born sat on the bed and looked around him, as frightened as if a hurricane were approaching.

He had taken the decision to return home for Anthuria's sake, and now it was proving to be a bad one and the return had all the makings of a catastrophe. He realized he was much more like his father than he had ever imagined and that now he was gone, he could not put up with the rest of the family. It had become the same as any other. The house he had grown up in had changed beyond recognition. His mother was a stranger to him – even Hosannah. They had woken up Fréda in the middle of the night for him to kiss, and he had not recognized his little sister with her round face and simpering ways, wrapped in a night-dress with a lace front. He stood up, got his feet caught in the carpet, stumbled against a stray pouffe and had the feeling he was suffocating.

Where could he flee this time?

On opening the window to get some fresh air, he clearly saw his father's face outlined against the black painted canvas of the night. Razyé's expression was the same as it always was: hard and sombre, transformed by the hint of a smile that seemed to be scoffing at him: 'My poor unfortunate boy. Is this why you came home? What are you going to do now? If I have any advice to give you, it's to go back where you came from. Or go somewhere else. As quickly as you can. From where I am, I can see what sort of a life is in store for you, mapped out for you in advance, and I can see you turning into a bourgeois complete with gaiters and a paunch. Soon they'll find you a girl to wed, white enough to lighten the race, and the sins of your youth will be forgotten . . . Is that what you want?'

2   Return to l'Engoulvent

For years, people in the area hastened their step or made a great detour so as not to be in the vicinity of the graveyard at l'Engoulvent when night fell. Those who lingered in the neighbourhood at that hour told of unnatural occurrences. In an instant the sky would darken as if a storm were approaching, while shadowy shapes slithered along the ground. At the same time cries and wails, as persistent and delicate as those of babies, rose up on one side, while opposite there were the bass tones of a man's voice lamenting and yelling lewd words. Some people claimed to have seen silhouettes in a strange light as bright as day wandering side by side, passing each other, blindly searching for one another. A sad and frightening sight! No doubt the corner was inhabited by spirits for whom 'eternal rest' was far from meaning 'peace', and who might very well turn their anger on the living. It was therefore with great surprise they learned that Razyé's boy – after so many years abroad – had returned to such a place to live. And with a small child into the bargain! People said the boy must be cracked in the head. It ran in the family. But since jobs had become as rare as gold nuggets in the riverbeds, a number of former plantation workers, tired of letting their cutlasses and hoes go to rust, went over and offered their services to First-Born. Like Justin Gagneur before him, he had them clear the tangle of scrub and thornbushes that covered the savanna around the house and plant it with vegetables. He also hired a woman to do the cooking, a woman as black as night called Graziella, who didn't know what Sundays and holidays were and sang from morning to night like God's nightingale as she banged her pots and pans.

Was it out of miserliness that First-Born didn't touch a thing at l'Engoulvent, so sorely in need of attention after all the years it had remained uninhabited, soaking up the sun and the rain? The walls remained cracked, the roof infested with bats and rats, and the beams gnawed away by termites. As for the iguanas, they continued to sleep in the yard in their scaly sheaths. First-Born chose for himself Justin Gagneur's old bedroom that looked out over the savanna, at the trees flattened by the fury of the wind and beyond the cliffs, the ocean that dashed to the four corners of the horizon, tucking up its muslin petticoat. The workers who toiled to make tomatoes, lettuce and carrots sprout from the stony soil quickly saw that every minute of First-Born's life was devoted to his daughter. He bathed her, powdered her, doted on and coddled her, and himself cooked her sweet potato and arrowroot pap. He placed her cradle in his bedroom and while she slept serene and radiant on her pillow, he would place his ear to her chest every five minutes to see whether she was still breathing. Shortly before dusk he would take her in his arms and walk with her to the edge of the cliff. The child looked straight out to sea, and without batting an eyelid, watched the soaring birds. Sometimes she uttered cries inviting them to play with her. Then she closed her eyes and, nostrils flaring like a grown-up's, she breathed in the scent of the breeze as it blew back to earth. When darkness started to fall, First-Born slowly walked back to the house where Graziella was waiting for them, singing in front of a great bath of leaves and water warmed by the sun.

No visitor crossed the threshold of l'Engoulvent. Except

for Irmine. Every Saturday morning, the day had scarcely time to slip on its light when she climbed down from her tilbury. The first few times she did not come alone. She had Fréda or Cassandre, when she was home from school, accompany her. The sulky looks of disdain the two girls cast around them indicated that they had not come of their own free will. Soon, under one pretext or another, their visits were few and far between and then stopped altogether. After having handed Graziella the baskets lovingly filled with all sorts of victuals by Hosannah, Irmine swooped down on Anthuria in order to examine her every aspect. She sharply criticized the way First-Born and Graziella were looking after her. Were they powdering her with moussache flour from cassava to give her a lovely skin? Were they smoothing her hair with palma-christi oil? When she finished her inspection, she headed for the graveyard. She spent hours and hours there, without drinking or eating, as if her body no longer counted, praying, crying, day-dreaming, planting lilies or trumpet flowers in pots, changing the water in the flower vases, scraping the wax with the point of a knife, fixing the candles in their holders and rethreading the pearls on the crosses and wreaths. All this time she spoke out loud and rambled on monotonously to an invisible listener about the routine of her days.

First-Born never accompanied his mother to the grave-yard. Once, when she wanted to take the child there, he had gone into a fit of rage. It was as if something there fright-ened him. The letters intertwined in stone – CATHY DE LINSSEUIL – RAZYÉ – had given him the proof he had been looking for. So the bad-mouthers hadn't just bad-mouthed. And the bad-talkers hadn't just bad-talked. He had guessed rightly. This reunion in death proved it: Cathy de Linsseuil and Razyé had loved each other. First-Born had once been furious at what the power of money and the

347

vanity of women could do, and time and again approved his father's vengeance. Oh yes, he had been right to put Guadeloupe to fire and the sword. Then one night, while he was listening to Anthuria sleep, with the window open on a sullen crescent moon, a thought had slipped into his heart. Razyé – Cathy de Linsseuil. Cathy de Linsseuil – Razyé. Who would ever know the truth behind this sombre love story? Who would know the fruit it had borne?

The fruit?

Ever since that day, questions and suspicions had begun to torment him. Thank God his Cathy was no longer on this earth to share his doubts and dread. She could lie in ignorance.

Because of this apprehension that was gnawing at his heart, First-Born no longer took care of himself and his smell trailed behind him like the smoke from a sugar-cane train. His forehead was half-hidden by a fringe of greasy hair. His beard grew picky-haired around his mouth. He dressed sloppily in drab, worn-out clothes. Those who had known Razyé when he was Razyé shook their heads, sighing. What a come-down! He who said 'Like father, like son' didn't know what he was saying. Boys are sent to shame the memory of their fathers. First-Born ignored the children, cautiously entrenched behind the fence, who yelled out on seeing him: 'Mi guiab'là dero, kayiman!'

He was absorbed by the thought of Anthuria.

Such a lovely child could not be cursed.

Maryse Condé is the author of *Segu*; *I, Tituba, Black Witch of Salem*; *Tree of Life*; *Crossing the Mangrove*; and *The Last of the African Kings* among others. She is the recipient of the prestigious French award, Le Grand Prix, Litteraire de la Femme, and a Guggenheim Fellow. She is a professor of French Caribbean Literature at Columbia University. She and her husband, Richard Philcox, who masterfully translated *Windward Heights*, divide their time between New York City and Guadeloupe.